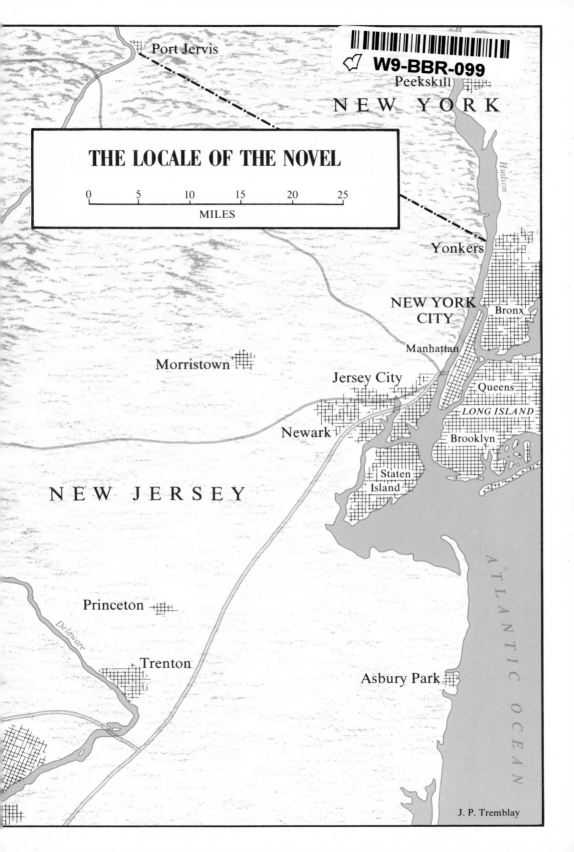

Port Jervis

Peekskill

N E W   Y O R K

Hudson

THE LOCALE OF THE NOVEL

0   5   10   15   20   25

MILES

Yonkers

**NEW YORK
CITY**

Bronx

Manhattan

Morristown

Jersey City

Queens

LONG ISLAND

Newark

Brooklyn

Staten
Island

N E W   J E R S E Y

Princeton

Delaware

A T L A N T I C   O C E A N

Trenton

Asbury Park

J. P. Tremblay

THE NOVEL

THE
NOVEL

James A. Michener

RANDOM HOUSE   NEW YORK

Copyright © 1991 by James A. Michener
Cartography © 1991 by Jean Paul Tremblay

Library of Congress Cataloging-in-Publication Data

Michener, James A. (James Albert).
The novel / James Michener.
p.   cm.
ISBN 0-679-40133-4
I. Title.
PS3525.I19N68   1991
813'.54—dc20   90-53489

Manufactured in the United States of America

24689753

FIRST EDITION

Book design by Carole Lowenstein

*To the Pennsylvania Dutch students
who attended school with me*

Contents

THE NOVEL

I

THE WRITER

HIS Tuesday morning, 3 October 1990, at half after ten, I typed the last sentence of the novel that will complete what the critics have taken to calling 'The Grenzler Octet,' as if I had planned from the beginning to write eight interrelated books on the same theme. No, that came about by accident.

In 1967, when I was forty-four, I imagined a compact little enclave in the Pennsylvania Dutch country, sixteen miles east to west, ten and half north to south, tucked in between the three well-known German cities of Allentown, on the north, Reading, on the west, and

Lancaster, on the south. It was such a well-defined area and so filled with fascinating rural people who adhered to ancient German ways and speech that, after defining it rather solidly in my first novel, I made use of it in the works that followed. I gave it a made-up regional name, Grenzler, and visualized myself as living within its boundaries, so that by the time I started this book, which I'm calling *Stone Walls* to evoke the obdurate nature of my beloved Dutchmen and their relationship to their land, I could imagine writing about no other part of the world, or of the United States or even Pennsylvania. As so often happens with writers, my imaginary terrain had become more real to me than the physical one that surrounded me.

Patting the completed manuscript as if to give it my final approval, I left my study, came downstairs to the kitchen, and shouted the great news: 'Emma! It's finished! Now we can start living again.'

My wife could not quite echo my enthusiasm, for she remembered the drudgery that had been required to polish my seven previous novels: 'I know what lies ahead. It's October 1990. We'll have a year of clean-up work—suggestions from New York, revisions, then proofreading—maybe a printed book this time next year. October 1991.'

But she did not wish to dampen my triumph, so with a bright smile she pointed to her oven, from which came one of those unequaled smells that make a Pennsylvania Dutch kitchen a hallowed place. It could have come from the making of apple butter, or the concocting of rich mincemeat or the baking of a pumpkin pie with nutmeg; this particular one was in my opinion the best of all: the tantalizing smell of rice pudding baked in the traditional Dutch way.

Opening the front door of her oven and using heavy woolen mittens, Emma drew out a handsome German cooking bowl of heavy brown ware, fourteen inches across and six inches high, flared at the top, so the sides were not perpendicular. In it she had prepared one of the glories of Dutch cooking, golden brown on top, speckled with raisins beneath the crustlike surface.

An Emma Yoder rice pudding was not one of those characterless affairs made with rice already boiled and a milky-thin custard with no raisins but maybe a little bit of cinnamon on top. For her no boiling but baking only, and that took time, plus careful attention as the pudding neared completion. That was why the container in which she baked it had to be much deeper than one might have expected, for after the hard grains of rice had cooked slowly for several hours until soft, and the raisins had been thrown in, and then the cinnamon, real cooking began, and at ten- or fifteen-minute intervals a beautiful brown crust would cover the top, the color coming from caramelized sugar in the mix. Then, with a long-handled spoon she would stir the forming crust back into the pudding, so that in time this tasty amber richness was mixed visibly throughout the entire pudding.

The art of making a true German rice pudding lies in starting with the right proportions of uncooked rice and rich milk; at the beginning it looks very watery, but as it bakes and the excess liquid vanishes in steam, the milk, eggs and sugar combine magically into one of the choicest custards of all cuisines. But what makes the German pudding so wondrous to the taste is the intermixing of caramelized crust and the raisins into the custard. A union like that does not happen accidentally.

'Make open the refrigerator,' she directed, falling back on a Pennsylvania Dutch idiom of her childhood, even though she had taught English in nearby Souderton during much of our married life.

'All right yet,' I said, mimicking her, but before she placed the pudding inside to be cooled she filled two small cups with the steaming richness; these she and I would eat as part of a ritual we had honored since the completion of my first novel decades ago. As we sat in our colorful kitchen—where we seemed to spend most of our lives—waiting for our feast to cool, she asked: 'Will the editing be easier this time?' and I said: 'Harder. As you grow older you have more to lose.'

'Were you serious when you said this might be your last one?'

'Positively. I wouldn't have the energy for another big one . . . nor the courage.'

Aware that these were moments of special meaning, she stopped behind my chair and placed her hand on my shoulder: 'Eight novels. First four so poorly received. Last four such triumphs.'

'Hold everything. I have serious doubts about this one.'

She sniffed: 'With your track record?'

'A writer's only as good as his next one. And I'm a bit uncertain about this one.'

'Is it so different? From your last three winners?'

'Yes. This time there're no personal antagonisms, as with the suspender men in *Shunning*, and no Pennsylvania Dutch mysticism, as in *Hex*.'

'You're turning your back on what made those books so popular? Is that wise?'

'I've pondered it a long time and I'm sure it's wise. This book's about the Grenzler land and how we Dutch cheat ourselves if we either abuse it or stray too far from it by breaking down our historic stone fence lines, our barn walls.'

'The ecology kick? Are you sure your readers are ready for it?'

'It's my job to make them ready.'

'Good luck, Roger Tory Peterson.'

It might seem strange to an outsider that I could be so far along in the writing of a manuscript without my wife's knowing much about it, but in our family we followed a strict tradition. I wrote my books alone, telling no one, not even my editors, what the subject of the next novel was. So Emma never knew until it was completed: 'I'll lend you my copy after I take Zollicoffer his, and mail a copy off to Kinetic Press in New York.'

'Sight unseen, I predict it'll be a smasheroo.'

'I like your elegant vocabulary.'

Gently she pressed my shoulder as she took her chair: 'When you teach high school kids, you adopt their vocabulary or they tune you out.' I said that I had supposed it was the teacher's job to impose her vocabulary on the class and she laughed: 'You really are from another generation.'

As we waited for the pudding to cool, I realized again how passionately I loved this little Dutch woman—she five feet two, I five five—for in the bad years when I could sell nothing I wrote she had enabled me to continue by teaching school in Souderton, and after each of the first four disasters she had said: 'Lukas, you're a real writer and that's a fine book. Sooner or later America has to realize it.' She had never wavered in her determination to support me during those years, and her words had been as important to me as the modest income she provided from her teaching, because she was a graduate of Bryn Mawr, one of our best women's colleges, and she knew what good books were. Sometimes when I worked alone in my study while she labored in her classroom, tears would come to my eyes, for I knew that she had wanted to pursue some career more glamorous and demanding than teaching in a rural high school, but she never uttered one word of complaint. She had given herself the job of keeping me alive so that I could write my books, and without complaining she had hewn to that line.

I have become impatient in recent years when I read of a sickness that seems to be infecting the young medical doctors of this nation. Before entering medical school, a would-be doctor marries a young nurse who will earn a small salary and support him till he gets started in his profession. Then, when the money starts rolling in and he finds himself at the center of his community's social life, he awakens to the fact that his wife is merely a country girl with no advanced education who does not do him justice in his new position. So he divorces her, shares none of his wealth with her, and replaces her with a younger and better-educated wife, with whom he can dominate the country club set.

Emma did exactly what the young nurses do: she enabled me to learn the skills of writing. Also, she was a better person than I in almost every respect. She went to a much better college—I attended the nearby Dutch school, Mecklenberg, which is a fine little college but no Bryn Mawr—and she had far greater inner courage and determination. Made of rose petals and granite, she kept us alive.

In a significant way, Emma had engineered the miraculous change in our lives, for when my fourth novel earned virtually nothing— certainly not enough for us to live on—she cried: 'Lukas, we're hexed.' I remember growling: 'You don't believe in that hex non- sense,' and I added: 'Our Dutch do themselves damage believing in witches and hexes—painting their barns with mystic signs to keep away devils,' and a spirited argument followed.

Emma's family history is a curious one. Her Stoltzfus ancestors, back in the 1650s, had lived in the Palatinate, the section of western Germany squeezed in between the Rhine and the French areas of Alsace and Lorraine. Illuminated by the religious fires ignited in the previous century by Martin Luther and Huldreich Zwingli, they had become fervent Anabaptists, who preached that it was both stupid and unbiblical to baptize children at birth: 'Only at age seventeen or eighteen is a human being old enough to understand the meaning of Christianity. Only then is he or she eligible to make a commitment and be baptized.' And they cited John the Baptist, Jesus himself and Saint Paul to support their claim.

On this fragile point of doctrine, plus their aversion to war and political interference in their personal lives, the original Stoltzfus clan was so persecuted, with some members even being executed, that they emigrated from the Palatinate, along with several thousand Yoders, Beilers and Zooks. William Penn, the inspired English Quaker, hearing of their plight, invited them to settle in Pennsyl- vania, which they did in 1697, when they promptly separated into two radically different religious sects. The Amish in Lancaster County adhered to the most rigorous biblical conventions—no buttons on clothing because soldiers' uniforms were crowded with them, no ostentation in dress or furniture, no mechanical contrivances that presumed to do a better job than God intended a man to do unaided, and little or no education because none was needed to farm and acquiring it made a person vainglorious—while the others who settled in my Dresden became Mennonites, who, like their Amish cousins, dressed mostly in black and favored chin beards but no mustaches, and allowed a much freer pattern of living. They could use buttons, musical instruments in church, and mechanical aids in farming or, in my day, automobiles, which were still fiercely opposed by the Amish.

Emma's entire Stoltzfus family from 1693 through 1890 were strictly Amish; my Yoders, from the same starting point to this day, have been Mennonites, who did not object when I said at age seventeen: 'I want to go to Mecklenberg College.' How Emma was able to leave her rigorously Amish family in Lancaster and attend Bryn Mawr is a magical story that I won't go into here. But she did. We met, discovered our mutual German background, and married. I never made a better move.

When I teased her about believing in hex signs to ward off evil influence, especially barn fires, she had said: 'You know, Lukas, if that word looms so large in discussions about our way of life, why don't you use it as the title of your next book and explore its significance?'

At first I dismissed the idea, but she returned to it repeatedly and some of the reasons she gave for deeming it viable stuck in my mind. One spring day, when Dresden looked like an enchanted place with blossoms, green fields and bubbling creeks, I reached a firm decision: 'I'm going to try the hex novel. And in your honor I'm going to name it just that.' But even so I had not allowed her to read it as it progressed.

My fourth novel, *Shunning*, which was entirely my creation, sold

1,607 copies. My fifth, *Hex*, which she had inspired, sold 871,896. Little wonder I respect her counsel.

Now as we prepared to dig into the cooled pudding, I warned: 'This could be a difficult year. Lots of pressures,' and when she asked why, I explained: 'People will suspect that this might be my final book. They'll want to mark the occasion in some way.'

'I didn't realize you were serious. This really is your farewell?'

'You know what our friend Zollicoffer says: "One too much is already three too many." '

Dipping with enthusiasm into the rich golden custard, I said: 'Granting that this is my last effort, I want to give it every support I can. Help it reach its proper level.'

'At the top, like the last three.'

'I don't mean in sales. Let Kinetic worry about that. I mean in the way the public sees the rounding out of my series.' As Emma rose to remove the little dishes, I caught her arm, drew her to me and kissed her: 'Thanks for helping me get this one finished.' Then I set in motion the ritual that had marked the completion of each of my previous novels: 'Let's get three bowls for what's left of the pudding. One for Zollicoffer, one for Fenstermacher, one for Diefenderfer. They're my living hex signs. They bring me good luck.'

It was ten o'clock before I pulled out of my driveway in our 1986 Buick and headed the short distance north to the farm of Herman Zollicoffer, carrying with me not only the three bowls of pudding but also two copies of my completed novel.

It had been my habit from the start of my career to take everything I wrote about the Pennsylvania Dutch to Herman for vetting. On that first day I had said: 'Please read this and check every word I say about us Dutch to see if it's right and in no way offensive.' Herman leaped at the opportunity, for he was a proud old Dutchman who wanted the language and traditions of his people to be honestly reported to the world.

Now as I neared his farm I reflected on the precarious situation every writer, even a successful one, finds himself in when he thinks his manuscript is completed. It must pass muster with an outside expert, in this case Zollicoffer; it's then torn apart by the editor; if it deals with especially contentious material, lawyers must scan for assertions that could be libelous; and finally some word wizard must check every sentence, every spelling. And when the book finally does appear, after all that loving attention, it can still fall flat on its face. I winced as I thought of famous American writers whose last offerings had been disasters. And I chuckled as I remembered the advertisement my neighbor Oscar Hammerstein paid for in *Variety* after his chain of awesome box-office successes, such as *Oklahoma!* and *The King and I*. In bold letters it proclaimed: I DID IT ONCE, I CAN DO IT AGAIN, below which he listed with title and dates of opening and closing some seven or eight of his earlier flops. If I were so inclined, I could run the same ad with the record of my early books. That would prove I had reason to be apprehensive about any manuscript I thought was ready for the printer.

These nervous thoughts were dispelled when I saw Zollicoffer's farm buildings ahead, for they were a solid representation of what the Pennsylvania Dutch stood for. What a curious term! It would be impossible for me to say 'the Pennsylvania Germans'; mind and soul would have revolted. But we were Germans; so far as I know, there was never a single Dutchman from Holland to come our way, so our name was a gross misnomer. It happened like this.

In the speech I learned in my Mennonite family as a boy we were the Pennzylwanische Deitsch, with the two vowels in the last word pronounced as they would be in *height*, and that's what we should have been called in English. But *Deitsch* was difficult to spell and pronounce, so it was quickly simplified to *Dutch*, which would obviously lead to endless error and confusion. However, it was so easy to say that that's what we became, and today I rarely hear the correct pronunciation. Herman Zollicoffer and I are archetypical 'dumb Pennsylvania Dutchmen,' except that we aren't really so dumb as others sometimes think.

My heart always beat a little faster when I approached the Zollicoffer farm, for it was the perfect example of what the Pennsylvania Dutch wanted. The barns—the heart of the farm—lay on one side of the rural road, while the house and its attendant buildings were on the other side. The two barns were painted red, of course, and were much larger than the house, which was a simple rectangular structure, three stories high, and painted white. It stood close to the road and was fronted by a generous porch supported by four white columns. Three rather small buildings clustered near the house: an old-style cooking shed, a deep cellar for storing foodstuffs, and a corncrib, each painted in some color neither white nor red. On the barn side of the road stood a substantial silo, and behind the house stretched the garden in which Mrs. Zollicoffer grew the vegetables she canned each summer and autumn for winter use.

West of the farm buildings marched seven glorious blue spruce, tall, magnificently colored and rounded out like plump Dutch housewives. Their unexpected presence told much about the Zollicoffers and my other Dutch neighbors, and since I had been involved in getting the trees to the farm I can explain exactly how that happened.

To look at the Zollicoffers and the way they lived you would have said: 'These two gross Dutchmen between them haven't a shred of appreciation for beautiful things.' Herman was a big man, close to six feet, who weighed about two hundred and fifty pounds. He had reddish hair, a copious beard, a clean-shaven upper lip, close-set eyes and a tremendous belly, which alone would have held up his pants, but, cautious man that he was, he wore both a belt and a pair of canvas suspenders. He favored thick socks and heavy shoes in which he waddled like a duck.

His wife, Frieda, was not quite as tall as he, but enormous in girth.

She wore shoes much like her husband's, heavy black stockings and a skirt that came to her ankles. I rarely saw her without an apron, which she tied tightly just above her ample stomach. In the early days she had worn the filigreed white lace headdress of the Mennonite women, but shortly after I came to know her she discarded this, preferring a sturdy bonnet. To watch the two Zollicoffers throughout a working day you would have concluded that all they were interested in was eating, and you would have been partly correct, for their appetites were prodigious.

But there was another side to the Zollicoffers that was just as strong. One day in 1938, when I was fifteen and picking up our family mail at the post office in Rostock, Mrs. Zollicoffer was there purchasing stamps, and since she was the best cook by far in our valley and I had been lucky enough to sample her culinary treats, I was always courteous to her. As we were speaking, a man I did not know approached and asked: 'Pardon me, but are you Mrs. Zollicoffer?' When she drew back, suspicious, he explained: 'I'm Hans Draksel. I have the nursery.'

'Yes! Up against Dresden yet.'

'The same. I have a corner of beautiful trees in what we nurserymen call "the Depression Block." '

'What's that mean already?'

'The trees we should have sold during the last eight years. Nobody had any money. They've grown tall, like trees do. This is the last season they could be sold. Either I get rid of them or we cut them down.'

'If they're beautiful, why do that?'

'To make way for the small trees that we can sell.'

'Why are you telling me this, chust so?'

'Aren't you Herman Zollicoffer's missus?'

'I am.'

'They tell me he's one of the few with any money in these parts.'

'We aindt in poorhouse.'

'I have seven of these fine trees, best that grow in America. Worth at least fifty dollars each . . .'

Frieda broke into a laugh: 'Fifty dollars for a tree. Such craziness yet.'

'And I offer them to you and Herman for three-fifty each.'

When all of us in the post office gasped, Mr. Draksel said: 'Yes. We missed those years when they should have been sold. Everybody missed them. Now you take them, Mrs. Zollicoffer, or we cut them down.'

'Well, now . . .'

'I know your place and Herman's. They'd look grand there. Big and blue and beautiful.'

He asked if he could follow her home and show her where the spruce could be planted to best effect. She said: 'The master makes all the decisions,' but he ignored her and invited me to toss my bicycle in the back of the truck and ride along to show him the way to the Zollicoffer farm. When Herman heard the man's story he appreciated immediately what the situation was, and I could see that he felt sorry for the immense reduction the nursery had to take on the seven trees. But he expressed no interest in buying them: 'What would I do with blue spruce? I'm not a millionaire.'

The man said: 'You could plant them along this little side road. A windbreak,' but Zollicoffer was stubborn and would have sent the man packing had not his wife suddenly joined us: 'Herman, take them already. At three-fifty we can afford.'

'What would we do with them already?' Herman bellowed and his wife shouted back: 'We could use them for nice,' and he told Draksel: 'Dig 'em up. If Frieda wants 'em, she can have 'em.'

So the sale was completed, and the next day Zollicoffer and I rode to the nursery and watched as two men dug out the seven beautiful trees, their blue-white needles shimmering in the sunlight. Mr. Draksel rode back to the Zollicoffers' to help plant the trees, and as the three of us were digging the holes Mrs. Zollicoffer surprised us by suddenly appearing and shouting in her loud voice: 'They're too near already,' meaning that we were planting them too close together. We ignored her, but she proved to be right, because three years later, when I was eighteen, I went back and helped Mr. Zollicoffer relocate three of the crowded trees and space out the line, just as she had advised that first day.

Now, when I see the spruce ruling the road like seven majestic queens dressed in blue robes, I think of the day when fat Frieda, a woman with no physical grace whatever, cried: 'Herman, we can use them for nice.' She knew what beauty was, and how small trees, overlooked in the Great Depression, could grow into towering spires to gladden the eye.

And Herman knew, also, but the focus of his attention was in another place. At the rear of his farm rested a collection of five enormous rocks, huge boulders really, shoved there forty thousand years ago, when ice shields reached down from Canada to cover much of what is now Pennsylvania. The terminal moraine, as this gigantic rubble is called, was the southernmost tip of the great ice field that totally submerged areas now occupied by states like Vermont, New Hampshire and New York. They were handsome rocks, and he had loved them since he was a child on this farm, just as his forebears had since the early 1700s. But his interest took a surprising turn, for he mowed all the grassland surrounding the individual rocks and made the place a rude garden in which the granite boulders were the flowers.

And he did more. Between the fields adjacent to his house and the big rocks lay a body of shallow water, a marshland fed by small springs, and along one edge he erected a small gazebo, which became known locally as Herman's Bench, and here his neighbors came to hold picnics. He too used it often, for toward the end of day he liked

to sit in his belvedere and watch the numerous water birds that came
to frolic in his marsh, with the great rocks standing guard behind.
Imitating his wife and her trees, he had converted his part of the field
into a kind of mammoth garden, for he too appreciated certain things
for nice.

Herman helped me enormously in my work by insisting that I never
use what he called with sneering contempt 'them made-up funnies
about us Dutch.' When early in our work together I first asked what
this meant he snorted: 'Comics down Lancaster way, never spoke the
Deitsch, sat around thinkin' up jokes about us that looked good on
the souvenirs they sell to tourists. Never was a Dutchman said any
of them.'

Over the years I compiled a list of what we both called the No-
No's. Heading it was the unquestionably amusing sign at the door
where the electric bell was out of order: BUTTON DON'T BELL, BUMP.
When Herman convinced me that no one had ever said that, I
replied: 'They should have.' Equally fake was the great statement by
a girl explaining that Elizabeth's vacation had ended: 'Her off is all,'
and he made me surrender one that I really wanted to use. It dealt
with a farmer who had both a wife and a girlfriend: 'He keeps Rachel
at home for cook but keeps Becky at the crossroads for nice.' Beneath
his contempt was the saying that had become popular on Lancaster
ceramics: 'We grow too soon old and too late schmardt,' and he
expected me to give up without his urging one of the famous ones:
'Throw the cow over the fence some hay.'

I argued with him about a sentence that I had heard my uncle say:
'Bose rotes is gute, but herns is more up' (Both roads are good but
hers is steeper). And it seemed to me that another was usable, but
he rejected it as spurious: 'Them is all but those aindt yet' (Those are
used up, but these aren't).

His strictures did not limit me in my attempts to convey the spicy flavor of my childhood tongue, for I had at my disposal a barrage of individual words that members of my own family had used in their unique way. *Make* was a universal word, used in scores of idioms: 'Make shut the door' and 'It makes rain.' *Aindt* for *ain't* rings in my memory as a word constantly in use by my parents, and *all* too, as in 'The bread is all, I chust better bake.' Words beginning in English with *j* became *chimmy*, *chust* and *chugular*, but many words with *g* were handled the same, most notably *Chermany*.

Already and *oncet*, the latter for *once*, were universal, as was the word of approval, *wunnerful*, as in 'She was wunnerful kind.' In my family a constant phrase was 'It wonders me,' and although we did not usually pronounce the normal *w* as *v*, we did the reverse by always saying *wery* for *very*, a word used frequently, and *walue* for *value*. *Friendlich* was a word we used a lot to indicate a person with a kindly nature, and of course we had our own way of pronouncing *somesing* and *Besslehem*.

If Herman Zollicoffer banished some of the locutions I might have used, his wife, Frieda, more than compensated for the loss by the richness of her speech. I rarely visited them without acquiring from her normal speech some gem of syntax, for she had been reared in a family that spoke almost no English and had gone to school with other children who also used Deitsch at home. Her speech was larded with German words, many of which I never learned, but I had decided early on that I would not sprinkle such words in my novels and would restrict myself to English spoken with a Deitsch lilt. In pursuing this tack, Frieda Zollicoffer was an invaluable help. Whenever I took out my notebook to record some barbarous but heartwarming expression of hers, she would cry in her loud voice: 'Look oncet, Herman, there he goes again already,' and she would warn me: 'Don't make games with me, yet,' and then burst into laughter.

She used idioms like 'Outen the cat' and 'It wonders me that she can eat so much,' and 'It ouches me!' when she nicked herself peeling apples. But as with all the Deitsch speakers it was her lyrical pronunciation of ordinary words that made her the archetypical resident of my imaginary Grenzler. She pronounced *w* as *v* and vice versa as my own family did. This was a term she often used, calling it *wicie-wersie* in a lilting way that made listeners either gape or chuckle. At other times she dropped letters in her exaggerated mouthing of a simple word. Thus *over* became not *ower* but a prolonged *ooo-er* in which her mouth performed gymnastics. Her *telewizion* carried its own translation, as did the compass directions *norse* and *souse*. She said *britches* for *bridges, veddink* for *wedding* and *zoop* for *soup*.

The Zollicoffers' kitchen had been my library and university, and as I sat in it this morning while they wolfed down Emma's rice pudding in great gulps, I remembered how indebted I was to them.

'Herman,' I said as I handed him a copy of the manuscript, 'I bring you the last of the lot. Give it a careful eye because I'm worried about this one.'

'You done good so far.'

'But this one's different. It's about our Dutch people wrestling with difficult ideas.'

'You got a good story, don't you? Nothing to fret.'

'I hope you're right. I have the original bundled up in the car. Mailing it this afternoon to New York. See what they say.'

Mrs. Zollicoffer broke in: 'The Mister enjoys readin' your stuff.'

'And you?' I asked

'Me?' she laughed heartily as she licked her spoon. 'I leave readin' to the Mister.'

When I left the Zollicoffers', I faced two choices for reaching my next customary stop, Otto Fenstermacher's farm, where I would trade Emma's rice pudding for a sampling of his scrapple, the best in Dresden. I could double back to Rhenish Road and head west

through the town of Dresden, or I could stay on our country road
until I reached Fenstermacher's.

Because the rural road was so colorful I chose it, and shortly after
passing under the Interstate I saw to my right the simple one-story
church that Emma and I attended. Valley Mennonite it was called,
and it could have had no more appropriate name, for it overlooked
the handsome valley that nestled between two low ranges of hills that
protected the town of Dresden to the north and south. From the
front porch of the church one could see endless miles of the most
beautiful land in Pennsylvania.

The site had been selected by the first Zollicoffers and Yoders to
settle in this region, and they had chosen well. A record kept by my
family explains how it happened:

> In 1677, the year Yost Yoder was released from prison with
> scars from torture marking his face, the Word of God seemed
> to arrive in our Palatine valleys in the person of a tall En-
> glishman of gentle manner who brought us news we could
> scarcely believe. His name was Wilhelm Penn and he said:
> 'In the New World the English king has given me a principal-
> ity larger than Bavaria, Württemberg, Baden and your
> Palatinate combined. There we live in peace. Each family has
> its own free land to till as it disposes. We have no army, no
> forced enlistments, no crushing taxes, no Lords to whom we
> must bow down. A free air blows from our mountains and
> a man's home is safe at night. And what should encourage
> you Mennonites most of all, in my lands each family is free
> to worship as it pleases, for we allow no Bishops to hand
> down orders which all must follow. We live under the rule
> of God, as each man in his heart interprets it.'
>
> Although young Penn seemed an honest fellow, we could not
> believe the promises he was uttering, so we sent Heinrich

Zug across the sea to inspect this new paradise and in 1681 he returned with news that kept us awake at night: 'The young Englishman has the land. It's even bigger than he said. Freedom does rule there, and we're invited to send him fifty families of good repute, who will each receive a large farm of the best land available.' The Yoder families decided that night to come to Pennzylwanische as we then called it and we have never looked back.

A later passage of extreme simplicity and devotion told how Valley Mennonite was established:

Almost the first thing Yost Yoder and Uriah Zollicoffer did when they reached our valley in 1697 was to select a site for their church in the wilderness, and it was Yoder who stood atop the little rise on which Valley Mennonite would later stand and cried: 'Let's build here so we can see our entire valley when we give thanks to God for our salvation.'

I spring from reverent people, which is why I have written of our Mennonites with reverence.

Today, as I looked at the old church whose roots dated back to 1698, I saw a modern building of the choicest kind: one story, built in the shape of an extended L, fronted by a spacious porch supported by five white columns. Architecturally it is a gem and I often speculate on why our Mennonites, who are so conservative in most aspects of life, are so liberal and almost radical when it comes to building their churches. Ours is a beauty, and I salute it each time I pass by.

The Wannsee, which stretches off to the north, is a handsome body of water graced at the far end by the buildings of Mecklenberg College. Then comes the village of Neumunster, the most fiercely Dutch of our settlements, after which the Cut Off drops quickly down to Fenstermacher's farm. This was in many ways the most memorable part of my ride, because from the Cut Off I could see the rare charm of western Dresden: the rolling hills, the spacious valley, the little roads, the farms, one perfect vista after another, all bespeaking the richness and stability of the Dutch country. Striking a jarring note in all this loveliness was the dilapidated Fenstermacher farm.

Otto's place dominated one of the most valuable spots in Dresden, where the important Rhenish Road intersected with the Cut Off. On these rich fields thrifty farmers should have been able to build fortunes, but the feckless Fenstermachers, starting as far back as the 1850s, were beset by one misfortune after another, and to keep themselves afloat they were forced to sell their precious land bit by bit. The family had started in 1709 with two hundred acres awarded them by William Penn, and to this fine start the early owners had added another three hundred acres, until ultimately they had what amounted to a small principality.

But later Fenstermachers made poor marriages that produced sons of little merit, so that while the Zollicoffers and the Yoders prospered on lands of smaller size and limited fertility because of the thrift with which they tended them, the Fenstermachers drifted constantly downward. This morning, when I came upon their farm after having enjoyed the glorious views from the Cut Off, I felt sick. The big barn was in disrepair. The house needed painting and the smaller outbuildings had been surrendered to slow ruin. It would have been difficult to find, in all of Dresden, a worse case of misguided husbandry, and I was ashamed to think that it was one of my fellow Mennonites who had behaved so ineptly.

And yet I liked Otto, enjoyed his witty companionship, and often told my neighbors: 'Otto's better at making scrapple than I am at making books.' When I drove into the messy yard fronting the unkempt house I hesitated a moment to consider one of the reasons I had made this long detour: on the face of the old barn, which ought

THE WRITER

· ·

22

soon to be torn down in an orderly way before some storm did the job haphazardly, rested three handsome hex signs, somewhat faded by weather but elegant in design. For some years I'd kept watch on those signs, waiting till Fenstermacher was willing to sell, and now, with my book done and the barn about to collapse, I wanted to make sure they were saved.

So when I entered the kitchen, so disorganized when compared with Emma's or Frieda Zollicoffer's, I told the Fenstermachers: 'I come on three missions. Emma sends you her rice pudding. She wants to buy three pans of your scrapple. And I want to talk about those hex signs on your old barn.'

As might be expected in a Dutch family, the food was tended to first, with plump Mrs. Fenstermacher crying: 'Emma's puddings we love, and since it's near dinnertime, Lukas, stop with us and I'll fry up a sample of Otto's new scrapple.'

The invitation was irresistible, for if there is any food I dearly love it's Dresden scrapple, cut thin and crisp-fried on each side. And Otto Fenstermacher's was the best in the valley, for no matter how his fortunes declined in farming and real estate, he continued to make scrapple of such high quality that he might have made a lucrative business of it had he been more sagacious.

When his hogs were slaughtered, and the scraps of the carcasses were combined with a few shreds of real pork thrown in to make the product respectable, Otto added fat, cornmeal, salt, pepper and spices, cooking the mixture lightly until it formed a grayish concoction that, when poured into elongated cake tins, hardened into a unique and delicious country delicacy. Culinary experts unfamiliar with it in childhood said when encountering it as adults: 'It can best be described as "the poor man's pork pâté" or perhaps "an hors d'oeuvre that's imaginative and cheap to make." ' We Pennsylvania Dutch thought of it as our national dish and felt sorry for people in states where it was unknown.

When Mrs. Fenstermacher flipped the scrapple to crisp the other side, which sent ravishing smells circulating through her kitchen, her husband and I waited at the oak table. 'Why do you want those hex signs?' Otto asked and I explained: 'Whenever I finish writing a book I need a change of pace. I work on hexes. But they must be old.'

'How old?' Mrs. Fenstermacher asked from her stove.

'Before World War Two. Even older. Real Dutch, not recent make-believe.'

'My father had four old ones on our barn,' she said and I reminded her: 'You were standing beside him the day I bought them.'

'That's right,' she cried. 'But you never told me what you did with them.'

Addressing both the Fenstermachers, because I could not guess which would agree with me and which would oppose, I said: 'I clean the boards, mend the damaged areas with epoxy—'

'What's that?' Mrs. Fenstermacher asked.

'Powerful new glue. Then I replace the missing paint very delicately so the repairs don't show, and break off the edges of the board so it looks as if it had been busted loose, not cut by a saw.'

'Then what?'

'I glue it onto a wooden panel, leaving a margin about six, eight inches on each side.'

'What's that for?' Otto asked, and I said: 'For the artwork. First I rough the panel, to make it look old like the hex. Sandpaper or pumice does the trick.'

'What artwork?' Mrs. Fenstermacher asked as she flipped her scrapple again to ensure a golden crust, and I explained the interesting part of the operation: 'On the exposed margin of the panel, I paint Pennsylvania Dutch designs. Old frakturs.'

'Like on birth certificates!' Otto cried. 'Distelfinks. Tulips. Hearts with prayers.'

Dutch society was short on all forms of art: not much music except

hymns of interminable length and little variation in the tunes; no
painting of portraits or landscapes; and absolutely no sculpture.
Biblical austerity forbade such display. But what we did have in
glorious profusion was pen-and-ink fraktur, depictions of a relatively
few symbols, endlessly repeated: birds, flowers, letters of the alphabet
and occasionally human figures. Fraktur had been used in the old
days to decorate birth certificates, school diplomas, genealogies and
other important documents.

'Why do you mix hex signs and fraktur?' Otto asked, and I explained: 'Because I'm making a painting. Old hex and new fraktur,
a beautiful blend and very Dutch.'

'What do you do with it?'

'Sell it, give it to a museum, place it in a public library.'

'Are you an artist, then, like on television?' Mrs. Fenstermacher
asked. 'French cap and all?'

'Only an amateur. But after a long sit at my typewriter, I want to
work with my hands.'

'People buy what you make? This hunk of barn sidin'?'

'I give most of them away. But yes, sometimes people buy them.'

'I thought you was crazy yet,' Otto laughed, 'offerin' me money
for that old sidin'. But if you sell them, more like I should charge
you double what you offered last time.'

Before I could answer, Mrs. Fenstermacher served us dinner, as
we rural Dutch called our midday meal, and she brought not only
perfectly fried scrapple with its side dish of applesauce, but also a
delicacy she had slipped into her frying pan at the last moment: slabs
of golden cornmeal mush, fried in butter to a deep brown and served
with a heavy Karo syrup. It was a meal for working farmers and
provided enough cholesterol to last a month, but as we Dutch say:
'If it aindt fried it aindt food.'

The mix of flavors was so delicious that I had to compliment the
cook: 'I can't tell which is better, Rebecca, your scrapple or your

fried mush,' and she replied: 'Scrapple was made by the Mister, mush by me.'

The pleasantness of the meal was marred by the noisy arrival of the Fenstermacher son, a loutish overweight young fellow of nineteen who bore the unusual but appropriate nickname of Applebutter. In Dutch communities, where only a few family names and even fewer first names, brought over from Germany, exist, it was possible for six or seven boys with only a few years' difference between them to have the same name. In my case there were three Lukas Yoders, and with the Fenstermachers three boys named Otto. It was the custom, therefore, to refer to Big Otto, Red-haired Otto, and Applebutter Otto, the ungainly son.

Before he sat down both parents jumped on him, his mother whining: 'You're suppose to be here at sittin'-down time,' and his father: 'You was goin' to help me take them boards for Mr. Yoder yet.'

Wolfing food and dousing his fried mush in a flood of syrup, he ignored me and shoved his empty plate toward his mother: 'More scrapple,' which she supplied. Finally he belched, pushed his chair back from the table and grunted: 'Let's get to them boards,' after which he clumped out, grabbed an ax and a crowbar and led his father and me to the barn that seemed about to collapse.

As Applebutter clung to his ladder and hacked away at the barn siding he growled at me: 'I don't see what good these'll do you—or anybody.' I tried to humor him by assuring him he was doing a good job, but my encouragement was useless, for at that moment he swung his ax and intentionally dug a deep scar across the face of the best of the three hexes. Eager to prevent him from doing further damage, I said: 'That can be fixed. You're doing a fine job,' and he hacked away at the last one without mutilating it. When it broke loose he climbed down, and again I tried to humor him: 'You helped me get three fine hexes for my work,' but he would not be won over. Leaving

THE WRITER

· ·
26

the barn without helping to load the boards into my car, he roared off on his motorcycle.

'Applebutter can be headstrong,' his father apologized, 'but he's better now than he was three years ago. The Missus spoiled him when he was young, fed him like a hog,' and I laughed: 'She fed you and me the same way. But it was good.'

As I prepared to leave, Rebecca brought out the three long pans of her husband's scrapple, the meat in each hidden beneath a quarter inch of solid white pork fat that had been rendered in the cooking, and I thought: A symbol of my region—hearty, nourishing, old-fashioned and good.

The third stop on my traditional tour on manuscript day was in some ways the most important, for at our little one-room store in Rostock I handed Mrs. Diefenderfer, the postmistress, the carefully wrapped package that contained my manuscript: 'To Kinetic Press, as usual. Return receipt requested.' These last three words, which slipped out like the lyrics of a song, meant that the package would be delivered only into the hands of the addressee, who would sign for it, after which the receipt would be returned to me as proof that it got there safely. This protection cost only an additional ninety cents, a postal bargain.

'Finished another big one?' Mrs. Diefenderfer asked and I smiled. After I handed her the crock of rice pudding she said: 'We'll have this for supper,' and then, closing her stamp window, came from behind the protective iron grille and led me to her nearby farmhouse, where we sat in the kitchen: 'We'll celebrate.' After summoning her farmer husband with a loud whistle, she served us glasses of cold milk and ample helpings of her famous apple brown betty with its luscious crust of breadcrumbs, butter, grated lemon rind and spices, all topped with her own heavy whipped cream.

LUKAS YODER
· ·

27

Raising her glass of milk, she offered a toast: 'To our good friend Lukas Yoder! May Book-of-the-Month Club take this one, too!'

'I'll drink to that,' I said, and after refusing a second helping of brown betty, I drove off muttering: 'I won't be hungry for a week.' Finishing a manuscript and mailing it off in Dresden was not a simple affair, but as soon as I reached my farm I kissed Emma, assured her that it was in the mail, and trundled off to bed for an afternoon nap, thinking as I fell asleep: I've been in four homes in the heartland. Yoder, Zollicoffer, Fenstermacher, Diefenderfer. Never entered by the front door. Never saw any room but the kitchen. Never ate better in my life. That's Pennsylvania Dutch.

That evening, after showing Emma my three fine hexes and assuring her that in view of the gorging I'd been doing I needed no supper, we sat with her little bound diary for 1990 and the two-page condensed edition for 1991, and tried to anticipate what our obligations might be for the year that loomed ahead. When she began to complain that dates associated with the publication of *Stone Walls* were piling up, I reminded her: 'This is the last book, and this will be the last year we'll ever do this. I want to give the book a proper send-off, every chance of success,' and she retorted: 'And it's my job to see that you come out of it alive.' On one decision she was firm: 'No publicity tour to eleven cities. Not at your age.'

'I agree. Too demanding—and I doubt it does much good.'

I did add one date of which she had not been aware: 'That museum of folk art in Williamsburg, the one named in honor of Abby Rockefeller, wants me to show eight or nine of my hex paintings. That's why I was so eager to get those three from Fenstermacher.'

She considered this for a moment and said: 'That could be a very pleasant trip south. They'd put us up at the Inn?'

'Better yet. In that wonderful colonial house DeWitt Wallace refurbished for them.'

'That would be most agreeable.'

I'd done several articles on Dutch country for the *Reader's Digest*, and the Wallaces, to show their gratitude, had invited Emma and me to use what was known as the Wallace House whenever we went to Williamsburg.

'In all decency we'll have to be in New York when the book is published,' I said and Emma nodded. 'And if publicity arranges for television crews to come here, which might happen, considering the luck we've had with our last few books, we'd have to agree.'

'They must come here. You can't be yo-yoing back and forth to New York every week.'

I leaned back and said reflectively: 'I doubt I would have much leverage in dictating to N.B.C. how they should run their network,' and she laughed.

I had just used a word that loomed large in our life as we entered our sixties; we both believed that in America the artist in any field was remunerated in large part by the leverage that society entitled him or her to exercise. Emma, who at Bryn Mawr had acquired a much more sensitive education than I had at Mecklenberg, which was after all primarily a church college, was strong in her belief that a writer like me wasted my hard-won prestige and fortune if I did not spend it on good social projects, or use it to help students gain a foothold in society, or, as she liked to phrase it, 'raise hell in the local community when you see it careening off in the wrong direction.'

But I had been reared to be so reticent that when she first voiced this opinion it did not occur to me that I had any leverage. But she educated me on that score, pointing out that wherever I had gone to autograph books long lines of admirers waited for as long as two hours while I scribbled names and exchanged greetings. 'For heaven's sake,' she and the store owner would plead, 'just sign your name, not theirs,' but I could not do that: 'After all, Emma, readers are the ones who keep you and me in business.'

I could not share even with her the true reason why I had tried to be kind and attentive to strangers who sought my autograph. On the publication of my fourth novel, *The Shunning*, my lively editor at Kinetic Press badgered her publicity department: 'Damn it, this man has written three fine novels and he can't get them off first base. Hell, he can't even get them *to* first base, forget coming around to score. So please, please, I ask on bended knee, this time give him a break. Arrange an autographing party at one of the big stores in his home district. Lancaster, Reading or Allentown. Please.'

When publicity checked populations they found that the three towns moved upward in increments of 25,000. Lancaster was smallest with 54,000, Reading next with 78,000 and Allentown the largest with more than 100,000, and Kinetic decided to approach the popular Hess store in the last city to see if they would arrange a modest celebration for me. They pointed out that I could be featured as a local boy, since our farm was only thirty miles to the south.

'I must say,' I confessed later when recalling the dismal affair, 'the store did everything right. Advertising, a sign in the window, a well-arranged corner with a baize-covered table and a pile of my books. I was the one who failed.' Since hardly anyone had read any of my first three books and almost no one realized that I was a writer, no one lined up to buy. I still wince when I think of it. 'There I sat like the Pope waiting to give benediction and maybe allow them to kiss my ring, and no one showed.' After about forty minutes on that doleful day, I heard the store manager tell some of the clerks: 'Form a line, walk past and say hello as if you were buying a book,' and later, when there still had been no sales, the same man told two women clerks: 'Here's seven dollars each. Get in that line of clerks and buy one of his damned books. Let everyone see you flash the money.' The sales were made, two of them, the only ones on that painful day, and even before they happened, I knew they were fake.

As Emma was holding her diary I said: 'Put down in December next year an autograph party at Hess's,' and she protested: 'You do it there every time. Why not some other store?' I knew the reason but did not explain. At the first party Hess had done everything right but had sold no books. Therefore when *Hex* was about to be published and Kinetic asked again if the store would like to host a party, since the novel dealt with their sales district, the manager replied, understandably: 'No thanks,' but when the book department sold more than two thousand copies at eighteen dollars each, the manager had a gracious idea: Hess would put on a gala celebration honoring their local boy on the sale of the three thousandth copy of the book in Allentown, and the customer who bought the lucky copy would not only be photographed with me as I signed it but would also receive a sales credit for a hundred dollars to be spent in the store that joyous day. As I told my wife that night: 'A man could become quite fond of Hess.'

As soon as the manuscript of my final novel left my hands and passed under the control of Kinetic Press, it seemed to take on a life of its own. Numerous duplicate copies were made of the unedited manuscript, and I was assured that they were being placed in the hands of what my editor called 'the opinion makers.' The hope was, Kinetic told me, that people in the trade would begin to say: 'The new Yoder is a hot item.' In the period between October and New Year's a variety of officials held consultations with associates to determine how their companies could participate in the launching of what my editor assured me was going to be 'the sensation of the coming season.' I hoped she was right.

Shortly after the New York offices opened in January, nine months before publication, I began receiving what seemed like daily telephone bulletins about the progress of the manuscript. They came from one or the other of the two brilliant young women who masterminded my affairs and whom Emma described as 'our Ministering Angels with their wands of gold.' The first was Ms. Yvonne Marmelle, the editor at Kinetic Press responsible for seeing that what I wrote was literate and good; the second, Miss Hilda Crane, the agent who handled my business affairs. Each was about forty, quite attractive, underweight and gifted with endless energy and sharp ideas. The only ostensible difference between them was that the editor preferred being known as Ms., the agent as Miss, but why I did not know, for I believed that Miss Crane had a husband hidden somewhere, while Ms. Marmelle did not.

Since my contract with Kinetic gave it control of sales to foreign publishers, the first excited calls to reach our house came from Ms. Marmelle, and now a curious routine developed that some will not believe. I had an aversion to talking about the financial aspects of my occupation as a writer, but Emma, who had always handled what money we had, or didn't have, took great interest in how we were doing, so the calls came not to me but to her: 'Emma! Fantastic news! Great Britain has just bought *Stone Walls*, seventy-five thousand dollars guaranteed.' A few days later came the exciting report that Germany wanted rights in that country, $110,000 guaranteed. France had had good luck with the last three Grenzler novels and wanted this one, as did Sweden, Spain and Japan. By the middle of February six more foreign publishers had come aboard, the most gratifying being the one represented by a call that Ms. Marmelle wanted to deliver to me personally: 'Remember how disappointed I've been over the fact that Italy took none of your three big novels? Well, they've not only taken *Stone Walls* for a fine advance, but they've also picked up the other three for publication at scattered intervals later. And they've paid the money on those others now.'

Because I was afraid of the deadly sin of hubris, remembering when my first books had been ignored by everyone, I masked the quiet satisfaction I felt at having Italy accept me at last and asked: 'How's the editing going?' and she snapped: 'Hey! Forget your work for a minute and let's celebrate,' but I reminded her: 'I have a year's hard work before me. Reacting to your suggestions, reworking rough parts—'

'You sure know how to kill a celebration, Mr. Yoder. Our work's on schedule, and I'd like you to come up here next week to discuss the first five chapters. If you agree with my modest queries, you can go home and start your drudgery.'

'At this stage every change I insert makes the final work a little bit better. That's not drudgery.'

'A few minutes ago you sounded as if it were. Now I want you to fetch a glass of wine. I have mine here, and we'll drink a glass to good old Italy.' I complied, for I liked this brash, outspoken woman, and as my glass made a clinking sound against the telephone we both cried: *'Salut!'* If I were to lose Ms. Marmelle I would be lost.

In the four days before I could get to New York Miss Crane called twice in her more reserved way to inform Emma that the *Reader's Digest* was considering *Walls*, as she called it, for a major selection in its popular Condensed Book series, and to reveal that a mysterious Japanese-Israeli film outfit had expressed interest not necessarily in *Walls* but in my work generally. She said: 'I'll be watching this one carefully. They have no track record but they do seem to be well funded.'

Coincidentally, that same afternoon Ms. Marmelle called to say that Kinetic had been in repeated touch with an Israeli book publisher who wanted to bring out *Stone Walls* but would need some kind of financial concession because of the cost of translating it into Hebrew. 'Help them,' Emma said without pausing to consult me. 'We like people who like books, and their people produced one of the great ones.'

To get to New York for business consultations with my Ministering Angels, I followed a set routine. In my younger days I had enjoyed hopping into my car and barreling along what were then considered the superhighways that carried me from Bethlehem through the Holland Tunnel and into Manhattan, where I parked my car in the same garage, trip after trip, for $2.50 a day plus a $.50 tip. As I grew older and the highways became more crowded, with the parking fee jumping to five and then seven dollars, I did what most sensible drivers in Dresden were doing. I drove myself in my old Buick to the nearby intersection of Rhenish Road and the Interstate, parked my car there and caught a commuter bus that whisked right through the tunnel and into the huge bus terminal on Forty-second Street, from which I could drop into the subway and catch a branch line of the Eighth Avenue that delivered me almost underneath the offices of Kinetic Press. A brisk walk through half a block of underground passages took me to an elevator that hoisted me to the eleventh floor, where Ms. Marmelle's office would be waiting with a comfortable chair in which I could sit talking with my editor.

It was a civilized way to travel, and on most mornings I used the two-hour trip to read some book on Mennonite backgrounds or the causes of the eighteenth-century flood of German immigrants into Pennsylvania farmlands. On this January morning I did no reading; instead I reflected on a subject that constantly perplexed me: How different the last few weeks have been for Yoder Senior compared with what they were twenty-four years ago for Yoder Junior, who was just starting out as a writer. Dear God, how I sweated out those fearful days when I had submitted my manuscript and waited.

And when they finally did report they didn't like it very much, 'but let's get together and see if it can be salvaged,' I drove out of the farm gate at seven, confident that if anyone could straighten out a difficult manuscript I could, but when I reached the spot where I could first see the towers of Manhattan, courage fled.

My editor, a woman much brighter than I, scared me, but she was most helpful, and together we whipped the manuscript into shape. But as it moved through the process of bookmaking I began to learn what fear really was, for I wondered if any critic would bother to review the book or any reader to buy it. None did.

It was hell before death to watch the book appear, flutter like a wounded bird and die. And to experience the same disaster four times! Those were not good years.

Remembering those destructive days, when one book after another failed, forced me to drop my head against the bus window and hide my face lest someone see my embarrassing tears. Finally I blew my nose and said to myself: If Emma hadn't had her teaching job, what would we have done? Just as important, if Kinetic hadn't stayed with me through the bad years, how would my life be ending now? But as I asked this, and the last farms near Somerville in the center of New Jersey vanished, giving way to the strip development that would continue to Manhattan, I brightened while shaking my head in disbelief and a kind of cynicism: Today what happens? Before the manuscript has been edited, or transferred into galleys, or assumed the form of a completed book, its future has already been determined. Publication abroad, probable sales to interested agencies at home. Maybe three hundred thousand first printing and hopefully many of them ultimately sold.

These days a book can be a success before it even appears. Book clubs, movies, television serialization, it all becomes so big. So unimaginable. And so damnably unfair. As everywhere else in America, the poor get poorer, the rich get richer. It's not good, it—is—not—good.

Despite my firm conclusion that American publishing was falling into disarray, I had not the vaguest conception of what might be done to stop the decline, and I could only lament: 'The time is out of joint . . .'

When I entered the familiar offices of Kinetic Press I felt as if I were a member of the firm, for in recent years they had done well by me, and I acknowledged the debt I owed them for having stayed with me till my books began to sell. As I rode to the eleventh floor and left the elevator to go to the office door bearing the small metal plate with the name YVONNE MARMELLE I felt that I was where I belonged. This was home.

Knocking gently, I pushed open the door and saw the woman to whom I owed so much. Slim and well groomed, with the New York look of one who had grown up knowing city ways, her personal appearance, the acquired part, was somewhat French, as befitted her name, but her manners and speech were strictly Manhattan.

When she saw me she jumped up from her chair, ran forward and gave me a huge embrace: 'Oh, Mr. Yoder, not ten minutes ago Book-of-the-Month Club called. They're considering *Stone Walls* for their main October selection!' She danced with me for a few moments to celebrate this quantum leap in her efforts to get my last book off to a dramatic start.

I found her effusiveness embarrassing, especially since on the bus my mind had been brooding about exactly this sort of inflated success. I looked past her shoulder at a remarkable painting that for me summarized what publishing was about. It showed a silk-screen reproduction of a feathery Monet landscape, which on the face of it had nothing to do with publishing, but those in the know shared its professional secret. Now I went to the Monet, unhooked the wire from the long glass-headed nail on which it hung, and turned it over, suspending the reversed painting from a tiny loop that had not been visible. With this maneuver the significance of the painting was revealed.

The back had been covered by a rectangle of the composition board artists use, and on it a chart had been lettered by someone who knew his job:

PORTRAIT OF AN EDITOR

YEAR	TITLE	ADVANCE	COPIES SOLD	ROYALTIES PAID ON HARDCOVERS
1967	*Grenzler*	$500	943	−$2,119
1970	*The Farm*	$700	1,107	−$3,147
1973	*The School*	$800	1,304	−$4,246
1976	*The Shunning*	$900	1,607	−$5,210
1980	*Hex*	$1,300	871,896	$1,307,844
1984	*The Creamery*	$200,000	917,453	$2,477,126
1988	*The Fields*	$500,000	1,000,000	$4,263,191
1991	*Stone Walls*	?	?	?

As the two who had been responsible for achieving these dramatic figures, Ms. Marmelle and I studied the data and shook our heads in disbelief. Then she showed me a feature she had added since my last visit: a heavy cloth that could be dropped to mask the last three lines giving the figures for the books following *Hex*: 'I don't want our experienced writers to know the advances we pay someone like you, especially if the man looking at the board has just been told that we can't allow him more than eleven thousand on what promises to be his next turkey. And I don't want young writers to get blinded by the royalty figures for your last two books.' She added: 'I may bring the artist back to make that last column Total Royalties Paid. As I'm sure you've already guessed, that would include foreign payments, book-club sales, any sales of subsidiary rights that come in, and on your books they can be amazing.'

At this point she dropped the heavy cloth and we stood before the chart contemplating the first five lines. For her part, she refrained from covering herself with glory for having fought so vigorously with Kinetic's top management to give me one more chance and then another and another. The figures spoke for her.

I had sometimes caught hints of the struggle she had maintained to keep me alive, for fragments of conversation were burned into my soul:

1967: 'Mr. Yoder, I did everything humanly possible to move *Grenzler* because I know it's a fine book. I failed.'

1973: 'Mr. Yoder, the very best I could do was another seven hundred dollars, but when I yelled, "I'll give him one hundred dollars of my own," they raised the ante to eight hundred dollars.'

1976:   'Mr. Yoder, listen to every word I say. You're going to be one of our best writers. Mr. MacBain isn't quite sure. Our salesmen don't believe it and I suppose your wife doesn't. But I do. Advance sales on *Shunning* are deplorable. But to hell with them. Go home and start that new book we talked about. Make every word sing, because this can be the one that breaks the logjam. You're a writer. Trust me.'

1980:   'Mr. Yoder, I couldn't sleep last night. *Hex* tells the story. If we miss this time, Kinetic will probably drop you, but I'm telling you that if they do, they drop me, too. I'll take you to some other house with me, and sooner or later we'll do it. But toward morning I did fall asleep, and so help me, I dreamed that *Hex* was going to knock them silly. Let's pray that the shrinks are right and that dreams do count.'

It had taken thirteen years of heartbreaking labor before we published a book that earned back its meager advance, and if Ms. Marmelle had not questioned my stubborn insistence on excessively building the backgrounds of characters and their milieus, I could never have acquired my skill in writing books that readers would cherish. The first five lines of the chart constituted a portrait of two people who'd had faith in their convictions.

'Do you want to see the figures I've penciled in as guesses for your last line?'

'Don't hex me.'

'They'd be reassuring.' But she put the paper away, for she had learned that I liked to hear neither bad news nor good. As I had said in the bad days: 'I write books. Things happen to them. In my mind the two facts are not related.' I had tried never to rail against the public's indifference when it ignored my early novels nor rejoice when it embraced my later ones: 'I write books and allow them to find their own levels of success.'

But she had one bit of news that she knew would give me as much quiet satisfaction as it gave her when it was faxed from Kinetic's London agent: 'Recent interest in Yoder's "Grenzler Octet," as it's being called in Europe, has enabled us to sell the first four novels to three countries that passed them over before, and *Shunning* by itself to four additional publishers who are now viewing it as perhaps his finest novel. I think I can guarantee that *Hex* will be a steady new best-seller across Europe.'

We did not linger to gloat over this good news, for we were two battle-scarred veterans constantly aware of the perils; I knew that a writer's reputation was only as good as his last book, while she had seen numerous examples of editors who'd had great successes but whose current stable of writers were producing nothing. Each of us had a lot riding on *Stone Walls* and we knew it.

So I was attentive during the nose-to-nose session that morning when she hammered at me from a page of notes detailing the things she had not liked in the opening sections of *Walls*: 'I like this story very much, Mr. Yoder, but I think it contains a weakness so serious it might damage sales.' That last word irritated me: 'You had adequate proof in those first years that sales don't worry me.'

'They worry *me*, but let me phrase it in a way that I know does worry you. The fault I'm speaking of, if not corrected, would cause your readers to be disappointed,' and now I had to listen.

'Your story line is solid, but its level is so exalted you've forgotten to create suspense. And the reason, I think, is that instead of focusing on your characters, you go chasing after abstractions. Because of this, I think the novel would profit from a subplot in which the reader could get involved.'

Although her ideas irritated me—and seemed almost an intrusion on my terrain—I'd had similar sessions with her on my other books and had found her to be right most of the time, so I had to listen, even though I did not like what I was hearing: 'How can I do it?'

'First, cut. Cut a good deal of the long middle section. That'll provide space for the subplot.'

'I don't have one. What lines are you thinking along?'

'No specific suggestions at this point. I'm just asking you to consider it.'

'Hmmm. I'll think about it.'

She continued: 'Oh yes, a technical point. You do not differentiate your female characters enough, and the problem arises, I think, from the fact that you do not take time to describe and define them carefully when they first appear. Nail them down. I don't advocate Fenimore Cooper's device—always a blond heroine opposed to a brunette villainess—but I suppose if we talked long enough that's what it would come down to. Use the Cooper trick, but mask it with switches and changes and sudden revelations.'

'I agree. Next?'

'You aren't going to like this one, but I can operate only on gut feelings, and I've had warning signals. If your readers have already read seven, or even only the three big novels, they pretty well know where things are in the Grenzler district—what a Pennsylvania Dutch farm looks like—how the landscape influences the behavior of the people who occupy it. You may have too much land and too few people. I think you could profitably cut sharply or even eliminate things like the long passage on why the geology of Berks County dictated how the dam should be built. And when the Troxels are forced to sell their farm, we know they'll feel despondent. Show that through their emotions toward one another, not their grief at leaving

a particular field that had been in their family since 1690. We already
know that, we've been over it with the clubfooted uncle. I'd cut the
descriptions and get on with the story.'

'I can't agree. This is a novel about the destruction of the stone
fences that defined a man's fields—the stone walls of his barn that
defined him.'

'Do you think your readers are interested in that much ecology?
They're expecting a novel, you know.'

'I hate that phrase *your readers* as if they were a special breed. If
a book sells a million copies, its readers are apt to be pretty much
of a cross section, don't you think?' ·

'I hope so, for your sake.'

'I think my readers, as you call them, also have serious concerns,
also wrestle with ideas.'

It had always been like that with us; she had no hesitation in
recommending the severest cuts or alterations, and I offered no
apologies when I felt I had to reject any of her suggestions. This was
not obstinacy; through the years I had built a vision of absolute
clarity as to what a book must be: its size, the number of its chapters,
and of supreme importance the significance of the theme, the characters, the plot, the manner of flow from start to finish and from one
scene to another. Also the way the book would look—its binding, the
color of its jacket, the look of its individual page. I did not talk about
these things to others, not even to my wife or Ms. Marmelle, but I
brooded over them constantly and it was my dedication to those
visions that had sustained me through the bad years when almost no
one but Ms. Marmelle believed I could write.

The virtue was not all on my side, not by any means. Ms. Marmelle
also knew what a book was, an object of beauty standing in racks in
bookstores across the nation and the world, waiting to be picked up
by buyers. She often told her writers: 'It isn't worth a damn unless
somebody is bullied into realizing its merit and not only buys it but

also says at the end: "I'd like to see what this guy does next time out." That's writing. That's publishing.' We had become a formidable pair, each instructing the other, each adding her or his magic to that confederacy of insight, talent, love of words, dedication to narration and skill in the managerial manipulation that produced fine books, and we shared an objective: to close the Grenzler series with a blaze of rockets. What we did not share, apparently, was the basic concept of the novel; she wanted to focus on characters and plot, I wanted to deal primarily with the land, the physical backdrop, that had served me so powerfully in the first seven novels.

At lunchtime, at a quarter past one, we were tired from the morning's concentration, and with pleasure at being out in the cold air, we walked briskly to an Italian restaurant tucked away on one of the side streets between Lexington and Third. There she recommended a light dish that she said the chef made to perfection, a tasty eggplant parmigiana. While we waited for it to arrive, she took my left hand and brought it to her lips: 'A day of celebration,' and I feared she was going to talk about some new sales triumph with *Stone Walls*, but she was thinking of something that she knew was far more important to me and, in a sense, to her: 'To think that fifteen long years after we published *The Shunning*, knowing it was a fine book, the world is finally accepting our original evaluation. Frankly, Mr. Yoder, I feared it would die unnoticed, and I'm simply overjoyed that Europe is discovering it.' Suddenly she flung her arms in the air and shouted so loud that others in the restaurant could not help hearing: 'Whee!' When customers stared as if to ask: What's up? she explained in a voice that carried: 'The good guys just won one!' and several raised their glasses to salute whatever victory she had achieved.

I laughed, not at her exhibition but at my oldest memory of *The Shunning*, which had to do with my wife's family. I said: 'I'd always known that Emma came from a rather motley background. Her maiden name was Stoltzfus, pure Amish from Lancaster County, headquarters of that strange and colorful people. Remarks she dropped accidentally led me to believe that her family had once been Amish, but they certainly weren't when I met her. She was typical Mennonite, proven by the fact that Emma's father operated a big garage in Reading, where *his* father had been a hidebound Mennonite, but also a sharp gentleman with a pfennig. I think Emma's father and her uncle owned their garage, but at any rate they had enough funds to send her to Bryn Mawr, which was itself unusual for people who were Mennonites and Amish. When I met her she was Episcopalian.

'After we married and I'd written my first two novels, Emma and I drove out to Lancaster and people who knew us whispered: "Aha, he's going to write about the Amish and make us look like fools." Not at all. I'd decided long ago that I'd never write about the Amish because it was too easy to make fun of them and their ascetic way of life.

'Well, anyway, while we were in Lancaster visiting Emma's relatives I heard frequent comments about two stern men everyone called "the Stoltzfus boys," and under my prodding a riveting tale unfolded. During the last years of the previous century, Emma's grandfather Amos and his older brother Uriah belonged to the most conservative branch of the Amish. Unfortunately, they became embroiled in a religious debate of almost mortal intensity. Uriah adhered to the fundamentalist branch, which taught, among other things, that if a man wore suspenders to secure his trousers he was guilty of vanity and a sinful addiction to self-adornment; his group held their pants up with ropes used as belts, used pins instead of buttons, and wore heavy beards.

'Amos, already a freethinker at age fourteen, would have none of this, so there was bound to be animosity between the brothers. Now, there was another slightly more liberal branch of the congregation, which had proposed a compromise: "Since suspenders are more effective than a rope in holding up a man's pants, we authorize them, but the man must wear only one brace over whichever shoulder he likes, because to wear two would be an act of vanity." Had Amos accepted this solution, an arrangement could have been worked out.

'Unfortunately, he insisted not only upon suspenders with two braces but he was also caught buying store-made clothes instead of having his wife sew everything by hand, and such blatant insurgency could not be permitted. Conservative brother Uriah so goaded his liberal brother Amos that the fight became known in the Lancaster area as "no-suspenders brother against two-suspenders," and shock waves swept not only the congregation but the Amish community generally.

'I asked people who were telling me this: "What happened?" and they said Uriah was so outraged that his brother should challenge the sanctity of his principles that he led a movement to ostracize Amos, his wife and their children. *Shunning* it was called, *Meidung* in German, and it was a terrible punishment, for it banned the stricken family from any intercourse with other members of the congregation: Amos could not talk with them, meet with them, eat with them, buy or sell from them, or worship with them. The ostracism was total, and what was worse, since it was only Amos who was shunned and not his family, his wife was forbidden to sleep with him. Emma's grandparents, a tough breed, could not tolerate this, so in fury they quit the congregation, the Stoltzfus farm of which they owned half and Lancaster itself. They moved to Reading; Amos shaved, affiliated with a Mennonite church, and since he loved horses, he opened a livery stable, which prospered.

'But as the years passed, they thought less about the money they were making and more about their happy days as members of an Amish community, so every autumn when the harvest was in, Amos sent a humble letter to his Amish church begging it to cancel his shunning so he might resume the membership he and his wife longed for.

'When the first letter arrived, in 1901, the elderly head of the congregation said: "According to Amish rules a member shunned can be rejoined to the church, but only if he comes back, throws himself on his hands and knees before the church leader, admits his sin and pleads for reinstatement." When Amos received this verdict, he told his wife: "Fair enough. I was headstrong years ago, and if this is the rule for repentance, I accept." But in the meantime, who had become leader of the congregation to whom Amos must bow and scrape and show tears in his eyes? His brother Uriah, whose tyranny had led to the banishment in the first place. Since Amos refused to humble himself before his self-righteous brother, he stayed excommunicated, shunned by all good Amish who wore no suspenders.'

I did not laugh when relating this bizarre tale, for I knew from my wife's experience that the stain of the shunning never left Amos and his family. He prospered, helped his son convert the livery stable into a garage and immersed himself in the more liberal Mennonite society: 'But his enormous loss ate into his soul. Spiritually he was an Amish man who wanted to die in the bosom of his church, but each year that his wealth increased he fell farther away from that austere faith. Each new device he purchased, such as an icebox, made it more unlikely that he would turn back, but even so, he continued to send annual begging letters to his old church and each year his own brother reminded him of the rules: "Come back, humble yourself on your knees before the head of the church, confess your sins and pray for our forgiveness and we will consult with the membership to see if they want you back." The yearly letter never reminded Amos that the head of the church who would adjudicate his guilt and innocence and before whom he must crawl was still Brother Uriah, but Amos knew this and died in exile.'

Ms. Marmelle, who had edited *The Shunning*, had not realized at the time that I was writing about my own family—that is, my wife's—and she said: 'I always wondered about that novel. After our disappointment with your first two tries I suggested that you write about the Amish; they were more appealing to the eye—the old-world costumes, the black buggies and all—but you refused, said you'd never ridicule a good people or use them for humor. Then you did write about them. . . .'

'But not for humor. The story overwhelmed me. I felt it had to be told.'

Ms. Marmelle said: 'The reason the novel's having a rebirth is what made it powerful back then. The last hundred pages, where Amos is succeeding dramatically in his social and financial life but experiencing tragedy in his spiritual one. You've written nothing better, Mr. Yoder, than those scenes in which he slips back into Lancaster to view secretly the farm his family had owned through four different centuries and on which he worked so hard to improve it. In the darkness he acknowledges that only his stubbornness about the suspenders is preventing him from ever assuming responsibility for that beautiful land again.'

I have never been comfortable when someone praises my work; I feel embarrassed, but the emotions of this day affected me, and as we finished lunch I said: 'The good scene was that one near the end. When he converts his livery stable into a garage. Says good-bye to the horses, his last association with the land. He is no longer an Amishman, not even a Mennonite. He's passed over into the real world.' I sat silent, relieved that my editor was making no comment: 'You know, Ms. Marmelle, Emma has never thought of herself as a Mennonite. She and her family dropped that designation when she went to college.'

Ms. Marmelle said: 'I like your tough little wife, from what I know of her on the telephone. I wish you'd bring her in to see me on one of your visits.' I nodded and she placed her hand on mine: 'In the office you wouldn't allow me to tell you about the wonderful news that's flooding our office. But Emma deserves to know, and it's so important to me that I have a right to tell someone.' Thereupon she revealed the estimates that were thrilling the people at Kinetic: 'Every contingency in your contract has already been met or is going to be met, and each one adds a million dollars to your guarantee. Book-of-the-Month, maybe. Softcover publication, assured. Foreign publications, assured. Three months at least on the *Times* best-seller list, a sure thing. And how many copies do you suppose we'll have for a first run? They're talking about seven hundred fifty thousand.'

Embarrassed, I said: 'You'd better have some good salesmen in the field,' and she said: 'You can tell Emma that I predict she'll be able to bank not less than five million from *Stone Walls*, and maybe six if there's a movie or television sale.'

'I wish you hadn't told me,' I said, and she laughed: 'I wasn't telling you. I was telling me—and Emma. We understand about these things.'

Suddenly she moved closer and spoke in a low voice: 'Do you accept hypothetical questions?'

'In everything except politics.'

'May I throw one at you?' When I nodded, she said: 'This is a hypothetical on a hypothetical. If Kinetic were to be sold tomorrow to some other huge conglomerate and the new bosses fired me, and I was able to find a new job with a new publisher, would you come along as one of my writers?'

'Of course, unless you had stolen Kinetic funds in going.'

'How about if I was not fired but felt that under the new conditions I had to quit?'

'Your ethical standards are mine. Of course I'd stay with you.'

'And now the daddy of them all. Suppose the new buyers were not Americans? Say Japanese or German? And I could not abide them and quit in a huff?'

'I might very well leave whether you did or not.'

'Understand, my questions were confidential and hypothetical.'

'My answers were neither. I take publishing far more seriously than even Emma realizes. With me it's not a game, it's not a matter of figures, it's one of the world's great professions, and I'm elated to be part of it.' I had said too much and was embarrassed, so with a voice as low as hers I whispered: 'I couldn't work without your help, and I never forget it.'

On this visit to New York I remained in town overnight, for it was obligatory that I have a session with my agent, with whom I had a distant, strictly business relationship. I'd had a humiliating experience with agents, having been grudgingly picked up at the start by one of the big-name men who, owing a debt to Ms. Marmelle, had accepted me as a client but only as a gesture to her. When this busy man saw that my first books foundered and that I had no gift for writing short, colorful articles, he dropped me by means of a letter, not even paying me the courtesy of a phone call. I was then adopted by a brash young man who was starting his own agency after having served an apprenticeship with William Morris, but although he talked big he performed little, and since he quickly saw that I was never going to be able to command in the writing business what he called 'important numbers,' he too dropped me, and in recent years, when the 'numbers' for my books became not just important but staggering, I have often wondered what the young man, whose business has succeeded, thought when he remembered the day he threw me out. Fortunately, Hilda Crane, a hard worker, offered to represent me and my fourth novel, *The Shunning*, which she liked. With hopes soaring she had submitted it to all adjuncts of the publishing business—Hollywood, television, newspapers for serialization—but persuaded none to take any interest. Continuing to have faith in it, she assured me that, sooner or later, it, or one of my other books, would be recognized for the fine storytelling it was. She had said: 'I'm sure I'll be your agent then, and we'll both celebrate.' She was delighted but not surprised when *Hex* became a runaway best-seller; with quiet glee she submitted it to the same agencies as before, and this time the responses were decidedly positive.

Miss Crane maintained a three-room office on upper Broadway— no glitz but lots of working files—and told me in jest: 'I might have to move into larger quarters because of the increased amount of work I have to do handling the many aspects of your last three books—and hopefully the next.' A woman of forty-four who could, depending on the time of day and whether the news that week had been favorable or disastrous, look either a radiant twenty-four or a dejected sixty-four, she was a quiet, stable influence in my life. Far less mercurial than Ms. Marmelle, she had warned me from the start about her professional behavior: 'I do not coddle my writers, nor help them in their divorces, nor buy theater tickets for them, nor arrange hotel rebates. Specifically I do not guide them or help them in the writing of their material. What I do, and do well, is accept what they've written, if they deem it ready, and find a market for it. If it can be sold, I'll sell it, and sometimes they'll be amazed at where it finally lands. House organ, manufacturers' journal, farm magazine, university magazine, I comb them all. My passion is to see things in print, and sometimes I'll sell an article for five dollars, just to get its writer into print. That's what counts.'

She received 10 percent of everything I earned, no matter how I earned it, and there was an understanding between us that I would accept no cash or check on my own without informing her of it and sending to her without being asked her 10 percent. For that fee she performed a number of mystifying services: most important, she negotiated fees for whatever I did, for it had been seen early in the writing business that one could not expect a writer to argue one day with an editor about the development of a manuscript and to come back the next day and argue with her over the fact that he wanted more money for what he was trying to get into publishable form. It was not only more sensible but also more profitable to allow the writer to worry about the quality of his manuscript and the agent to worry about getting a just price for it.

In addition to negotiating royalties, Miss Crane also handled subsidiary sales, licensing arrangements if any became necessary, obtaining and renewing copyrights and a score of other services. On some weeks she might send me three letters or even four, each dealing with some technical publishing matter about which I knew little but which demanded legal attention. In a normal year she earned her 10 percent, but this year, if the figures Ms. Marmelle had recited at the end of our lunch prevailed, Miss Crane would earn at least half a million dollars from the fellow she called 'my quiet little Dutchman,' and she would have done little specific work to justify that fee. Ms. Marmelle, on the other hand, would have served as midwife on the manuscript, babying it along and whipping occasional chaos into literary order. She would be intimately involved in whatever success the manuscript achieved, yet she would earn only the relatively modest salary that Kinetic allowed her.

This seemed most unfair, but once I heard Miss Crane justify the percentage she earned from another writer with this logic: 'I have nurtured him like my own child, negotiated constantly improved deals for him, seen that he wrote for the right journals at the right time, and ensured that his reputation moved constantly upward. Without me he might have fumbled along without focus.'

The person to whom she was speaking asked: 'But couldn't his wife have handled these matters just as effectively?' and the question alerted me, for I suspected that Emma could have done so. However, Miss Crane had a withering response: 'Whenever a writer uses his wife as his agent, it's a sign he's on his way down. A writer doesn't need a loving hand. He needs a tough one.'

She offered her questioner one more justification: 'The ten percent

I collect from a writer like Lukas Yoder enables my agency to represent beginning writers who earn me nothing, and to nurture them till they establish a foothold. Yoder keeps the young ones alive until they become Yoders.' As I listened I was mindful of one humiliating fact: In my first thirteen years as a writer, my three different agents earned from my efforts a combined total of $496.10, and they must have spent five times that much on postage and phone calls. I did not begrudge Miss Crane her present massive fees, but I did hope she was doing what she said, spending some of my money on the cultivation of young writers.

Today when I entered her office she seemed a mite more reserved than usual, but when she detected my own hesitancy she said briskly: 'Mr. Yoder, I'm so glad to see you. We have much to discuss,' and before I was properly seated she said in her best professional voice: 'There's good news and there's bad news. Which first?' When I shrugged, she said: 'Very well. The good,' and briskly she ran through the sales she had completed since last speaking with Emma. As she turned the sheets on which her notes had been jotted down, I sat admiring her, rather than listening to the details, in which I was not interested. In her office she was always well groomed, wearing fairly expensive but not flamboyant business suits usually with some small accessory on her left lapel. She was a handsome woman, hair not yet gray-flecked, no flabbiness under the chin, and eyes not yet jaded by the repetitive nature of her business. She was, I said approvingly to myself, a reassuring person with whom to do business, but my final judgment as she droned on about subsidiary rights was more impersonal: 'She looks like a good eighth-grade English teacher who has been promoted to principal of her junior high school.'

'But that's all preamble to the exciting news, Mr. Yoder. Have you seen that sleeper film about the Amish? Low-budget but it won some Oscars, I believe. At least it was nominated. *Witness*.'

'Heard about it, haven't seen it.'

'Took everyone by surprise. Excellent actors—you may not have heard of them—and a believable story, but the hero of the film was your Amish country. The camera shots of the fields and barns made it delectable.'

'I hear they treated the Amish with respect. No cheap humor.'

'That they did, but what's important to you is that the success of the film awakened interest in your properties. An outfit named Argosy Films, put together by a Japanese financier with oodles of money and an Israeli cinematic genius, wants to take an option on *The Shunning*, and if I read their motives correctly, they want to do a film in the great tradition. Careful development of character, shots showing the beauty of the land, the spiritual triumph of the ugly brother, who remains Amish, and the deterioration of the good brother, who gains financial success but loses contact with the soil.'

I leaned forward: 'At least they know what the story's about. If it had been one more Hollywood outfit wanting another option on *Hex*, I'd not have been interested.'

Miss Crane, smiling austerely, picked another sheet from her pile of memorandums relating to me: 'That's what I was going to take up next. An entirely new Hollywood outfit, this time with some German funding, wants on option on *Hex*. They have a writer under contract who's positive that this time he can lick the story line.'

'How often have we heard that?'

Miss Crane winced, for I had touched upon one of the frustrating but in a sense amusing aspects of her business, and mine. *Hex* had been such a sensational success as a book that the various motion picture companies operating at that time, many of them now vanished, fought to gain rights, but when one finally did, for $185,000, nonrefundable, it promptly discovered that the action of the book was so spasmodic, the scenes so fractured and the characters so inflexible that no story line suitable for a motion picture could be hammered out. The project was abandoned and the payment written

THE WRITER

. . . .

52

off as a loss, but I did keep the money because Miss Crane had been vigilant in drafting the contract. The rights also reverted to me.

In the eleven years that followed, numerous companies felt at one time or another that they could 'lick the *Hex* problem,' and each, in succession, took an option, paying a standard fee of between five and ten thousand dollars, which gave them exclusive rights for a stated period, after which they had to either go ahead with the picture or drop the project, thereby forfeiting the trivial option money.

At any one time since the success of *Hex*, Miss Crane had had two or three options working on various books in the Grenzler series, and each brought in a few thousand dollars, but none matured into a real contract. With my interest aroused so often but being invariably disappointed, I could no longer express enthusiasm when Miss Crane telephoned that yet another film company wanted an option on *Hex* or on any of the other successful books. I always advised: 'Give them the option now, take it back next year, and pass it along to someone else the year after that.' I had little hope that a picture would ever be made, and in fact had not much interest in whether it was or not.

She could not be so blasé: 'Mr. Yoder, always remember that everything good that happens to a book—the plays, the musicals, the movies, the TV series, the deluxe editions—begins with three talented guys sitting around a barroom table, and one cries: "Hey, wouldn't it be great if we could get rights to that Yoder book and persuade Newman to play the lead and Streep the heroine? And get Kazan to come back for one great final stab?" and one of the men says: "I know Streep. She loves Yoder's work. Told me she could visualize the whole Amish scene, like in *Witness*. Told me she wished her agent had gotten her that part." And the third guy says: "I know Jerry Herman, and he's been looking for a period piece, American history like what he used so effectively in *Dolly*, and I'm sure he would jump at the chance to tackle *Hex*." Then the man who knows

Newman says: "But Paul can't sing," and Jerry Herman's friend says: "So we'll get some kid who can." '

She also told me: 'Every blind alley we've gone down has started with those three guys in a bar saying: "Hey, wouldn't it be great if . . ." But remember, every good thing that's happened started that way, too. First man said: "Hey, I read this book called *Anna and the King of Siam*, very colorful setting. Now if we could get an English-looking dame in her forties and an actor who could look Oriental," and the second man said: "I know this guy Yul Brynner and maybe he'd be interested," and the third says: "But what you're talking about would cry for music, and my brother-in-law has an in with the lawyer for Rodgers and Hammerstein . . ." And *that* time it wasn't all futile options. It was a masterpiece, so you mustn't laugh off any queries. Creative geniuses are a slap-happy lot. Treat them with respect.'

'I would be most interested in the group that wants to do *The Shunning*—if they intend to do it the way you said.'

'Mr. Yoder, remember that I said *hope to do*, not *intend*.'

'I know, but you did make it sound enticing. Give them encouragement.'

She had several other matters to discuss concerning my *Stone Walls* and the avenues she hoped to explore, but as always I lost interest in the complex details, preferring that either Miss Crane or Ms. Marmelle dispose of them; I was rarely disappointed in their decisions, for I had explained early in my association with Miss Crane: 'I think a writer does best when he directs his entire attention to his typewriter. That is, if he trusts his agent—and I trust you.'

I had tried to maintain the same kind of placid relationship with Kinetic Press. Its recent contracts with me had been fairly important, considering the sums involved, but each had been disposed of in less than three minutes. Kinetic or Miss Crane would call regarding details, Emma would call me to the kitchen phone, and I would

listen to the details and say: 'Sounds O.K.' and the deal would go
into effect. Of course, after it had been agreed upon in principle, the
Kinetic lawyers and Miss Crane might argue for several months over
minute details. In recent years Kinetic was preoccupied with new
forms of reproduction, innovations like audio books, mechanical and
distribution processes not yet even in commercial existence but
looming on the horizon. When the formal contract finally arrived,
it might run to sixteen pages, most of them dealing with matters that
had never been mentioned to me, but later I would discover to my
gratification that some new process that had exploded onto the market had been covered by some agreement Miss Crane had hammered
out years before.

When I heard Miss Crane's summary of the good news I asked:
'This sounds so good, what can be bad?' and she coughed nervously,
then leaned forward to speak to me directly: 'Not really bad news,
Mr. Yoder, but disturbing. Really, quite disturbing.'

'Shoot. I'm a big boy.'

'Three ominous warnings, all focusing on the same problem. First,
the *Reader's Digest* called yesterday after you left Ms. Marmelle to
say they were not taking *Walls*. Their editorial readers said their
subscribers would be disappointed. Too much preaching, not enough
story line.' I brought my fingertips to my lips and waited for the next
blast. 'Today the Book-of-the-Month Club called to say that they
would not be taking the novel for October, nor later. Same kind of
reasoning: "Yoder fails to provide the gripping personal histories for
which he has become famous in his last three novels. Our readers
would be disappointed." And we've heard from the big chains—
Dalton, Walden. They've cut their pre-pub orders by two thirds.
Their experts made the comment that could prove most damaging
if the others picked it up: "Yoder has gone back to the well once too
often." That could hurt.'

When she leaned back, but with her hands extended on the desk as if to ask, So what do we do, Mr. Yoder? I looked at her, tried to smile and said quietly: 'Three body blows, no?' and she said: 'Indeed. And since we can assume that word of these decisions has swept the industry in New York and California, we could find ourselves in deep trouble.'

'I don't see why. Three big customers lost in the United States. Three big sales in Europe.'

'Mr. Yoder! That's not a comparison. A watermelon to a lima bean. A book makes its reputation in the United States or it dies. I repeat, this is very serious.'

'Not to me. Anyway, if it's as bad as you say, why didn't Ms. Marmelle warn me?'

'Because when you were with her, the bombs had not yet exploded. Late yesterday and today, they have. And yesterday she didn't know that her own Kinetic had already cut back the initial print order from the planned seven hundred fifty thousand to a mere two hundred fifty thousand.'

When I heard this I had to laugh: 'A mere two hundred fifty thousand! Do you know what that would have meant to me in the ugly years before you became my agent? I'd have flown to the moon.'

'But as you just said, you're a big boy now. The industry expects big things from big men. Kinetic hangs great hopes on you. So do I. If this book can be saved, we've got to make every effort to do it. In ten minutes we're having a meeting in the next room.'

'Who's we?'

'You, me, Yvonne and Mr. MacBain.'

I was astonished that she would have been bold enough to convene such a meeting without consulting me and said so, but she squelched that: 'I didn't call it. Kinetic did, and the fact that they're coming here, not us there, is proof that they take this far more seriously than you seem to.' Since she had never before spoken to me like this, I realized that she was no longer merely my representative but also a tough-minded professional agent who could not afford to have it said in publishing circles that she had allowed one of her clients to fall on his face. In the meeting about to occur she would be fighting for her survival as well as for mine.

The session was most embarrassing, for Ms. Marmelle had to retract almost everything she had said yesterday: 'Mr. Yoder, I am sorry. I didn't hear the bad news until this morning.'

'I don't consider it bad news. Unfortunate, yes. But with the big European sales it's already a success.' And then I added an unfortunate conclusion to my sentence: 'For me.'

'Not for us,' Mr. MacBain said sharply, and when I looked at that grave magisterial face whose frowns and smiles had been so important to me throughout my writing life, I felt ashamed at having placed my interests so far above his. At a half-dozen crucial meetings in my career it was his willingness to listen to Ms. Marmelle's defense of me that had saved the day; others at Kinetic had been willing to dump me—only he among the managers stood firm, and I revered him for it.

He was in his late sixties now and, if rumor touched the truth, in the ugly position of having three or four conglomerates interested in the possibility of buying Kinetic, a marginally profitable company. Each reasoned: 'We could pump in substantial funds so that Kinetic could gamble with the big boys. And we'd give them sophisticated management so that bottom-line profits would be ensured.' Actual bidding for Kinetic had not yet occurred, but subterranean calculations were under way, and it seemed probable that an offer of some kind would eventually surface. If the offer was so high that the stockholders were tempted by unexpected profits, they might vote to sell the company, whoever the bidder might be and whatever his credentials were for operating a publishing business. When that happened, Mr. MacBain, regardless of his past brilliance in steering Kinetic, would be out of a job and out of publishing.

To have my novel, the company's major fall offering, collapse in the American market would be disastrous, for the perceived value of the firm would plummet in publishing circles, and I was aware of this. So if my *Stone Walls* could be salvaged in any of the three major markets in which it had been so unceremoniously rejected, Kinetic as a firm, MacBain as its president, Ms. Marmelle as the senior editor involved and Miss Crane as my agent might all be saved a major embarrassment. I could see in the faces of the others that this was not going to be your congenial publisher's meeting, and I could not anticipate what I might be advised to do, nor how I might react to pressure.

Mr. MacBain started by summarizing the situation: 'Negative reports from three major markets with devastating effects on pre-pub sales. Where did our in-house estimates of this manuscript go so badly wrong?'

'I fear we may have assumed that any novel by Mr. Yoder was assured of wide reception. Obviously, we overestimated his popularity.'

Humiliated by having such matters discussed in my presence, I had to protest: 'I think the sales that come in will be gratifying. I don't have to shoot for the moon every time.'

Somewhat icily Mr. MacBain said: 'You'd better inform him about the revision in the print order we had to make,' but when Ms. Marmelle began, 'From an initial belief that we could sell seven hundred fifty thousand—' Miss Crane interrupted: 'I've already warned him. Now down to two hundred fifty thousand.'

'Fearful reduction,' Mr. MacBain said. 'Tell me, why does everyone think there's something seriously wrong with this manuscript?'

To my surprise Miss Crane, not my editor, answered. In clipped sentences she laid out the driving force behind my novels: 'His four big novels, beginning with *Shunning*, focused on strong characters involved in powerful human dramas. We all remember the two brothers fighting over principle. In *Hex* there was that near witch, the burning of the farm, the resistance of the wife. In *The Creamery* there was the almost mortal fight over ownership, and in the *The Fields*, which so many readers loved, there was the gallant effort of Huddle Amos to protect his farm against the claims of his cousin and the false testimony of his church elders. Readers could choose sides in a Yoder novel. There was always a hero to cheer for.'

MacBain startled me by defending *Stone Walls*: 'I cheered for the three farmers who would not sell their land, who wouldn't allow their fences to be bulldozed.'

'But where there's three,' Miss Crane pointed out, 'the effect is diluted. The reader doesn't cheer for any specific actor in the company.'

'Is the story, then, defective?' Mr. MacBain asked, looking at me as he spoke.

When no one answered, Ms. Marmelle said hesitantly: 'I fear it's a case of exaggerated expectations . . . and misguided ones. The big markets look for a standard Lukas Yoder tale about his Pennsylvania Dutch. They do not want a lecture on ecology. When that's what they get, they feel defrauded. As simple as that.'

In the silence that followed, everyone looked at Mr. MacBain, and after a painful pause, he said: 'Mr. Yoder, we cannot lose this novel.'

'You're not losing it,' I said, but he obviously feared I would repeat the fact that I was not unhappy about the way things had worked out so far, for he interrupted me: 'Tell me, Mr. Yoder, can you think of any revisions that might lessen the disappointments the outside readers have reported?' Before I could respond, he added: 'I don't mean recasting the novel. I liked it as it is. But I do mean making it, with the minimum amount of reworking, into more of a Yoder novel, more of what the public expects of you, and has a right to expect.'

When this question was thrown at me I sat facing three fine people, to each of whom I was indebted, and deeply. They had molded my professional life and had tried to steer me in proper and profitable paths. I could see that each eagerly wanted me to revise my novel, to bring it into paths that would be more familiar and comfortable to the reader. But I had written *Stone Walls* as the culmination of my Grenzler novels, showing people returning to the land and abusing it with malls and condominiums instead of nurturing it as they should. The charge was true that this time I had villains instead of heroes, but sometimes villains need to be identified. I could not alter this completion of a grand design I had intended from the start of my first novel, nor would I. But before I could voice my decision, Ms. Marmelle spoke.

'During our editing, Mr. MacBain, I foresaw the difficulties we're discussing this morning, and I proposed a variety of relatively simple changes that would maintain a better balance between what we might call fiction and science, but for his own good reasons Mr. Yoder rejected them, and reluctantly I had to agree with him. It's his novel, not mine.'

The president of Kinetic turned and asked me directly: 'Mr. Yoder, could those proposals be resurrected? Without damaging the force of the novel?'

'No,' I said and with such firmness as to terminate the discussion. MacBain, interpreting my answer accurately, rose, bowed to Miss Crane and said: 'Well, what we must do is go forward and try our best,' and he left the room, followed by Ms. Marmelle and Miss Crane, and I accompanied them as an act of courtesy. As we stood waiting for the elevator Mr. MacBain took me aside and said quietly: 'I'm disappointed, of course. This book means a lot to me. But I'm not unhappy to work with an author who knows his own mind, who stands for something. Not many around these days,' and he jumped into the elevator before I could respond.

It was a gloomy ride home. I remembered none of the good news Ms.
Marmelle had shared with me that first day, nor the heartening
reports from Europe and Japan, for I was beset by two fearsome
questions: Was I being arrogant and self-centered in my dismissal of
Kinetic's problems? And worse, were the outside readers right? Had
I lost my touch? Was I an old farmer who had gone to his well once
too often?

The first question tormented me so acutely that I returned to it
repeatedly as the bus carried me across New Jersey. If Kinetic had
been so good to me through the years, did I not owe a compensating
debt? And if a notorious failure of *Stone Walls* subjected Mr. Mac-
Bain to increased pressure from corporate raiders, was I not obligated to offer him some help by contributing maximum sales figures
from my novel? The answer to both questions had to be Yes, and I
wondered if I should now accept the suggestions Ms. Marmelle had
made last year that I had rejected so peremptorily. I still thought not,
but without the firm resolve I had voiced in the meeting. I wanted
to discuss this with Emma.

The second question was far more personal. I can honestly state
that I had not secretly begun to doubt my capacity to write generally
as well as I did when I composed *Shunning*. I could still write. But
I must admit that from time to time when I was out walking I had
wondered if perhaps the parade had passed me by. I wouldn't concede that I had gone to the well too often, but perhaps I had gone
to the wrong one. Perhaps there were other, fresher literary reser-
voirs that I had not discovered. Perhaps time had passed me by.
Perhaps *Walls* was outmoded and lacking in interest. These are
terrible questions for an older writer to have to ask himself.

By the time I reached the bus stop where my car waited I had
resolved nothing. Indeed, I was more rattled than when I left New
York, and stepping out into the cold January night air, I was eager
to hurry home for the consolation I had always found there: Emma's

reassuring stability, my old typewriter on its own table, my work-shop with its little bottles of acrylic in their proper places. I would not disturb the tranquility of that haven tonight by discussing the distressing matters that had surfaced in New York, but early tomor-row I'd want to talk frankly with Emma and Zollicoffer, my trusted advisers.

The next day, bundled in warm clothing, the three of us sat down together at a site Zollicoffer reserved for important meetings and reflections, the belvedere overlooking the boulders that dotted the marsh in back of his house.

'I need the advice of you two,' I said. 'You've both read the manuscript in the past few days and must have formed opinions. I'd like to hear your judgments, but first let me tell you what happened in New York.' Repeating only the bad news about the three adverse critical reactions and the distressing loss of prepublication sales and orders, I concluded: 'At a solemn meeting yesterday of all concerned, including Miss Crane, they agreed with the outside critics. The new novel is not as interesting as the former ones that readers liked so well, and they think I should rewrite it to provide more human interest.'

'What did Miss Crane say?' Emma asked almost angrily.

'Her exact words were: "I must agree with them, Mr. Yoder. I don't think it came out of your top drawer." '

'She ought to have her mouth washed out with soap.'

'The problem is, was she right? Is there something basically wrong with the manuscript?'

For some moments we sat looking at the ice spots where water had frozen and at the giant boulders, which made us seem so puny, and it was this sense of the power of the land about which I had written that encouraged Zollicoffer to blurt out: 'Lukas, it's the best of the lot. At last you write like an honest Dutchman who knows where he's at and what he is. Don't change nothin'.'

Emma was even more forceful: 'I read it while you were in New York. Couldn't put it down. It deals with real people facing real problems. The other novels had a sense of history. *The Creamery* dealt with the 1920s. *The Fields* could have happened now, but you placed it in the thirties, to catch the depression. But this one is today's story. It's our blood and guts, and I agree with Herman. Change nothing.' As soon as she said this, she chuckled: 'Oh, edit it—as always. I marked some frightful grammatical errors. But the main thrust? Let it stand. It's as solid as those rocks out there.'

I was heartened by these votes of confidence, but I could not completely trust them, for they came from amateur readers. There was, however, one woman in Grenzler whose literary opinion I respected and often sought. She was Martha Benelli, a thirty-five-year-old divorcée who had kicked her hard-drinking husband out of the house and taken a job as the Dresden librarian. A graduate of Penn State with an M.A. in American lit., she had an infectious love of books, especially novels, and had proved invaluable to me as someone who could track down almost any tome I needed, no matter how arcane. Born a Mennonite with the family name of Zigenfusser, she knew Pennsylvania Dutch material better than I and took pleasure in introducing me to old books she enjoyed.

When I handed her my copy of the manuscript I said: 'You've helped me so much on this, I wondered if I could persuade you to skim it and give me your opinion?' When she reached for the sheaf of paper as if it were a baby, I faced an embarrassing moment, but I had to forge ahead: 'I'm asking for a professional opinion, and I'd be honored if you'd accept a fee of two hundred dollars.' To my delight she did not, out of modesty, beg off: 'You know I'd do it for nothing, but I could use the money,' and she must have read late into the nights because two days later she telephoned her report.

'A substantial change in direction, *n'est-ce-pas*? High time and wonderfully successful.'

'Will readers stay with it?'

'They'll devour it. Especially those familiar with your work. They'll see it as a logical progression.'

'Not too cerebral?'

'Mr. Yoder, a large proportion of readers are far more cerebral than most critics think. Schlock does seem to dominate the best-seller lists, but there's always that reassuring handful of really fine books that finds a place there, too. I know. I circulate the good ones.'

'Could I drop over and talk with you?'

'For your hundred dollars you've earned the right to a whole seminar.'

I drove directly to the library, which was nestled in a park at the edge of town, and found her waiting for me with my manuscript on her desk, some of its pages flagged with yellow strips containing her recommendations regarding certain passages. Before she could go into her reactions to the novel, I spelled out the negative comments it had received, then asked her opinion.

'I can understand why the big chains might draw back from this one. It's not perfect and perhaps it's too different from what went before. But it's a corking good read, with the additional advantage of having a solid content. Obviously people in these parts will gobble it up, but so will readers across the country.'

I then confided that three quite knowledgeable experts had recommended that I rework the novel to make it more acceptable to the usual customer of the big chains, and she snorted: 'To hell with that. You've felt driven to do something new and wonderfully rich. If they don't like it now, they will, down the line.'

She then proceeded to defend her editorial recommendations, and as she lectured me I thought: What a solid, rosy-faced Dutch girl she is! Flaxen braids that would be at home in the Palatinate. And a sharp mind. Dresden does produce good citizens and that's what this novel is about. If she and Zollicoffer like it, for their different reasons, it can't be as bad as New York says.

When I left, my mind was made up. I would call New York to

inform them that I would not do the rewriting they had suggested. I was not unhappy with that decision, but the call was delayed, because when I reached home at eleven-thirty Emma told me: 'Herman was so helpful the other day, and has been through the years, that I invited him and Frieda to lunch with us in town. He said he didn't want dinner in a public restaurant, but you know Frieda. Always ready for a new meal in a new place, and we're to pick them up as we drive into town.'

Our route took us along the back road to Neumunster and the Cut Off, and as we came down the slope leading to the intersection where the Fenstermacher farm lay, we saw to our disgust that a big bull-dozer was at work knocking down the very barn from which I had rescued my three hex signs only a few days ago.

None of us in the car were particularly distressed to see the wooden sections of the old barn go, because generations of improvident Fenstermachers had allowed that part to fall into sad disrepair, but when the bulldozer started to attack that handsome stonework from which the wooden sections arose, Frieda cried: 'No! No! Save that one yet,' for with her stolid appreciation of nice, she could visualize the various uses to which the lovely wall with its engaging shadows and rugged protuberances could be put. When the massive machine plowed ahead, crushing the wall, she almost wept: 'They could have let it stand already.'

My attention was focused on quite another matter, for from the hidden side of the barn there now emerged a second red bulldozer, smaller than the first but easier to operate. On its seat perched the Fenstermacher boy Applebutter, using his machine to knock down the remaining wooden portions, crunching them beneath the treads of his dozer. As I watched him I thought he represented much of what I had written about in *Stone Walls*: An oaf like him wouldn't attack stone. Too difficult. He'd always go for the easier wood. Then suddenly I shouted: 'No! Stop!' and leaped from the car because

LUKAS YODER
· ·

65

Applebutter's machine was heading directly toward a fallen section
of the wall that contained a splendid red-and-green hex sign of the
size best suited to form the central section of one of my paintings.
'I want that! Applebutter, save that sign!' He must have heard my
cry, for I was close to him when I shouted, and surely he saw me
waving my arms, but he headed his dozer right at the fallen hex and
pulverized it with his massive treads.

At lunch I said little, for ideas and images were coursing through
my mind, and it seemed to me that this latest example of the humiliation of the land and its buildings was exactly the focus of concern
in my manuscript, so I excused myself to telephone Ms. Marmelle
in New York: 'I stayed awake last night, pondering our meeting the
other day. I think I understand the points you and Mr. MacBain
were making, and I assure you I've reviewed them painfully. I agree
with what you told MacBain: "The story line could be modified with
a minimum of trouble. Mr. Yoder and I know exactly what could
be done." You were right. It could be done, but it would be very
wrong to try. Insofar as the big ideas are concerned, we'll let the
novel stand as it is,' and after a few courtesy exchanges I hung up.

The discussions I'd had in New York, my moody reflections on the
trip home, and my decision regarding the sanctity of my manuscript
propelled me into an evaluation of my life as a writer, and that
evening as I sat in my study facing my typewriter but not using it,
I started thinking:

'How strange! My life is kept in a cocoon guarded by three women:
Emma, Ms. Marmelle, Miss Crane. I remain here in my study with
a typewriter and allow them to make the decisions. So far they've
protected me admirably, and I have no regrets, but I doubt that a
macho man would be content with the arrangement. I am.

'I live in a world that changes so rapidly I can't keep up. I'd not like to guess how books will be printed or distributed twenty years from now. That was pretty scary, my article for the nature magazine in California. Candace put it on a floppy disk here in Dresden, delivered it by phone to a compatible word processor in Los Angeles, where they made some editorial changes and sent it on, again by phone to a printing firm in Palo Alto, and they set it automatically into type and printed it in the magazine. Amazing.

'On my typewriter I print the symbol *m* to represent a significant part of the idea I'm playing with. Then my secretary reads my symbol and uses her word processor to implant on her floppy disk not my symbol *m* but but the electrical representation of the concept *m*-ness. By telephone that electrical representation is lifted across the continent to a compatible processor in Southern California, where it is massaged editorially, as they say, and sent by another telephone call to the printer in Northern California.

'Now, what the printer receives is still merely an electrical impulse that says: At this point in the finished product we want some visual representation of *m*-ness, but we don't know in what typeface, what size, or what leading between the lines, nor do we know how long the lines will be nor how many to a page. All we know is that it's a lower-case *m*, not a capital *M*, because if we wanted that, the electrical reminder would be entirely different.

'So the Palo Alto printer puts the California version of my floppy disk in his printing machine and cranks in a handful of instructions: what typeface, whether normal, boldface or italic, what size, what leading between lines, etc., and when all the instructions have been entered and acknowledged, the machine does the rest. Wherever my original concept of *m*-ness appears, that miraculous machine translates it into a clear mark on the printed page. I communicate with my readers by electrical impulses.

'If the essence of my manuscript resides in the electrical impulses on that floppy disk, the narrative could be lifted off and distributed in almost any form that have been devised. Indeed, the time may come, and very soon, when there will be no necessity to bother with the intermediate form of a book; the material on the original floppy disk might leapfrog in some mysterious way right into the home of the intended reader. No writer in 1990 can visualize what form his or her book might take by the end of this century.'

As I leaned back from my silent typewriter I felt as if I knew more about the mystery of writing than ever before: 'I may not understand technical miracles, but of one thing I'm sure. Regardless of how the industry handles the symbols of the writer when he gets through assembling them, no matter how the book of the future is going to look, it'll still need women and men who know how to move words about, how to tell a story, how to keep a narrative flowing.'

My self-esteem had been wounded by the negative news in New York, but as I pushed myself away from my typewriter I had an abiding consolation: The writer will always be needed, to remind others who can't write what really happened and what it meant. *Walls* is a powerful statement, and ten years from now, readers will embrace it.

As Emma and I went to bed I told her: 'In the discussion with you and Herman at lunch the other day I left out one fact that you ought to know. The reverses in New York mean that you and I are three million dollars poorer than we were last week. How does that shake your apple tree?' and she said: 'I can't feel the difference. But I'm sure of one thing. Readers aren't stupid. They're going to love this book.' And with that reassuring thought, we went to sleep.

The weeks following my two-day visit to New York would prove the most productive of this exciting year. Each morning I rose at seven, dashed cold water on my face, combed my hair, brushed my teeth, drank a large glass of unsweetened grapefruit juice and went directly to my typewriter, where I worked without interruption until twelve-thirty, by which time I was exhausted.

I had before me some fifteen to twenty closely typed pages of Ms. Marmelle's queries and suggestions relating to a hundred-page segment of my manuscript, her questions having been submitted in a format she had devised during her first days at Kinetic. A page of my manuscript as printed out by the word processor invariably contained twenty-six lines, the first thirteen of which she designated by arabic numerals starting at the top. The bottom thirteen she indicated by the numbers 13 down to 1, starting from the middle, but each designated by an asterisk, 13*, at the middle, down to 1*, at the bottom. Her notes for any given page, say 37, thus became:

37-4	subject and verb do not agree in number
37-11	cannot find antecedent of pronoun *its*
37-11*	on page 19 you say twice Marian is blue-eyed, how now brown cow?
37-3*	I like this bit very much and recommend you consider restating in later chapter to remind the reader

Hour after hour I grappled with the problems she had identified, the blatant weaknesses she had spotted in the flow of the narrative; sometimes I agreed with her suggestions, quite often I saw no merit in them, but one type of criticism I attended to without exception:

49-11*	I see what effect you're trying to achieve in this paragraph, but don't believe you've caught it. Last half sags, drags. Idea good, execution not. I'd redo this, maybe the entire page to catch and maintain the right mood.

Sometimes as I strained to perfect a troublesome paragraph, recasting and rearranging the five sentences, I would smile and think: I wonder what the young people who say so blandly 'I want to be a writer' would say if they saw this pile of her queries, my responses and that growing pile of my attempts to improve what didn't work?

This kind of intense work placed such heavy demands upon my mental and nervous systems that by midday I felt thoroughly depleted; I would push myself away from my desk, abandoning the rest of the manuscript, and wander down into the kitchen, shaking my arms and hands as I went. Turning on the radio that Emma kept in the kitchen, I would listen to the twelve o'clock news as I watched her prepare my dinner. In Dutch families the meals are breakfast, dinner, supper—a hangover from the colonial ground-clearing days when men worked with axes and ropes felling trees from dawn till midday and came in famished, expecting a big meal. Even today the Mennonite men, who do their heaviest farm work in the mornings, want not lunch when they stop but a full dinner.

Emma modified this routine for me, because she had learned that a big noon meal of fried foods, two glasses of milk and a slab of apple pie made me lethargic in the afternoon, and that was counterproductive. She gave me small meals, but when Fenstermacher's scrapple became available in the winter months, she did make a concession: three days a week she served me two thin slices of the delicacy, nicely browned in butter, with an oversize cruet of molasses on the side. But she refused to serve dessert, no matter how light, at dinner; she saved that for supper.

When I saw that this day I was to be favored with scrapple, I expressed pleasure: 'Did a lot of good work this morning, and I'm ready for something good. Smells as if you had it cooking.'

She sat with me as I ate, eating her own single slice of scrapple with a taste of ketchup on the side, and asked between bites: 'What really happened in New York? You've told me only the bad part of the story.'

'Ms. Marmelle said . . .'

'Has she ever been married? Why the Ms.?'

'I don't know. Many young women in New York offices use it.'

'How old would you say she is?' On and on went the questions, moving on to business details, until she had a fairly clear understanding of what had transpired in the two meetings, except that I told her nothing about the various bits of good news I'd had about the foreign sales of *Stone Walls*, the many new editions of my older books, and the financial success of the book here at home, even before the manuscript was completed. I deplored such talk from anybody, so I invited her to telephone the two offices to learn at first hand what was happening. I had learned that such calls placed her in the heart of my career and gave her a strong feeling of participation.

But one thing I had learned was too good to keep secret: 'Something did happen that pleased me very much. A motion picture company with an odd partnership but lots of money is taking an option on *Shunning*. They say they want to make what they call an art film, well cast, with careful attention to detail and a spacious development. I'd like that, so if they telephone, I want to talk with them.'

I had touched upon one of the few points of friction in our marriage: Emma had such a proprietary interest in both my career and my well-being that she insisted on opening incoming mail and answering phone calls so that she could talk briefly with whoever wanted to speak with me, thus learning for herself what was happening at Kinetic and Miss Crane's. But in recent years it had become her pleasure to tell whoever was calling: 'He's at work now. Call back later.' This gave her a sense of shared power in my work and also of control. Of course, if I heard her doing it I would lift the phone in the study and interrupt to take the call. This irritated her, and she would growl when the conversation ended: 'I'm trying to protect you. They can call later,' and I would ask: 'Why have them make two calls?' and her reply would be: 'You're busier than they are. Besides, they have a secretary to make the call in the first place.'

With Ms. Marmelle's critical calls an agreement was reached: 'I want to speak to her as soon as she calls,' and Emma nodded, but even under that arrangement she managed to ask the editor two or three short questions before she alerted me.

After lunch each workday I read *The Philadelphia Inquirer*, and three days a week, more or less, Emma when shopping would purchase *The New York Times* and I would enjoy it, especially the column that reported news and gossip relating to publishing: 'I learn a lot more about Kinetic from the *Times* than I do from Ms. Marmelle.' Recent news had not been reassuring; whispered rumors continued that Rockland Oil, the huge conglomerate that owned Kinetic as a kind of bizarre appendage to its other interests in petroleum, wood pulp and paper mills was eager to off-load it, because its profit yield was so modest it was out of place in what was known as 'a go-go outfit.' Who might be interested in buying was unspecified: 'But among those known to have been nibbling are at least two overseas consortiums, attracted by a bargain when the dollar is so low in comparison to their currencies.' That news was not reassuring.

About an hour after lunch I took a short nap, a habit I had acquired in my mid-fifties when I found myself tiring at three each afternoon. My doctor at the time, an older man, had said: 'Even a short nap relaxes the tension, restores the zip,' and that proved true in my case. 'Strange,' I told Emma, 'on Monday and Tuesday I had no rest of any kind in New York, all excitement and lunches with lots of talk and big ideas, but I didn't feel a bit tired.'

'You sure look it now.'

'I feel it. If the phone rings, you handle it. I need a rest.'

When I woke I could not remember where I was, and for just a moment I thought it was morning and that I was late rising. Jumping out of bed, I hurried to the bathroom, then saw the sunlight outside and realized where I was and what time it was.

Slipping into old work clothes, I went not to my upstairs study but to the ground-level workshop attached to our main house, a self-

indulgent convenience I had added when royalties from *Hex* came
tumbling in. It contained a long workbench backed by a Masonite
pegboard with stainless-steel hooks for my various tools. In heavy
black paint, carefully applied, I had drawn the outline of each major
tool so that I could assure myself at a glance when I finished work
that everything was in its place. The bench had not only a vise
powerful enough to handle an airplane wing but also a small drill
press and a power saw. A reasonably good workman, I had constructed many of the small gadgets that made our farmhouse a place
of convenience and comfort.

But now my interest focused on the three hex signs I had acquired
from the Fenstermacher barn, and as I inspected each I was satisfied
that they were going to yield three exceptionally good paintings.
Each was about four feet square, large enough to have been seen by
the driver of a distant wagon in the early 1900s, and each had enough
of the original paint to convey both the design and the color, yet not
too much to kill the effect of a mysterious symbol from another day.
The designs varied, each intended for a different compass direction
on the barn, each qualified to ward off a specific danger.

I used extreme care in dealing with the signs once the excess wood
had been removed from around them. My job was threefold: to
strengthen the old wood by a judicious injection of special epoxies
applied deep in the exposed seams with a hypodermic needle; to
preserve the original colors in their weatherbeaten condition so as to
create the appearance of age; and to enhance the colors, but so
delicately that the result was not conspicuous. When these processes
were completed properly, the ancient hex seemed to leap off the
restored wood, and then came the segment of my artistic effort that
I enjoyed most.

Selecting a big slab of Masonite that had been laminated with a
veneer of some lightly veined and softly colored wood like bleached
oak, I affixed my hex with a powerful epoxy so that it filled the

middle of the slab with about six to eight inches of blank wood exposed as a margin in each direction. Then with a set of fine brushes and the bright colors the Pennsylvania Dutch preferred—scarlet, cerulean blue, a vivid green, a sparkling yellow—I began to decorate the exposed margins with fraktur, that curious mix of alphabetical letters, designs from nature and geometric framework that had originally been used to decorate precious family documents. As drawn and painted by traveling artists in the eighteenth century, the frakturs were folk art of the highest quality, and I believed that I was reviving its best elements in my paintings.

My specialty was big Gothic letters highly ornamented with examples of wildlife, such as tulips and goldfinches, or with sparsely used geometric patterns. With a restraint that the old-time artists never practiced, I kept my fraktur spare and neatly distributed about the edges of my central hex, but on days when I felt especially happy with my work I would finish a painting with unusual care, drawing and then painting seven or eight specimens of wildlife, nicely scattered and in brilliant colors, and label each with its name in old German script, using stencils I'd cut years ago, which enabled me to letter the flowers and birds in exquisitely spaced and inked names: *distelfink* for the finches, *dullaboona* for the tulips, *hertz* for the hearts. Those were the prized paintings.

At the start of this year, 1991, I had completed twenty-one of my big hexes, and if I could complete the three Fenstermachers, *XXII* through *XXIV*, I'd have two dozen in circulation. I kept none at home, but I always promised Emma: 'Next time, a special one for you.' I gave them to friends, sold a few at the Rostock post office, and donated four of the best to museums in the area, including the great concrete castle in Doylestown, where the crafts of the German region were housed in grand profusion. Two museums far from the Dutch region had expressed an interest in my work, but I had not built up a surplus from which I could supply them. I refused to sell a painting for personal gain on the grounds that to do so would put me in competition with real artists who might need the money. I made my living from my books, so I gave whatever money I did occasionally make from the post office sales to the Dresden library for the purchase of books on Mennonite and Amish history.

About five in the afternoon I would leave the shop, return upstairs to the study and work for an hour and a half on a manuscript, stopping well before seven so that I could join Emma at that hour for supper. I ate sparingly, listened to the news, took a short walk with the dog along the darkened road leading to Rostock, and was in bed before ten.

I cherished this regimen of a man who loved to write books but who also wanted to preserve the art of his people, and I told Emma: 'When I come down from writing at noon I think: This is the best job in the world, but when I come in from working on the hexes I think: I'm happier doing this than anything else.'

She said: 'I often feel the same way when I've baked an especially good pie,' and I said: 'I don't catch the analogy,' and she became angry.

'A good pie is just as important as a good hex,' she snapped, and I apologized: 'Emma, I didn't mean that. I meant I was giving an alternative, writing as opposed to painting, but you didn't give any second choice.'

'Go to bed,' she said.

When I was deep into my corrections on the manuscript and receiving regular calls from my Ministering Angels, I was shown an unexpected word portrait of myself. Emma returned with the morning mail and burst into my study flourishing a magazine and crying: 'Hey, Mr. Celebrity! Here's a story about you, photograph and all,' and she thrust before me the magazine, opened at the appropriate page. There I was, looking up at myself in color, surrounded by glossy type.

The story was not about me. I had merely served as what some editors call a *frinstance*: 'Your article is about authors who've done well on the contemporary scene. Give us a for instance.' The report was a thoughtful account of the radical change in New York publishing, written by a clever freelance, a young woman who had followed the rumors. At some point she must have interviewed either Ms. Marmelle or Miss Crane, who had cited me as a typical older writer who had kept his head above water. Intrigued by what she heard, she must have gone to the other woman to verify what the first had said and decided that I was a good choice for a frinstance. Thus I was permitted to see what my two associates thought of me; quite properly in our business, they had not informed me that they were giving the interview.

Ms. Marmelle had said: 'Sometimes the little Dutchman's an iceberg. Gives the impression of being indifferent, no matter what's happening to him or his books. But he does reveal a passionate interest whenever the actual publication of his book is involved. He wants to see the typeface, check the length of the line, satisfy himself that the paper's opaque, verify the mapwork. He also wants to see the jacket, the artwork, the blurb. But even if he's disappointed he never makes waves. "Does this look right to you?" is about as far as he'll go.

'I thought of him last week when one of our authors—he works with another editor, let's call him Renford—blustered in here raising hell about everything. I overheard him delivering ultimatums, threatening to take his immortal work to Simon and Schuster, and when I was finished eavesdropping I burst out laughing because he's six foot three, dumb as an ox, and I compared him with my little Dutchman, five five and never raises his voice. The goon's last book sold eighteen hundred copies, the Dutchman's a million one, and I wanted to butt in and tell the ranter: "You ain't earned the right to throw your weight around. Tell me in a quiet voice what it is we can do for you."

'But I kept my mouth shut. And do you know why? My Yoder gets a year older every January and the other editor's goon may become our next hot item. In this business you never know.'

She gave another portrait of me: 'I think Yoder acts a lot, parades the indifferent bit. When I told him at lunch the other day that maybe a Japanese-Israeli film company might want to make an artistic picture of his old novel *The Shunning*, his eyes lit up like Hallowe'en lanterns and I was so relieved to see him show emotion that I instinctively shouted "Whee!" and people in the restaurant stared at us. He didn't care. Raised his glass to everyone who offered us a toast and continued smiling the rest of the meal.

'Later he told me: "*Shunning*'s important to me. If the team you mentioned wants to do a real film, honest in all details, no cheap shots at the Amish, let them get the rights for bottom dollar. We'll defer our take until it proves itself at the box office." Publishing profits from producing guys like my little Dutchman.'

When the freelance interviewed Miss Crane, my agent provided another view: 'Lukas Yoder's a special case. We never address him by his first name. When I did at first, he winced. I think it was because as a Mennonite he was uneasy about having a strange woman be so familiar. And he never calls me Hilda, always Miss Crane. Very disconcerting, sits in that chair and listens to a dozen things I've done for his books and all he does is nod. But once, when I showed him the jacket for the Berlin edition of *Hex*, he cried: "Now, that's a jacket!" and when I asked why, he said: "Their modified Gothic lettering makes it look Pennsylvania Dutch." He constantly amazes me. Won't allow publication parties and refuses to go on the road to publicize his books. Yet he answers his mail, every piece, no matter how inane. When I chided him about the waste of time and money he looked surprised: "Miss Crane, so far as I know, everyone who sends me a letter has bought one of my books or checked it out from the local library. My job is to encourage him or her to read the next one."

'You may be interested in how I acquired him as a client. When his first books did poorly, two agents in this town dumped him and now shudder with regret when one of his big books comes out. I found him huddled under a rock, his ego shattered. But I'd read *The Shunning* and thought it magnificent. I'd always wanted to represent writers like that, and so help me, a week later I heard that he'd been dropped by his agent. No, I won't give the name. Within the minute, I telephoned him and said cold turkey: "Mr. Yoder, you can write. *Shunning* was magnificent and I want to be your agent. I see great years ahead for you." '

The young woman writing the article took responsibility for the next quote: 'Neither his editor nor his agent was willing to talk about Yoder's financial success with his recent blockbusters, but others familiar with the industry assured me that Yoder alone probably accounts for 60 percent of the Crane office's yearly take. Miss Crane did say: 'When I call him on a business deal, he agrees to everything in about two minutes. But he's not stupid. He then turns me over to his wife, Emma, and she hammers at me for an hour. I can tell you that she runs everything—the farm, the book contracts, the bank account, and Yoder too, for that matter. The other day I told my assistant: "Your job is to keep Lukas Yoder happy—even more important, keep Emma happy." '

I was not displeased with what my Ministering Angels said about me, but since they both described me as little, I must point out that I am taller than Miss Crane and almost as tall as Ms. Marmelle.

The work continued unabated through the rest of the winter, week after week, and as I reminded Emma several times: 'The thing's not even in print yet. We have to read galleys and I don't see how they can deliver copy to the German publisher on schedule.' She said: 'They have a building full of bright people in that office on Madison Avenue, it's their problem,' and in late April she brought home from the post office a large flat package that contained the first visible proof that a book by me might truly be appearing in the fall. It was a rough of the proposed jacket showing a green meadowland with lettering that carried a hint of German Gothic, and it seemed to both of us about as clean and appropriate a cover, with just the right intimations, as one could have wished to devise.

'They've got it right,' Emma said, 'and on the first try. Miraculous.'

Telephone calls from my two Angels continued on a regular basis, Ms. Marmelle keeping me informed on the progress of the manuscript and its appendages through the publishing process, and Miss Crane telling Emma about some minor financial coup. The former reported that the maps of the Dutch country that would form the endpapers were being worked on by the highly regarded Jean-Paul Tremblay, who would be sending preliminary drafts within a week. She said also: 'We've sent out feelers to the stores as to how many specially autographed editions at fifty dollars each they think they can handle, and the response is surprising. Looks as if the final estimates will run to nearly two thousand.'

When I heard this I warned: 'I told you I'd do only one thousand. Do you know how much work that is? Murderous. I could never handle two,' and Ms. Marmelle said: 'We'll accept your thousand and prorate them.' Some days later she called with alarming news: 'Somebody in our Midwest shop, without consulting me, promised that big bookstore in St. Louis that you'd be glad to sign a special gift edition for them, boxed, seventy-five dollars, and they've mailed out a lot of brochures. Present estimates indicate that this may involve another thousand.'

'Tell them to rescind the offer. I can't sign that many.'

'Mr. Yoder, I don't know how this snafu was allowed to happen, but it has. The letters are out and the orders are flooding back in.'

'That'll be your problem,' I said sternly. 'I'm beating my brains out down here trying to make this manuscript letter-perfect. Rewriting whole passages. Corrections on every page. And I don't want to be heckled because of an error that one of your people made.'

In a quiet, conciliatory voice, she reminded me: 'Through the years Inglenook has been one of your strongest supporters. Thousands upon thousands of copies. Don't dismiss them out of hand. We'll work something out.'

'I'll do five hundred, but that's tops.'

'Thanks, that may satisfy them.'

Miss Crane's calls were of a quite different character, for the people she dealt with spoke as if the book were already in print, and when Emma gave me summaries of her calls, I shivered: 'They think that when I submit my manuscript in October 1990, things mysteriously jump ahead to October 1991 and Voilà! There's the finished book! Does she have any idea that I'm working my tail off in the interim?'

The idiom was not irrelevant, for day after day I sat at my typewriter in the greatest discomfort. I had tried a soft cushion, but although it helped, I had the frightening feeling that it was eating me up, that the chair was in command, not I, and I discarded it. I liked the stiffer seat, even though it did require frequent moving about to relieve my numbed bottom.

When my Ministering Angels telephoned with the latest news, they avoided any reference to the fact that rumors were circulating through the industry that my latest novel was such a severe disappointment that the initial print run had again been reduced. But apparently this information was widely known, for one of Emma's casual Bryn Mawr acquaintances with affiliations in the book business called to say that it was too bad about my novel but that my regular readers would probably find it interesting. So we lived with a Damoclean sword over our heads, and one day Emma snapped: 'A nasty way to end a writing career, but we did have those great years. Who can complain?' and I grinned: 'Not I.'

One of Miss Crane's calls was a welcome interruption: 'Exciting news! Argosy Films has paid the money on the option we talked about regarding *Shunning*. Their top people want to fly in to A.B.E. and talk over their plans to do a really fine film. Can I tell them to come?'

There was really no time in the year that I welcomed interruptions; either I was writing a book, which was murderous work, or I was editing one, which demanded all my attention and energy. So I routinely turned down suggestions that interested people fly in to consult with me. I was always glad to see my two Angels in New York, but they had become members of our family; the rest Emma fended off. However, I did want to encourage these men who might convert my best novel into a respectable film: 'Arrange it. And tell them not to rent a car. We'll pick them up.'

The A.B.E. Airport was proof that sometimes government officials can do things right. Perched on a huge field capable of handling big jets, and convenient to the three Dutch cities, Allentown, Bethlehem and Easton, it linked the Dutch country with the rest of America and the world. On a Thursday in April, Emma and I waited there at eleven in the morning to greet the Japanese and Israeli tycoons who proposed making the film that I had always wanted to see done. *Hex* and my other novels had not excited me as potential motion pictures, but as I told Emma while we waited for the United Airlines jet to fly in: '*Shunning* has something important to say, and I'd like to see it said on the screen.'

We had no trouble spotting our guests, for the two men with such different backgrounds looked almost like twins—short, a bit over-weight, with a dark complexion, bouncy steps and heads that constantly twisted about in an effort to inspect everything, a longtime habit that had projected them into strange adventures, including the making of movies.

After introducing my wife, I said, 'We're most happy to see you. We have arranged to drive directly to a rather nice inn at Dresden, where we invite you to lunch. They have a quiet room where we can talk later.'

'Agreeable,' the Israeli said, 'but Mr. Saito and I came here to take *you* to lunch.' Emma said: 'Fine.'

As our Buick eased onto the Interstate and headed southwest she gave them an introduction to our area: 'This is the Grenzler my husband writes about. Our farm, in the family for centuries, is just to the south, but we're heading for the beautiful little town of Dresden, the capital of Grenzler, you might say. It's an old Dutch village, with streets laid out in a grid like Philadelphia's, but with several beautiful avenues winding in and out. In the center we have what we call Der Platz, a village square, and lining it to the north a splendid old inn with the crazy name the Dresden China. You'll understand when we get there.'

She explained there were two ways to enter Dresden from the Interstate: an imposing one with ramps leading right into town and a modest one along Rhenish Road that provided glimpses of the beautiful countryside. Our visitors, opting for the latter, had a chance to see the lovely rolling fields to the north and the spires of Dresden, but what pleased them most was the winding avenue in town that led them to Der Platz with its monument to the town's Civil War veterans. It was in the grandiose style of the mid-nineteenth century, with four soldiers guarding the compass points.

'And this is the Dresden China,' Emma said as we drew up before the elegant white inn that occupied one entire side of Der Platz.

The dining room, where lunch waited, was a charming space, decorated in a pastel blue against white walls and ecru curtains, but its main feature was a row of glass cases along two sides of the room, each filled with Meissen figurines, a few originals from the great period of the 1700s, most of them the cheaper but still beautiful reproductions from the late 1800s. The display was so attractive that Mr. Saito, a connoisseur of Japanese ceramics, walked immediately to the nearest case, studied the figurines for some minutes and then called for his Israeli partner to join him.

Mr. Saito told him: 'Look here! This illustrates exactly what we don't want to do,' and after the Israeli had inspected the chinaware, the two men joined us at the table. No sooner were they seated than Mr. Saito said: 'Providential! That case illustrates everything we want to avoid,' and he pointed to a shelf containing seven rather garish china figurines representing a German artist's conception of a scene at the French court at Versailles: noblewomen making believe they were shepherdesses, but gross in form and heavy in coloring.

'I do not like German ceramics,' Mr. Saito said. 'For me delicate Oriental ware, especially the austere celadon of Korea. The same our film. I want it to be not heavy German but delicate, gentle, like a celadon bowl.'

Such talk bewildered me, but Emma used it as an excuse to pay the Japanese a compliment: 'You speak beautiful English, Mr. Saito,' and he explained: 'When my company goes international, the directors import an Oxford professor teaches me English. Fourteen hours all day; nothing but English. That way I learn.' He smiled: 'But the Oxford man tell me: "Keep it simple," so I use all verbs in present.'

Before either of us could comment, the Israeli broke in: 'Me too. Only Hebrew till seventeen. Then I have to learn English, bellboy at the King David in Jerusalem.'

The determination of these men to learn a new language in order to excel in their new profession encouraged me to think they might be capable of creating a work of beauty, so I told them: 'We're eager to provide you with every assistance.' When Emma asked: 'Do you intend to keep my husband's two major characters?' we received an introduction to the shorthand used in Hollywood, for the Israeli, the practical member of the pair, said: 'Indeed we do. We think the older brother like Rod Steiger, same appearance, same villain look, whether he wants it to show or not. Smirky, too. Now the younger brother, we see him as Maximilian Schell, more frail but man of tremendous character, like in Lillian Hellman film. Did you happen to catch him, the one in which Jason Robards plays her lover, the writer guy?'

For the rest of the discussion it was Steiger and Schell conducting their feud in Lancaster County in the 1890s, but the conversation was interrupted by the bellboy, who informed the Israeli: 'We got one and it's set up in Room 217 ready to go.'

Mr. Saito said: 'We bring two films we want you see. They show better than words what we after,' and they called the bellboy to lead us to the room where a rented VCR was already hooked to the television with the shades drawn.

The Israeli said: 'These films, great simplicity, much beauty. First is *Barry Lyndon*, made in 1975 after a Thackeray novel.' Lowering his voice he said: 'Anyone could make *Vanity Fair*. Simple characters. But look what Stanley Kubrick does, very subtle.'

Mr. Saito added: 'We do not show whole two hours, but this worth seeing,' and within minutes of starting the VCR we were transported to an English countryside peopled with believable characters caught in slowly developing situations that charmed but did not exhaust, as the typical costume dramas did with their violent swordplay. Emma and I had heard of neither the novel nor the movie, but we were soon captivated by its mesmerizing loveliness, and when, after forty minutes, Mr. Saito cut it off, I said: 'I can imagine my story done that way,' and the visitors said they had hoped for such a reaction.

'Next one,' Saito said, 'proves it can also be done without no costumes,' and into the VCR he placed *A Room with a View*, made in 1985 by the adventurous Merchant-Ivory company. Based on a novel by E. M. Forster, it was entirely different from the first, with no special emphasis on landscaping or costuming. The routine views of Florence and the English countryside were utilized in such a way as to underline and strengthen the story line, which involved ordinary people caught up in ordinary matters. It was such a sensitive film that we almost protested when it was halted midway.

'We do at least as well,' Mr. Saito said as his partner raised the shades, but Emma wanted to know: 'Did either film make money?' and the visitors said almost together: '*Lyndon* flopped,' but then the Israeli said: 'We shall see that ours does not.'

Looking at his watch, Mr. Saito asked: 'Is it possible you drive us to the Amish area, right now, so we see it with you?' I said: 'Yes, but we have to move. This time of year light fades quickly.' Emma herded us downstairs and out to our old Buick, but we were held up by Mr. Saito, who ran back to the inn: 'I got to have my cameras.'

Properly adorned with two Nikons, he grinned apologetically: 'If we make film, take pictures of scene for writers.' He then asked Emma: 'Would you mind, Mrs. Yoder, ride in back? I must see landscape,' and she said brightly: 'That's no problem, because I'm driving. We're heading into my country and here's a map for you to follow,' and she whisked us southwest along the Interstate through Berks County's rolling hills. As she drove she told Mr. Saito: 'The two brothers in *Shunning* were my ancestors.' When he turned to stare at her she said: 'Well, my family way back. The younger one was my grandfather.'

Before the visitors could respond to that amazing revelation, Mr. Saito cried: 'Stop!' and we were faced by a typical American sign: YOU ARE ENTERING LANCASTER COUNTY. RICHEST FARMLAND IN AMERICA. Whipping into position his camera containing color film, he said as he left the car: 'All Japanese carry cameras. This Japanese carries his for most important purpose.'

Since his Nikons had battery-driven motors that advanced the film at amazing speed, he was able to shoot almost as rapidly as he could swing the camera to catch the various aspects of the landscape, and since it also used an oversize cartridge providing not thirty-six shots but seventy-two, he was not afraid of running out of film. But as soon as he was satisfied with his color shots, he switched easily to his black-and-white and continued blazing away at the county in which his company would be doing much work in 1991 or '92.

Back in the car he became more selective, and he had a sagacious eye for scenes he might want to recommend to whomever the company chose to do the film. Peremptorily he would cry: 'Stop here! Landscape speaks!' And out he would jump, clicking like mad. In the course of an hour, as light began to fade, he changed rolls four times in his color camera, three times in his black-and-white, giving him well over six hundred shots. When he was finished with the Amish country he was going to have a full record of what it looked like in April.

Emma and I were struck by the extreme courtesy Mr. Saito showed, and the Israeli too, to any Amish he encountered. Never did he photograph them without permission. However, he did place himself inconspicuously behind a tree to take shots of the black horse-drawn buggies as they filed along the country road, snapping furiously but in a way that would not embarrass the bearded, black-frocked travelers.

Emma developed such a high regard for our gentlemanly visitors that she was inspired to say: 'You know, the farm where the brothers lived, the old Stoltzfus place, still exists. Would you like to see how the land sits? The buildings have been modified, of course, but it's still there.'

Mr. Saito almost jumped out of the Buick, thinking the farm was at hand, but she restrained him, and by dodging down back roads she brought us to the farm where the old struggle over moral principles had been fought, and Mr. Saito said as they remained in the car to survey the scene: 'Not suspenders drive them apart. Entire scale of values men believe in.' Leaning back in his seat to study the setting, he said quietly: 'I see things in pictures. The idea of this area captures me. But never, never do I visualize it so perfect . . . low hills . . . a stream . . . the barns. Come, we catch it all while still light.'

The two men leaped out of the car and began clicking their cameras in all directions, striving to catch the exact look of the old Stoltzfus farm, where the socioreligious tragedy had occurred, but at one point, when Mr. Saito was standing near me, he stopped shooting, studied the wonderful fields that constituted the farm and said aloud: 'So much empty land, so few people,' and I could guess at what must have been going through his mind, coming as he did from a tiny overpopulated country.

Then, to my surprise, he took the Israeli by the arm and they walked boldly to the farmhouse, spoke briefly with the owners and were apparently told: 'No, you cannot photograph here.' Without argument they nodded to the Amish family and withdrew, but as soon as they rejoined us the Israeli asked Emma to step out, and with his white handkerchief and Mr. Saito's he deftly fashioned what from a distance looked very much like the white bonnet worn by Dutch women. Placing this on Emma's head and adjusting it skillfully, he made her resemble one of her female ancestors, and as she moved here and there in front of the barns and buildings the two men snapped her, and at certain moments when she moved in an unexpected way and at such a distance, I saw her as living and moving in the days of the feud.

We drove back to the Dresden China in darkness, had an early supper and went upstairs to Room 217, where we spent two hours viewing the last halves of *Lyndon* and *Room*. Viewed so soon after having seen the real landscape of *Shunning*, the films reminded us of what might be accomplished with the Amish story, for as Mr. Saito said: 'I am awed by beauty of your land. Drama of the brothers,

I understand that when I read book in Japan. But I do not realize they battle for land of such magnificence.' I had to break in: 'I wrote the story, and it wasn't land they were struggling over, it was religion,' but Mr. Saito replied: 'You think it is religion. It is really recovery of his land that make Amos willing to crawl back and beg forgiveness.' Turning to his partner, he said solemnly: 'We shoot it as an epic of the land, because the land we see today has epic quality.'

As they walked Emma and me back to our car, Mr. Saito said: 'Not bother with us in morning. We hire car from the inn and scoot over to airport.' Kissing Emma's hand, he concluded: 'You are not ashamed when you see our film,' and we drove home willing to accept that prediction, for we knew we had been in the presence of two sensible and sensitive men.

In subsequent weeks the A.B.E. Airport saw various groups of strangers fly in, rent cars, and set off to look for Rhenish Road and the Yoders. Why were they bothering to interview me when the received wisdom was that my novel was a flop? Because both Ms. Marmelle and Miss Crane, determined to protect their own interests as well as mine, were building every backfire they could, calling upon old friends for help, sending out letters saying how exciting my novel was, and using every other imaginative ploy to nullify the big adverse blows.

Most effective was goading media people to come to Dresden to see that I was still alive and in possession of whatever faculties I once had. Some had been dispatched by Ms. Marmelle, others by Miss Crane, but all made their final arrangements with Emma, who became almost hoarse giving instructions on how to exit the airport, catch the Interstate headed west, and watch for Rhenish Road and the sharp turn back east: 'If you get lost, ask anyone. They'll know our farm.'

Two reporters from German television hired a three-man technical crew in New York and brought them down for what such groups always swore would take at most forty-five minutes: 'Fifteen minutes' setup, thirty minutes' shooting and we're gone.' But when they saw our inviting living room and learned that I had an outside shop in which I painted, they spent two hours choosing camera angles and lighting them properly. Shooting and reshooting took another hour and a half; reverse shots of the same scene, focused not on me but on my questioner so that it would look like a dialogue, took more time, and my work was totally disrupted.

Emma always protested in advance, groused when they rearranged her furniture, but finally served them drinks, and in the end almost made herself a member of their crew, asking about their families and looking approvingly at photographs of their children. When they asked, at five in the afternoon: 'Would you accompany us to dinner?' I wanted to say 'No, thanks,' but Emma was so eager to remain with them and hear their stories that I had to say, rather sourly I'm afraid: 'The day's gone. I guess we can spare the night, too,' and in we went to the China, where the Germans found the dining room so colorful they took a whole new series of shots of me posed against the Meissen figurines.

As we drove home I grumbled: 'What a waste of time,' but Emma reminded me: 'We have a lot of readers in Germany. This is how we nurture them.' Since we also had a lot of readers in Great Britain, the B.B.C. flew in a crew for a session much like the Germans' and another workday was wasted, but the men were so delighted with Emma that again she urged me to accompany them to dinner at the China, where conversation about Diana, the Princess of Wales, and the new movie about Christine Keeler was lively. I supposed that such interviews might help in the foreign distribution of my books, but I wasn't too sure; when the visitors returned home and wrote to thank us for our hospitality, I noticed they always referred to Emma, not me. Later a Japanese television crew wanted to come down, spurred no doubt by Mr. Saito, but Emma had to say 'No,' for she had her own plans and they could not be disrupted.

Each spring the women who had been classmates at Bryn Mawr in years past held reunions on the college grounds, where they renewed old friendships, recalled good times, and, not incidentally, provided the fund-raising staff of the university with current addresses. For many years Emma had missed these annual meetings, at first because she had no money to spend on such frivolities and later because we were too busy concentrating on my career. In the early years she could imagine her former friends asking at the picnic: 'Whatever happened to that curious Stoltzfus girl, Amish I think?' and someone would say: 'She's teaching school in some small town.' She could imagine their feeling smug, with husbands who were directors of great companies or heads of departments at major universities.

This would be the forty-fifth anniversary of her graduation, the kind that alumnae like to return to, and early on she let it be known that not only would she be coming but her husband too would be trailing along. She did not rub it in; she did not phrase it 'my famous husband,' but that's how she intended it to be read, and that's how it was. She knew that her classmates would be hauling along scores of my books.

Prior to the reunion she made a secret call to Miss Crane from a pay phone in Rostock: 'This is Emma Yoder. As you know, Lukas asks me to take charge of his income—taxes and all. Am I right in assuming that we'll be making a great deal of money this year?'

'Not as much as planned but more than you'll know what to do with.'

'I'll know what to do with it.'

———

If we took the lovely winding back roads of the Dutch country, Bryn Mawr was a mere thirty miles south and slightly to the west of our farm, so we did not have to leave home till shortly after five on a Friday afternoon to arrive in time for the intimate dinner prior to the festivities, and it was with quiet satisfaction that Emma, the insignificant little teacher of English in the Souderton schools from 1946 to 1984, made her appearance with her husband in tow. Few of her former classmates remembered her, but some were familiar with the photographs that appeared on the backs of my books, and soon everyone knew that Emma Stoltzfus had arrived.

Before the group sat down to the dinner, many women crowded up to congratulate Emma and ask me for autographs. Some asked if we had children, to which Emma replied with a gentle tap on one of my books. The highlight of the evening, however, came unexpectedly and was therefore doubly effective; the president of the university, a lively young woman, moved away from one table of diners and said with bubbling enthusiasm: 'Your class of 1945 can be proud of yourselves. The treasurer informs me that you've made an anniversary contribution to our Alumnae Fund of $1,178,000.'

Gasps greeted this astonishing information, but they became even more audible when she explained: 'This was made possible because of a magnificent gift of Emma Stoltzfus, '45, who sent me a registered letter this week containing this little goodie,' and she held aloft a check on the Bank of Dresden. 'It gives your college the nice round sum of one million dollars.'

Among the reactions none was more astonished than mine. Later, during the applause, I whispered: 'Where did you get that kind of money?' and she said smugly: 'I earned it. When you told me, "Take care of the money," first thing I did was give myself a salary.'

Late Saturday night as we drove back home with Emma at the wheel, she said: 'It was as fine a reunion as one could have imagined. So good to see the girls again.'

I said: 'I thought you hammered it into me, never use the word *girls* for mature women,' and she said dreamily: 'To me they will always be nineteen.' Silence. 'And I think they were glad that I came back to be with them,' and I said: 'You bought your way back,' and she said: 'Yes. I did. But with money I helped earn. Forty-five years ago when I first started teaching in Souderton I laid plans for last night. Grandiose plans. I refused to come back empty-handed, nor did I.'

There was no time for celebration of her triumphal return to Bryn Mawr because on the next Monday Emma received an urgent call from Ms. Marmelle: 'Emma, there's hell to pay. I'm not allowed to discuss it, but Mr. MacBain is flying down early tomorrow with two men who must talk to Lukas. They'll rent a car at A.B.E. and I'll draw them a diagram of how to reach your farm. Set the day aside. It could take that long.'

'Tell me one thing. Are the men lawyers? Is this a plagiarism suit or something like that?'

'On my word, it's not. Lukas is not in trouble, we are,' and with that she hung up, letting Emma stew through the rest of Monday.

Our family had two strategies from which we never deviated: first, face a catastrophe head-on and grapple with it and, second, analyze situations in advance so that we're never blindsided with a blow to the head. Nine years ago, at the first indication that Emma might have cancer she went into the hospital for extensive and expensive exploratory probing, which proved that she did have a growth. Fortunately, it was benign, but we had it removed anyway. On a less serious level, we tried to anticipate how we would react if a book did poorly, or if there was a considerable lag in production. We strove always to be in command of any situation where panic might be triggered so that hysteria could be avoided.

At both dinner and supper we tried to guess the meaning of that cryptic last sentence: 'Lukas is not in trouble, we are,' and by the process of elimination we concluded that it could only involve those stories we'd been reading in *The New York Times* regarding the probable sale of Kinetic Press, possibly to a foreign buyer, and we spent a good deal of time pondering what reaction we would have to such a distasteful sale.

Early Tuesday morning, much sooner than we had expected, Mr. MacBain drove his rented car into the farm entrance and waited for two men in blue suits to alight. Emma, watching the strangers approach her door, whispered: 'They look like federal agents,' and she was trembling when she let them in.

The introductions were both stiff and tentative, as if the visitors did not really care to meet us: 'This is Mr. Schulte of Inglenook in St. Louis, the biggest bookstore in many states out there. And this is Mr. Fregosi.'

When the three were seated, MacBain wasted no time in introducing their problem: 'We find ourselves in a most serious mess, I can describe it in no other way. Mr. Schulte, please show him the flier you mailed out.' From his folder the bookman produced a well-designed enticement to the store's customers, which said that Inglenook was fortunate in being able to offer its longtime patrons a rare opportunity, an autographed copy of Lukas Yoder's final novel in his 'Grenzler Octet,' autographed and boxed, for a mere seventy-five dollars.

'Well presented,' I said as I handed it back. 'Price seems outrageously high,' and to myself I added: Especially for a book that's going to be a dud.

'Not at all, as it turned out,' MacBain said. 'Now, the two operative words we're here to discuss are *mailed* and *autographed*. Both Inglenook's lawyers and Kinetic's assure us that when you offer to sell something in a letter that you send through the mail, that becomes a binding contract if the acceptance by mail is accompanied by a check. Fix this in your mind, Mr. Yoder. If Inglenook accepts money from its customers and then fails to perform, even if Inglenook returns the money, they've committed a fraud.'

Quietly I asked: 'How could something like this happen? I was never consulted. So far as I can see, I'm not obligated in any way.'

When everyone stared at MacBain, he was forced to make a humiliating confession: 'In our attempt to offset the unfavorable publicity we spoke of in New York, we sent a flier to all our sales reps: "Do everything possible to help us see that *Stone Walls* is launched with a maximum shove." Our man in the St. Louis region took this literally and told Mr. Schulte: "I'm sure Mr. Yoder would be delighted to autograph a tip sheet if you wanted to offer your customers a special edition." Without any authorization from you or us, our man said that.' In the silence we looked glumly at one another.

Then MacBain continued: 'We must understand the full legal complications. Mr. Schulte's lawyers and mine agree on this. The Kinetic salesman who made this commitment became, at the time of doing it, an agent fully authorized to speak for his employer, Kinetic, so if lawsuits or criminal penalties are instituted, they will fall on Kinetic, not on Inglenook. Is that how you understand it, Theodore?'

'Precisely. I can crawl out from under, not because I want to pin it all on you, MacBain, but because I have to. In this affair, I'm blameless.'

'And now we get to the sticky part. No one knows exactly what the law is or what the courts might hold. But when our agent made this offer to Mr. Schulte, he not only obligated me as his employer, but might also be considered as having obligated you, Mr. Yoder. You may be legally bound to autograph the books that have been ordered through the mail and paid for by checks sent through the mail.'

I gulped: 'And all because one of your salesmen was loose-tongued?'

'Yes.'

'Have you shot him?' Emma asked and MacBain replied: 'No, but next week I may.'

Mr. Schulte broke in: 'We all must keep the devastating facts in mind. We sent brochures by *mail*. Our clients returned their checks by *mail*. So we're obligated to perform or else.'

'And I'm dragged in by the tail?' I asked, and when both MacBain and Schulte nodded, Emma broke in: 'Nobody's said how many customers ordered the books.' In explanation Mr. Schulte said something that changed the color of this day, this year: 'Because Ms. Marmelle had slipped us a Xerox of the manuscript, something she rarely does, I and our leading salesmen read your novel, Mr. Yoder, and we deemed it so sensational, so exactly what readers are going to want this year, such a leap forward for you, I might say, that we ran this follow-up,' and he handed me a clipping that made bells ring in heaven: 'Everyone on our staff who has had the honor of reading an advance copy of *Stone Walls* has said: "This is the best Yoder yet." Order your special copy now. Only seventy-five dollars.'

Tears did not come to my eyes but I did breathe deeply: 'And how many responded?'

'Nine thousand.'

'I can't believe it.'

'Mr. Yoder, readers treasure your books. And word has seeped out that this may be your last. Everyone will want a copy of the regular edition, and nine thousand not only want the special edition but have already paid for it.'

'Signing that many sheets would take days, maybe weeks. My hand would drop off.' I was gratified by the vote of confidence from my readers but appalled by the magnitude of the task that confronted me.

The gloomy silence that followed was finally broken by Emma, who had a habit of wanting facts on which to chew: 'What kind of figures are we talking about here?' and from his portfolio Mr. Schulte produced numbers that stunned us: 'Nine thousand copies at seventy-five dollars a copy, that's $675,000. We've never had anything close to this.'

Emma asked: 'Why would anyone be crazy enough to pay that for an ordinary book?' and Mr. Schulte said: 'It's not an ordinary book. It's probably the best novel your husband has written and possibly his last, and this may be news to you, but there are thousands of people out there who love your husband, the mannerly way he behaves, a reminder of the days when authors were authors and not exhibitionists. . . . I doubt if the orders will stop at nine thousand, because those readers interpret this as a gentleman's farewell gesture.'

'And your flier stressed that interpretation, didn't it?'

'The selling of books is difficult. We grasp at straws—honorable ones.'

Emma did not care to have him explain what was included in his definition of *honorable*. Instead, she turned to MacBain and asked: 'If we accept his figure of nine thousand, what would that mean to us?' and the president of Kinetic said: 'We'd better move into the other room, if we may. Such figures are trade secrets—their circulation could damage us.'

When he was alone with us, he asked me: 'You know, of course, what the terms of your contract state?' and he was astonished when Emma said: 'No. He never attends to such matters.'

'But you signed our contracts. I have them in our safe.'

'Yes,' I said, but Emma broke in: 'He never bothers to read the figures. Wouldn't remember them if he did.'

'Where are the contracts?' he asked and I said: 'I don't know. In a file somewhere.'

Turning to Emma, he asked: 'Do you keep them, Mrs. Yoder?' and she said: 'He won't let me. Says no good comes of brooding over contracts, and I think he's right.'

'For your information, then, your contract is the same we've had for all your last books, ten percent for the first fifty thousand, fifteen percent after that. But this one does have a special kicker we give to no one else. After five hundred thousand, sixteen percent. So if this deal goes through you could earn $108,000.'

'With that fatal start,' Emma said, 'this book will never reach five hundred thousand.'

'From what we hear in the field, it will do better. Schulte's reaction is what the other independent booksellers are telling us, and when the big chains get the word, they'll come back in line. Your husband can do himself a lot of good by fulfilling this implied obligation.'

'And go to jail if he doesn't?' she asked and MacBain replied reassuringly: 'Our lawyers told us that while our agent *might* have become your agent when he made the promise, the likelihood is that since you were at one remove and knew nothing of the deal, you would very probably be exempt from culpability. But not for sure.'

When we returned to the living room the time had come to bring Mr. Fregosi into the discussion. He was introduced as a wizard from Boston's Route 128, the so-called Loop of Genius because of the bright young men from Harvard and M.I.T. who clustered there to realize their technological dreams. He was soft-spoken and gave an impression of credibility: 'The picture is not pleasant—in fact, it's quite ugly. But we do have one thing in our favor,' and he handed me his copy of the Inglenook flier with the word *auto-graphed* underlined in red: 'It does say *autographed*, clear enough, but it does not say either *personally autographed* or *autographed by hand*, and I can assure you that that provides us with an out that is foolproof.'

Taking from his briefcase a handful of papers, all different, he distributed them: canceled checks, diplomas, bond issues, hand-signed copies of ordinances and half a dozen other important forms. After we examined them he said: 'We've known for some time that governors of states, C.E.O.'s of corporations and university presidents simply cannot sign all the documents placed before them, especially salary checks. Quite a while ago bright boys invented machines that would enable the C.E.O. to sign, with many pens acting as one, fifty documents at once. The papers you have there are examples of how well that old machine works. Now look at this improvement,' and as we studied a different set of papers all apparently signed by T. Wellford Jackson, for the signatures were identical, he explained: 'This time our geniuses took only one signature of the man but with their magic machine they can reproduce it as if by hand, a thousand times if necessary.' And before we could express our wonder, he distributed a third set of papers, still signed by T. Wellford, but this time each of the signatures was visibly different from the others. The differentiating details were minute, to be true, but there they were, seventeen different signatures. 'What our boys have been able to do is to take one basic signature written out in longhand by Mr. Jackson and vary it by lasers into about four hundred slightly different signatures. Look at them, how handsome they are on their documents.'

While Emma inspected each one closely, Mr. Fregosi continued: 'So now you see the position you're in. If Mr. Yoder gives me ten samples of his handwriting, just ordinary samples with the natural differences that arise, a long *Y* here, a shorter one there, I can produce four thousand different signatures, all his, all original.'

Before I could protest, Fregosi added: 'There's no deception. Court cases have established in the case of the older system that the signatures it produces are signatures. And thank heavens, Mr. Schulte, you didn't say *personally autographed*.' Speaking directly to me, he said: 'The store's lawyers, Kinetic's lawyers and ours have given this a clean bill. If you go ahead with this we are legally safe, especially you, Mr. Yoder.'

'It's still a fraud,' Emma blurted, 'and I'll not allow Lukas to be involved in it.'

'The alternative,' said MacBain coldly, 'is sitting down and signing nine thousand copies, maybe ten by the time they're through opening the mail.'

To break the tension, Schulte said brightly: 'Let's all duck out and catch some lunch.' MacBain said: 'Ms. Marmelle told me there is an excellent inn in Dresden,' and the five of us started for the rental car, but before I left the house I excused myself, then returned in a few minutes, without explaining my brief absence.

The visitors were pleased by the Dresden China and spent much time inspecting the Meissen ware, but the lunch itself was a nervous affair, with everyone waiting for me to reveal my decision, and I could see that the men were distressed when I began: 'This is palpably immoral. We'll be delivering a shoddy product.' The visitors looked furtively at one another, but were visibly relieved when I continued: 'However, I see no option but to agree to your escape proposal and shall pray that it's legal.' When the men breathed audibly in relief, I took from my pocket an unsealed envelope: 'But I could not in good conscience accept even a penny royalty on those contaminated books. Here's a check, carefully dated as of today, and I want Mr. MacBain to mail it on his stationery dated tomorrow to the president of Mecklenberg College, Bethlehem, Pennsylvania 18016, with the notation: "For the college's library fund." I would not want the money ever to enter my account, and insist upon getting rid of it well beforehand.'

The luncheon did not end on a happy note, and after dropping us off at our farm the visitors hurried back to the airport.

———

When the better part of a week was lost in June, I began to wonder if I would ever again be allowed to correct galleys because I was taking an inordinate amount of time checking the proofs for *Stone Walls*. But I worked diligently in such hours as were available and was sometimes surprised at how effective some of my corrections were but dismayed by how many required repeated efforts before I got them right. I worked with special care because I knew that this was my last chance to perfect the narrative, and I was sardonically amused at those who referred to writing as if it were an act of supreme inspiration. Writing is fiendishly hard work.

The June interruption began when Ms. Marmelle called with the exciting news: 'Things are beginning to break our way. Schulte in St. Louis now has eleven thousand acceptances of their seventy-five-dollar offer. Independent stores are ordering like mad. We're going to lick this thing yet. And best of all, C.B.S. has heard about your hex paintings and has alerted publicity that they'd like to do a substantial segment about you on their Friday-morning *At Home* show.'

'Is that a respectable show?'

'Mr. Yoder, it's a gem! Don't you ever watch TV.?'

'Not till nine at night. The old movies, if we can find one.'

'Publicity has worked their keisters off to arrange this, and we'll be lucky if they go ahead. They come to your place—all shots in your own home—Emma to be featured prominently as your helpmate—and they do it with distinction, class. Do say you'll agree and I'll handle details.'

C.B.S. in New York phoned to tell us that our portion of the show would air at eight-thirty Friday morning of this week, and I said: 'Fine. I'll work through Thursday noon, consult with your advance people for a few minutes in the afternoon and go to bed early so I'll be fresh for the camera on Friday.' Emma planned to do the same, bringing in her helper on Thursday afternoon to straighten things.

Our plans were somewhat disturbed, because on Wednesday morning at eleven a monster truck pulled into our driveway, hauling behind it a huge three-part generator to provide the electricity required for what had to be done. Four electricians arrived in private cars to rewire our entire house, and when Emma shouted: 'Why are you disconnecting our wires?' they explained: 'We can't run the risk of a power blackout in the middle of the show.' Black wires coiled through the house like cobras waiting to strike. Plans were made to disconnect the telephone and to substitute three different wires direct to the studio in New York.

Just before dusk that day a truck, even larger than the first, the kind one saw at important football games, pulled into the farm, and when Emma cried: 'Hey, what's that?' she was told by the driver: 'We call it the command post. Everything operates out of here.' And as night fell, an armed policeman on hire from the Dresden department rode up in his own car to guard these valuable properties till dawn.

About ten on Thursday, three camera crews dispatched by C.B.S. in Philadelphia arrived, and there were now on the site two huge trucks, a smaller one and six private cars, but the director and her staff had not yet arrived. They flew down from New York, rented a car, and pulled in before twelve. They went right to work scouting the place and agreeing on camera positions and angles: 'I see this as a three-part setup. First, Mr. and Mrs. Yoder in their gracious living room with colorful German decoration. Chat-chat-chat with New York. Then, of course, we see him at his desk, because, after all, he is a writer. Chat-chat-chat with New York. And then the surprise. We switch to the studio with him explaining what he does with the hex signs. Chat-chat-chat including an explanation from him about what a hex is.'

When this program was agreed upon, she moved swiftly to the big decisions: 'Obviously we'll need three cameras. Living room, down-

stairs; study, upstairs; workshop, in the yard. Sounds simple. But I
also want an outside shot, the Yoders inviting us into their house.
We must have movement. Zig-zag-zoog, no static talking heads. So
how can we have a camera out here to catch them inviting us in, and
still maintain the three we need for the guts of the show?' After some
discussion it was agreed that the camera responsible for the workshop was best qualified to start at the entrance and then sprint over
to the art area and be ready when I walked into it, prior to the closing
scene, but for some reason I did not understand, the cameraman
would have to run backward, so a helper had to be on hand to guide
him over the wires and grass. They tried this several times and found
it practical.

At twelve-thirty that Thursday, waiters from the Dresden China
appeared with elegant box lunches for everyone and a large icebox
filled with canned drinks, nonalcoholic. The crew ate voraciously
while Emma and I sat in the kitchen with the director and her
principal assistant. 'We do this every Thursday,' the director said.
'Wrap it Friday at ten, fly home to Long Island, fly out to the next
assignment on Wednesday, or if it's close at hand like this, on Thursday morning.'

'Where do you head next week?' Emma asked.

'Where is it, Frank?'

'Seattle. For that famous bone specialist. Speaks with a Viennese
accent. Has a smile as big as a full moon.'

After lunch the director wanted to run through the movements,
not once or twice, but six or seven times, because the actions of half
a dozen people besides Emma and me had to be coordinated, and
although I did not have to memorize lines, I did have to establish
a set path through the myriad wires and adhere to it, and this I was
unable to do. Finally the director had to warn me: 'Mr. Yoder, you
are not strolling from this room to your study, and then on to your
workshop. You must walk a carefully defined path.' When I proved

unequal to the task, she said calmly: 'We've had this before. Great
men can really screw up, Mr. Yoder, so as soon as we finish a scene,
Frank here will grab your left arm, pull you back and guide you
directly to your next shot and vanish before the camera catches him.'

'That would be better,' I said, but that night when everyone was
gone except the policeman guarding the trucks, I said: 'Emma, I'd
hate to make a fool of myself before all the people who might be
watching. Grab my left arm, pull me backward and lead me through
the maze,' and when she had done this five times I caught the rhythm
and felt more secure.

On Friday morning at six the director wanted to run through all
the procedures once more, but as she was about to do so, Frank came
in breathless: 'We can get no signal from New York into Mr. Yoder's
earphone. Yours is all right, but he won't be able to hear the questions New York will be asking. He'll look very stupid if he just sits
there not saying anything.'

When Frank started to wring his hands she said: 'Frank, remember our rule. We never have disasters, we have problems,' and within
a few minutes she was holding a huge sheet of cardboard on which
she printed the questions she would direct the interviewer in New
York to ask. Standing where I could see her, while the cameras could
not, she assured me: 'I'll point in sequence to the questions being
asked in New York,' but this seemed so cumbersome that I asked:
'Why not let me see her asking the questions, even though I can't
hear her. Then I'll know when it's my turn to speak,' and the director
gave me alarming news: 'No good. You never see the people in New
York. All you get is her voice. And today apparently you're not
going to get even that.'

'Oh my God!'

'Now, Mr. Yoder, I get the feeling that you're a real pro. And I
know you've faced emergencies before. Let me give you one hint.
When I point to the questions you can't hear, speak with great

enthusiasm and keep on speaking, whatever you want to say, till I flag you for the next question. Then shut up. After a pause, I'll point to what's being asked and you bang into it again.' When panic showed in my face, she leaned over and kissed me: 'You're going to look back on this as one of the triumphs of your life.'

Staring at her in total confusion, I said: 'This new problem has completely driven out of my mind how I'm supposed to walk backward into the next shot.'

'That's not your problem. That's Frank's. Words? You look to me. Feet? Rely on Frank.' Then I asked: 'But if I can't hear through the earphone, why do I have to wear it?' and she said: 'To look good. If it wasn't there, all the pros would know we were faking it.' She stopped, stared into my quivering eyes and said grimly: 'You and I are pros, Mr. Yoder. We do not screw up.'

The interview ended at 0849 and before 0900 calls started on the reactivated lines. Acquaintances from all over the country, especially Emma's Bryn Mawr friends, called to assure her: 'You looked tremendous! Delivered your lines like an actor.' Several people wanted to purchase one of my hex paintings, and an art magazine called to see if we had any color negatives of my work.

By ten the wires were gone, normal electricity was restored, and the phone calls from people who had called C.B.S. had been forwarded by the very system that had not functioned while I was on the air. I could not remember who some of the callers were.

At noon the mammoth trucks were gone, headed to the Interstate and their next assignment, and at a quarter to one the director and her personal staff were sitting around our kitchen table chatting, drinking beer and feasting on scraps from the refrigerator, including fried toast, honey and cold milk, followed by huge wedges of a German apple pie Emma had purchased the day before from the Diefenderfers at the Rostock post office.

As the New York people drove off, the director gripped my hand:

'You didn't damage yourself this morning, old man. Anyone who saw you would say: "That son of a gun knows what he's doing." Books and paintings and polished speech, you're a triple threat.'

Just as I was about to tackle my final batch of galleys in mid-July I was sidetracked by an interruption I welcomed: the director of the Abby Aldrich Rockefeller Folk Art Collection in Williamsburg, Virginia, telephoned to say that they had an unexpected vacancy in their schedule of exhibitions and would like to display almost immediately eleven of my hex paintings that they'd been able to assemble, but only if I'd agree to add the three they understood I'd been working on and had not yet disposed of. I explained that I'd finished only *XXII* and *XXIII*, but I thought I knew where I could borrow back *XVII*. They were delighted: 'We have a handsome brochure at the printer's—a substantial pamphlet, really—and posters we had intended to use later. We'll paste on the proper date and expect you and Mrs. Yoder with your three paintings on Wednesday next, for the opening on Thursday.'

'We'll be there.'

I took pleasure in exhibiting my paintings in a fine museum like the Williamsburg, for to do so brought the art of my people to an entirely new population; as I explained to Emma while driving south to Virginia: 'When they read my books, all they get is my impression of what our Dutch were like. When they actually see the hexes, torn bleeding from living barns, they see something that was a vital part of our experience,' and I added: 'Living in the Wallace House again isn't an interruption of work, it's a vacation. I don't like to tear myself away from the galleys, they're top priority, but the paintings also stand high.'

When we drove up to the museum, we encountered a surprise, for the director said: 'A delightful young couple runs a bookstore here in town, the Colonial. When the Cutworths heard you were coming to us for the exhibition tomorrow afternoon, they asked if they could arrange a small party at their shop tomorrow night, an informal affair at which local booklovers would drop in for cider, gingersnaps and good talk. I accepted on your behalf.'

'I didn't come here to peddle books. Folk art was the attraction.'

'You'll have discharged any obligation to us when you finish your presentation. I encouraged the Cutworths. Told them we rarely get a two-fer in town, artist and writer, and we should make the most of it.'

'If you're not doing it because you're trying to please me.'

'Mr. Yoder! I'm going to be at their party and looking forward to it. Their shop is one of the most civilized places in Williamsburg.'

When we drove about the elegant town on our way back to the Wallace House, we saw several posters proclaiming that Lukas Yoder would be at Colonial Books on Thursday night for an informal discussion with booklovers familiar with his work.

The fourteen paintings from my *Hex Series* made a striking display for the Thursday afternoon show, and the carefully prepared brochure with three of the older works reproduced in color gave an accurate account of what the writer called 'Yoder's dual personality, the author of the popular "Grenzler Octet" and the plastic artist who created the imaginative *Hex Series*.' The show was a success, and after sharing a light dinner, the curator drove us through the quiet streets of Williamsburg, where every house seemed to be a museum, and to the main street leading down from William and Mary College, where a surprise awaited me.

The section of the street near Colonial Books was so crowded with people that two policemen had been called to extra duty. When the curator asked one of the officers what the police were protecting, the man replied: 'The bookstore. They're all carrying books.' When Emma from her seat in back inspected the people near her car

THE WRITER

. . . .

106

window, she whispered: 'They have your books, darling . . . some
have shopping bags full of them.'

What had been planned as a quiet literary evening had turned into
something of a crisis, with many in the crowd pressing forward to
buy whatever books of mine the store had for sale, while harried
clerks tried to tell them that the stock had been virtually exhausted
by three that afternoon. However, the enterprising husband of one
of the clerks had jumped in his car and sped to neighboring communities to buy up what copies he could, and he had phoned from his
last stop to say he had found about forty and would be bringing them
in promptly. In the meantime the curator deposited us at the front
door and drove ahead to find parking.

Since I am not the kind of author who is easily recognized, when
I climbed out of the car and started toward the bookstore, people in
line protested and one man shouted: 'Back to the end of the line,
bub!' to which Emma said with a wink: 'He's the bub who writes
those books you're carrying,' and she tapped the two novels he was
holding.

'It's Yoder,' someone said in a low voice, and while no one
cheered, there was scattered clapping of a restrained sort, which I
acknowledged with some embarrassment.

Inside the shop we encountered consternation, for the Cutworths,
the owners, were engulfed by the crush of people, their hopes of a
quiet evening of genteel discourse blasted. Their store was jammed,
everyone waiting with books to be autographed that had not been
purchased there, and there were no copies on hand to sell to those
who had come empty-handed.

When we saw the Cutworths, whom we identified by the anxiety
on their young faces, practical Emma elbowed her way up to them
and introduced herself: 'Don't you think you'd better arrange a table
where he could sit and do some signing?' and they said: 'We hadn't
planned it this way,' and indicated a circle of chairs in the back of

the shop near which stood a table with gingersnaps and two rather small pitchers of cider. 'We expected a few friends.'

With a practiced hand, Emma cleared the table and directed Mr. Cutworth to move it forward to a spot at which the customers could be organized into a line. The announcement of the autographing had brought out not the fifteen or twenty booklovers the Cutworths had anticipated, but close to three hundred; some of them were motivated by mere curiosity, but many were true fans of the Grenzler books. After all, the books did deal with a colorful area not far to the north that many of them had visited. As with the case of the St. Louis autographs, most of the people in line had heard that this would probably be my last book, so they were lured here by two impulses: to say hello to a writer with whose work they were familiar and to get his signature on a first edition of one of his books in hopes that it might later be of value. When anyone told me of the latter reason I nodded gravely but did not point out that the book he carried had been issued in a first edition of 500,000 and it would be miraculous if one could find a copy that wasn't a first.

I signed till my right hand was numb, and since I liked to look directly at the person requesting my autograph and exchange a few words, the process went slowly. This irritated Emma, who whispered: 'Sign the things. Don't hold little cocktail parties with everyone who comes by.' I could never explain to her or to bookstore people who gave the same advice that at such moments I was not in Williamsburg or St. Louis autographing books by the hundreds, I was back in the Hess store in Allentown on that terrible day when not a single customer showed up. The difference between then and now was that more than a million people had read each of my last three books and many of them had found them meaningful and their author a responsible man. They were people to whom I was indebted, and if they had come out on a warm evening for an autograph I had to give it in a way that was not perfunctory.

The poor Cutworths had abandoned any hopes of this being a literary evening; this was book mania with no relationship to what they considered their civilizing function in the community. Intermittently they had seen in the street outside members of the local intelligentsia, especially certain distinguished professors from the college who had been invited to participate in the conversation, and were not surprised that these booklovers, shuddering at the sight of the mob, passed on.

Now a cheer broke out, for the clerk's husband who had gone scouting for books returned with word that he had brought back sixty-three Yoders, and he and Mr. Cutworth went out into the crowd and sold the lot as quickly as they could lift each book in the air.

At such signings—Emma and I attended about two a year—she served one function that I applauded. When there was a long line, she moved back and forth bringing forward to the head any woman who was pregnant, or had a child, or anyone, man or woman, who was physically handicapped. Invariably when she did this, the queue cheered, as if she had done a good deed, but she declined credit by saying: 'My husband insisted on this,' even though the idea was hers.

At the end of two hours there were still many in line, so Mr. Cutworth and one of the policemen went to a certain point in the line and marked it with a chair: 'We'll have to stop here.' Emma, hearing murmurs of complaint, went to those excluded and told them: 'Give us your address and Mr. Cutworth will get you the books you want, if you have your own my husband will send you a special bookplate signed with your name and his.' Cutworth, taken by surprise, eagerly agreed, and some forty people gave their names and left, reasonably content.

I signed for another half hour, then indicated that the police should close the doors. When they did, Emma invited the officers inside, and they and the Cutworths and the man who had corraled the extra copies gathered about the table and finished the ginger-snaps. 'I'm sorry about what happened,' I said. 'It wasn't planned that way.'

'I should have anticipated this,' Cutworth said. 'We do sell a lot of your books.'

'We rarely see such an orderly crowd,' one of the policemen said. 'Especially in a college town.'

Mrs. Cutworth said: 'I saw quite a few college students in line. Those who had no books always said: "I'm so sorry you ran out. I was going to buy one," but I think they were just looking.'

When Emma and I walked down the historic street to our private house, I was overcome by the solemn majesty of this town, rescued from thoughtless ruin by the imagination of the Rockefellers: 'When Jefferson walked this street he saw it much as we do. George Wythe might have strolled here with his law students. It's proper for a republic to maintain a memory like this,' but when I entered the house I spoke only of this night: 'I feel so sorry for the Cutworths. They'd planned a quiet literary evening and would have been so much happier if they'd had some proper author who sold eleven copies of his books in Williamsburg. What we had tonight was a riot, but I'll not soon forget some of the things they told me.'

'They talked even more with me,' Emma said. 'I'm so proud that in a little town like this, where they have no call to like either you or your books, they came in such numbers.' We went to bed as soon as we reached the second floor, and I was so exhausted from the show at the art gallery and the confusion at the bookstore that I fell asleep immediately. But toward three in the morning I found myself awake and thinking not of this day's triumphs but of how important the public reception of *Stone Walls* was going to be in my life and for MacBain and Kinetic: 'If I insisted on doing it my way, I've got to do everything possible to make the book as flawless as possible.' And I swore to do so. Not wanting to waken Emma, I slipped quietly out of bed, reached for my briefcase and crept downstairs to the dining room. There I took out the last batch of galleys of *Stone Walls*, and on a colonial table made of burnished cherry wood that Jefferson might have used for a similar purpose, I began scribbling on the galleys, praying that I might be inspired to add something that would make the kind of book I wanted more appealing to readers who insisted that it be written the way they wanted. I certainly did not write only to please readers, and *Stone Walls* proved this, but on the other hand, I did not ignore them, which was why so many had come out tonight.

My rustling of the papers must have awakened Emma, for toward five in the morning she appeared at my elbow like a lovely little ghost: 'Oh, Lukas! I told you a dozen times, "Do not bring galleys. This is to be a vacation." And here you are at God knows what hour, as if you were a struggling beginner.'

I told her that in the last stages of seeing a book through the press, every writer is a struggling beginner, but in my own case, haunted by the negative assessments, I was doubly the beginner: 'I'm scared. Just as I was when we started. I can't run the risk of making even a small error,' and she said: 'All right. Finish that galley, but then you must come back to bed. We'll stop at Rostock on the way home and mail the proofs to Ms. Marmelle.'

II

THE EDITOR

MY LIFE as a rowdy New York tomboy ended on a cloudy October day in 1955, when, at the age of eleven, I was painfully transformed into a self-taught intellectual.

An unruly gang of six youngsters were playing a noisy game of stickball in a three-walled, brick-lined cul-de-sac in the Bronx. A version of baseball, this is a game that uses a broom handle as a bat to hit a spaldeen, a pink rubber ball named after the Spaulding Company, which made them, and when a well-hit ball ricochets off the walls, the game can become a real test of skill.

As always, I expected to be chosen first when the teams were made up because I was spectacular not only at bat but also in the field, for then I was constantly on the move and the batter couldn't tell where I was going to wind up. This meant I was always ready to dash full speed toward what looked like a sure hit, leap high in the air, and snare it with my extended right hand. Older people watching me sometimes cried: 'The lady Joe DiMaggio!' I liked the last part of that name, but not the lady bit. My aspirations did not lie in that direction.

Whenever a game was about to start I said a little prayer: 'Please, God, let me be chosen today,' because if I was, my day was made or even my week.

In the early days the boys had not wanted me in their game and said so: 'This is a man's game. Girls keep out.' But one day they were short one player; a red-headed Irish boy of twelve, Earl O'Fallon, insisted that I be allowed to play, and to prove his conviction that I would contribute to the game, he chose me for his team.

When I excelled, the other boys whispered that he was soft on me, and a viperish boy no one liked made up a jingle that he took pleasure in chanting in a high-pitched voice whenever I came to bat:

> 'Shirl, Shirl, the goofy girl!
> No one loves her but a stoop named Earl.'

And if I popped up an easy fly for the other team to catch, its members would join the poet in the chant to tease O'Fallon and me.

I have always believed that O'Fallon wanted to ignore the teasing, for I knew he liked me, but the viperish boy had another taunt that Earl could not ignore: 'Why should a good Catholic boy be sweet on a Jewish girl?' When others asked the same question he could find no answer, and one day he startled me by snapping: 'You shouldn't be out here playing with boys,' and he refused to choose me for his team. In fact, he told the other boys: 'I never liked her.'

But because I was so good, the other boys did choose me for their team. One day when Earl was at bat during a crucial game, he gave his broom handle a mighty swing that drove the spaldeen toward the far brick wall. This was exactly the kind of ball I often caught with a spectacular flourish, but even as I ran with great strides toward the spot in the wall where the ball would come, I remember telling myself: 'Don't catch it. He will really love you if you don't catch it.' But the rhythm in my running was so irresistible that I loped over, leaped high in the air, and snagged it with my right hand.

Instead of cheers I heard 'Shirl, Shirl, the goofy girl,' and I was so confused that I ran toward O'Fallon to tell him: 'Sorry I robbed you of a sure homer,' but this irritated him doubly, and when I reached out to shake hands as a gesture of friendship, all he could hear was the chanting of his opponents—'Nobody loves her but a stoop named Earl'—and he lashed out with both hands, caught me just below the neck and pushed me heavily against the very wall where I had leaped to catch his hit. Losing my footing, I stumbled, flew backward against the rough brick and saved myself at the last moment only by throwing out my right arm to absorb the impact. In that awkward moment of smacking into the wall, I heard something snap and I fell to the pavement, my arm broken, while the viperish boy continued to chant: 'Shirl, Shirl, the goofy girl.'

What hurt most was that O'Fallon did not come either to help me or to apologize, while my own teammates, afraid of being held responsible for my accident, fled the scene. Left alone, I headed home, cradling in my left hand my limp right arm. In this wounded way, with no tears showing, I climbed the steps to our second-floor tenement home and told my mother: 'Mom, I think something happened to my arm.' And I played no more stickball.

If I had to break my arm, I did it at an appropriate time, for during my convalescence I came to realize that I could not continue my tomboy ways and associate with the rowdy boys; I had to remain indoors, and this projected me unwillingly into the world of books, an area I had not explored before. My tastes were simple, those of a girl of seven or eight. I still found pleasure in fairy tales and the childish novelettes of adventure. I rejected as 'icky' any story in which girls showed a sentimental interest in boys, but when I explored books written specifically for boys, some strong intuition told me that I was heading in the wrong direction. It was then, as I became twelve with my broken arm, that I accepted the fact that I was a girl and grew hungry to read about girls like myself.

In this discovery I was assisted by my uncle Judah, a tailor who loved books, for he recognized the alteration in me: 'The library's filled with elegant books for a girl like you,' and when I asked: 'What kind?' he brought me, charged to his own lending card, *Anne of Green Gables*: 'You read this at your age, Shirl, you'll never forget it.'

'I don't like you to call me Shirl.'

'I'm sorry—I won't call you that again. But it *is* a good book, Shirley.'

When I took it from him I hefted it and said: 'It's heavy and it looks long. I don't think I'd like it.'

It was only with difficulty that he restrained himself from slapping me, but he did growl: 'You're not wise enough, Shirley, to make a judgment like that—based on nothing. Read the book, you'll like it.'

I laughed: 'You sound just like Mom. "Eat it, you'll like it." '

'Well, you do like it, don't you?'

'When it tastes good, yes.'

'This book will taste very good.'

With the opening of that book, leaning it against my broken right arm as I turned the pages with my left hand, I entered a new world, one that I found increasingly wonderful. I could visualize myself as this winsome Canadian orphan, which led me to go to an atlas to see just where Canada was; I also studied the map to determine where Heidi and Hans Brinker lived, and in this way my physical world expanded at the same speed as my emotional one. Without knowing it, I was growing to love books.

My horizons widened in all directions when one afternoon Uncle Judah took me to the public library and showed me the almost endless shelves of books for children, but my tastes had now matured to the point where I gravitated naturally to the section labeled YOUNG TEENS, and there for the first time selected for myself, with a little prodding from my uncle, a novel written with adult serious-ness about a girl much like myself but two years older. *The Vacation*, it was called, and I noted that it was by a woman writer; it was about a city girl of fourteen who spends a summer vacation with an aunt in rural Maine. A colt is born, a baby girl is left an orphan, a boy wants to take the girl to the movies but is told 'Next year,' and an ailing aunt dies. But what was most important was that the novel created an overwhelming sense of reality: Antonia was a living girl whose friends called her Tony, a name she despised, and her summer relatives were as real as my own family. It was such a sensational experience to become so familiar with other people's lives that when I took the book back I asked the librarian: 'Did all this really happen?' and she explained: 'It happened, but only in the mind of the writer. And, of course, in your mind, too. That's what a novel is. The exchange of dreams.'

After such a fortunate introduction to the realm of fiction, I became an addict and read voraciously down the endless line of books for teens, but my real adventures came when Uncle Judah offered me a proposition: 'Shirl, I mean Shirley, I'll give you a dime for every book in this row you read,' and he led me to SENIOR HIGH, where the maturity of style and the level of adventure and emotional content took a quantum leap upward. Along with this new avenue of exploration, Uncle Judah arranged for me to get my own library card, assuring the woman at the desk that this leggy child was fourteen. When I lugged home my first two near-adult selections, my mother cried: 'What kind of a book is this for a little girl to read?' and she wanted Judah to take the inappropriate books right back to the library, but he argued: 'If a girl doesn't grow up now, she may never grow up,' and I kept the books.

By the time my right arm was mended and the cast removed, I was a confirmed bookworm who knew a good novel from one that did not take itself seriously, and one day as I approached thirteen I announced to my family, including Uncle Judah: 'When I grow up I want to be a librarian and know all the books on the shelves.'

When I was nineteen, a recession in the clothing industry forced my father's employer to lay him off for the duration of what was prom- ised to be a 'temporary slowdown.' When the bad times showed no signs of abating, my father had to tell me: 'Darling, there's no escape. You'll have to quit college for the time being. We have no money and no possibility of finding any.'

I was just finishing my freshman year at C.C.N.Y., that wonderful college that takes the children of poor people and turns them into leaders of the nation, and if I was desolate about leaving school, my teachers were, too. But Professor Fineschreiber, who himself had been educated in the New York system, ending with a doctorate in English from C.C.N.Y., told me on the sad day of my departure: 'Miss Marmelstein, your education does not end today. It's just beginning. When you get a job, and you will, because you're a survivor, spend at least one evening a week, and better two, going to free concerts, free lectures, free talks at the museums.' He added: 'Take into your heart and mind the richness this great city provides free, and in the end you'll have a better education than most of us.'

My father gave me encouraging news: 'They're laying off old men like me at the shop, but they're hiring young women. Laurelsohn promised me that he'd give you a job till the recession ends, then he'll take me back.'

Early on a Monday morning I boarded an IRT subway train and headed south for Times Square and the northern end of the city's famed Garment District, but as I walked south on Seventh Avenue and saw grown men like my father pushing clothes racks on wheels up and down the streets—bumping pedestrians on the pavement, dodging cars in traffic—to rush garments from one location to another, I felt a great repugnance for such an insecure way of life. Halting amid the throng, I mumbled: 'I refuse to be trapped in a life like this. There's a world of books, of ideas, and I'm going to fight my way into that world.'

I fled the area with its crowded streets and enormous vitality, but I did not know where to try next for a job. Then I remembered vaguely that one day a lecturer visiting Professor Fineschreiber's class had said: 'There's this nest of publishers on Madison Avenue who help set the intellectual agenda for the nation. . . .' That's all I remembered, but the words burned in my mind: 'the intellectual agenda for the nation,' that's what I wanted to be involved in! And I strode purposefully east on Forty-second Street—not realizing at that moment how important that bustling thoroughfare was to become in my life—and turned north at Madison, where I found in succession Random House, in its stately mansion close to St. Patrick's Cathedral, and two other firms whose names I recognized. But a little farther on I saw Kinetic Press's dashing logo, with its fluid swirly K.

I had stopped at each of the three previous houses, asking if they had any openings for a young woman who could type and take dictation, but had been rejected. At Kinetic I took the elevator to the third floor and spoke to a friendly receptionist, who said: 'Not a single opening,' but as I started to leave, the woman said: 'Did you say you could take dictation?' When I nodded, the woman said: 'Wait just a moment,' and she dialed a number.

'Pauline, did I hear you say you could use a girl if she knew shorthand?' After a silence, the receptionist said: 'I'll send her up. Presentable. Says she's had one year at C.C.N.Y.'

On the fifth floor I was interviewed by a Miss Wilmerding, an older woman who asked the essential questions so rapidly that I had the sensation of facing a machine gun. But her questions and my enthusiastic replies established the fact that I was a responsible girl on the verge of becoming a capable young woman. 'Two further questions. Are you planning to remain in the city indefinitely?' When I nodded, she said: 'And most important of all, do you have a family you can fall back on if trouble should strike?' And I said: 'The family's falling back on me.'

The woman said: 'We have nothing right now, but you seem to be the kind of person we'd like to get into the firm. Come back on Wednesday.'

That evening at supper I lied to my family: 'Nothing right now at the factory, but maybe later,' and I shivered when my father growled: 'Damn that Laurelsohn.' I had to object when he wanted to call the foreman: 'Don't make him angry. I'll go back Wednesday.'

I spent Tuesday in a manner that set a pattern for my adult life: I went to my familiar public library and consulted for eight unbroken hours books on the publishing, editing and marketing of books. I spent several hours tracking down entries regarding Kinetic Press, and at the conclusion of my labors I knew when it was founded, by whom and with what intentions. I could rattle off the names of a dozen now-dead writers who had made it famous and another dozen still living. In each group I had recognized only three names, but other reference books provided thumbnail sketches of all twenty-four, some of whom slowly came to life when I saw their photographs or read the lists of their books.

When I went to bed that night I told myself: 'I want to work in publishing. Even if I have to scrub floors.'

On Wednesday the receptionist on the third floor at Kinetic recognized me and said: 'Go right up to five, they know you're coming.' There Miss Wilmerding said without further questioning: 'We do have that opening I spoke of the other day, but as you can guess, it's at the bottom of the ladder. Nothing glamorous.'

'To work anywhere is a salvation,' I said. 'But to work with books, that's a privilege.'

This answer pleased Miss Wilmerding, for it reminded her of things she had said in her late teens, and her ambitions, dreamlike though they had seemed at the time, had come to fruition: 'What is it you would like to become in the years ahead?'

'An editor—working with authors—seeing books come alive with my help.'

Miss Wilmerding leaned back, smiling indulgently, and delivered the speech she had utilized so often in giving young women guidance as they started their first job with Kinetic: 'Every year, Miss Marmelstein, we employ the brightest young graduates of our finest women's colleges—Vassar, Bryn Mawr, Smith. They all want to become editors. They all have A's in English. And without exception they start as secretaries, or gofers, or paper-pushers. No hope whatever of becoming editors.'

I fought back any sign of disappointment at hearing my ambitions shot down, but then she added: 'However, any young woman I've hired who really wanted to become an editor eventually became one.'

'How does it happen?'

'You work at your menial job. You watch what others do. You educate yourself. You listen to book talk. And by force of personality and intellect you make your superior see that you're a very bright, capable person who loves books. At the start it seems it cannot possibly be that you will ever find an opening. At the end it happens, because we seek dedicated people. Couldn't run a major house without them. But do study and learn.'

Back home that night I waited till supper was almost over, then said: 'I got the job today.'

This caused great excitement, with my father crowing: 'I told you that Laurelsohn could be trusted. Where's he starting you? Fabrics?'

'I'm to be an editor. A book editor.' When the entire family gasped, I added: 'At Kinetic Press. One of the best.'

Uncle Judah cried: 'This house is blessed.'

Blushing, I warned: 'Well, not exactly an editor. Not yet. I start at the bottom and work my way up.'

'How else?' Uncle Judah asked, and my mother broke out a bottle of inexpensive wine, and toasts were drunk to the new publisher of Kinetic Press.

I really did start at the bottom, serving in a kind of secretarial pool, now working in one office where an employee was absent, now in another, but always in some function relating to the making of books. As I worked I strove to accomplish two goals: to make my superiors realize that here was an exceptional recruit and to learn from them as much as possible about publishing. Gradually many in the big building began to say: 'That new kid, you can depend on her.'

During one exciting week I served as a replacement in the small, crowded office of Miss Kennelly, whose door had the sign SUBSIDI-ARY RIGHTS. Her job was to be like an old-time peddler, hawking her wares, except that she remained in her office, telephoning anyone who might conceivably want to purchase from Kinetic the rights to publish or use a Kinetic book in some special way. Sales to paperback manufacturers, magazines, book clubs and newspaper serializations all fell under Miss Kennelly's supervision, and, with the changes that were overtaking the book business, her role was becoming increasingly important.

During the five days I helped, I listened as Miss Kennelly participated over the telephone in a bidding war for book-club rights to a Kinetic romance that used nineteenth-century techniques to tell a twentieth-century story involving two competent modern women, a bewildered man and a fifteen-year-old girl caught in the vortex of tangled relationships. In the midst of frantic phone calls in which Miss Kennelly seemed to be the only one maintaining her cool, a secondary competition began over the right to reprint the same book, which seemed sure to be a big winner. In the midst of the dual crisis Miss Kennelly, intensely occupied with book clubs, gestured to me: 'Handle the paperback people. Tell them there'll be a decision by four-thirty this afternoon.'

I leaped into the fray, fending off agitated callers with statements like: 'The author is aware that you've taken his last two books and is mighty proud of that fact. Naturally, he inclines toward letting you have this one, too, but there are considerations about which he doesn't know—complicated ones. We'll get it sorted out by four-thirty. But we do need to know one important thing. Have you given us your absolute top bid?'

Like a fisherman keeping four baited hooks in a stream, I tried to keep my four possible purchasers nibbling until Miss Kennelly finished with the book clubs and grabbed the other phone: 'Yes, Miss Carstain, my able assistant Miss Marmelstein did give you such figures, but there happen to be others that have just surfaced. She did not hold back anything relevant. She just didn't have the latest data. Our big brass has reached new conclusions that modify everything.'

At the end of the hectic day in which this sharp-minded juggler had earned Kinetic nearly a quarter of a million dollars by her adroit management of rights, her office was crowded with officials who praised her coolheadedness. Mr. MacBain, head of Kinetic, said: 'What we appreciate, Miss Kennelly, is how you pick one winner from the pack but manage to retain the friendship of the others, so that we can go back to them next week with another deal.'

The smiling Irishwoman, savoring the accolades, said: 'At the climax I couldn't have handled all the bidders without the help of this young person, Shirley Marmelstein. You'd have thought she was an old pro.'

Mr. MacBain smiled at me and asked: 'What department are you in?' and I said brightly: 'I'm a floater. Learning the secret of what makes a good book a salable one.'

'If you find out, please tell me.'

When the party broke, Miss Kennelly, realizing that neither she nor I could unwind after the excitement, said: 'Let's celebrate. My treat,' and as we perched on stools in a bar frequented by editors of various houses, I heard for the first time the knowing chatter of young men and women engaged in my new profession: 'Miss Kennelly! I hear you hit the trifecta!' A reporter who covered publishing for *The New York Times* stopped by to say: 'I'm not asking for figures, but I would like to quote you as saying that while you didn't want to gloat, you were delighted, since this meant that *Tricorn Anxieties* is assured of a huge best-sellerdom.' Miss Kennelly beamed: 'I said it, word for word, as you just gave it.' The *Times* man toasted her: 'You'll go far.' But as he was about to move on she tugged his sleeve. 'An interesting sidebar is this bright gal, Shirley Marmelstein. She was catapulted right into the middle of this frenzy, first week on the job, and the success of the pocketbook part of the sale is largely due to her improvised skill.'

The reporter asked for additional facts, then said: 'Wait right here till I call my photographer,' and two days later I was able to show my parents the dramatic story NOVICE HELPS SWING MASSIVE DEAL, accompanied by my photograph. The column dealt primarily with the role that was increasingly being played in New York publishing by bright young women, and I was cited as an example.

When the week ended and I had to move on to other assignments, Miss Kennelly told me: 'You're the best I've ever had. I'd ask for you permanently, but the budget won't allow it.' She said: 'Keep your eye on this job if I should ever move on.'

'Are you leaving?'

'I've engineered some spectacular sales under difficult circumstances. Other houses know who was responsible.' She dropped that subject and said: 'In one house after another, across New York, there are young women like me who started as nothing, wound up handling the automatic paperwork associated with subsidiary rights. In those days we were paper-pushers only, filling the blanks in the final deal, and if we did well the company made five thousand dollars, if poorly, only four thousand dollars. But you heard the figures for my day last Wednesday. A fortune. So now the big companies find that their drab little secretaries who handle subsidiary rights have become some of the most powerful kids in the industry. If you ever get a chance to move into this office, grab it. The future lies here.'

My immediate future was far less dramatic and infinitely less important. At all publishers a constant barrage of unsolicited manuscripts arrives in the mail—'over the transom' is the phrase—and because almost none of these have merit, they fall into what is usually called 'the slush pile,' that forbidding heap of cardboard boxes, each containing a novel. Almost none of the manuscripts ever appears as a finished book. In fact, most of them would never even reach the attention of a senior editor, for those well-paid experts cannot waste their time on such unpromising material. Protracted studies at various houses have proved that only one manuscript in nine hundred that come in over the transom ever becomes a book, but case histories abound of how manuscripts that were rejected by half a dozen firms, or even more, have become best-sellers. So the hunt through the garbage continues.

At Kinetic a Jewish editor had named the accumulation of these pathetic works Mount Dreck, and now I was in charge. Assigned to a reception desk on the fourth floor, I answered phones, took notes for the editors, did typing when called upon, and faced each morning when I came to work that mountain of boxes, each containing someone's dream. I would lift one box after another, glance briefly at its contents, shudder, and, if return postage had been included, place a formal rejection slip in the box and mail it back to the sender. If there was no postage, the box and its contents were tossed into a bin that was emptied each night into the huge trash receptacles waiting in the basement.

Like previous beginners who had excavated on Mount Dreck, I began with a determination to find diamonds in the junk. I vowed I would give every unknown who had mailed his or her novel to Kinetic a fair chance at publication, so it was with an anticipation of discovery that I lifted each box from the pile on the floor at the right-hand side of my desk, but as soon as I saw that the manuscript was hopeless, I placed it in the growing pile at the left-hand side, from where it would either be mailed back or be tossed into the trash. My experience was not a happy one, for most of the manuscripts were so dreadful that a look at one page was sufficient, and on some mornings when I was especially alert I might inspect fifty novels, finding them equally deplorable. At noontime I would feel remorse for having destroyed the hopes of so many, and after lunch I would refuse to read further, since the experience was so frustrating.

I learned several tricks in sampling the junk. If the first page contained more than one misspelled word, I became suspicious, even though I was aware that some fine writers, such as F. Scott Fitzgerald, were miserable spellers. If a manuscript had bizarre punctuation, I rejected it, and I was especially hard on any that was coy or unintentionally juvenile. A typical sentence justifying instant rejection might read:

> His mother-in-law was a fine woman (!) who he loved dearly (Ha-ha!) but she was such a batleax that he tryed to get her out of the house as soon as posibell.

More often the manuscript was technically respectable, but the story was so poorly told that no amount of editing could give it a chance for publication.

However, occasionally I would come upon one that would make me say to myself: It's better than I could have done, and then I was obligated to draft a short typed note summarizing the reasons why I thought someone higher in the editorial hierarchy should look at this one, and when the messenger came on her next round, she would carry that box to the desk of some editor who would cast a more practiced eye on it and even, perhaps, write to the author suggesting a conference. Then I would feel the thrill of being in the process of actually selecting and publishing books.

But when at the close of 1964 I had been in charge of Mount Dreck for several months, Miss Wilmerding at personnel summoned me to a review meeting and opened with a startling statement: 'Miss Marmelstein, we hear only the finest reports about you. Three different departments in which you've worked, including subsidiary rights, where you did the fine job the *Times* wrote about, have said they'd be glad to have you back when an opening occurred. We'll remember that. But there has been one complaint, voiced by three different editors who liked your work otherwise.'

When I leaned forward, honestly eager to learn about my deficiency, Miss Wilmerding said: 'When you read the crud at Mount Dreck, you're sending on to the editors about three times as many manuscripts for them to worry about as you should. Remember what I told you: publishers find one reasonably acceptable manuscript in nine hundred. You're sending forward one in every hundred.'

When I looked astonished at both the reprimand and its cause, Miss Wilmerding said: 'Don't lose your enthusiasm. What you must do is sharpen your critical judgment. Ration yourself to three in nine hundred, and sooner or later you'll spot a winner. And by then the editors will have learned to respect your judgment.'

As I was about to leave, well chastened, Miss Wilmerding stopped me: 'Sit down, please,' and the way she smiled at me proved that in some way I did not understand she liked me: 'We all feel you have a bright future with this house, and Mr. MacBain thinks it's time to make you eligible for our advanced study program. Here's a list of seminars on publishing given each winter in New York. Columbia, N.Y.U. and the New School. If anyone took all those courses, she'd know far more than I or any of our editors do.'

I studied the titles of the courses and saw at least seven I would have profited from, but I had to confess: 'Those fees are pretty steep,' and Miss Wilmerding said: 'But we pay the fees,' and for the moment I could not speak.

That night I almost flew from the subway exit to our apartment in the Bronx, and when I got there I ran right past my mother and threw myself into Uncle Judah's arms: 'Everything you told me has come true. Because I read the books you got me after I broke my arm, and studied the way you said, they decided at Kinetic to try to make me a real editor.'

'You told us you already were.'

'Well, I lied. What I really am is a glorified secretary, once removed.' I had not the courage to confess that I was marooned on Mount Dreck.

'So what's different?'

'They're sending me to night school! To study editing.'

He stopped playing solitaire, shoved the cards aside and asked: 'Is that significant?' and I said: 'Very,' and he asked: 'How are you going to pay for all this?' and I shouted: 'They pay!'

To Uncle Judah those two simple words made a universe of difference: 'In this world, everyone is ready to tell you what you should do, on your money. Advice is cheap. But when they tell you what to do and add "We'll pay," that means something,' and we spent half an hour dissecting the hierarchy at Kinetic, with me explaining who really controlled destinies and what promotions I could logically expect as the years passed. At least six times he interrupted: 'And you're sure they pay for all this?' When I gave my final assurance, he leaped from his chair, took my hands and waltzed me around the room, shouting to my mother, who had been listening: 'She's going to be an editor!'

This fact had a profound effect on him, for he was older now and more inclined toward having sentimental feelings about family.

He said: 'It's like you were my daughter, and I want to warn you about one thing. Sometimes you talk like an illiterate Jewish girl, no family background. The Marmelsteins have always been educated people, and I want you to clean up your pronunciation.'

I had not even a hint of what he was talking about, but then he began imitating the way I pronounced that cluster of words so difficult for people with my Bronx background: *singing, clinging, winging, bringing*. I was aware that I, like other Jewish girls from the Bronx, pronounced the *ng* in these words the way one pronounced it in *linger*—that is, *ling-ger*. There is no way, using the English alphabet, to indicate exactly how such words as *singing* should be pronounced. And the way a girl like me pronounced *singing* made it something like *sing-gingg*, with a *g* sound preceding the second syllable, instead of the correct *sing-ing*.

At any rate, Uncle Judah commanded me to stop pronouncing the words that way: 'When you say that, Shirl, I mean Shirley, it lights beacon fires for anyone who hears: "Ah, here's that nice Jewish girl from the Bronx." With one word you've imprisoned yourself inside a category.'

What he said almost frightened me, because with the brief taste I'd had of promotion within a corporation, I did not want to stigmatize myself in any way: 'How do I correct it?'

'I had the problem when I wanted to become your father's outside man, selling to the important stores. With a name like Marmelstein I was Jewish enough and clearly from the Bronx. I didn't need a calling card like *sing-gingg*.'

'What did you do?'

'I made up a nonsense formula that I said over and over as I rode the subway to work: "The birds were singing and they went winging, bringing music to the clinging vines." You sing that yourself maybe five thousand times, you grow so scared of those words that you become almost afraid to say them. And when you do say them, you say them right.'

He had other phrases that I, as practically the vice president of Kinetic, must drop: 'Just quit saying *all right already*. It's not correct,' and he outlawed numerous other Jewish idioms.

'But I am Jewish,' I protested. 'And proud of it.'

'Me too, but half the buyers I worked with were not. I wanted to give them one less reason for saying no. And while we're on the subject of words, if you're smart you'll start right now to learn as many new ones as you can—big words—unusual ones—popular words of the moment: *paraplegic*, *parameter*, *peripheral*. Talk big, you look big.'

He also thought I ought to dress in a more managerial style, and in this field he was an expert, and kept a collection of perhaps a dozen glossy magazines that had published special issues on clothes for businesswomen. One that caught my eye, and apparently his, too, for he referred to it several times, was a magazine devoted entirely to what its editors called 'the executive look,' and after I had studied its pages I got an idea of what he was trying to say: 'A businesswoman can acquire the proper look without spending an extra cent if she uses her eye and her brain.'

On three successive Saturdays he took me to shops where former customers of his sold women's wear and asked the owners to instruct me about fabrics and design, and about suits that gave maximum value. During these visits he allowed me to buy nothing, but when my instruction period ended he asked my mother to prepare a special Saturday-night dinner so that he could make a little speech: 'Now that we have a high-toned business executive in our family, I want her to be properly dressed as she climbs the corporate ladder.' I started to say: Hey, I'm just a gal in charge of Mount Dreck, but fortunately I kept my mouth shut, and he continued: 'Tonight I'm handing over to our young genius a fund I've been collecting for some time. On Monday after work, she and I will start to buy her what I call "an executive wardrobe," bottom prices, top quality.' And he handed me a check for three hundred dollars.

I can see him now, leading me to one shop after another and telling the owner: 'My niece is on the executive track in a big corporation and I want you to show her two, three suits, highest quality, lowest cost.' At the end of the week I had a wardrobe that Joan Crawford would have envied, with sixty dollars left over: 'Put that aside for a wedding dress.'

Two weeks later that dear man, who had given my life such dramatic turns for the better, was dead. He left an estate of a few suits—top quality, bottom price—a shelf of books, and less than fifty dollars. But when I wore to work the attractive clothes he had bought me, so trimly tailored and of such excellent material, people in general began to take me more seriously.

The work in that winter of 1965 became the kind that in later years of a gratifying career one can look back on as the experience that made the difference. Kinetic, sensing they might have a winner in me, agreed to pay my tuition for two different courses, one at Columbia and one at N.Y.U.

In the first I learned the overall principles of editing, a mix of information on contracts, schedules, publicity, libel, and relations with book clubs, reprint houses and bookstores. Nothing was profound, but everything was instantly applicable to my job.

The second course, entitled *Editing the Manuscript*, was taught by a skilled woman from Simon and Schuster who distributed at the start of her seminar a thirty-two-page Xeroxed copy of a sample chapter from an imaginary novel. It contained a plethora of errors, half of which I could not see on my first reading, but under her tutelage many of the basic principles of editing emerged, with my copy of the chapter becoming covered with corrections.

The editor had several points on which she was adamant: 'Sentences must have grammatical structure. They must preserve parallelism. Once the tense is established, it must be maintained to the bitter end. Pronouns must have antecedents that can be instantly recognized, even by the careless reader.' She taught me that a well-constructed paragraph, with sentences in place and each word within the sentence properly used, was a creation of beauty: 'It's the basic unit of human thought, a format unto which can be poured your most exalted conclusions, and also your most impassioned depictions of human relationships.'

When one older student complained that we were wasting too much time on a certain passage, she snapped: 'That's the real name of this course. How to whip the author's inadequate paragraph into an acceptable one. Parallelism, coherence, integrity of verbs, respect for pronouns, and the elimination of superfluous adjectives and adverbs, that's what I'll be talking about all winter.'

She did not bother with spelling—'We have machines and little books which handle that'—nor was she fanatical about sticking to standard word usage, but certain New York idioms used by her young editors irritated her, and once when she heard me ask a fellow student: 'Can you bring this to her?' she exploded.

'Damn it. You *take* a thing from here to there. You *bring* a thing from there to here, and if you misuse the two in your speech, you sound illiterate. But if you allow it in the manuscript you're editing, it proves you're not ready for the big time.'

Hungry for even bits of knowledge about my chosen profession, I absorbed all that my teachers offered, and one day after work I stopped by Miss Wilmerding's office to report: 'Those classes you allowed me to take, they're sensational!'

'That's how we ensure that Kinetic keeps on top of the field.'

'Thank you for telling me about them,' and Miss Wilmerding said: 'You earned them.' But one weekend when I was reflecting on my progress, I awakened to a disturbing fact: 'What I'm learning is mechanical, the rules of the game, how to handle a manuscript—if one ever comes along. What I need to know is how the manuscript got there in the first place,' and when I queried my friends, two different students—one at Columbia and one at N.Y.U.—said the same thing: 'This wizard Evan Cater's giving an intensive course at the New School. Six hours on Saturday, four on Sunday for four weekends.'

'Who's he?'

'There are about four real editors in New York. Hiram Hayden used to teach a fabulous course, trained half the fine writers in town. Cater's his replacement, some think. I'm going.'

I decided to pay out of my own pocket the fee for this February course, and on four successive weekends I spent hours listening to the brilliant lectures of this quiet sixty-year-old man as he explored the psychological and mental processes involved in constructing a novel, and like the woman editor at N.Y.U. who ignored misspellings, he ignored the mechanical aspects of writing. Writing was a cerebral process that evolved not primarily from the brain but from the soul. The goal of writing was a communication between the souls of the writer and the reader, and mastery of the art consisted of the ability to utilize those symbols that would ignite flames in the reader's soul. Any ambition less lofty was beneath his contempt.

He used for references Dostoyevsky's *The Idiot*, Thomas Mann's *The Magic Mountain*, Flaubert's *Madame Bovary*, and Faulkner's *The Sound and the Fury*, distilling from them the lessons he sought to impart on Saturday and Sunday. And Monday through Friday I remained awake late into the night consuming these masterpieces as if they were spiritual manna.

Cater did other imaginative things to blast us from our lethargy. With assistance from the famous Apollo movie house on Forty-second Street, he arranged for a showing of classic films and recommended that we find the time to see six of them: 'And since they're shown as double bills at the Apollo, this involves only three long evenings or afternoons.' He was especially keen that we see the first one, *The Passion of Joan of Arc*, of which he said: 'Filmed in 1928 by the Danish director Carl Dreyer, it goaded the cinema into entering the world of art. He photographed the great Falconetti as Saint Joan, in close-ups, minute by minute, allowing terror and triumph to cross her face. He allowed the porcine faces of her French and English prosecutors to explode off the screen. No excess motion, no hysterics, just those magnificent faces epitomizing ten centuries of church history and persecution.'

Cater was equally insistent about a film in the third pair, calling it 'perhaps the finest movie ever made, *Les Enfants du Paradis*.' Shot in secret during the Nazi occupation of Paris in World War II, it depicted a broad mix of people involved in a kind of vaudeville theater in Paris during an earlier revolutionary period, the children being the noisy occupants of the cheap seats in those upper galleries called *paradis*. There were three main characters: a ravishingly beautiful and complicated woman played by Arletty, a white-faced mime played by the emerging star Jean-Louis Barrault, and a posturing actor played by Pierre Brasseur; the interlocking relationships, including a tragic nobleman, formed the movie. In speaking of it, Cater made an important point: 'Remember that I said I thought it perhaps the best ever made. It blew my mind. You may not agree. But your job as would-be writers is to see the movies and plays and operas that blow *your* minds. Try to associate with people who are more intelligent than yourself and seek out work that explodes your sensitivities.' He also wanted us to see *The Informer* as an example of the psychological intensity that could be achieved through the proper use of a setting.

Now I learned what Professor Fineschreiber at C.C.N.Y. had told me about getting an education from the streets of New York, for I haunted Forty-second Street with its multitude of good cheap movie houses between Seventh and Eighth and the free Public Library at Fifth, where I could find almost any book that I might want to consult. The street was a university available to anyone who wished to utilize it, and I was voracious. I saw not only the movies Cater had arranged for his students to see but also a rich medley of the best from most of the European filmmakers, and if I now have a fairly good sense of narrative, it's partly because I saw how dozens of the best minds in the film industry had spun their magic. But once when I stayed after class to thank Cater for having brought the street to my attention, he said: 'Movies and books *are* important, yes, but if you want to probe the secrets of great writing, you must pay attention to music and painting, too.'

'Is life long enough for all that?' and he said: 'Why else were you put on earth but to explore the finest fruits of human endeavor?'

What he explored and preached as the supreme goal in the writing of fiction was the creation of characters who were entirely credible and valid, and he believed that this could best be done by showing the alterations that occur in a character as he or she undergoes various experiences. 'Fiction is growth,' he repeated.

When the last session on the last Sunday in February ended, I remained after class to tell him: 'I'm in training at Kinetic Press to become an editor. You've taught me what to look for in a manuscript.'

'In one word, what is that?'

'Intensity.'

'Good. What are you editing now?'

'I handle the slush pile. At Kinetic we call it Mount Dreck because it does build up.'

'It builds up everywhere, Miss Marmelstein. Your job and mine is to keep it from putting down roots right through your floor, getting a foothold.'

'I'll try,' and at Kinetic the editors to whom I now forwarded the transom novels for further consideration noticed that starting in March I had cut down the rate of my recommendations to the more acceptable three per nine hundred.

One morning during the winter of 1967, when I was twenty-three and the recipient of so much praise from those supervising my work that I knew I was being considered for a promotion to a better job, I picked up a standard cardboard box with its customary well-typed manuscript. Before I had finished the third page I cried to Janice, a new employee, who was delivering interoffice mail: 'This one justifies the care we take,' and I handed her the pages I had just read and together we discussed the obvious merit of the writing. She had had two years of college and in that time had acquired a sense of what a book should be.

'This one knows what he's trying to do,' Janice said. 'Who is he?' I inspected the wrapping of the box and said: 'Lukas Yoder, Rostock, Pennsylvania.'

After Janice moved on to the next floor, I continued reading the manuscript, and that evening before going home I telephoned the mailroom: 'Tell Janice to hurry back to Floor Five, reception desk,' and when she appeared, fearing that she had made some mistake, I said: 'They've been giving me hell for sending too many manuscripts from the slush pile. Will you read three or four chapters of this and tell me in the morning what you think?'

Delighted to be at last in touch with books, Janice accepted three chapters and the box in which they had come. In the morning Janice was waiting at my desk with an excited report: 'Compelling. In three chapters he defines Grenzler so that I can hear the Dutchmen talking and see their barns.'

'I said almost the same thing at one this morning.' I thanked her and said: 'You've helped me a lot. Come back in an hour. I want you to take this one by hand to some understanding editor.' When Janice took the elevator to the upper floors, I sat at my typewriter drafting the report that would launch Kinetic's famous 'Grenzler Octet.'

> Clarice: I've not bothered you for a long time, but I've come upon a manuscript that begs for your understanding attention. It's about a small corner of Pennsylvania, the Dutch country, and it depicts a colorful and wonderful pattern of life. Good dialogue, some in dialect but not excessive, and characters with whom you can get involved.
>
> It is written by a man of whom we know nothing, but we do know that he can write literate English and that he seems to have a solid understanding of how a novel is constructed. Please humor me, and give this one a careful eye.
>
> Shirley Marmelstein, Mount Dreck

When Janice returned the manuscript three days later, the curt note said: 'Not for me, I'm afraid.' Irritated by this flat dismissal, I told Janice: 'Wait right there!' and banged out a copy of the note that had accompanied the manuscript to the first editor. I snapped: 'Please take this to Julia right away.'

After my manuscript, for I was already calling it that, was returned a third time, I was preparing to circulate it once more when Miss Wilmerding called: 'Miss Marmelstein? Can you join me immediately?' and I left a fourth version of my forwarding letter unfinished. When I reached personnel, I found awaiting me not only Miss Wilmerding but also one of the senior editors, a Miss Denham, who supervised the small group of junior editors who were learning their profession.

Miss Wilmerding went directly to the point: 'Miss Denham tells me you have very stubbornly circulated one of your slush-pile manuscripts three times, despite the fact that it's been rejected by some of our ablest editors.'

'I'm convinced it's a first-class effort. It contains what fiction needs,' and when the two women asked: 'And what is that?' I gave an impassioned rehash of what I had learned from Evan Cater's February course at the New School. When I finished, somewhat flushed by my enthusiasm, Miss Denham said: 'I agree with you. Miss Rodgers, the last editor you sent the manuscript to, told me what you were doing, so I looked at the manuscript myself, and you're right. It does have promise. Much work to be done, but that's what we're here for.' Turning back to Miss Wilmerding, she said: 'Tell her, Pauline,' and the personnel manager said: 'We've been delighted with your growth, Miss Marmelstein, and the reports we've had from your classes. Mr. MacBain's given authority to move you into a junior editorship, so as soon as we can find someone to take over your duties with unsolicited manuscripts . . .'

I wanted to leap out of my chair and shout 'Whee!' but looking at the two rather staid women so much older than I, I realized that my joy might be wrongly interpreted, so I said as modestly as the situation permitted: 'It's wonderful news—what I've been working toward.' Then I remembered Janice and said: 'May I make a suggestion? The new mail girl on our floor, Janice. She's responsible and has shown a serious interest in what I've been doing.'

'How is that?' Miss Wilmerding asked, and I said: 'In her spare time she hangs around my desk, eager to know what I'm doing—to look at manuscripts.'

After consulting a file, Miss Wilmerding said: 'I think that might be arranged, but you must say nothing to her. As for your move,

Miss Denham has some ideas,' and the senior editor delivered news that burst in the room like fireworks on the Fourth: 'Since you're so enamored of the Pennsylvania Dutch work, you'll move to my floor and start by seeing if you can get the author to whip his work into shape. If you can, you'll present it to the editorial board to gain their approval, and then to the salesmen to see if they can show any interest. When that's done, whether you succeed or not, you'll be fledged as an editor.'

For some moments I sat silent, knowing that I ought to say something but not at all confident that I would strike the proper note. What I wanted to do was the same as before, to leap and shout 'Whee!' but once again I feared this might not be proper, so with a broad grin, which I could not control, I told the two older women: 'This is a day I've dreamed about. I think I'm ready. I'll not let you down.'

'One word of caution,' Miss Denham said. 'Never fall in love with a manuscript or with its author. Hold both at arm's length. They don't love you, and in the long run your success depends on your ability to judge each of them critically—at a distance—at arm's length.'

When I returned to my desk I quietly took from my typewriter the fourth incarnation of my report on the Yoder, carefully reboxed the manuscript and began cleaning out my desk. That done, I telephoned the mailroom and asked Janice to join me; when she appeared, I said: 'Let's have a drink,' and I said this in such a conspiratorial way, not meaning to do so, that she asked: 'Not bad news, I hope?' and I smiled: 'I think not.'

At the bar I said: 'I'll break your neck, Janice, if you say a word—not to anybody. But I have reason to believe that very soon they're going to take you off the mail bit and have you take over my desk. Your first leg up.'

'That would be wonderful!' So again, after swearing her to secrecy,

I addressed her as if I were an old, experienced hand indoctrinating a neophyte: 'It's an exciting job. You're the first person in the house to see the manuscripts,' and with that I proceeded to analyze the numbers: 'Of nine hundred manuscripts that come in over the transom, the big houses find only two or three worth bothering with.' I also told her it was important to recognize the one fine work that does sneak in. And I coached her on which of the Kinetic editors were most sympathetic to beginning writers.

At the conclusion of my lecture, with Janice's eyes aglow with hope, she asked: 'But what's happening to you?' and I, who had been afraid that she might never ask, said modestly: 'They're making me an editor. Beginning level, of course, but I won't stay there long. And I'll bet you won't be on Mount Dreck permanently.'

'I'll drink to that, Shirl.'

'Please, I despise that nickname. Sounds so stupid . . . especially if I'm to be an editor.'

'Apologies,' and we drank toasts, each to the other's boundless future.

The junior editors who had rejected *Grenzler* when I sent it to them from Mount Dreck continued to express doubts when I joined them with the manuscript, and their negative views permeated the office, so that I encountered constant difficulties when trying to gain approval for my maiden effort. But I never lost heart regarding what had become my crusade, nor in the inevitability of its final success.

However, when I applied in due course for a money advance for my writer, I ran into frontal opposition: 'Your suggestion of fifteen hundred dollars is preposterous, wholly outside our parameters. Advances like that are reserved for authors with proven records.'

'What can I tell him? I understand he could use the money.'

'So could we all. You're authorized to go up to five hundred dollars, but only when you feel certain we'll get a finished manuscript.'

'But we already have the manuscript.'

'I said "finished." '

I understood my position, and when the others were gone I defined it: I'm convinced it's already a fine manuscript. But before I can persuade others, it's got to be as professionally crafted as possible. Until it is, I can't assure him he's got a contract, nor can I even tell him we'll give him an advance. What I can do is telephone him and give him a word of personal encouragement.

When I heard my unseen, unknown man speak in a low, unemotional voice and agree quickly with every suggestion I made, I thought: We're going to be a team, and this encouraged me to tell him: 'Mr. Yoder, if we work out a program to accomplish what you've just promised, in return I'll promise you two things. You'll have a firm contract with Kinetic. And when I'm convinced you can do what you say, Kinetic will give you a cash advance and we're off and running.'

When I heard the gasp of joy, I uttered two warnings: 'The advance will not enable you to buy a Porsche. And when you see me, don't gasp like that. I'm very young.' I heard a reassuring chuckle. 'But I'm also very determined that you and I are going to publish a wonderful book.' He said he felt the same and I ended the conversation. 'So you'd better come up here right away.'

He arrived on a Monday morning in March 1967, and when he entered my small office he did gasp, for I must have appeared even younger than I had said. Years later he told me: 'I suspected you would turn out to be an arrogant New York girl who would hold in contempt my rural ways,' but by the time I invited him to lunch at a modestly priced restaurant, we had already formed that rapport which would become celebrated in Kinetic annals. At the end of a long day, when he understood the changes that I considered essential

THE EDITOR

. . . .
140

before the contract could be signed and the advance paid, I walked him out to the elevator and down to the first floor, and even to the entrance of the building. I was loath to have him go because he was my first author and therefore precious to me: 'Mr. Yoder, rush the first four chapters to me and it's in the bag,' and he replied: 'I'd expected someone a bit more austere, with a vocabulary more formal—but with only one tenth of your vigor and enthusiasm.'

Nine days later at ten in the morning the four chapters arrived, a prodigious amount of work having been done on them, and the next morning at ten-thirty I sent Miss Denham a report:

> Lukas Yoder of *Grenzler* has resubmitted the first four chapters elegantly revised. Please issue a standard contract with authorization for an advance of $500 payable immediately.

When the legal papers arrived at my desk for signing, I was surprised to find that I would not be forwarding them; that would be done by Miss Denham's people, who explained: 'The *Collier's* scandal alerted us all. Years back they had an editor who did not forward checks to his writers. He thought he needed the money more than they did. And he even fabricated authors who wrote what he said were wonderful imaginary articles, and by cashing their checks he got rich before anyone detected the fraud.'

'Can I phone Yoder and tell him the contract and check are on the way?'

'Yes. Miss Denham is meticulous about ensuring they're sent out promptly.'

I telephoned Mr. Yoder and said: 'Marvelous news, for you and me. I just verified the contract and initialed the authorization for your check. As of this minute, they're both in the mail.' Our partnership was sealed.

In the winter of 1968, when I applied to Miss Wilmerding for company funds to attend a course at the New School on 'Advanced
Aspects of the Novel,' that careful watchdog said: 'Haven't you
taken a course from this fellow Cater before?' and I replied: 'Yes, and
that's why I'm developing into an editor who knows something—or
am attempting to know.'

'It's a pleasure to help, but I see you've also asked for the course
at N.Y.U. on "Editor and Printer, a Team." '

'Yes, I want to know how an edited manuscript becomes a finished
book.'

'Approved. Kinetic's proud of you, so do not allow the poor sales
of your novel on the Pennsylvania Dutch to distress you. Editors and
authors alike sometimes start slowly.'

'Thank you for the vote of confidence, but I wasn't so slow on that
murder mystery. Besides, Yoder is back at work on a follow-up that
I'm sure will be a smash.'

I'm afraid that that year Kinetic did not get its money's worth
from the tuition fees it paid for me, and it was not the teacher's fault.
It was mine, because after the first night's lecture, when I was riding
home on the subway I suddenly thought: Hey, I'm solving everybody's problems but my own. I helped Miss Kennelly with her
paperback sale. I got Janice her promotion. I certainly helped Lukas
Yoder make contact and I helped straighten out that woman with
the mystery she had started so well and ended so poorly. But what
in hell am I doing for myself?

My anxiety concerned me. Here I was, twenty-four years old, with
no prospects, not even a nibble on the line. The problem was, I didn't
know any young men, and it began to look as if the sixty dollars
Uncle Judah had left for my wedding dress would be locked up
somewhere gathering interest while I failed to attract attention from
anyone in pants. I had been attracted to one of our editors, a promising fellow in his late twenties who specialized in nonfiction. Sigurd
Jeppson was his name, and I had hopes until they were dashed one

night when I saw a bright young woman editor from *Harper's*, who was waiting for him in our lobby, embrace him passionately. She was from Smith, I learned when I made some frantic phone calls—honors in English, a hefty allowance from her parents and a summer place in Vermont. When I heard about that combination I heard doors closing.

And then, on the second night of that winter's class I saw him! He was sitting off to one side in the row in front of me, so that I could catch a good look at his handsome face, dark hair and intense concentration on what was being said. At the break in the middle of the session I practically threw myself at him and learned that he was three years older than I and twenty years more sophisticated regarding the real problems of life and writing. He was Benno Rattner, a second-year dropout from Columbia, which made him somewhat like me, but he was also a veteran of the early stages of the Vietnam war, which made him completely different.

I told myself: Now this is my kind of guy! and at the end of class I hung around hoping there'd be a bull session, and my luck held out because there was one. He spoke in a quiet controlled voice and tried in no way to dominate the discussion, although he must have known that with his Byronic looks and tone of authority he easily could have.

It didn't take me long to spot a major source of his charm: he really listened to what other people said, and if he had to disagree he did so with the gentlest, warmest smile, flashing his perfect white teeth. The person he was contradicting might want to fight back, but would be disarmed by that smile and his look of genuine friendliness— doubly so if the person was a woman—me, for instance.

He always spoke in defense of the most far-out opinions, as if he were taking off from where Cater had stopped; he said that in fiction he sought the ultimate explanations, the weirdest behavior, the most complicated motivations: 'We're not talking Aesop's fables any longer, are we?'

He was especially contemptuous of current war fiction: 'It won't do any longer to have the good old platoon, one black, one guy from Brooklyn, one sensitive gay, a weak-willed lieutenant and a nails-hard sergeant in a do-or-die attack on the Beau Geste fort. The Foreign Legion is dead, isn't it?'

'What do we want in its place?' a young professor from a New Jersey college asked, and my eyes grew wide when I heard Rattner reply: 'We want a book with men who are spiritually torn apart by the six things they have to do in one day: First, listen to a Catholic chaplain drip his treacly words over a coffin being shipped back to, say, Minnesota. Two, stand at respectful attention when a colonel from the Deep South addresses his unit, two-thirds black, as they prepare to move forward against a jungle position. Three, shoot an eleven-year-old gook kid out of a tree for sniping at the Americans. Four, spread gasoline over rice paddies to set them ablaze and starve out the peasants siding with the Commies. Five, stand at the ready around the perimeter of a village that has been napalmed from the air and shoot the gooks—men, women and children—as they try to escape. Six, write a letter in your tent at night to the folks back home. And in your novel, make every one of that cast a real person in the year 1968. The kid in the tree, the colonel, the old woman trying to escape the flames, the young pilot who dropped the napalm, and, above all, you as the narrator.'

'You think you could write all that?' the professor asked, and Rattner snapped: 'It must be done. If one of your students doesn't do it, I may have to.'

When the talking ceased, I moved to be near him and said: 'You make sense. I'm an editor, and people like me are looking night and day for writers like you.'

He stared down at me and said: 'I'm not a "writer like you." I'm not in any category. I attended this seminar to see if I can learn how to be like me, unique, one man alone with a tremendous story to tell, if I can get it together.'

'What I meant was, all publishing houses seek unique you's. Others aren't worth a damn.'

'Where do you edit, if you're telling the truth?'

'Kinetic.'

He smiled at first, then broke into a laugh: 'Now, that's a coincidence, the kind they warn us not to use, isn't it?'

'How so?'

'Two days ago I submitted five chapters and an outline to Kinetic.'

'To whom?'

'To Kinetic. I mailed it in.'

'Oh, no! You're too bright to have done that. Do you know what happens to manuscripts that come in over the transom?' With half a dozen of Cater's students listening, I explained how unsolicited manuscripts were treated at the big houses. 'At Kinetic we call our pile Mount Dreck, and it's appropriate. Only three manuscripts out of nine hundred are seen by real editors.'

'Aren't you a real editor?'

'When I handled the Dreck? No, I was nineteen years old, finished one year at C.C.N.Y.'

'So my majestic effort stands no chance?'

'None. But what's your name? Benno Rattner? You mailed it two days ago? I'll check to see if it's still hiding in the manure pile.'

As the others started to drift off he said: 'If you hadn't told me you were with Kinetic, I was going to invite you for a drink. Can't do it now, it would seem like currying favor, wouldn't it?'

'I'm immune to cozening,' I said, not wanting to lose contact with this exciting man and his warm smile. 'And I'd enjoy hearing more of your ideas.' So as we walked briskly south on Fifth Avenue in the wintry air, I said, 'You have an unusual vocabulary. *Currying*,' and he said, 'How about *cozening*?' When I explained that I had acquired mine by being diligent in my job, he said: 'I was born with mine. An educated Jewish family that did nothing but talk—uncles and aunts, too.' When I made no reply he said: 'I suppose that when we get to the bar you're going to say: "Tell me all about Vietnam." '

'No,' I said, with a slight edge to my voice. 'Because I want us to get started right I'm going to ask, as a professional editor fascinated by these things: How do you propose, in a limited space, to define each of your characters? The boy in the tree, the black soldier who refuses to fire at the villagers.'

With that beginning the two of us talked till two in the morning, bouncing ideas off each other, rejecting any concepts in circulation before the sixties, and tentatively applying the principles Evan Cater had been elucidating. Anyone listening would have concluded that Rattner had the more penetrating grasp of psychological factors and that I had the surer grasp of how to apply them to fiction, and it would be clear that we each respected the other.

When Rattner started to pay the tab, I said: 'We go Dutch,' and he asked: 'You're sure you can afford it? I have an allowance from my folks,' and I said: 'I have one from Kinetic.' At parting he said: 'I really can't ride with you all the way north to the Bronx, but this has been a meaningful evening. A respite from the empty days in Vietnam.'

'They didn't sound empty,' I said, and with that I headed toward the subway, but he tagged along to ensure that I made it safely through the night shadows of Washington Square. At Eighth Street, before I descended underground, I said: 'I'll check Mount Dreck for your manuscript. Did you enclose return postage?'

He bristled: 'Don't patronize me. Of course I knew enough to include return postage.'

'When did you mail it?'

'Delivered it by hand three days ago.'

'You said two.'

'That was last night.'

Usually on the long ride north I read the next day's *Times*, but on this night I sat with hands folded, reflecting on how exciting it was to meet a dynamic young man who knew about books, and suddenly I sat upright: He could be for real! Maybe he's the one I've been waiting for! Musing on this happy thought, I had to suppress laughter as I remembered how I spent one whole winter fantasizing about the convoluted tricks I might use to lure Evan Cater away from his wife and into a passionate romance. And the jolt I experienced when I learned that he had never been married, nor was likely to be.

'But Benno,' I mused, 'he makes such solid sense. A would-be writer, too, with something to say.' As the train approached my station I thought: If he submitted his manuscript by hand, I must see if it's still in the house, and I felt a pang of anxiety when I remembered a recent conversation with Janice, who had replaced me on Mount Dreck. When I asked how the work was going, she had said proudly: 'I often move out a whole day's arrival of crap by nightfall.' I hoped she had not exercised such diligence during the past few days.

In the morning as soon as I checked into my office on the seventh floor I hastened down to five to speak with Janice: 'Last night at the New School I met this young writer, and when he heard that I worked here he said out of the blue: "I submitted a manuscript two days ago." It was unsolicited, and had return postage. And I wondered if you had disposed of it yet.'

'Did you get his name?'

'Yes. Benno Rattner.' When I repeated the name very slowly, Janice cried: 'I'll be damned! Look at this memo!' And she showed me the kind of note I had often typed out:

> Miss Marmelstein: You being up on problems of the young, I think you might want to look at something that just came over the transom. I don't think you'd be wasting your time, but of course it isn't a completed manuscript. Janice Croop.

When I asked: 'Where's the manuscript now?' she said: 'Could be on your desk. Rachel picked it up first thing this morning,' and I sped back to my own floor.

When I found that the manuscript was not there, I asked testily: 'Has Rachel delivered the interoffice mail yet?' No one could remember, but shortly she came in with galleys for the contemporary romance that I was editing plus the memorandum from Mount Dreck with the Rattner manuscript attached.

I grabbed at the box, which was so similar to the hundreds I had once handled, and placed it almost reverently in front of me, shoving aside pages of other manuscripts to provide space. Then, simply staring at it before daring to inspect the pages, I uttered the prayer that editors invoke when approaching any effort by a writer they know and with whom they will work: 'I hope it's good.'

Ceremoniously I put aside the memorandum, lifted the top half of the box and placed it flat on my desk so that I could slip the bottom half containing the manuscript itself inside, thus ensuring that I would not lose the top half if it became necessary to mail it back. As I performed this routine maneuver I noticed two things: a small glassine envelope containing postage stamps had been Scotch-taped inside the top, and because the manuscript was only a partial one, the empty space left had been filled with crumpled tissue paper.

The first paragraphs demonstrated why Janice had rescued the manuscript from Dreck, for they contained a parade of vivid images: an immediate setting of the scene—a rice paddy in Vietnam—and a lone woman in a cone-shaped straw hat working on her knees. Since I was now a practiced editor, I also saw a defect that Janice might have missed: the paragraphs were not properly organized, lacking a lead sentence setting the agenda with the rest of the material reinforcing the concept, action or mood.

He knows how to use images to great effect, but not how to keep things moving forward, I thought; however, I could not lay the chapters aside to pursue my schedule because I kept hoping that the first chapter was merely kaleidoscopic scene setting and that in what followed there would be greater development of the plot. That was not the case, and before lunch break I typed out my report for Miss Denham:

> Rattner, Benno: *The Green Morass*. Timely tale of Vietnam, powerfully different. Wonderful images and word usage, weak on construction and lacking forward movement, at least in this sample. Recommend letter expressing encouragement if better organization can be ensured, and offer personal interview regarding manuscript if he desires.

It was twelve-thirty when I finished my six-paragraph analysis, which led to the conclusion that this incomplete manuscript might well become a book Kinetic would want to publish if the author received firm advice at this critical juncture. Satisfied with my work, I tossed my report in the out-box, repackaged the manuscript with its tissue-paper filler and looked at my watch: 'Goodness! One-thirty! I've almost missed lunch.' As I started for the door my eye fell on the Manhattan telephone directory, and this brought me to a halt. After riffling through its pages, I reopened the box I had just set aside and sought the address, which was a number on Bleecker Street. I hadn't seen any Rattner on Bleecker Street in the directory, but I studied the listing of Rattners again, thinking that Benno might be living with his parents. I found nothing to confirm this, so obviously I could not give him a call. I returned to my desk and typed out a brief reassuring note to Rattner advising him that I had rescued his manuscript from the slush pile and had found it interesting. I would speak to him after our next session with Evan Cater.

During the next several years, 1968 and into 1970, I was caught up in a hurricane of emotion, in both my professional and my personal lives. It was not a negative period, for if the tempests sometimes knocked me down, they more often lifted me to dazzling heights.

As an editor I worked intimately with Lukas Yoder in the completion of his second novel, *The Farm*, helping him to refine it, and this was joyous, rewarding labor, but at the same time I wrestled unproductively with Benno Rattner and his Vietnam manuscript. The Dutchman was a patient, almost plodding worker, who kept his eye on an unwavering target toward which he progressed despite all interruptions; the Vietnam veteran was so mercurial, exploding in contradictory directions, that he seemed to be following not a point of light but an entire aurora borealis that flashed in all sectors of the sky. And whereas a mere word from me would set Yoder on the right track and encourage him to do many pages of difficult rewriting, my slightest word of criticism would emasculate Rattner for a week and he would shun the typewriter. So each month the Dutch farmer trudged purposefully toward the completion of his novel, while the Vietnam veteran thrashed about, lost in the jungles of Southeast Asia and waiting for the flash of inspiration that would rescue him.

This contrast between the two approaches to writing—professional expertise gained from long practice as opposed to amateur improvisation depending upon flashes of insight—was painfully apparent to Rattner, who heard me mention Yoder's name frequently, and always in a sense that seemed to denigrate him, Rattner. Unintentionally I would wound him by saying that Yoder was now reading the galleys of his forthcoming novel, which contrasted with the fact that Rattner was still far from having a manuscript in good enough shape to send to the printer, a fact that irritated both him and me. In fact, every reference I made to Yoder was so inescapably to Rattner's disadvantage that one day he snapped: 'I don't care to hear any more about your goddamned Dutchman and the swill he turns out.' I wanted to reply: 'You'll be lucky if you can turn out anything half as good,' but I controlled my irritation with this handsome, talented man who was struggling so honestly if ineffectively to solve his problems.

This difference between the staid middle-aged Yoder and the tempestuous young Rattner was further heightened by the fact that I had fallen deeply, deliriously in love with Benno. This was an experience completely unlike my mild romantic speculations about Sigurd Jeppson and Professor Cater; this was a total involvement with a young man who was wonderful in every respect. He was handsome, intelligent, dedicated, stimulating to be with, and outstanding in any group. I had never fantasized that anyone like him could be interested in me, and sometimes in class I would look at some of the other young women editors—they were a classy lot—and wonder: Which one of these beauties will take him away from me?

I remember as if it were yesterday our first kiss. We'd had a great lecture by Cater, followed by an informal seminar in a Washington Square bistro, at which Benno was nothing short of brilliant as he held forth on one of his idols, Stendhal, and the magical way in which the tortured Frenchman could reveal people caught up in diverse emotions. Afterward Benno walked me to the Eighth Street subway station, where he had several times before said good night to me with apologies: 'Wizard girl, I simply cannot take that long ride up and back just to bid you farewell. You're worth it, but I'm not equal to it. Mr. Rattner sends his regrets.' This time he was about to throw in some extra persiflage when he suddenly caught me in his arms and kissed me passionately: 'You *are* worth it! You're something wonderfully special,' and I was so breathless I had not the words to tell him how special *he* was to me.

On the dreamlike ride north, my basic insecurity overwhelmed me, for I began to torment myself with doubts: Why should he be interested in me? How could a man as sophisticated as he possibly want to continue talking with me rather than with one of the more educated and worldly women? My self-esteem fell so low that at work the next morning I phoned Miss Wilmerding to ask if I might see her to discuss an important personal problem. She said rather primly: 'That's my job. Come on down,' and I think she must have been surprised when she heard how banal my worries were: 'I'm self-conscious about never having finished college. As you know, I tried to catch up. But am I learning enough, I mean doing well enough in my studies, to tie down a job as a permanent editor?'

She laughed: 'Miss Marmelstein! The night courses you've been taking under our sponsorship, and the reading I know you've been doing on the side—goodness, I'm sure you've given yourself much more than an ordinary master's degree in literature. Believe me, you're miles ahead of some of the most successful editors here in New York.' She smiled warmly and added: 'And even some of the men or women on our own staff. Brains you have, I assure you. Experience in the trenches, that comes later, for all of us.'

As I left, feeling more than reassured, she walked with me to the door: 'What I'm about to say is outside my bailiwick, but you're to be commended on your improved personal appearance. I wish I weighed what you do and looked as good in my clothes.' Giving me a motherly pat, she sent me back to work, and all that day, whenever I passed a door or a wall whose glass provided a reflection, I tried to catch a glimpse of myself, and what I saw I did not dislike.

That Friday night, at the close of our class, Evan Cater asked me to remain behind a moment: 'I understand that you're a full-fledged editor at Kinetic. That's quite wonderful for one so young.'

'I feel very young—inadequate really. You see, I had only one year of college.'

'My dear young lady, the way you conduct yourself in my class, you already have a doctorate in what really counts. You're one of the best.'

I must have blushed, for he said quickly: 'That was a horrible thing for me to say, just before asking you for a favor. But in one of my other classes, the one for beginners that you took, there's a young woman with enormous talent, if I'm any judge, and I wondered if you might take a look at her manuscript, nine tenths finished in my opinion, and help her escape the junk pile.'

'I'd be honored to help, Professor Cater. Your classes are lifesavers. Also, I trust your judgment.'

'I'd hoped you'd say something like that, and on that chance I brought the manuscript with me.' That young woman, as gifted as someone like Sylvia Plath, proved to be my find for the year.

So when I saw that Benno Rattner had waited for me while I talked with Professor Cater, I joined him with more confidence than I had before. I was competent, I was educated, I had a secure job, and I was, if I said so myself, not bad-looking. To have those attributes and to be twenty-four and at the center of the intellectual life of New York—what a magnificent experience, especially since I had proof that a young man was interested in me.

That night when we reached the Eighth Street station we lingered near the entrance for almost half an hour, at the end of which he said casually: 'My apartment's just over there,' and we both knew that on this night I would not accompany him there, but that on one of these Friday nights I would.

Three Fridays later, when my affection for Benno had exploded in directions I had never before experienced or indeed contemplated, firm decisions were reached. He had been brilliant in his adaptation of Cater's ideas and when the subsequent bull session lasted till two, he suggested as we took our customary walk toward the subway: 'It's silly of you to ride all the way to the Bronx at this time of night, isn't it? Why not take it easy at my place? And go up in the morning?'

My reply came so quickly that it could have been rehearsed: 'That's a good suggestion. I'll check your place out tonight and think about it for next week.' When we reached the subway entrance we continued past till we reached Bleecker, where in a newly erected building Rattner occupied an apartment his parents had purchased for him, and as soon as I saw the Persian rug, resplendent in white and blue and gold, the two filled bookcases, the Fisher hi-fi and three big Monet reproductions, I thought: How wonderful that he has tastes like mine.

Locked in Benno's arms, I did not even think of leaving. But when I finally got up to take the long subway ride home, something strange happened. I reached for the doorknob to go, but it was as if some powerful force prevented me from grasping it. Turning to Benno, I said in a whisper: 'Oh, Benno, it's so wonderful here with you. I can't go.' Running forward to take his hands, I met him with such force that he fell backward onto his bed, dragging me down with him, and there was no further thought of going home that night.

The next Friday morning when I left for Kinetic I took with me two large suitcases, which I kept with me when I attended Cater's seminar. Benno, seeing them as I entered, raised his eyebrows questioningly, and I nodded. That decision to live with him was one of the most satisfying I would ever make.

The year 1970 brought a series of niggling little problems, none major in itself, but premonitory when combined with the others. I worked at fever pitch to get three of my books to press on time, then spent extra hours with Yoder helping him make last-minute adjustments to his text, for we both realized that how this book fared was vital. At the same time, Benno was struggling with a complete rewrite of his novel, retitled *Green Hell* at my suggestion, and the labor was proving its own special Gehenna, one known by writers whose efforts are becoming so tangled they often feel they are doubling back on themselves while dragging behind them some fearful incubus that will not break loose. Composition at the initial stage can sometimes be a soaring experience, when all the birds of heaven accompany the writer on his flights, caroling as they rise with him; undirected rewriting is aimless slogging in the trenches, and four times out of five it is unproductive.

But Benno and I did know nights of joy, as on Fridays, when we

would catch some of the holy fire that Evan Cater shared so generously. When he finished his seminar we would invite selected students to our apartment for drinks and a continuation of the debate,
and on two occasions Cater joined us, elaborating essential points till
one or two. On one such night, when Benno and Cater were sitting
side by side, I had a fleeting memory so preposterous that I almost
burst out laughing: it was a memory of that winter when I dreamed
about luring Cater into my bed! Look at him, a waning old man,
brilliant though he is, and then at Benno, a young tiger with the
entire future before him. Well, girls have to grow up, but it's amazing
the crazy paths they sometimes follow in doing it.

On other nights I attended some technical class relating to publishing at N.Y.U., and when the class ended I would almost run through
the streets to get back to the apartment, where Benno would be
waiting with cold drinks and warm affection. At such times going to
bed was sheer joy, and I could imagine myself with no other man,
so perfect was our relationship.

It would be difficult, even now, for me to explain why we did not
marry. I had acquired an imaginary portrait of 'the liberated
woman,' and to tell the truth, I did at times vaguely realize that I
was better adjusted to the modern world than Benno and sensed that
in marrying him I would be adopting a burden that might in time
prove worrisome or even destructive. Put simply, I was stronger than
he, and an instinct that protects women warned: 'Beware of that
one.'

Why he did not insist on marrying me is more difficult to explain,
but I caught glimpses of his fear that since I was an established
performer, he could not hold his own with me until he had success-
fully written and published his novel. We would then compete on
equal terms. But the irony was that the agent who must help him
finish his job was the very person who was a threat to him. This made
each of us wary about solidifying our relationship by marrying.

However, we were by no means incompatible. We enjoyed arguing about books and analyzing what Evan Cater said in his seminars. We had equally exalted notions as to what a really fine book could accomplish. And we looked forward to jumping into bed. We were a happy pair, the only visible difficulty on the horizon being that neither his parents nor mine would accept our living together.

With a chain of carefully calculated disclosures I had prepared mine for what they would consider 'the awful truth,' the fact that I was living not in my own apartment but in his. They had not yet met Benno, and when they finally did they asked bitterly: 'If he's so wonderful and has what you call "a God-given talent," why don't you marry him?' and I replied: 'I'm fighting to establish myself first.'

And when Benno explained to his parents that a girl named Shirley Marmelstein was sharing his apartment, his mother said: 'That's a funny name to go with your fancy apartment. Sounds like a sales-clerk at Bloomingdale's.' He assured them that I was one of the ablest young editors in New York and a genius. 'Good,' his mother said. 'So marry her and have genius children.' He promised that he would think about that, but in the meantime he made no effort to introduce me to his parents.

It seemed that our idyllic love affair could be relied upon to produce one tempestuous moment each month, such as the time when Lukas Yoder's *The Farm* was totally ignored by the important journals of opinion and given faint praise by the daily press. When Benno was callous enough to say: 'I see your world-famous Dutch-man has fallen flat on his ass again,' I screamed: 'At least he had a finished book with which he could fall on his ass.' A bitter row ensued, and for two days neither of us spoke to the other. But in the morning of the third day I said: 'Darling, remember. When you ridicule Yoder's failure, you ridicule me, too. It's my book as much as his, and I'm desolate that it's been ignored.'

I spoke with such feeling that he reached for me and kissed my fingers: 'I was a shit, wasn't I?' And then he flashed that million-dollar smile. As I descended in the elevator on my way to work I thought: At least we care about books, and Benno sees things so clearly he'll whip his problem. But it does drag on.

The next three-year stint, 1971 through '73, saw me nail down my position at Kinetic with a series of solid books that I had personally discovered and nursed to success. Word circulated at Kinetic that 'Marmelstein has the three essentials of a fine editor. She can spot the flashy novel that people will want to read. She can pick current subjects for strong nonfiction books and find the writers to do them. And best of all, she can produce a book that people will still want to read fifteen years down the line.' One afternoon in 1972 Mr. MacBain came out of his way to stop at my desk: 'Miss Marmelstein, some of your books already show signs of having legs. Steady sales are what keep us going. Keep snooping in corners.'

It was this vote of confidence from the head of our company that emboldened me to combat the entire editorial board when they wanted Kinetic to drop Lukas Yoder because of his two failures. I ranted: 'The successful books I've found and published prove I have a moderately keen sense of what a good book is. Trust me, my author is going to break through one of these times because he does a solid job.'

'You mean stolid.'

'Yes,' I agreed, forcing a smile. 'He *is* stolid, like Dreiser. And one of these days he's going to write his *American Tragedy*.'

'Never in a hundred years.'

Without rancor I pressed on and with such knowledge of the trade that by sheer force of will I persuaded my colleagues to give Yoder another chance, and another advance to demonstrate their faith in him. I received grudging approval for only eight hundred dollars and had to be content, but when I accepted I had to make a little speech: 'One of these days we'll agree that this was the best eight hundred dollars we ever invested.'

Since it was generally known throughout Kinetic that I was emotionally involved with Benno Rattner, my fellow editors did not badger me about his nonperformance as a writer, nor did they even ask whether he proposed handing back the small advance our company had given him.

But Sigurd Jeppson, who had served in Vietnam and who closely followed events related to that war, had some thoughts that were potentially helpful to Benno. Sigurd had been outraged by the hideous events at Kent State, where young soldiers of the National Guard had, in his impassioned words, 'murdered four innocent students in cold blood' while they were protesting the war. During one editorial meeting he said: 'I believe the nation's ready for a hard-hitting exposé of the whole Vietnam fiasco. It could head in either of two directions: a devastating assault on the horrors of field combat or a kind of Dos Passos's *42nd Parallel*, in which the author looks at the impact of the shameful war on a selected chain of American towns, ending with four villages in Vietnam itself.'

When other editors said they would welcome either of those two approaches, predicting success for whichever author got to the market first, Jeppson volunteered: 'I'd be interested, Miss Marmelstein, in talking with your writer about either concept that might catch his fancy.'

Defensively, I replied: 'Mr. Rattner does not wait for things to "catch his fancy." He has a most vivid imagination—like most good writers.'

Jeppson was not deflected by my dismissal; he had served in Vietnam and knew the field and its ramifications: 'I thought that if he was bogged down in one direction, a fresh start might break him loose—set him free.'

'He's on a powerful track of his own devising, from what I've seen recently of his progress.'

'Good. But if he ever comes by the office, I'd be pleased to exchange notes with him,' and he said this so generously and without animus that when I returned home I told Benno: 'You might want to hear what he has to say. Different view of your war.' But this simple suggestion so agitated him that for the first time I saw a decidedly dark aspect of his personality, almost frightening, for he growled combatively: 'I refuse to traipse through Kinetic for your friends to commiserate with me over writer's block. Invite him here.'

I did, and only Jeppson's determination to be helpful prevented the evening from being a social disaster. But philosophically it was a terrible disaster, for Jeppson, unlike Benno, represented the new type of American veteran returning from an overseas war: he was bitter about the contempt being shown the Vietnam veterans and angry at the politicians who had allowed, or, as he said, 'encouraged' the debacle to occur. He made every accusation that the Vietnam veterans would voice in the years ahead, and pleaded with Benno to write a novel that would 'expose this shameful episode in our history.'

Benno affected not to understand what Jeppson was talking about: 'You make it sound so complex . . . filled with cabals . . . treason. I didn't see it that way at all. We were sent overseas to do a job against the Commies, kill gooks before the slant eyes killed us. But we were so badly outnumbered and led by such stupid doozies that we got the crap kicked out of us and came home.'

Jeppson, staggered by this analysis of the war he had seen in such a different light, and by the snide smile at the end, asked: 'Is that the kind of book you're writing?'

'I'm not writing any "kind of book." I'm trying to translate experiences into words.'

'But is that how you interpret your experiences? Our good guys killing their bad gooks?'

'I guess that's about right.'

'How can you construct a book on those principles?'

'I don't construct books. I allow them to write themselves.'

'Have you ever finished a book?'

'I've read most of the good ones.'

'I meant, written one? To the end?'

'I wouldn't recognize the end if it bit me. I see life as a continuum. The general who is a horse's ass in Vietnam comes home and continues to be a horse's ass, but this time he's in the Senate.'

'So you don't see any merit in the two designs I suggested?'

'None. They'd have been just dandy in 1919 after World War One or in 1946 after World War Two. But in 1972? Relating to Vietnam? Real writers would laugh you out of the bookstore.'

'Do you think you'll ever get into the bookstore? The way you're heading?'

The question was so brutally on target that Benno rose and said: 'After that insult, there are only two things you can do. Cut your throat or get the hell out,' and he showed him the door.

Unwilling to see a colleague dismissed so uncivilly, I walked with Jeppson to the elevator: 'You wanted to present your petition to the emperor and you did. Thanks for being so even-tempered. My apologies, Sigurd,' and Jeppson said: 'Wake up, Shirley, your man will never finish his novel. Men like me assess his kind in the first three minutes. A born loser.' With a wild, uncontrolled swing of my baseball arm, I smacked Jeppson across the face and stalked back to where Benno was pouring himself a shot and laughing at the empty-headedness of our visitor.

In 1973 I assisted Lukas Yoder in publishing his third novel, *The School*, and it was such a dismal failure that even Benno commiserated with me over its swift demise: 'I read it, darling, and found some very good parts in it. I saw what he was trying to do, but he sure as hell didn't do it.'

'He has a marvelous idea for his next novel—'

'You mean, they're going to let him do another? Your shop must be filled with masochists.'

'They'd extend you the same courtesies, Benno, if only you'd buckle down and finish your manuscript.'

'When an author buckles down, what he gets is Yoder's tripe. Eagles soar, darling, they don't grub around in local color and cute dialects.'

I could not afford to fight with him this time in defense of Yoder, nor with anyone at Kinetic, for I knew I was on delicate ground. Since Yoder, writing exactly the kind of books I had encouraged, had produced three dismal failures, I knew I would encounter difficulty if I tried to persuade the management to bother with him any longer, and sure enough, when the editorial board convened I saw they had decided to force my hand in two instances.

First: 'It's ridiculous to keep your Rattner hanging on the hook. Cut him loose and let him swim away. If you don't want to write the letter, Mr. Jeppson will.' I said nothing, for I realized that in this climate I could not defend both Rattner, with his diminishing chances of ever producing a publishable manuscript, and Yoder, with his inability to sell the fine manuscripts he did produce. Regarding Benno I did not argue back.

'Now, with your man Yoder, the returns are in from the steeple-chase. He hasn't made even the first jump. The race has passed him by. Only sensible thing to do, drop him.'

One editor asked: 'Hasn't his agent cut him loose?'

'Yes, two of them, and one of these days they'll be dreadfully embarrassed.'

'Miss Marmelstein, we see no hope for this kindly man. He knows what sentences and paragraphs are, but he seems not to have a clue as to what a readable book is.'

Despite my pleas, Yoder would have been dropped from the Kinetic list had not help arrived from two quarters I least expected. Just as the vote was to be taken, Jeppson checked in: 'I do believe Miss Marmelstein is right. Yoder knows how to write. His time will come, I'm sure of it.'

That made the vote nine against, two for, and Lukas Yoder was dead, but at this moment Mr. MacBain coughed a signal, and when we turned to hear what he might advise, he said quietly: 'When I finished *The School* I had a strong feeling that this was the kind of book we could very well be selling fifteen years from now. I believe that what Jeppson said is true. This man's time will come,' and with that surprising support I was allowed to keep my Dutchman on our list.

When the meeting broke, I approached Jeppson: 'You were more than gallant. I appreciate it,' and he said: 'Dismal development about Rattner. Do you want me to write the letter?' and I smiled ruefully: 'He'd take it as an additional insult. I'll have to do it.'

'Don't let his smile disarm you.'

That night I waited for a propitious moment when Benno and I had finished our pizza and beer and were listening to a Chopin scherzo. Quietly, as if what I had to say was important but in no way vital, I said: 'Rather unfortunate news, Benno. Kinetic has decided to cut you loose. You keep the advance, of course, but the association is ended.'

'They see no hope that the manuscript . . .' his voice trailed off.

'Will ever be finished? In printable form?'

'I suppose that's what I mean . . . what they meant.'

'It's the end of one highway, Benno, but after the meeting I consulted with Suzy Jenkins in subsidiary rights, she knows everybody. Assures me that she'll have another publisher for you by the end of Friday.'

'Would that be sensible?' he asked so tremulously that I knew he was wounded, and I also knew that this was not the moment to desert this gifted man who most desperately wanted to write: 'Of course that's the right thing to do. A new publisher who can see *Green Hell* in better perspective, a fresh editor who can provide clearer guidance. It could make a difference.'

That night in bed we were extremely close, two young people in New York who were tasting triumph—mine—and defeat—his. The next morning, three days before the day promised, Miss Jenkins, of sub rights, rushed in with news that a friend of hers at Simon and Schuster had volunteered to take on Rattner and his Vietnam novel: 'She said they were real hot at S and S for the big 'Nam book. They're sure it's coming and want to grab it.'

'Can I alert him?'

'Yes, it's a Miss Crippen. She's waiting.'

When I called the apartment and started to tell Benno the exciting news, he cut me short: 'Simon and Schuster would never understand what I'm trying to do. They're only after the sure best-seller.'

'Benno, I've told you a hundred times. If you get your Vietnam book done—the right way—it'll be the best-seller on that war. The nation is hungry for a solid statement. Hollywood, television—' I had said exactly the wrong words.

'I'm not interested in hype. I'm interested in writing a great novel. S and S green stamps can go to hell,' and he slammed the receiver.

His childish rejection of every effort by a well-wisher to help so depressed me that when I left the subway and started for our apartment I had not the courage to face my whining adolescent. Instead I wandered through the Village looking into the faces of men who passed and wondering: Is he one who takes arms against his sea of troubles? Or is he a quitter? A policeman stopped me: 'Excuse me, ma'am, but you don't seem like a night-stalker. Anything wrong?' and when I replied: 'Only everything,' he walked me home and said: 'Go inside. Things'll get better.'

In my distress I could not face Benno and spent the next half hour prowling back and forth in the bright lights outside our apartment-house lobby, with the doorman watching me. I interrogated myself: 'Here I am twenty-nine years old and successful in most of what I do, but I find myself baby-sitting two men who can't get it together, an immature young lover who will not try and an aging codger like Yoder who tries incessantly but can't hack it.' Suddenly I shouted to the night air: 'What in hell is wrong with you, Marmelstein? Always hooking up with losers? Are you a woman from some old-style novel convinced she can detoxify a drunk husband or be the successful muse to a doomed poet? Does this betray a genetic weakness?' Grimly I decided it did not: 'Benno Rattner can write if he conquers his malaise. Lukas Yoder is bound to break the sound barrier. And I can help them do it.' With that resolve I ran the few steps into our building, so eager was I to embrace Benno and help him get the monkey off his back.

In the weeks that followed, after I had apologized to Miss Jenkins at Kinetic and Miss Crippen at S&S, Benno and I attended Cater's Friday seminars with added intensity of interest, and in the discussions that followed, no student was more brilliant than Rattner in the analysis of the novels Cater had discussed. And on the happy occasions when the class was continued in our apartment, with Cater drinking grapefruit juice, Benno was obviously pleased to hear the brilliant critic say: 'I do believe, Mr. Rattner, you could teach my class as well as I do,' and several of the listeners applauded.

This year Cater was tackling in systematic form Erich Auerbach's remarkable book on the craft of writing. *Mimesis* he had called it, the art of mimicry or the representation of reality, and in it he used nearly two dozen of the world's greatest authors to elucidate points: Homer and Petronius, Rabelais and Cervantes, Stendhal and Virginia Woolf. He was what one student called 'a pretty brainy guy,' and although some students could not follow either Auerbach's close reasoning or Cater's explanations, both Benno and I relished the tautness of the work, which tested our mental sharpness. With others of like mind, we continued the Friday-night sessions in the apartment, with Benno providing drinks and snacks. In such gatherings he glowed, and gave evidence of living on the edge of thought, of wrestling with the fundamental problems of narration.

When the class touched upon Auerbach's opinions of Balzac and Stendhal, Benno surprised even me with his wide understanding of these supreme Frenchmen, and when Cater asked: 'How did you get to know them so intimately?' he replied: 'In Vietnam you had to read something, and you quickly ran out of the comic books the military provided.' Later another student who had been in 'Nam explained that whereas the military did provide comics for its numerous illiterates, it also provided quality paperbacks for those who could read: 'I too read both the Frenchmen in 'Nam, but I confess I never got out of them the hidden things that Auerbach proposes, and I'll bet Rattner didn't either, until the German pointed them out.'

Unfortunately Benno heard of this assessment and at the next meeting of the seminar he confronted his fellow veteran: 'I suggest we have a written examination right now, you and I, to determine who understands what,' and the other veteran backed off, since he had seen that Benno was becoming unreasonably pugnacious.

Matters were not helped when another classmate somewhat older than Rattner and an editor for a small house that did avant-garde fiction asked to see Benno and me after the discussion: 'I've been listening to you, Mr. Rattner, and you have a fantastic sensitivity about writing. I understand you have a manuscript on the Vietnam war, and we'd be honored at Gallantry if we could take a look at it.'

'It's not really in shape yet—'

'Most of what we publish isn't when we first see it. Whipping it into shape is our job. And with your comprehension of the problem . . .'

'Not ready,' Benno said in tones louder than necessary, and he would have stalked off if I had not stopped him: 'Dear, I believe it is ready, and we'd be delighted to have Gallantry take a look. To publish with such a house would be a distinction.' Afraid of what Benno might do with his manuscript if I left him alone with it, I suggested to the editor: 'Why not come over now, and we'll box it up?'

In that way *Green Hell* reached a house whose editors were best qualified to impose order on chaos, and the editing leaped ahead with such promise that both Benno and I felt our problems had been solved. But when more practiced editors delved into the copy they quickly saw that considerable work still had to be done before it could be offered to the public as a book.

An editorial meeting was called that led to the transfer of the manuscript from the enthusiastic younger editor to a no-nonsense man adept at handling experimental works, who invited Benno to his office, where he laid out a master plan for the salvation of what he said was 'possible material in impossible form.' His suggestions seemed to Benno so intrusive, and even insulting, to a writer of his stature that he grabbed the manuscript from the editor's desk and shouted: 'We're not making a confection out of this. We're making a novel,' and out of the building he stomped, with the manuscript under his arm.

At the next seminar the young editor apologized: 'I'm sorry our Mr. Peterson was so harsh. He lets his experience affect his manners. I'd be honored to give it another try,' but Benno said: 'It'd be the same thing repeated. Happens in all the houses publishing schlock, doesn't it?' The derogatory word and the smile were so inappropriate for the trailblazing work Gallantry did that its editor looked in amazement at Benno and then broke into laughter: 'You must not read our catalog, Mr. Rattner,' and another escape door clanged shut.

In the months when I was doing perhaps the finest editorial work of my life—assisting Lukas Yoder in fashioning his best novel, *The Shunning*—I was suffering miserably with Benno. Dispirited and no longer trying to convert his notes, many of them brilliant in the judgment of experts who saw them, into a coherent narrative, he was not getting out of bed till one in the afternoon, at which time he drank heavily, but not quite to the point of drunkenness. In the late afternoons, having read the *Times* and done the crossword, he listened to Brahms and Chopin, alternating those masters with a set of records he especially liked, 'the best' of *Aida, Don Carlos* and Wagner's *Ring*, and as the familiar arias soared through the apartment, he sometimes felt a glow of euphoria that masked the dismay he felt at being unable to convert into words the majestic ideas that filled his brain. Once he cried: 'They had the same problem. To put into musical notes the glorious sounds they heard in their heads. How did they do it?' And then came the terrifying question: 'Why can't I do it?'

He was aware of the perilous condition he had fallen into because of his dependence on me, and one morning, while I was getting our breakfast, he surprised me by confessing as he shivered in his bathrobe: 'I had a horrible dream. Lost my temper. Went wild. Shouted accusations. And threatened you, even though I knew, as I was doing it, that I could not survive without you. I know how important you are to me, darling, and I'll do nothing to endanger that.' I was so deeply moved by these words, which described our situation so accurately, that I lingered over breakfast, chatting with him about our life together and assuring him that I needed him just as much as he needed me.

That morning I went to work late, and when I returned in the evening and was preparing our supper, he resumed the conversation in a voice that almost trembled: 'Shirley, we've been on dangerous ground. And I swore an oath this afternoon. I repeat it now: "I will never, on pain of death, do anything to endanger my love for you. If I lose you, all that remains is nothingness . . . the dark night. . . ." '

He took my hands and kissed them, and I was so elated that he had foreseen the dangers that I actually sang as I cut string beans for the cheese dish he was helping me make. Then I inadvertently destroyed the mood by saying: 'I do believe Yoder has leaped over his last hurdle. This time he's got a winner, I'm sure.'

I heard Benno gasp. Unable to stand the oppressive name that haunted our relationship, he screamed: 'Don't ever mention that goddamned Dutchman again,' and he lunged at me, obviously intending to hit me in the face. When his shaky fist came within inches of my cheekbone, I grabbed the long knife I had been using and thrust it toward the middle of his throat. Had he lunged one step closer, he would have impaled himself. We both realized this, and stared at each other in terror. Each dropped the weapon—Benno his fist, I my knife—and that night as shadows darkened in the unilluminated apartment we whispered haltingly to each other about our lives and about the intense love we felt for each other. Toward midnight he asked: 'Would you feel safer, darling, if we married?' Before I could answer he explained: 'I can provide for you because I have more than enough investments. You wouldn't have to work.'

'I want to,' I said without hesitating. 'I love seeing books come to life.'

'So do I. But I can't seem to do anything about it.'

'I'll do the creative work for both of us.'

'You don't insist on marriage?'

'At age thirty-one, no. At age thirty-seven, when I might fear it was all slipping away, maybe. And at forty, when it has slipped away, Yes! Yes!' I shouted these words and kissed him vigorously. Then I said: 'But let's not drown the moment in sentimental tears. Benno, if you had struck me tonight I would have killed you. In my family, honor is all. My father would never have escaped from Nazi Germany had he lacked the courage to sacrifice his life like that'—I snapped my fingers—'in defense of what he perceived as his basic human dignity.'

When he made no reply I said almost coldly: 'Get your life in order. I love you and want to remain with you.'

The unprecedented harshness of my implied threat was a measure of the fear and confusion I felt over the fact that Benno had come close to striking me in the face with a clenched fist. This was so outside my experience that I had no way of assessing its significance, but I remembered how Uncle Judah had once condemned husbands who beat their wives: 'No Jewish man ever strikes a woman. Unthinkable. We hear of Irishmen who do it now and then when drunk.' Well, he was wrong. Benno Rattner came within a hair of slugging Shirley Marmelstein, and the latter was terrified by the thought.

Why didn't I walk out that night, especially since I wasn't married to him? I cannot explain, except that I loved him and that when he smiled that smile at me I simply melted.

And my threat worked, for when he realized that I might one day just leave, he no longer menaced me, but this restraint seemed merely to direct his aggressions into other channels. Within a few days he was involved in another imbroglio and again it was he who initiated it. Kinetic's young editor Jeppson, who felt so strongly about Vietnam, had written a letter to *The New York Times* bewailing the lack of attention and justice the veterans of that war were suffering, and Benno found his statement so objectionable that he sent off a blistering retort, charging Jeppson and most other veterans of Vietnam with being crybabies and self-appointed critics of the military who were perilously close to committing treason:

> Throughout history real men have gone to war. Most of them probably wanted to remain home, but they went. To defend

the things they held worthy. They took their lumps grinning. If they made it back they considered the war the greatest adventure of their lives and knew they were the better for it. The way the Vietnam veterans cry the blues makes me sick. And I'll bet the rest of the nation reacts the same way.

He signed the letter with his full name, adding: A REAL VIETNAM VETERAN, and proud of it.

When the girls at the office showed me what he had done, I was outraged and could hardly wait till I returned home to berate him: 'You thoughtless clod. Jeppson offered to help you. Later he did help me when I was in a tight spot. And you ridicule him. Benno, he's just as much of a man as you are, and don't you forget it.'

Doubling his fist, he sprang at me, but I sidestepped and he banged into the wall. I said quietly: 'We agreed there'd be no more of that,' and he blandly excused himself: 'Forgive me, I've been drinking.'

At his mention of this unfortunate word, which symbolized so much of his problem, a flush of remembrance swept over me, and I heard again my uncle Judah talking with me privately on the night he gave me the money for my wedding dress: 'I want to see you married, Shirl. And you ought to pick out your man quickly, when you're in full control of your senses, because I fear you may become one of those sentimental Jewish women who pass up all the good men who might want to marry them but beat the bushes trying to find some derelict they can save. They pick drunkards, psychos, men who will never hold a job, wife beaters, weirdos. They convince themselves that they alone can save this poor fellow who the others don't understand—and they waste their own lives in this futile attempt.'

I remember that at this point my uncle fell silent, then started to laugh mirthlessly: 'I watched three fine ladies dedicate themselves to the reform route. They were going to save heavy drinkers, and all the while there I was—available, sober and with a good salary, without the necessity of any salvation job. They could never see me. They were determined to save someone, and I was already saved.'

I asked him why he'd never married and he said almost bitterly: 'I was invisible. They saw only the lurching drunkards, who'd provide them with a noble life's work.' He ended this unpleasant summary of a lonely life by taking my hands and saying solemnly: 'Shirl, I've seen signals, little things, that make me fear you may be one of those women who will always search for some weirdo to save. Let me tell you one thing. There are five hundred young men in New York right now—Jews, Catholics, Protestants, Republicans—who would surrender two fingers from their left hand to marry a fine girl like you. For God's sake, Shirl, find yourself one of them, someone you won't have to save.' I listened, but I did not hear.

And then salvation came our way: Evan Cater stopped by our apartment with a tempting invitation: 'I teach a course at N.Y.U. and I have to be in Chicago for two weeks. Class meets three times a week, and no one I know could handle it better than you, Benno. Would you be interested?'

I almost leaped forward to answer 'Yes!' on his behalf and was delighted when he agreed: 'That would be an honor,' and arrangements were made: 'Two weeks, that's one sixth of the term, I'll give you that percentage of my fee. Subject matter? Six lectures on six novels, you've mastered them all, *Passage to India, Tin Drum* and I'd like you to include my notes on *McTeague*. Class meets for only an hour, and the people do enjoy the last twenty minutes of lively question and answer.'

Arrangements completed, Benno dug into the six novels, reading *McTeague* for the first time and enjoying it. As time approached for the first Monday-afternoon session, I realized that he might be a bit nervous and asked: 'Would you like me to come along?' and he snapped: 'I don't need a baby-sitter.' That night when he came home, five of his students had trailed along, and hours after the class on the novel had ended they sat at mute attention as he expounded further on various subjects. I served lemonade made from crystals and as they filed out at a quarter to seven I heard one say: 'That guy's terrific!'

It was so obvious to me that Benno enjoyed the class that I wanted to see him teach. I slipped away from work on Wednesday and slid into the rear of his classroom, from where I heard a brilliant exposition of *Tom Jones* as the archetypal picaresque novel. I could see that he was proud of his ability to identify subtleties that others had missed in the novels. I had never heard him use words more effectively, and he displayed an unusual skill in leading students to conclusions that would not have occurred to them a few minutes before. It was a bravura performance, and when I saw the manly way he comported himself, his charming trick of using his smile to make the students feel at ease, I thought: No wonder I love that gorgeous hunk, and I would have been willing to wager that half the girls in the class were in love with him too.

That night when the students had left the apartment, I said joyfully: 'Benno, I think we have it! You're tremendously good at this teaching bit. The students are going to tell Cater, and I'll bet you can land a steady job. You have so much to share.'

He was not excited by my suggestion, and showed a diminished enthusiasm for his Friday class, which I was not able to attend. That afternoon he invited no students to the apartment, and when I got there I could see that he had been drinking. When I asked him how the lecture on *Madame Bovary* had gone, he shouted: 'I don't want to teach others how to write. I want someone to teach *me*,' and he announced that he was damned well not going back to that stupid class come Monday.

Failing to make him realize the dreadful thing he was doing, especially his violation of the trust Cater had placed in him, I spent the weekend trying to make him change his mind, but all I received was a stream of profanity of a kind that I would never have allowed in any book I edited. I tried in vain to track down Evan Cater to seek his advice and could come up with no solution but to inform Kinetic that I was occupied Monday, Wednesday and Friday from two to four and teach the class myself.

When I told the students that Mr. Rattner was indisposed, they groaned, so that I started behind the eight ball, but I turned the class into an informal seminar on how people only a bit older than they wrote and published books, and I had at my fingertips so much behind-the-scenes chatter about the trade that I held their attention. In the next session I dealt with grammar, at which I had necessarily become something of an expert, and on Friday I enlisted the aid of Suzy Jenkins, in charge of our subsidiary rights, and between us we told of a dozen exciting auctions of Kinetic books, three that we won and three that we lost because of our ineptitude.

The second week was not a disaster, but it was not what Evan Cater had intended, and when he learned of Benno's juvenile behavior a coolness developed between the two men and we saw him no more at our apartment.

In this unhappy way we passed the next years, with me rising steadily in the hierarchy at Kinetic while he moped about our apartment during the afternoon and attended one class or another at night. It was the year 1976, when Yoder's *Shunning* proved to be a commercial failure and I threatened to walk out of Kinetic with all my writers if the house did not extend its contract with my cherished Dutchman; it was also the year when Rattner made a wholehearted effort to finish his novel. He had been freed from his writer's block by some curious reasoning that he developed by himself and certainly with no input from me, for it ran counter to everything I believed about editing: 'Darling, I see it so clearly now. I've been on the wrong track. I listened to you advising me how to write my book. Then I listened to Evan Cater, how he would do it. Then the people at Gallantry kept yakking at me, and I suppose if I'd taken that offer at Simon and Schuster they'd have given me the vital word that would break me loose. The fact is that the writer must, entirely by himself, solve the big problems. He must generate a clear under-standing of where he's heading and how he proposes getting there. Claptrap from editors merely muddies the water.'

I was sure I could cite a dozen historical instances in which knowledgeable editors did help tremendously, but I judged that this was not the time to name them because he continued: 'So as of today I become my own man, with my own guiding star. This novel is going to be finished my way, and to hell with the smartasses at Simon and Schuster.' I did not point out that he had never spoken a word to anyone at S&S, nor they to him.

But in the mornings he was inspired to get out of bed when I did and sit at his typewriter throughout the day. The few ideas he shared with me about alterations in his story line sounded sensible and, I must confess, more original than any suggestions I had made months before. When I saw the pile of neatly typed pages building up I told myself: 'He's really going to do it! He knew himself better than I did.'

But then things slowed down. When I left for work, he would still be in bed, and when I returned at night—at Kinetic we worked late—I would see no increase in the pile of manuscript but there would be *The New York Times* folded back at the crossword puzzle, which he had apparently spent some hours trying to do in ink with-out making corrections. Most ominously, glasses showed that he had been drinking: he used a new glass each time he moved about in the apartment.

The day finally came when he did not leave his bed at all but lay there for hours in a drunken stupor. That did it. I was unusually exhausted one evening when I saw him still under the covers, for I'd been involved at Kinetic in irritating discussions about how we might cut costs to make our corporate overseers happy, and I was in no mood to humor a grown man who was acting like a baby. Slapping him to make him pay attention, I threw a wet towel at him and growled: 'Wash your face and clear your eyes. We have something to discuss.' Propping him up with pillows, I said: 'There'll be no more nonsense about your working on a novel that doesn't exist and never will.' The sharpness of my words startled him and he began in a whimpering way to assure me that . . . 'Cut it out,' I said bluntly. 'We've been down that road too often.'

He astonished me by leaning on his left elbow and gesturing grandiloquently with his right arm as he delivered a wildly poetic exposition of what a novel ought to be, and he sounded more logical and inspired than Evan Cater and Erich Auerbach put together. He was so persuasive that for a moment I was transfixed, but then he smiled at me mischievously and asked like a boy of nine who has been caught misbehaving: 'Isn't that so?'

Waving my hand across his eyes to break the spell he had generated to mollify me, I said: 'I've learned the hard way what a novel really is. It's sixty thousand carefully chosen words, and if you can't put them down on paper in a meaningful way, you have no novel.'

Dropping his pretense, he said so softly that it was almost a whisper: 'Sixty thousand words would be just the right length for my novel. I've been trying to make it too long. Tomorrow I start cutting back.'

'You'll never do it. Stop daydreaming, Benno, and make believe you're a man.' But once I had spat out these words, I was terrified at their finality and became the befuddled woman that Uncle Judah had foreseen: I wanted to save this lost soul.

Gently I combed his black hair with my fingers and helped steady him as he climbed out of bed. 'Benno, my dearest, your dream is finished. Help me attain mine.'

Benno was so demoralized that he did just that; he put aside his manuscript and helped me edit the novels I was working on. Since he had a good critical sense for narrative and an even better eye for grammatical construction, he created the illusion that we were a team, but his work habits were so erratic that I could not rely on him to complete any self-assigned task on schedule. After a while I abandoned the illusion of teamwork and became just one more hardworking New York woman who was striving to bolster emotionally her shattered unemployed man.

At this dismal point, in 1978, I visited for the first time the small Grenzler town of Dresden to work on Yoder's fifth novel, *Hex*, for which I had vibrant hopes, and as soon as I saw the Dresden China, at which I would be staying for the next three working days, I fell in love with its rural charm, its white-and-blue decor and its glass cases filled with Meissen objects. At my first meal I was given a table in a corner formed by two of the cases at right angles so that I sat surrounded by beautiful shepherdesses, country swains and posturing members of the German nobility.

'No wonder Mr. Yoder loves his Grenzler if this is a sample,' I said, and my daily drive east to the farm where we worked on the manuscript showed me the rich lands about which he wrote. But the visit had its bitter overtones, for as I watched the close intimacy enjoyed by the Yoders—the sensible division of labor, the respect each had for the other, the shared leadership and the tremendous amount of work they accomplished—I could not help thinking: How can these two achieve with such apparent ease the kind of meaningful companionship I sought so desperately with Benno? Why can Yoder, relying on Emma's help, complete his manuscripts, while Benno, who receives much more assistance from me, completes nothing?

Back in New York with my besotted but loving partner, I worked twelve and fifteen hours a day, afire with the conviction that *Hex* was going to be the breakthrough for the Yoder I had fought so diligently to protect. When, at last, the accolades and the sales and glory streamed in, I reveled in the joy that reigned at Kinetic.

At the height of the frenzy, when on each Monday morning officials at Kinetic would proudly inform the media: 'We go back to press tomorrow for another fifty thousand of this runaway,' I suffered near exhaustion from excitement and lack of sleep. 'Take three days off,' Miss Wilmerding of personnel advised, and I did. But as I rested in bed the phone continued to ring with glad tidings regarding *Hex*, and at one point, when I thought Benno was out of the room, I shouted after replacing the phone: 'Another hundred thousand! Yoder, we've done it!'

Benno, hearing the hateful name that had haunted him in these weeks of triumph, stormed over, pulled me out of bed and bellowed: 'I warned you not to say that name in this house.' When he raised his fist I screamed: 'Benno! No!' Just in time he refrained from striking me, but he vented his fury by giving me a mighty shove in the chest, which should merely have sent me spinning more or less harmlessly into the opposite wall, but my feet caught in my nightgown and I tripped on the Persian rug. To break my fall, I threw out my right arm and smashed it against the sharp back of the sofa, breaking a bone in two places.

When I left the hospital and returned to my apartment, a contrite Benno tearfully apologized: 'Darling, I never meant to strike you, you know that.' There was nothing I could say, so he continued: 'All I did was push you, not hard. It was your nightgown . . . the back of the sofa. I would never harm you, sweetheart.'

When he asked what I was going to do, I said: 'Go to work tomorrow.'

'But they'll ask about your arm!'

'Simple fracture. I'll tell them the truth. I tripped on my nightgown, fell against a sofa.'

'You won't tell them about me?'

'Why should I?'

'I thought you might.'

'Wouldn't it make me look stupid? To remain with a man who treats me the way you do?' Suddenly, when tears threatened to overcome me, I fought them back, for I had never been the kind to cry. 'Do you know what I kept saying while the cab carried me to the hospital . . . when you couldn't make it downstairs to help me? I said over and over, "But I love him. He's the only man I've ever loved. And we can work this out." '

My words so awed him that he swore in that solemn moment that he would cherish me, and to prove that he was the man I'd met at the New School, he would finish his Vietnam novel and invite me to edit and publish it, if not with Kinetic, then with some other good house. He said: 'I have no more illusions, darling. It's not a great novel, but it's a damned good one . . . potentially . . .' I smiled at his sad optimism, but I did want to help him defeat his self-doubts, so against inner warnings I said: 'I think that maybe this time you can do it,' and the very utterance of those words lifted me into believing that this damaged man could save himself and that with one gigantic final push he could complete the job: 'Benno, we'll make this one hell of a book.' Why was I willing to persist in what must have seemed to my friends at Kinetic this inane folly and self-delusion? Because in a somewhat comparable situation I had rescued Yoder and I truly believed I could repeat the success with Benno.

In the weeks that followed I led two lives, each resonant with satisfaction: in my office I was swamped with continuing good news about *Hex*; in my apartment, where I must not mention that name, by reassuring news regarding Benno's resurrection. He had definitely tried to cut down on his drinking and kept no alcohol in our apartment, but late one afternoon he ambled into a Village bar for what he termed 'a quick fix that Shirley doesn't need to know about.' Two hours later he wove his way home with a tall red-headed man in tow, the kind of winsome talker one meets in bars, but this one was different. 'I'm Arthur Jameson,' he said when Benno failed to introduce him. 'President of Pol Parrot Press and profoundly impressed by your husband's philosophy, Mrs. Rattner.' When my astonishment revealed that I could not imagine why Benno had created such a favorable impression in his near-drunken state, Mr. Jameson volunteered an explanation while Benno went into the bathroom to drench his face in cold water.

'When your husband wandered into the bar I paid no attention, but when I overheard him tell the bartender that he was fed up with Vietnam veterans crying the blues, I had to comment, for those were my sentiments, too. One exchange led to another, and the more I heard your husband speak, the more I liked him. At one point I said: "Sometime ago a chap had a letter in the *Times* castigating the whimpering attitude of the noisier Vietnam veterans," and he said: "Who do you suppose wrote that letter?"

'When I learned that he had written it, and that he also had a novel on the subject three-fourths done, I asked if I could accompany him home and dip into the parts he'd completed.' He stopped, smiled at me and said: 'In bars when the beer flows, lots of men have written novels. But when you walk home with them, the novel vanishes. In this case, is there one?'

I avoided the direct question: 'I know your press well, Mr. Jameson. It does distinguished books—like your translations of German authors and that one about the revolution among American Catholics. You must be gratified when books like that catch on.'

'Thank you, ma'am, for your support. But does your refusal to answer my question about your husband's book mean it doesn't exist?'

'Wait a minute, Mr. Jameson! Did Benno tell you who I am?'

'In public bars, gentlemen never discuss their wives. Who are you?'

'Lukas Yoder's editor at Kinetic Press. And as an editor I assure you that Benno not only has a novel nearly completed, but it's also very good. Gutsy, if I may say so.'

He bowed: 'If Lukas Yoder's editor says so, I must accept the verdict. She knows what a readable book is. Now, may I see part of it?'

'I thought you'd never ask.' As he laughed at my enthusiasm I went to where we kept the precious papers, but at that moment Benno returned from the bathroom, saw what I intended to do and shouted: 'Leave it! It's not ready for—'

I cringed, expecting a scene in which the sensitive author protects his immortal pages, but Mr. Jameson asked gently: 'Isn't it the job of the publisher to say whether it's ready or not?' and to my delight, Benno subsided, saying: 'It's the Vietnam book you've been looking for. That I guarantee.'

So while I threw together some sandwiches, cookies decorated with marzipan, and wine, this distinguished publisher, who had fallen into our laps as it were, rapidly turned the worn pages of Benno's masterpiece and mumbled through his sandwich: 'Hey, this is for real! Pardner, you know what war is.'

And so, as a result of this meeting in a bar, Benno's nearly completed manuscript found yet another home with a major publisher who was determined to see it in print. Mr. Jameson handed it over to an experienced woman editor who reported: 'The first three chapters are exactly what we've been looking for,' and this so excited Jameson that he took Benno and me to dinner, where he explained the plans he had for vigorously publicizing the novel: 'The *Today* show. Maybe *Good Morning America*, and I'm sure Ted Koppel or *MacNeil / Lehrer* will want it for its controversial nature.'

'It is a novel,' I reminded him, but he said: 'Yes, but it deals with one of the hottest subjects of our time. One that's been sadly distorted. Your husband, Mrs. Rattner, is going to be wanted everywhere. We'll see to that.'

As a consequence of this heady conversation, Benno did something so bizarre that I suspected the old instability was returning: he went to court and had his first name legally changed to Bruce on interesting grounds. 'Benno sounded too Jewish, and if my book is a smash like your other fellow's, it might work against me when I appear on national television.'

'Why Bruce?'

'Good clean name. Lots of young men I know are Bruce.'

'You're crazy! Crazy as a loon, but you're also a darling.'

As Bruce Rattner, he shaved more regularly, drank even less, was amazingly considerate of me, and seemed to be working with some effectiveness on his novel. But on a bleak day in mid-December, while I was celebrating with Kinetic officials the astonishing fact that orders for *Hex* had leaped past the half-million mark, a young man working in my office interrupted: 'Miss Marmelstein, an urgent call from Mr. Rattner's editor at Pol Parrot,' and I left the celebration prepared for the latest catastrophe.

'Miss Marmelstein? I found your name on a memorandum from Mr. Jameson. Forgive me for bothering you but I thought you'd better know. Our board decided this morning that our contract with Rattner was not going to work. He's done none of the revising he agreed to do. He's not even tried to correct the big errors. He's ignored every bit of help I offered, just tinkers with stray items here and there. It seems to me that Mr. Rattner just doesn't give a damn, and I said as much to Mr. Jameson, who lost his cool: "Let him keep his damned advance. But cut him loose." '

'You didn't! Not in the holiday season!'

'Had to. I asked Mr. Rattner to meet me this afternoon and when he arrived I told him: "Sorry. Your association with Pol Parrot is terminated. Keep the advance." '

'Not like that! What did he do?'

'He whimpered. Pleaded to see Mr. Jameson. I told him Mr.

Jameson was in Denver, but he would not accept that and started saying things like: "I know he's in the office. He wants this book. He wants the truth about Vietnam." He started bellowing, made quite a racket. I had to call my assistant to show him to the door.

'When my assistant saw that Rattner was making trouble, he astonished me by the harsh things he said: "You insist on knowing what Mr. Jameson said about you? That in a saloon you're an in-spired philosopher, but at your typewriter you're a horse's ass. Here's your manuscript, take it, hit the road, and don't come back. You had your chance, but you screwed up." '

When I heard this report I knew that I had to hurry down to Greenwich Village and find Rattner so that I could give him what-ever support he needed, but meetings at Kinetic kept me pinned there, and as a wintry dusk settled over the city I thought numbly: Poor guy. He's out there somewhere, lugging a manuscript no one wants, and my heart ached.

Subsequently several people told me that they had seen Bruce that snowy afternoon, plodding aimlessly about the Village, and he appar-ently went into a drugstore to use the pay phone. Dusk had already fallen when he called Kinetic, asked for me and started blubbering as soon as I answered. Never before having heard him cry with such abandon, I realized that this was serious, but I could not console him: 'They said it was no good, that I was no good. Everything's falling apart, it's dark outside and I need you. More than ever, darling, I need you.' Before I could give him encouragement, he hung up, and as I stuffed manuscripts away so that I could rush to help him, I saw the darkening sky: What a hell of a day to inform a man he's finished. A week before Christmas.

Running into the street, I flagged a cab: 'As fast as you can to Bleecker Street.'

During the dash south, I did not once consider leaving Rattner; I thought only of what I might do to stabilize him, support him in his loss of dignity. He was a fine man, one with a remarkable brain that was superior even to Evan Cater's, and I loved him.

As I ran toward the entrance to our apartment house I saw the doorman out in the street trying to pick up sheets of paper, which I recognized as parts of 'Green Hell.' 'What happened?' I shouted, afraid that Benno might have been hit by a car.

'Mr. Rattner. He came home staggering like, but not drunk. I told him: "Your papers are scattering," but he walked right past me. Heard not a word I said.'

'Where is he?'

'Upstairs.'

Fumbling with my purse, I extracted a handful of bills and gave them to the doorman. 'Gather all the pages. They're valuable,' and with that I ran to the elevator, summoned it, and was irritated almost to the point of screaming by its slowness in arriving.

'We're fixing Number Two,' the doorman explained as he came in with a messy batch of manuscript. 'Getting ready for Christmas, remember?'

When the lazy lift finally carried me to my floor, I rushed to our door, inserted my key on the first try, and ran into the apartment, where I found Bruce face up on the Persian rug, covered with blood. Grasping the sharp kitchen knife with which I had once come close to killing him, he had tried twice to stab his heart but botched it. In what must have been terrible pain, he had then thrust the knife deep into his Adam's apple.

In the months following the funeral, when I was forced to find an apartment closer to our office, for without warning Bruce's parents sold his apartment and evicted me, I underwent a transformation. Realizing that with the phenomenal success of *Hex*, now with more than eight hundred thousand copies in print, my life had reached a watershed, necessitating numerous decisions. I was now, at thirty-six, one of New York's top editors, able to shift to any company I might choose, provided that I brought Lukas Yoder with me. I was invited to panels discussing publishing, where young writers in the audience sought me out, and sometimes, when Rattner's face replaced theirs, I would feel dizzy and ask myself: What is happening to me?

My transformation was taking one turn that astonished me, but whenever I thought critically of my two men, Rattner and Yoder, I discovered that although the latter had become what columnists called 'one of the hottest properties in the business,' with probably more triumphs ahead, I could express no intellectual interest in the kinds of predictable books he wrote. His plans for *The Creamery*, sixth in line of his Grenzler novels, were, to put it bluntly, dreary. The same formula, the same fetching characters, the same enchanting material about the Pennsylvania Dutch, the same sprinkling of risible dialect. I thought: I could almost write the book myself. But I could see no social contribution it would make.

What really interested me were the ideas illuminated by Evan Cater and Benno Rattner, who saw the novel as an explosive thing, filled with surprises and glorious revelatory scenes, crammed with unique interpretations of normal behavior and prosaic explanations of what seemed bizarre. I could visualize unlimited horizons for the kinds of books Benno had dreamed of writing, works sparkling with vivid ideas, stormy with challenges. What I now sought in a novel was not another prose poem about Grenzler real estate but an explanation of how a sensible person like me could have wasted so many years with a self-destructive whiner like Benno Rattner, helping neither him nor myself. When I reflected on this surprising switch in my priorities, I reflected: 'Keep at it, Lukas, you adorable fellow, so reliable, so removed from sharp knives. You do small trouble in the world and perhaps a smidgen of good. But, Rattner, you were right. In every argument we had about books, you were right. You saw things the rest of us never dreamed of, and it killed you. You could dream it, but you could never write down those sixty thousand organized words.'

One night I cried aloud: 'I'd like to find just one young man with your vision, Rattner. I'd give my life's blood to help him get started properly, feet on the ground, head among the stars.'

At the conclusion of these incandescent thoughts I performed an act as bizarre as Rattner's. With the help of a lawyer and an understanding judge I had my last name shortened legally to Marmelle. When the judge, a jovial Irishman, asked: 'Now, why would a lovely lass like you want to do such a thing?' I explained: 'I'm proud of my family and heritage, but my parents and uncle are gone now, and so is much of my past. I want to make a fresh start.'

'With a French name? Will a French name help?'

'It sounds better. And while we're at it, let's make the first name Yvonne. You cannot imagine, Judge O'Connor, how many Shirleys there are in New York, all Jewish and all called Shirl. I despise that name.'

'So would I, Shirl,' Judge O'Connor said: 'Greetings, Miss Yvonne Marmelle.'

'I'm going to make it Ms.,' I said and the judge said: 'If you had to have my permission for that, I wouldn't give it.' The judge and I smiled, and that afternoon I circulated this announcement to those who might be interested:

> To assist me in my business relationships, I have this day had my name legally changed from Miss Shirley Marmelstein to Ms. Yvonne Marmelle. Wish me luck in my vita nuova.

III

THE CRITIC

N COMPILING these somewhat
scattered notes, written as I approach my fortieth birthday, I
have had only one ambition: to
explain how a gangly red-headed
Mennonite farm boy whose
Pennsylvania Dutch parents had not finished high
school became a member of Phi Beta Kappa, a critic of
American literature, the head of a writing school and
a visiting professor at Oxford. It was not an easy route.

After a dozen years of teaching the advanced course
on writing at Mecklenberg College I find that nine of
my graduates have become professional authors, and a

tenth, Jenny Sorkin, about whom I have the most ambivalent feelings, seems assured of publication by Kinetic Press next year.

A graduate who landed a Literary Guild Selection with her first novel wrote this description of my class for a journal that presumed to teach amateurs how to become professionals:

> It was a class for serious students only, never more than fourteen a semester, and since each session lasted ninety minutes you could be sure he would call on you, so we went prepared. We girls thought he was a very odd type; he had never married and we could guess why. He was quite tall, but very thin, with red hair that would not stay combed and eyes that preferred not to look at you unless he was about to ask a question that might reveal how stupid you were. His clothes? Well, yes and no, sloppy but clean, but always of a style about ten years back. A strong baritone voice that went up in scale when you least expected it to, and where the average professor might display a sense of humor he offered a taste of bile. We girls sometimes cried in his class when laughter was directed at our mistakes, and several boys told me they wanted to sock him, but one, a football player, said: 'We held back because a real blow might of broken him in half.'

A young man who now taught in another college said: 'Streibert had one virtue that eclipsed his faults. The moment you entered his class he let you know that no matter how he behaved, he was on your side. Come hell or high water, he fought for you, was determined that you become a writer, and would do anything to assure your success. He got me my job. When you enrolled with him he offered you a contract: "Bide with me and I'll show you how it can be done." '

Another graduate who has published two rather good novels said:

KARL STREIBERT
· ·

187

'You could see it in his face. He willed that you produce something meaningful. And I got the curious feeling that he saw us as his last chance. He'd wanted to be a novelist, you know. Failed miserably. Published one and it was murdered. Never went back. After that I think he realized that his life would be justified if he helped his students succeed.'

I feel quiet pride when these former students report: 'I would never have made it if I hadn't taken that class with Professor Streibert.' I know it sounds as if I were touting my own teaching, but I'm not. In interviews they never say what a charismatic person I was (I'm not), nor how brilliant my analyses of literature were. No, they always say: 'That mural he had painted on our classroom wall made all the difference.' Because when a young would-be writer finished memorizing that damned mural, and passed the drill on it, he or she had a visceral understanding of what great books were. One student said, 'I'd read a dozen novels before coming to grips with Professor Streibert's mural, but I hadn't caught any of the hidden meanings.'

Students who entered my class later than Christmas 1983 invariably commented on the mural, the typical evaluation being one delivered by a graduate named Timothy Tull, who would achieve considerable fame at Mecklenberg and in the publishing world. He said: 'My writing life began when I sat in Streibert's class, studying that awesome mural, analyzing it privately until I caught a sense of what literature in the grand sense involved. It invited me into the actualities of life and showed me how a great writer dares to use the facts.' Another student said: 'Streibert's mural, a preposterous thing, which the college authorities wanted to paint over, taught me more than any normal class I've ever had. There was the world of human behavior, stark, cruel, infamous and dramatic.'

One sharp interviewer who'd done some writing was not satisfied with these generalizations and asked: 'How specifically did the mural help you become a writer?' and a young man explained: 'He con-

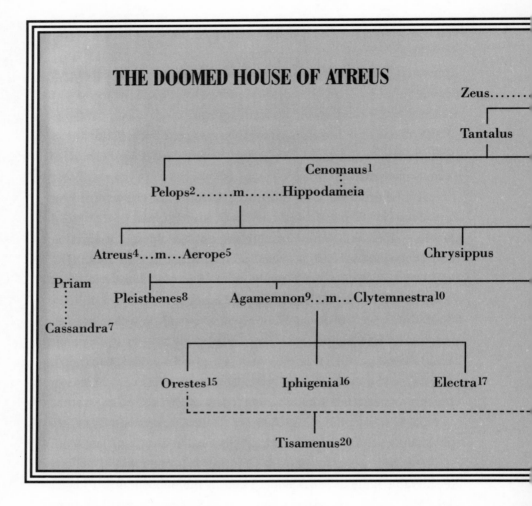

THE DOOMED HOUSE OF ATREUS

Zeus........

Tantalus

Cenomaus[1]

Pelops[2].......m.......Hippodameia

Atreus[4]...m...Aerope[5]

Chrysippus

Priam

Pleisthenes[8]

Agamemnon[9]...m...Clytemnestra[10]

Cassandra[7]

Orestes[15]

Iphigenia[16]

Electra[17]

Tisamenus[20]

0. A goddess whose parents were either Cronus and Rhea or Oceanus and Tethys.
1. Had an incestuous desire for his daughter and killed any young man seeking to marry her.
2. His father cooked him alive and served him to the gods.
3. Her twelve children, sons by Apollo, daughters by Artemis, were slain before her eyes.
4. His fratricidal strife with Thyestes dooms his house.
5. She conducts a liaison with Thyestes and exacerbates the quarrel between the brothers.
6. Atreus, in revenging his wife's faithlessness, serves Thyestes his own sons for dinner.
7. She is slain by Clytemnestra at the killing of Agamemnon.
8. He is sent to kill his father, Atreus, but is slain by him.
9. He is slain by Aegisthus and Clytemnestra.
10. She and her lover, Aegisthus, murder her husband, Agamemnon. She is slain by her son, Orestes.
11. Helen of Troy and sister Clytemnestra marry brothers; Helen also bigamously weds Paris.

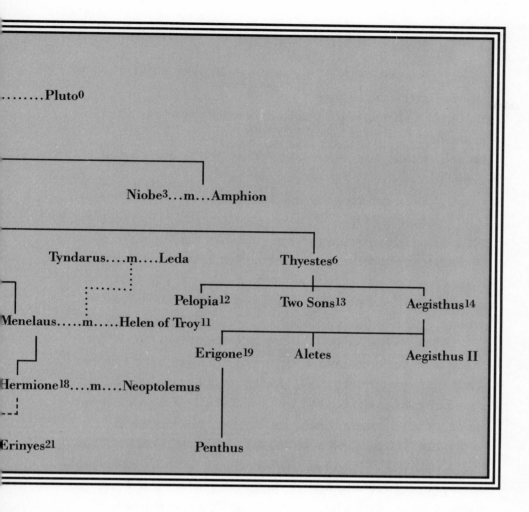

........Pluto[0]

Niobe[3]...m...Amphion

Tyndarus....m....Leda   Thyestes[6]

Pelopia[12]   Two Sons[13]   Aegisthus[14]

Menelaus.....m.....Helen of Troy[11]

Erigone[19]   Aletes   Aegisthus II

Hermione[18]....m....Neoptolemus

Erinyes[21]   Penthus

12. She commits incest with her father, Thyestes. She is thus both sister and mother to Aegisthus.
13. These two children are cooked and served to their father, Thyestes.
14. Becoming the lover of Clytemnestra, he murders her husband.
15. To avenge the murder of his father, Agamemnon, he kills both his mother, Clytemnestra, and her lover, Aegisthus.
16. Her father, in order to gain a favorable wind for his ships, sacrifices her at Aulis.
17. She helps kill her mother, Clytemnestra, goes mad, tries to kill her sister, Iphigenia.
18. Soon after her husband is killed by Orestes, she marries the murderer.
19. After seeing her brother Aletes slain by Orestes, she has a son by Orestes.
20. He was the son of Orestes and Hermione, widow of a man Orestes had slain.
21. They are Furies, avenging deities, who torment criminals. They haunt Orestes for his matricide. They can forgive a husband killing his wife, but not fratricide, patricide or matricide.

ducted a drill. Pointed at you cold turkey and shouted: "You're number seventeen and tomorrow you're going to kill your mother, the Queen. What do you say to yourself when you lie awake at three in the morning?" And you had to stand, usually a man playing a woman, or vice versa, and you had to become her, and speak as she might have spoken.' The interviewer had interrupted: 'A way to teach, I grant, but what did you learn?'

The young man said: 'That unless you have a strong sense of blood coursing through your veins when you write, significance won't be in the words you write. I learned that writing is an act that draws upon every part of my body. Streibert told us: "If you can't throw everything into the pot when it begins to bubble, you'll never be a writer." '

A woman writer told the newsman, 'Mecklenberg itself didn't want to obliterate his mural, but some girls from good Lutheran families objected to it on moral grounds, although great literature is full of heinous goings-on. Streibert said: "If it goes, I go," and so it was allowed to remain—thank heaven, for it showed me the way.'

My mural was entitled THE DOOMED HOUSE OF ATREUS. It covered a wide spread of wall and consisted of an intricate genealogical chart showing the members of the Greek family upon which the focus of early Greek literature rested. It showed the father of the gods, Zeus, marrying the earth goddess, Pluto, who gave birth to Tantalus, who sired the man Pelops, of whom Milton sang. The sons of Pelops, Atreus and Thyestes, were bitterly estranged, and their actions and feelings fueled the brooding tragedies that preoccupied Homer, Aeschylus, Sophocles and Euripides, and laid the groundwork for all subsequent literature.

Those fateful names loomed before the students—Agamemnon, Menelaus, Clytemnestra, Cassandra, Helen of Troy, Orestes, Iphigenia, Electra—and after each name appeared a bright red numeral, from 0 through 21, so that students could trace the awful tragedies. There it was, all spelled out, the hideous doings of the Atreides.

On a Tuesday in February 1989, when students who had come into my course at the end of the autumn semester had their first meeting with me, I launched my introductory lecture on the essential nature of literature. After stressing that it dealt primarily with human emotions and passions, I said: 'If you cannot imagine the emotions that drive your characters and identify with them, you'll never be a writer. Regardless of how horrible their behavior, how noble, how self-sacrificing, how banal, you must goad yourself into putting yourself not only in that character's situation but also in his or her heart.'

At this point in my introduction to the chart I have a ritual. I designate without previous warning some would-be writer to imagine himself or herself one of the Atreides caught in some terrible dilemma and to recite either his hero's speech of the moment or his unspoken reflections, as if writing dialogue for a story in which the ancient Greek appeared. On this day I chose as my first actor a young woman about whom I had had mixed reactions. A transfer from the distinguished writing school at Iowa, she had brought with her a finished novel of quality, but she had the nasty habit of wearing form-fitting T-shirts that carried across her chest provocative messages that might have been considered amusing in Arkansas or Oklahoma but seemed out of place in Mecklenberg. Her name was Jenny Sorkin, and on this day emblazoned across her chest was the challenge: WHAT YOU SEE IS WHAT YOU GET, and I judged that now was the time to test her merit.

'Miss Sorkin,' I said abruptly, 'you are Number Fourteen, and you have been asked to lunch by your sister, Number Twelve, whom you have just discovered to be your mother as well. I want you to speak in two distinct voices, one that your mother-sister hears, the other that only you hear. You have entered the room where she waits to serve you and you speak.' Before Miss Sorkin, a normally brash young woman, could collect her thoughts I shouted, standing close to her: 'Go!'

I realized that she had been given a most difficult assignment. She was required to be a man and he was to find himself in a shattering situation, and I feared she might not be able to handle it. But I was in for a shock because Miss Sorkin had been studying the mural and had learned that her man Aegisthus[14] was one of the real swine of Greek tradition, the seducer of Queen Clytemnestra[10] and the murderer of her husband, Agamemnon.[9] So with a skill that astonished the class, who had not previously taken favorable notice of her, she became a man, adopting an oily and sycophantic approach to his sister and establishing himself as a weasel. Then the voice dropped to an Iago-like snarl as he contemplated killing his sister for the wrong she had done his mother through her incestuous relationship with Thyestes,[6] their father.

She spoke four times in each voice, and at the conclusion all of us in the room were satisfied that Aegisthus[14] was capable later on of killing not only his sister Pelopia[12] but also his king, Agamemnon.[9] I led the class in applause, concluding: 'I have a suspicion, Miss Sorkin, that despite your T-shirts you might become a writer,' and again the class clapped.

I then made the subsequent points I wished to hammer home, and they came as a shock to students who heard them for the first time: 'Throughout the remainder of your lives you are to be the guardians of literature, the ones who combat censorship in all its forms. If some Baptist women's group in Oklahoma protests that a book or a play quote deals with ugly themes unquote, I want you to remind them that some of the greatest literature the world has ever known, the stories that got us started, were founded on the behavior of this gang of scoundrels,' and I jabbed at the mural: 'Murder. Matricide. Incest. Betrayal. Patricide.' Halting dramatically, I said: 'So do not listen if anyone presumes to tell you what decent literature is and what is forbidden. And if you need strength to fight them, remember this mural and the names of the men who relied upon it for their inspiration: Homer, Aeschylus, Sophocles, Euripides. They showed us the way.'

Then, with a sudden leap, I pointed at a young man: 'Mr. Cates, you are Number Seven and you're having tea with Number Ten, but because you are a seer you foresee that she is going to murder you. Two women's voices, please. Their conversation.' Cates was not the impassioned actor Miss Sorkin had been, but he had subtle insight as to what the two women were up to, and when he finished their dialogue I said: 'Less dramatic than Aegisthus, but you know what you're doing, Mr. Cates. Your heart is attached to your mind, and vice versa. The story you submitted for entrance made me think you might make it. Your performance today doesn't change that estimate.'

I then proceeded to my third message from the mural: 'Shakespeare wrote three majestic studies of murder—*Hamlet, Macbeth, Othello*—but I strongly doubt that he himself ever committed a murder. He didn't have to. Watching the prisons and the hangings, he deduced what murder signified and allowed his fevered brain to do the killing. Homer imagined and Aeschylus daydreamed. They didn't have to commit these horrors.' And then I slammed the wall and said, 'You don't need it here. You need it up here, in your head, and down here, in your heart, and way down here in your guts and your loins.' Several students remarked later that when I said this I seemed 'to grow in majesty . . . no longer a skinny red-headed Dutchman but one of the Atreus family . . . maybe Orestes awestruck by the terrible duties he was about to discharge.' Another said: 'From that moment on, when he challenged us to become the Atreides, everything changed. We saw literature in a nobler and more passionate light.'

In the silence following this episode on the opening day of the winter semester, I said quietly: 'Mr. Thompson, you are Number Sixteen on a summer's afternoon in Aulis and you see your father coming toward you. You are not sure what he is about to do, but as a sensible girl you have an idea. You do not speak to him, but to yourself. What is it you say in these last moments of your life?'

Thompson was not equal to the assignment. He had studied the mural so assiduously and with such a powerful sense of identification that he became Iphigenia, beautiful daughter to the king and queen, and the thought that he was about to die so overwhelmed him that tears flooded his eyes and he stood mute. When it became obvious that he would not be able to speak, some students grew restless, others embarrassed, but I in my gentlest voice resolved the impasse: 'Excellent, Mr. Thompson. You may have come closest of all to the truth, because it's probable that our beautiful princess in Aulis that day, realizing that her father was about to kill her, did what you have just done. She wept.'

I was born in 1952 on a farm near Reading to a German family that had followed not the strict Amish discipline of using nothing automotive for their farms, or buttons on their clothing, but the gentler Mennonite tradition that was stoutly conservative but also prudent in business activity. We did use buttons and motor cars, but both had to be a funereal black, as were our clothes and German-style hats. There was one exception: women wore beautiful lace bonnets, and the care with which they made them differentiated the meticulous housewife from the slovenly. There were not many of the latter.

Strongly imbued with Mennonite tradition as a boy, I had overlaid it with a straight-A academic record in the public schools of Reading, where I acquired such a solid grounding in mathematics, science, history and French that my teachers knew from my first year in high school that I was going to be eligible for scholarships to the best universities. And as graduation approached and placement officers from schools like Pitt, Penn and Syracuse saw that I had not only been class president and one of the mainstays of the school band because of my skill with the trumpet, but also was more than competent in three languages—German, English, French—and passable in both science and literature, they were not content merely to offer me scholarships; they contacted alumni in the area to persuade me to accept.

When the scholarship offers from three major universities rested on our kitchen table beside one from a small college, it was my mother who made the decision: 'Penn and Pitt are out, because Philadelphia and Pittsburgh are godless places, and I doubt if Syracuse is much better. Poppa and I think you ought to turn down these three offers and go to Mecklenberg. It's God-fearing and Lutheran, and there you couldn't fall into evil ways.'

When I said: 'But they haven't offered me a scholarship,' my mother snapped: 'They will, when I talk with them,' and on a memorable day in April, Momma and I drove the ten miles to Mecklenberg. As we passed through the beautiful German countryside with its reassuring names from the old country—Fenstermacher, Dresden, Wannsee—we were put so at ease that when we reached the stone battlements of Mecklenberg College we were satisfied that if the school wanted me, we wanted it. 'Poppa would like this,' Momma said, and when we faced the admissions officer, Momma had no hesitation in spreading before that gentleman her three sets of papers: 'This shows what he did in class, this out of class, and these three letters are the scholarships he's been offered. But we're a Christian family, Professor, Mennonites by persuasion but very respectful of you Lutherans . . .'

'I'm a Quaker, Mrs. Streibert.'

'What's that?'

'Protestant. Sort of like a Presbyterian or a Baptist.'

'Nothing wrong with them. What do you think, Professor?'

The officer hesitated, shuffled the documents, then smiled: 'I'd say that if these papers are authentic, and I'm satisfied they are—I'd say we'd be lucky to get your son.' Mother was not one to be satisfied with vague promises, not even from a smiling Quaker in an official position: 'What we mean, coming so far, could Karl get a scholarship here, same size as these others?'

'I'm empowered to make only limited decisions, Mrs. Streibert. I can't even say on my own that he can get a scholarship at all. But from the look of these papers I can assure you that it's ninety-five percent certain. We seek boys like your son.'

'How much?'

I could see that the officer had become accustomed to hardheaded Pennsylvania Dutch parents discussing matters of importance. He smiled: 'Mrs. Streibert, the college does not allow a relatively junior staff member like me to spend its money. A committee does that.'

Mother shoved the four scholarship papers forward. 'You see those figures?' Without answering, the officer pushed them right back: 'Mrs. Streibert, those figures mean nothing.'

Mother was astonished and showed it, but the officer quickly explained: 'You've noticed that the figure from Penn is much higher than the one from that small college. Doesn't mean a thing, because the total costs at big Penn are much higher than those in the small one. If we took time to compare, I could prove to you that this smaller scholarship is a better financial deal for Karl than the larger ones from Penn, Pitt and Syracuse.'

'Are you saying that your costs to us are lower, too?'

'Much.'

'Then your scholarship—'

'If the committee approves one.'

'I understand. It's only maybe. But yours will be lower?'

'Much. Because living in this part of Pennsylvania is a lot less expensive than living in a big city. Let's put it this way, Mrs. Streibert. You know that the stores in Lancaster, Reading and Allentown have to keep their prices competitive. Or sensible Dutch farmers like you and your husband will seek out only the bargains, and the high-priced stores will go out of business. Penn, Pitt and Syracuse are competitive, but so are we. That I can promise you.'

'But you can't promise a scholarship, and if you do give one, you can't promise how much?'

'No, but you can believe every word I've told you today.' As he was about to lead us from his office he stopped and said: 'Karl, you haven't told me what you think.'

'I want to come here,' and later I was told that when we two were gone, he wrote on my application: 'This one we want!'

I believe the college never regretted its decision to offer me a full scholarship and a waiver of fee for the extra courses I elected to take after I saw my grades at the end of my first semester. I found my classes easy, science as well as literature, and since I was already proficient in two foreign languages, I had free time to pursue courses that I might otherwise have missed. The record of my first three years was so uniform it was monotonous: in each of my six semesters I received four A's and one B Plus. I was proving to be so precisely attuned to college work that I could predict exactly what my professors expected and how much effort it would take to do the assignments and pass the examinations. Some of my teachers considered me close to a genius, but others, more perceptive, tabbed me as an ideal work machine, totally capable but totally uninspired. I allowed neither group to see me as I really was.

My attention to study limited the time I could devote to nonacademic activities. I played trumpet in the orchestra but refused to try out for the school band. I lent my strong baritone to the glee club, but found acceptable excuses for not participating in trips away from campus; I avoided going even to the church concerts the Mecklenberg students traditionally gave in Allentown and Lancaster churches, for I did not feel easy leaving my studies for even those short distances.

My social life was uneventful: no fights, no brawls, no surreptitious drinking, no card playing, and very little traffic with the opposite sex.

As a reasonably presentable if awkward young redhead with a well-cared-for body and a reticent but pleasant smile, I suppose I was acceptable to the stolid German girls from our part of Pennsylvania who crowded the campus, and since Mecklenberg had a well-deserved reputation as an encourager of sensible courtships that ended in marriage, some of these young women could understandably have speculated in their nighttime talk sessions: 'Who is Karl going to settle on?' as if I were a meadowlark seeking a mate.

During my first two years I remained totally unattached, but as a junior, that best of all college years, I started seeing a fine German girl from Souderton named Wilma Trumbauer, and once when her parents visited the campus they and Wilma invited me to lunch at a famous country restaurant, the 7&7, halfway between Allentown and Reading. I went, but I was too naive to realize that this was intended as an encouragement to my supposed courtship. When days passed without my following up in any way, or even letting Wilma know that I had been pleased by the lunch, she dropped me and was soon thereafter engaged to a more responsive Mennonite senior from north of Allentown. When I heard of the betrothal I said: 'That's nice,' having no awareness at that time of the part I had played in her decisions.

In my senior year, when I was determined to nail down an A or an A Plus in each of my ten classes, I ignored girls altogether. I was a young man who moved alone, but I was not lonely, for in a course called The Modern English Novel I was experiencing one of those intellectual awakenings that students sometimes encounter in their early twenties. Unlike others who discover the joys of learning in their teens and become self-directed dynamos in their first days in college, I had been one who fumbled along, doing well in whatever class I took but headed for no visible goal. This class changed that.

The professor was a man in his early sixties, a graduate of Penn who had taken his master's at Chicago and his doctorate at North

Carolina. Never a top-flight scholar, Paul Hasselmayer had landed a routine appointment at Mecklenberg and had proved to be such a reliable workhorse that he was kept on, finally becoming chairman of the English department because abler young men did not want to waste their time on the paperwork that job entailed—they spent their time writing books that would carry them off to better jobs at Indiana, Colorado, or, if they were really fortunate, to some prestigious Eastern school.

Hasselmayer, from a German family in the Lancaster area, could justly have been called a drone. For decades he had been teaching an old anthology called *From Beowulf to Thomas Hardy*, and he long believed that literature in English culminated with *The Return of the Native*. But during his mid-fifties he suddenly came upon a series of novels outside his customary purview. In rapid succession he read D. H. Lawrence's *Women in Love*, Arnold Bennett's *Old Wives' Tale*, and Aldous Huxley's *Point Counter Point*, followed by three powerful American novels, Frank Norris's *McTeague*, Theodore Dreiser's *An American Tragedy* and Ellen Glasgow's *Barren Ground*.

That autumn he gave a series of enthusiastic lectures about his recent discoveries, and the effect on me was overpowering. The sounds of those harsh voices that were new to me broke me out of my lethargy. I was awakened by the skill of the English writers Lawrence and Bennett. 'They present a life so different from what we see in this area,' I said, and I talked with friends that summer about how much I had lost by not having familiarized myself with these writers earlier.

My major attention, however, was directed to the American writers. I had never before heard of *McTeague*, which I found a compelling story of a miserable dentist in California, and although I had seen references to *An American Tragedy*, I had concluded that it was nothing more than a sensational bit of gutter probing; that it was a grand novel in the great tradition of storytelling surprised me. I also spent some time reading the short works of Edith Wharton, which pleased me enormously and led me to read three short novels of Henry James, as a result of which I concluded that *The Aspern Papers* was just about the finest novella in the language.

When I voiced this opinion in class, Professor Hasselmayer suggested that I write my term paper on the James story, but I attempted a more elaborate topic: *Henry James* and *Thomas Mann: Two Novellas Based in One City.* I wrote some four dozen pages analyzing 'The Aspern Papers' and Mann's 'Death in Venice,' which I had read in a German course, and describing how the authors had used Venice to powerful effect. It was a city I had never seen but understood intimately, thanks to the evocation of its colors and meanings by the two masterpieces.

What especially caught Professor Hasselmayer's attention was a long passage in which I analyzed the narcotic effect of Venice on James, Mann and their protagonists. My writing assumed a lot, made shrewd guesses and at times confused the living authors with their imaginary heroes, but it also revealed an analytical mind. I had transformed a reading assignment into the portrait not only of two short books but also of a student's mind pole-vaulting from one level of thought and expression to an entirely new plateau.

Summoning me, Hasselmayer said: 'A remarkable paper, Mr. Streibert. You've seen into the heart of the literary process. I would now like you to try your hand at a more difficult subject matter. Compare *The Old Wives' Tale* and *Point Counter Point* in the same way. I mean, how do these two vastly dissimilar men utilize dissimilar locales to achieve their common purposes?'

It was work on this paper, which consumed several months, that determined my future, for whereas I could see Bennett's famous Five Towns of industrial England as counterparts of Pennsylvania's three

Dutch towns—Lancaster, Reading and Allentown—which made comparisons and understandings fairly simple, I was astounded by the polished glitter of London and its inhabitants as described by Huxley. 'What kind of people are these?' I cried in frustration as I labored to untangle their lives and motives. And when, for instruction, I delved briefly into Huxley's other novels, I withdrew almost in horror from an amoral world I could not comprehend.

At the height of my bewilderment, with my paper not only unfinished but also unfinishable, a more sophisticated student told me: 'You can't understand Huxley unless you first understand André Gide.' I had never heard of the Frenchman, nor did the college library have any of his books, but the library in Reading did have two, *The Counterfeiters* and a brief work called *The Pastoral Symphony*. The first repelled me with its portrait of a decadent society, but the second enraptured me with its pristine, controlled storytelling. As weeks passed and I burrowed into the difficult parts of my paper, I awakened to the fact that *The Counterfeiters* had profound meaning for me, while the shorter work seemed no better than a French version of *Ethan Frome*.

When Professor Hasselmayer read this second paper he told me: 'Mr. Streibert, you have an amazing ability for penetrating the heart of a piece of writing and also the mind of the man who wrote it. What are your plans after graduation?'

'I have no idea.'

'I do. What foreign languages do you have?'

'German from birth, French well beyond the conversational level.'

'My goodness, you're well on your way.'

'To what?'

'To a doctorate. In literature.'

'What would that mean?'

'Three years at Chicago, or Columbia, or maybe, best of all, Harvard.'

'Would that be very expensive?'

'Not for you. The top schools are hungry for young men of proven ability.'

So before my final semester ended, I again had offers of three fellowships to the universities that Professor Hasselmayer had named and to whose English faculties he had commended me. For a sensible reason, I chose Columbia: 'Huxley taught me that I knew nothing of London. Gide, that I was ignorant of Paris. Time I learned what a major city is.'

That summer the gentle hand of André Gide lay heavily upon me, for I read, in the original French, *L'Immoraliste* and then moved on to Marcel Proust's *Du Côté de Chez Swann* and a sampling of the later books of *À la Recherche du Temps Perdu*. I spent the entire summer without inviting even one young woman to dinner, and when I left for New York in September I had not yet kissed a girl. But my knowledge of books, especially novels, was profound.

My years at Columbia were explosive, for I had excellent professors who led me into the broad boulevards of learning so much grander in design than the limited country roads I had known at Mecklenberg. I learned early that my proficiency in languages, especially German, made it easy for me to master the early tongues from which English was derived, and my progress in pre-Chaucerian language was so rapid that two different professors suggested that I specialize in that branch of study. This I might have done had not the beacon light of my career arrived in New York from Oxford University to teach for six months, beginning with the fall semester of 1977. He was Professor F.X.M. Devlan, born in Dublin, educated at Cambridge and Berlin, holder of a chair at Oxford and an opinionated luminary on the English literary scene.

He was a rotund little man with a puckish smile, a monk's tonsure, which left a fringe of hair above his eyes, and an ingratiating Irish brogue. A leprechaun, really. He started his six months at Columbia with a running high dive smack into the center of controversy. At a public gathering he gave a reprise of the teeth-rattling lecture he had given three years earlier at an Oxford symposium and which would now be quoted extensively in American newspapers. I had not met him prior to the lecture, but I took a front seat in the hall and gasped at his iconoclasm:

> 'If you desire to learn the secrets of meaningful narration, there are only four English novelists worth reading. Chronologically, by date of birth, they are Jane Austen, George Eliot, Henry James and Joseph Conrad. You will notice that two of them are women while the other two are not English.'

When the shocked whispering ceased, he proceeded to extol his four selections, coming close to revealing that he thought *Middlemarch* the best novel in the language, but he was also laudatory of Henry James and his severely controlled type of narration. He said of Conrad: 'With a golden net this Pole who never wrote a word of publishable English till he was in his forties captured the soul of Africa and the islands of the Pacific.'

Having justified his choices, he made a daring move; he identified four customary favorites whom he considered unacceptable in that they wrote only of life's facile surface:

> 'My attitudes toward literature will become clear when I share with you the names of four novelists whom some of you may hold in high regard but whom careful analysts dismiss, not as trash, to be sure—that's far too harsh a condemnation—but as mere purveyors of fiction not worthy of serious attention. They are, again in order of birth, William Thackeray, Charles Dickens, Thomas Hardy and John Galsworthy. These men are facile and inviting and entertaining,

but they provide the reader with no substance and should be reserved for a summer's light reading.'

There was audible opposition to this annihilation of old deities, and two professors who specialized in precisely those four highly regarded Englishmen felt constrained to leave the hall, but as they departed, Devlan said puckishly: 'Goodness, what a lack of commitment. At Oxford, seven stalked out,' and he proceeded to demolish both the works and the undeserved reputations of the four he rejected. During this part of his lecture the rumblings continued, for he revealed himself to be an arrogant, inflammatory exhibitionist. But those were the very characteristics that had prompted Columbia to invite him to cross the ocean.

A highlight of the evening came when a Columbia professor observed: 'You've given us four you anoint and four you condemn. In American fiction, who would the comparable eight be?' and Devlan replied: 'A most penetrating question. But that's why I've been invited over, isn't it? To learn something.' He said he would be spending his six months in New York wrestling with just that question: 'And I invite each of you to start racking your brains to determine whom you will place in my eight American slots, the good and the bad. I'll be doing the same, won't I?'

And that was the beginning of one of the liveliest six months I would know, for F.X.M. Devlan quickly spotted me as a young American with the kind of sharp mind prized by the English universities. Inviting four of us graduate students, two young women and another young man, to work with him, he initiated a seminar in which we analyzed past American fiction. Toward the end of his stay in New York the group had identified eight American writers who might be eligible for the saved, eight who surely deserved to be condemned, and at his last session this fiery Irishman told us:

'You've looked into the heart of writing. You're far ahead of where I was at your age. But now comes the difficult part. Each of you must coldly and critically nominate the four whose example you will follow in your teaching and writing and the four you find unprofitable and stale. And you must adhere to those judgments, because I assure you, you are in better condition to make those choices now than later. The freshness of youth is a marvelous lens through which to see the world. You see better now than I do at my age, and remember that after the age of thirty you will discover few new truths. Do it now or surrender hope.'

When we pressed him: 'Now tell us your eight American candidates,' he fended us off with a roguish smile: 'Do you think I'm crazy? If I told you what I thought I'd probably not make the plane home in one piece.'

'But you will tell us later, won't you?'

'Tell you? No. But I will write a companion essay to my first one. Remember the sovereign rule. Never say it. Write it. Of the ten million great stories that have been told to admiring friends, especially by Irishmen in their pubs, literature consists of the five thousand that were written down. If it's not written, it doesn't exist.' And he left New York with his secret American list intact.

In Devlan's memorable four-student seminar in 1978, one of our two women was an attractive graduate from Grinnell College in Iowa, whose name was Kathleen Wright. One day when I was in the library stacks looking for a book, I overheard Kathleen and a friend discussing my role in class, and I had the strange, almost unworldly experience of hearing myself described almost as a character in a book. What I heard staggered me.

'Sandy, what's the matter with Streibert?' Kathleen asked. 'I find him so easy to be with and unbelievably bright, but he seems a hollow man. He reacts to nothing except books.'

Sandra chuckled: 'When you grow up in San Francisco you hear that problem from all your girlfriends. "What's the matter with Paul? He won't look at me, and he's such a neat guy." '

'And your answer?'

'Each group of girls develops five or six criteria for judging men, and when you apply them intelligently you get your answers.'

'Like what?'

'Now remember, Kathleen, we're talking in a San Francisco ambience. The girls there have a dozen code questions.'

'Translate.'

'Answer these questions. Have you ever seen him with another girl?'

'No. Just men and not many of them. He's a real loner.'

'Does he quote his mother more than his father?'

'Yes, he does. His mother seemed to fight for his education, at least so he says, but I've never seen her on campus.'

'Do you catch him eyeing you when you appear not to be looking?'

'No.'

'Does he go out at night? Alone? Looking around?'

'I really can't say, but when I have seen him he seemed to be on his way to the library—or the bookstores on Broadway.'

'You'd say he was not a night prowler? Looking for the easy pickup, male or female?'

'Male?'

'Kate, where do you think my questions have been leading? I think you've got your eye on a mama's boy who won't marry till he's in his late forties, if then. Take my advice. Get off that racecourse. You're not on the inside track.'

Kathleen contemplated her friend's questions, then asked: 'Are you saying he's queer?' Her question so shocked me that I wanted to cry out. But Sandra did it for me. 'For God's sake, Kathleen,' she snapped, 'give up that backwoods stuff. Half the really swell guys in San Francisco don't like girls at age twenty, nor at forty. They're great people and every girl I know has two or three of them as friends—some of the most reliable friends in the world. Accept Karl as the brilliant man he is, and do what you can to help him get started, but don't wait around expecting him to marry you.'

'Who said marriage?'

'You did. By implication.'

'Is it so obvious that I'm fond of him?'

'Sticks out all over.'

'And you think nothing constructive can come of it?'

'Constructive? Yes. If he becomes head of a department at some good college, he might remember you and offer you a job. Sweetheart? Bedfellow? Husband? Not a chance. Not one.'

'What should I do?'

'Look elsewhere.'

In the months remaining, Kathleen was courteous and even friendly with me, but it was obvious that she now saw me only as an impersonal scholar who was going to do superlative work for my doctorate. We would probably be friends, perhaps even write to each other as our careers progressed, but that I might one day want to marry her was totally improbable, and both she and I knew it.

In 1980, two years after Professor Devlan had returned to Oxford, he sent a letter that astonished me:

> I have located a traveling bursary for which you may be eligible—Germany, France, Italy, England, to finish your education—and I may be able to break away toward the

close of your journey to join you for a jaunt into Greece. Please arrange your schedule so that you can accept. You need the civilizing impact of these great areas.

It seemed amazing that the famous British professor would even remember me, let alone go to the trouble of arranging a fellowship of such interest, and at the first opportunity I hurried home to consult with my parents about the practicality of accepting such an invitation. Mother displayed her common sense by pointing out: 'Karl, the offer hasn't even been made. You're jumping the gun, already.'

My life at college and the university with learned people had made me uneasy when my parents used Dutch idioms, like repeated *already*s, so I replied rather abruptly: 'Speculation. But if Professor Devlan says he'll do something, he'll do it.'

'Have you told him you'd go already?' Mother asked, and when I replied: 'No, I wanted to ask you and Poppa what you thought,' she asked: 'How well do you know this man?'

'He was my professor for half a year, surely you remember that. Best I ever had.'

But she was worried: 'I saw this terrible show on television. What a Turkish prison was like. It was horrifying.'

'Mama, those two college boys, smart alecks I'm sure, they were smuggling drugs.'

Poppa asked a more pertinent question: 'I thought your big job this year was to find a teaching spot for next year. Stick to the main task, son. Stay home and land a place to work.'

Slightly irritated by having to reveal a secret that I had intended sharing at the end of my visit, I said: 'My old professor at Mecklenberg, you remember him. Hasselmayer. He's retiring and has nominated me to take his place. So energetically that the administration has agreed. I have a job for next year, a wonderful one.'

Poppa responded: 'Then I think you should go to Europe. A fine chance to see Germany, where you come from.'

'I'd be even more interested in France and Italy.'

'They're all right,' Poppa said grudgingly.

'And especially England, since I'll be teaching English.'

'Makes sense, but they're very stuck-up.'

My mother returned to her major concern: 'Why would this man Devlan—how old is he?'

'Mid-forties, maybe.'

'Why would he want to travel with a youngster like you?'

'He's a scholar. He loves literature, and he recognizes that I do, too.' I paused, then added: 'And maybe he wants to refresh his judgments on American writing. He spoke once of doing a major essay.'

With the approval of my parents—Father's lukewarm, Mother's reluctant—I sent a cable accepting Devlan's offer, closed down my rooms at Columbia and boarded a Pan Am plane for England, where I spent a frantic week taking bus tours to the Wordsworth Lake Country, Shakespeare's Stratford, Hardy's Wessex and especially the back alleys of London made famous by Charles Dickens, whose work I did not like but I might one day have to teach.

I then crossed the Channel to Germany, where I spent a leisurely week absorbing the cultural treasures of my family's homeland, then on to France, where I tried to catch a glimpse of Stendhal, Flaubert and Balzac without much success, because whereas England makes it almost impossible for the visitor to miss her great writers, France makes it impossible to see hers, but I respected the general savor of France with her grand buildings and imposing museums.

By bus I traveled from Paris to Rome, poring over maps each mile of the trip and fixing in my mind the geographical features about which I would be lecturing for the rest of my life: 'Paris, Lyon, Grenoble, Les Alps, Genève, Firenze, Siena, Roma.' I tried to use only the local versions of the familiar names, and I was so assiduous in my study that France and Italy, at least the parts I traversed, were permanently locked into my imagination. Just this one bus trip more than justified my summer in Europe.

Although I had been reared in a family, a regional tradition and a local college that had turned their backs on Catholicism, and with reason, because their Protestant forebears had been badly treated during the Reformation, I now found Roma, as I insisted upon calling it, a city incredibly noble and historically rich quite aside from its close connection with the Vatican. Strolling with guidebook in hand, I could visit in the course of any one day pre-Christian ruins, heroic memorials of the great emperors, others dating from the time of Christ, churches from the time when civilization was darkened, monuments of the Renaissance, memorials of the papal states, and the grandiloquent vestiges of Mussolini's rampage. Does any other city offer so much? I asked myself as I wandered from one historic site to the next, and as my eight days drew to a close I suddenly realized that I had spent them all in Roma, not venturing into the countryside on a single exploratory bus trip. 'Roma is enough,' I said, and I went back to the Vatican to spend an entire day in its museums, awed by the wealth of sculpture and the variety of the paintings, about which I knew little except that the Sistine Chapel, with its magnificent ceiling and walls, was worth more than a couple of hours. I assumed at first that Michelangelo had done it all, but when even my untrained eye began to detect differences in style, I asked a European tourist what the facts were, and the man said in German: 'I do not speak English,' whereupon I repeated my question in idiomatic German, and he, a Swiss, turned out to be an art historian who felt that Perugino's exquisite painting on the wall was just as good as Michelangelo's on the ceiling.

Hours passed, and when gongs sounded to mark the end of day and the closing of the treasure house, the Swiss gentleman suggested:

'The afternoon's been so pleasant, could I invite you to share supper with me?' and I was pleased to escape eating alone again. I expected the man to lead the way to one of the many restaurants in the area, but instead we walked to a minor hotel, where the chef was prepared to serve in the man's room an excellent meal of saltimbocca, thin slices of veal and prosciutto, with a first course of the best spaghetti I'd ever had.

'I see you like plenty of cheese,' my host said, and when I replied that I liked anything with a salty flavor, the man cried exultantly: 'Then you'd love anchovies!' and he called for a small salad with plenty of anchovies. They were so unbelievably good that I wanted to be sure I understood how to spell the name: 'Anschovis, anchois, acciuga, anchovy,' the man said. 'Different in every language.'

The meal ended on a high note, followed by a protracted period of suspended animation in which I began to feel ill at ease. Then my host asked gently, in German phrases that were unusually friendly: 'So, why not spend the night here? I have an extra toothbrush and you can use my razor,' and as he issued this invitation—a sensible one since I had already revealed that I was doing nothing that night, or any of the other nights, and my own hotel was a distance away— the man smiled at me engagingly. He slid his hands caressingly over my shoulders and in this unsubtle manner revealed his intentions. I was twenty-six and had never before that night experienced such a sensation, neither with a woman nor with a man, and I was terrified. When it became apparent that I was supposed to undress and climb into the narrow bed with him, I panicked, forcefully pushed him away and bolted for the door. Before I could break away, the man held on to my left wrist and pleaded in a quiet voice: 'Please! It's no big thing. And it's very pleasant, really,' but with a powerful wrenching movement of my arm I broke free and galloped down the stairs, not trusting the tardy elevator to rescue me from a distasteful situation.

When I reached my own hotel, with the familiar woman at the desk, it seemed like a refuge in a storm, a sensation that was enhanced when the woman handed me a telegram that had arrived while I was at the Vatican. It was from F.X.M. Devlan and said: ARRIVING AT YOUR HOTEL TOMORROW AND OFF TO GREECE. A warm feeling displaced the fear I had just experienced, for I thought of Devlan not only as a mentor but also as a trusted friend.

We drove slowly up the spine of Italy that first day, reaching Florence at dusk. Devlan, in his good Italian, asked a policeman where we might find lodging. The officer laughed: 'Maybe two hundred places. The one on the corner, a nice mix of good beds and better food.' When we checked in, the concierge seemed delighted to have guests who would be taking two rooms, and Devlan, who was conducting negotiations, made no demurral: 'Two rooms it is,' and after an excellent evening meal, we talked briefly and headed for sleep, each to his own room.

We spent the next day visiting the sights of Florence, and I was amazed how familiar Devlan was with the Uffizi Gallery, which he said was one of the top three museums in the world: 'If you're to be a first-class teacher of English in your little college, Karl, it's obligatory that you know the fine arts, and music, and architecture and the whole great swirl of man's aesthetic efforts on earth. And you really cannot know Dante unless you know Firenze and imagine him wandering among other hill towns. You ought to come back to Italy every summer for three or four years, for postgraduate wisdom.'

Devlan was rhapsodic about the Medici Chapel on whose walls a Renaissance painter had displayed a glorious procession of Medici princes, factotums and horsemen: 'Here comes great Italy marching into your arms, bringing you its significance and its story.' I appreciated the chapel more than I had the Uffizi.

That night as we dined in a restaurant on the banks of the Arno, Devlan reminisced about Cambridge, his early days at Kings College in 1951, a time of rations and postwar tensions. 'Poor Cambridge!' he said. 'It's been treated harshly in recent years, all the old sores scratched raw again with those revelations about Anthony Blunt.'

'What sort of man was he?' I asked, and Devlan told me of the famous Cambridge spies—Philby, Burgess, Maclean, Blunt—who had formed fast friendships at Cambridge in the 1930s and then had fallen under the spell of Russian Communism, so that when during World War II and later they attained positions of strategic importance in Britain and the United States, they betrayed the crucial secrets of both nations to the Communists: 'They were traitors of the most egregious sort,' Devlan said. 'Cost the Brits and the Yanks enormous losses and the death of many Allied spies.'

'Why would they have done what they did?' I asked, as night darkened over the city, and Devlan replied: 'Spirit of the times. If I had been their age, I jolly well might have joined them. As an Irishman I despised what England had always done to my country. I would have joined them not because I loved Russia but because I hated England.'

Devlan then began to talk about his attitude toward art: 'The artist must always be somewhat opposed to society—against received knowledge. He must be prepared to explore strange alleyways, to rebuke accepted wisdom, to confuse and challenge and reconstruct new patterns. The artist is by nature a semi-outlaw. Van Gogh assaults our sense of color, Wagner our inherited ideas about what acceptable sound is. Those young men of Cambridge were artists in their lives, none better, and they cut right across the heartland of life.'

Before I could unravel this perplexing philosophy, he continued: 'And the master of them all was Anthony Blunt. Imagine. In the heart of the enemy, London, he achieved high office in military

THE CRITIC

. . . . `. . . . .
214

intelligence. And at the same time he received a knighthood because he served as Surveyor of the Queen's Pictures—he was a great scholar on Poussin and other French landscapists. And all the time he was either passing the most critical information to the Soviets or protecting his fellow conspirators from being caught. His loyalty to his friends was impeccable, but that was understandable, because he loved them.'

Devlan rocked back and forth, his salt-and-pepper Caesar's haircut bobbing over his eyes, and after a long while he asked: 'Karl, have you ever heard of the remarkable statement of our great novelist E. M. Forster? Wrote *A Passage to India*—you simply must read it. He was a Cambridge man, you know. My college, Kings. Well, Forster said, and his words appear in many contrasting forms, but I remember them this way: "If the time ever comes when I must choose between betraying my country or my friend, I hope I shall have the courage to betray my country." ' He let these complex words hang in the air for a long time, then added: 'That may be one of the profound statements of this century.'

I wrestled with this evaluation, then asked: 'Are you speaking about your own friends, Professor Devlan?' and the Irishman said: 'I was never a member of any clique. They'd never want an Irish lout. But in my own way I feel about my friends exactly the way he felt about his.'

'To protect them you would betray . . .'

Devlan did not reply. Instead he said in an entirely different voice: 'Karl, the life of the artist is invariably "us against them." People at large don't want artists, don't understand them, never find them totally acceptable till they're dead. The novelists you've thought about so deeply, all of them, they were athwart the grain, and the moment they tried to conform to the grain, they lost their forward thrust—they were doomed to mediocrity.'

'What is it you're not telling me?' I asked, almost in desperation, and Devlan said: 'The famous Cambridge Four, brilliant beyond compare, daring like no others, jugglers with nerves of steel—they loved one another. They were a brotherhood, and they will resound in history when their detractors are forgotten, because they stood for something.' Rising and walking toward the river, he said to no one: 'They were my Cambridge fellows, my peers and my preceptors.'

'You don't mean you want to be a spy? To betray your nation and others?'

'Of course not. I mean I want to live with a burning intensity—to have the courage to pay whatever price is exacted.'

After a long walk along the riverbank, we returned to our hotel and in the reception area we each hesitated when accepting our individual room keys, but nothing eventuated and we went each to his own bed.

I did not sleep that night. Twisting and tossing, I tried to absorb what had been said in the quiet restaurant, to winnow wisdom from the chaff. When morning broke over the city I had identified those truths that would animate my teaching life: 'An artist is a creative man who cannot and indeed should not lead a normal life. He should find sustenance from trusted friends like himself. His task is to provide society with a fresh and sometimes necessarily acid portrait of itself. And the highest good in this world, the behavior by which a man is judged, is that he be loyal to his friends, no matter what the consequences.'

When light filled my room I riffled through my gear to find a pencil and scrambled about to locate a piece of paper on which I could write in complete sentences, lest I forget them, my four maxims. But when I read them over I noted a serious omission in the last and added a postscript: 'I suppose she could be a woman, too.'

That evening, as we approached Venice and located the mainland depots where cars were parked while their drivers transferred luggage to one of the vaporettos, those noisy water taxis that plied the canals, Devlan said: 'Venice is a city for lovers,' and I said (rather childishly, as I realized later): 'I call it Venezia,' and he reprimanded

THE CRITIC

· ·

216

me: 'Henry James called it by the English name. He set the rules.'

That night I made no protest when he told the concierge: 'Double room,' and I was content when Devlan accepted the single key and led the way to the second floor.

The first day in Venice passed for each of us as if we were encased in a golden dream. I had never before experienced sexual passion and its force staggered me. I was like the little Mennonite girl of my home district who allows herself for the first time to be led into the hayrick. I could not believe the wonderful thing that had happened to me and that might have happened years ago if I had been more attentive to my innermost feelings. But, most of all, the beauty of my relationship with my admired professor erased the frightening ugliness of my earlier encounter with the Swiss traveler.

To Devlan, forty-seven years old and thick in the waist, the fact that a young man in the richness of youth should have flown across the Atlantic to meet with him in Rome, and that they should now be headed for two or three weeks in Greece, must have seemed almost inconceivable. He told me that frequently in recent years he had wondered: 'Is it ended? Have the glorious nights I used to know come to a close? And then'—he looked out toward a canal where lovers in gondolas passed—'in New York to meet a brilliant young American with three languages and a rare gift for words, and I, this aging Irishman, had recognized instantly that the young fellow was afraid to break into life, yet secretly eager to do so. I noticed at once that he was not easy with girls and probably never would be, and it then occurred to me that if I could get the young man to Europe and immerse him in the richness of cultural exploration, the Irishman might, just might, be blessed with one last fine relationship.' He paused, then added softly: 'And it has happened as I had contrived. Dear God, it has happened.'

Although our first day in Venice had been for me the beginning of a new life, it had been spent in an unfocused euphoria, but the second day was one of clear, aesthetic delight, for it focused not on Devlan and me but on Venice itself and the significant role it had played in world literature. To me the day was especially meaningful, for it illuminated my early study *Henry James and Thomas Mann: Two Novellas Based in One City*. This had led to my fellowship at Columbia and thus to my friendship with Professor Devlan.

We walked through narrow footpaths that lined the canals, hoping to find James's decaying palace in which the American litterateur struggled with Juliana Bordereau and her ungainly niece, Miss Tina, in his effort to win possession of the cache of papers relating to the dead poet Jeffrey Aspern. As we walked, Devlan remarked: 'The rather unpleasant English authority in the novel, John Cumnor, who also wanted the papers, could have been me, and the young American could easily have been you.' Our search for houses that fitted the description in James's tale became an investigation not into Venetian real estate but into a tangle of fictional lives that seemed more real than the lives of those living Italians who passed us on the narrow walkways.

'That is the job of fiction,' Devlan said with great intensity. 'To put down on paper a chain of words, words that anyone could find in an ordinary dictionary, which will bring to life real human beings in a real setting. Of the half-million words in English, which ones shall we use to describe that old house fronting this rather smelly canal to make someone who reads them on vacation in Zambia not only see the setting but also catch its psychological importance? The words are available, just pick them out of the mass, but be sure to put them in the right order so you achieve the sought-for effect.'

We spoke of Mann's story, of a Venice plagued by cholera.

'But today there is no cholera,' I said.

'Ah, but there is. A deadly cholera is pervasive in all Western societies, a cholera of popular culture, spewing off the presses and through the airwaves, deadening everything, cheapening all. It engulfs us and will in time strangle us.'

Devlan elucidated the fear he had for the future of civilization, and said what he believed creative artists must do to prevent that miserable slide into mediocrity: 'The great enemy is popular acceptance, because that proves the artist has settled for the least common denominator. The mission of the artist is to elevate himself through study and insight to the highest attainable level and then to communicate with his peers, to seek them out, to exchange concepts with them, and to write or paint or compose so as to illuminate the problems that concern them. Serious art is a communication between equals on exalted levels. Nothing else is worth trying.'

I saw the implications of this concept: 'But I caught from things you said at Columbia that publication was the terminus of any writing. Now you say it's nothing. Which do you mean?'

'Remember my lecture that aroused such a storm? George Eliot is a treasure, Charles Dickens a mountebank. Cling to Joseph Conrad, reject John Galsworthy.'

'But where does that leave publishing? Surely the dissemination of books by the authors you dismiss achieves some constructive purpose.'

'They're soporifics, *pasatiempos*. They do little harm and no good.'

'Then what is publishing for?'

'Real publishing is for the conducting of a dialogue between equals. When you sit at your desk, visualize your audience, your readers. As an intellectual—and you can be one of the best—you're obligated to communicate with the brightest minds of your generation, with thoughtful men and women in Berlin, Leningrad, the Sorbonne and Berkeley.'

'But the publishing industry is able to exist only because it sells to the multitudes books you seem to despise.'

'No, no! You have it wrong, Karl. The industry sells junk so that it will keep available its presses for publishing the great dialogue. Imagine a network of brilliant minds occupying centers like Buenos Aires, Tokyo, Madrid, Moscow, Dublin and the two Cambridges. Rare intellects cluster there, striving to keep this world together. Talk with them, give them encouragement and such illumination as you've been able to assemble through your own brilliance. And to hell with the rest.'

We discussed this principle regarding what Devlan called 'the best minds' as we drove slowly around the top of Italy, into Trieste and south through Yugoslavia and its funereal town of Sarajevo, then into the two Macedonias, where we paid our respects to Alexander the Great, who had been nurtured in these areas. As we traveled, first one driving, then the other, the time would come in late afternoon when I would become impatient for the day to end so that we might find some quiet inn and slip into bed.

Now we entered Greece through the historic northern city of Thessaloniki and even the skies seemed to change, for as we traveled dreamily down the peninsula ancient names loomed up as reality, and I was ashamed that Devlan was familiar with so many more than I. 'Product of a classical education,' Devlan said, 'and a good one, not just the light brushing you would get in the States.'

Before we reached Athens, Devlan said: 'Turnoff for Sparta,' and he showed me the ancient canal at Corinth, a beautiful sight from the high roadway. As we crossed the famous waterway to gain entrance to a secondary peninsula, I could imagine in the water below the passage of ancient Greek warships on their way to one battle or another, flags waving, slaves tugging at the oars.

Sparta was a mournful disappointment, little more than a bleak remnant on the plain where battles had raged, and Devlan said: 'I wanted you to see what happens when a society surrenders itself to a military dictatorship. Spartan children were under military discipline from age seven. All decisions were made by military juntas. Best armies in the world, conquerors of everything. And in the end the dictatorship strangled itself, because free men can always best a tyranny—not defeat it, outlast it.'

As we probed the area and came upon sad collections of mean buildings, none exhibiting the grandeur of Greece or even the victories of the Spartan armies, Devlan said: 'When I was in the United States I had the mournful feeling that eighty percent of your people would welcome a Spartan dictatorship if it promised to improve the schools, discipline the minorities, put women back in their place, install a religious supremacy and terminate the silliness of the Bill of Rights. Many modern Americans would leap at such an offer, it seemed to me, which is why I wanted you to see Sparta. Because what you see here is what such a choice always leads to.'

When we reached Athens, Devlan searched briefly for a small hotel he had frequented on previous visits, and when the owners saw him they ran forward to assure him that the room for which he had wired ahead was waiting. As he led me to it, he said: 'When anyone who can read, or has heard of history and man's long struggle to achieve meaning, comes to Greece he feels in his heart: "I'm coming home." We're home, Karl, from a journey that started long ago at Columbia.'

We spent the next ten days in Athens engaged in the most intense and concentrated discussion of my life. It constituted an advanced seminar on the novel in all its aspects, a Socratic conversation that started each day with a breakfast of Greek yogurt, dark slices of toasted Greek bread and a dab of Hybla honey, and ended only when sleep took command at midnight.

We discussed the novel as if it were a treasure beyond compare, spending one entire day on the problem of how best to narrate a

known story—that is, from whose point of view, a subject on which
Devlan had acquired firm tastes: 'Worst of all is the form in which
an author interjects from time to time his own sly comments. How
objectionable it is when it first breaks the flow of the narrative, how
repulsive at the end of a long tale when the convention actually
creaks like a poorly loaded hay wain. Never do it yourself, never
allow a student to do it, and when you review books, castigate it.'

From an intense life of study he had acquired mixed views on the
novel narrated by an unknown, unspecified, all-wise superintelli-
gence: 'Godlike figures in any aspect of life bore me. And the infinite
intelligence that presumes to explain all human activity no matter
how bizarre grows tedious. And yet I have read an occasional book
cast in this mold that has enchanted me—*Middlemarch*, for example.

'I've liked books that were told from the point of view of the
nameless village idiot who sees all but comprehends nothing. You are
never sure who he or she is, but you grow to trust the honesty of the
reporting.'

When he had analyzed four or five alternate approaches, I asked:
'And what about the most famous of all, the one that Henry James
advocated, the concerned colleague, a knowing friend of the family,
but not an intrusive participant, who can use the pronoun *I* and thus
inject some humanity into the narrative? Seems to me it creates a
curious sense of reality. What do you think?'

Devlan contemplated this question for some moments, calculating
which exact words he should use to convey the nuances he intended:
'Obviously, that's the best device of all, but I didn't want to ram my
opinion down your throat. For it carries with it deadly inflections.
The temptation is great to have your all-compassionate observer be
a nonparticipant not only in the lives of the characters he's watching
but also in the full flood of life itself. To put it bluntly, Karl, men
like you and me in telling a story choose a narrator like ourselves—

never married—never parenting—never in the army—usually with no defined occupation—never any dirt under our fingernails—superior to everyone we talk about—and damned dull people to spend the six days with that it takes to read the novel.

'If you ever write such a book, you can have your main character a superaesthete like us, but you must have as your observer a man who runs a shop and is trying to pay off a large mortgage before his three children start university.'

I interrupted to make a stupid statement: 'I'm not interested in shopkeepers,' and he replied: 'Then I fear that no one will be interested in your novel.'

At another point Devlan said, 'I don't believe critics should try to write novels.'

'Why not?'

'Because we know too much.'

'But novelists are always trying to serve as critics.'

'And usually making a hash of it.'

We had a long discussion on what themes were effective for a novel, and he made two points: 'Any activity of which human beings are capable is just material for a novel.'

'Do you mean that—*any*?'

'I can think of none that I would bar.'

'Even incest?'

'Greek tragedy is replete with great dramas involving incest. Treated with fire and fury and retribution.'

'I don't know much about Greek tragedy.'

'Well, this summer may be one opportunity to rectify an oversight that could be inhibiting later on—when you come to grips with the inner meanings of literature.'

His second caveat on theme, forcibly stated, was: 'Any novel about an abstract concept is bound to be a bad one. If you must deal with an abstraction, write an essay. In your novel, write about people, not prototypes. If you can show them trapped in the abstract principle you may find yourself with a very strong tale.'

At some point in almost every discussion, when I realized that Devlan was striving to teach me all he knew, I suspected that he had the idea that I might be his successor as a critic who really grappled with the essence of narration, and this suspicion was strengthened when he produced a paperback on the tenth day, one that had been well thumbed: 'I pass this along as a graduation present, Karl. You're ready now to memorize it—as a permanent guide.' It was a long, reflective essay called *Mimesis*, by a German scholar, Erich Auerbach, who had collected a series of brilliant narratives starting far before the birth of Christ and ending post–Virginia Woolf. He minutely analyzed each style, pointing out where the writer had succeeded brilliantly and where he or she had foundered. Devlan said: 'Auerbach does your work for you,' and later, when I dipped into the essay, I quickly saw what he meant.

It was then, on the night of our eleventh day in Athens, that I told my mentor: 'These days have been miraculous, a binding together of scattered and diverse ideas. You've taught me at a new level. I'm beginning to think I may be ready to be a professor.'

Devlan said: 'You've proved it these last few days.'

Men acquire wisdom in two ways: by patient accumulation and analysis of the evidence available and by epiphanies that in an instant illuminate continents and centuries. My two-week excursion from Rome to Athens with Devlan was an example of the first sort; what happened on the fifteenth day was a stunning example of the second.

Devlan saw on a bulletin board in the office where he went to cash traveler's checks that in the theater of Herodes Atticus, near the Acropolis, a touring German company had been invited by the Greek Cultural Commission to give an open-air performance of

Agamemnon, by Aeschylus, first performed in Athens in 458 B.C. The poster explained that the play would be given in German, but with Greek flutists and drummers to accompany the chorus. Without consulting me, Devlan purchased two of the best seats and hurried back to inform me of our good luck in being able to see one of the world's great tragedies in its proper setting.

As soon as I heard the news, at which I rejoiced, I reacted as Devlan must have expected: 'Where can I get a copy of the play to read?'

'I told you. It's to be in German. You'll understand every word and I won't.' But he had carried with him a book that he valued, an American volume, handsomely printed, which contained in modern translation every tragedy that has come down to us from Aeschylus, Sophocles and Euripides. Since each of the dramatists had composed and put on the stage nearly a hundred plays, for a publishing house to boast 'the complete Greek drama' seemed arrogant until one realized that only a handful of tragedies by each of the writers had survived: seven by Aeschylus, seven also by Sophocles, nineteen by Euripides, with scattered parchments containing references by name only to well over a hundred.

Devlan, who knew the plays well, especially the great trilogy of which *Agamemnon* was the opening part, gladly surrendered the treasured book that had accompanied him to Greece on three previous occasions, and I spent the afternoon reading and memorizing the characters I was about to see: 'Agamemnon, the king of kings; Clytemnestra, his adulterous wife; Aegisthus, the miserable cousin of the king, who has become the lover of Clytemnestra during the King's long absence at the Trojan War; and Cassandra, the beautiful doomed prophetess, daughter of Priam, the defeated king of Troy, and brought back as Agamemnon's mistress.'

Well before the time to leave for the short drive to the theater, I returned the anthology to Devlan: 'I'm ready,' and off we went to hear the German troupe.

As night settled over the hills in which the action of the tragedy might have taken place more than two thousand years before, the audience, composed mainly of tourists eager to see a Greek play in such surroundings, watched as the sentinel crawled out upon the roof of the palace, and lay prostrate but hunched forward on his elbows. As the sky darkened and stage lights came on in subdued colors, the watchman began orating in German so strong and clear that I was startled: he could have been shouting at a Lancaster festival, and in that instant I accepted German as the speech of the old Greeks and became one of them as the sentinel spoke words that some German classical scholar in Heidelberg had translated, and which now I converted almost automatically into English:

'I have been lying on this roof for a year like a hound, watching for the Atreides, propped on my elbows. I know far too well these starry skies. Even so I must watch for the beacon fire that shall bring us news that we have won the war at Troy.'

Then came the powerfully prophetic words hinting at the tragedy soon to envelop the doomed house of Atreus:

'To keep myself alert I like to hum or sing but always my song turns to lamentation for this House, no longer nobly governed as it used to be.'

Now the stage was enveloped in flames. The signal fires have leaped across the hills. Troy has fallen! The Greeks have triumphed! And great Agamemnon has come home, clothed in glory. But the sentinel knows that tragedy awaits:

'The war is over. The beacon fire has caused my dice to throw three sixes. The King's dice fall lucky, too. He is home. I say

no more. *My* tongue tells no secrets, an ox stands on it. But
if this house could talk, there'd be a tale! My words are only
for those who already know, for those that know not, I speak
not.'

His job done, the sentinel vanished and then, for the first time, I saw
one of the glories of the Greek stage: the chorus of elders, sages of
the district, came forward gravely to chant and sing and dance
sedately, accompanied by the flutes, providing the audience with the
many historical facts it needed in order to understand the dramatic
action that was about to unfold. They told a long and tangled tale
covering the past ten years, when members of the House of Atreus
were absent from Greece, fighting terrible battles at Troy. So much
had to be explained—and there was nothing more sad and difficult
than the story of Queen Clytemnestra's favorite daughter, the radi-
antly beautiful Iphigenia, whose father, King Agamemnon, sacri-
ficed her at Aulis in order that his Greek ships would receive a
favorable wind for passage to Troy:

'The captains, mad for war, showed pity none for her sad
pleas, nor listened to her cry of 'Father!' Her prayer finished,
her father signaled to his henchmen who dragged her off,
holding her like a young sheep high above the altar. . . . What
followed next I neither saw nor tell.'

After this piteous prologue the flutists departed and the dancing
stopped. Clytemnestra, one of the most powerful figures in Greek
drama, moved majestically onstage, striding like a man, prepared
to greet her husband, the king, after ten years' absence, during
which she committed adultery with Aegisthus. When she announced that Troy had fallen, the leader of the chorus, a wise old
man, spoke:

LEADER: What makes you so sure? Does a dream inspire you?

CLYTEMNESTRA (*harshly*): I take no stock in silly dreams.

With that this forceful woman took control of the action with such vigor that the leader said in admiration and envy: 'Lady, you speak like a man who understands.'

In my first experience with a Greek chorus, I was awed by the power that twelve old men in priestly robes could exert. I recognized them as a force required in the dawn of fiction when primitive passions were encouraged to run wild among the principals, but only if they could be kept in check by the admonitions of the chorus. And as I listened to their thundering imprecations and warnings, I realized that modern fiction had lost something of significance in abandoning that concept. For me, that night, they were the heroes of the drama. And to hear them in the German that might have been used in the unfolding of a tragedy located in the Lancaster-Reading area—concerning a group of fifteen Amish elders maybe, in the black costumes and flat-brimmed hats of our epoch—created an image that stayed with me.

In the final words of the great drama, Clytemnestra, like political leaders throughout history, boasts that the House of Atreus has never been on safer ground and that its future prosperity is assured.

When the lights of the stage went out and those of the theater came on, I remained in my seat, stunned by the artistic vigor of this ancient masterpiece.

The next day I scurried through the local bookstores, seeking guides to classical literature, and at Devlan's suggestion I spent time in the British Reading Room consulting the various Oxford and Cambridge dictionaries of classical lore. On improvised sheets of paper I began the construction of a master chart showing the deriva-

tion and composition of what I termed The Doomed House of
Atreus. When it was complete, covering two pages, and I felt trium-
phantly that I had dug down to the bedrock of literature, I had a
somewhat deflating experience. One afternoon as we explored the hot
countryside south of Athens, Devlan began laughing: 'You and I
would be such bores to an outsider eavesdropping on our conversations. All we do is beat the hedgerows over this or that minute point
in literature, while real life, the basis of literature, stands exposed all
about us.' Just then we rounded a bend and there, near some cottages
by the road, were three barefoot peasants, two women with their
skirts tied about their waists, a man with his trouser legs rolled up.
As we slowed to watch they climbed into a huge vat shared by the
community, for it must have been costly to build with oaken staves.
There they began to trample grapes brought in from nearby vine-
yards, and they were such a vibrant group that Devlan cried: 'Voilà!
The stuff of literature! The same three thousand years ago as now.
You don't need Greek kings and instructions from Henry James
when you have stompers of grapes.'

When the time came for F.X.M. Devlan to board his plane for
London while I took mine for New York, I said: 'You're sending me
home prepared to teach,' but Devlan spoke of more important matters: 'Save your salary and let's meet here again next summer.' And
on that promise we shook hands, but just before we parted, the
Irishman confided: 'My famous lecture about the good and bad
novelists. That wasn't my idea. It came from a teacher I had. Look
him up, he's worthwhile, F. R. Leavis. But I improved on his idea.
I added the four bad ones. Now it's your job to improve on me. Add
the Americans.'

I began my teaching at Mecklenberg in the fall semester of 1980 and
established such immediate rapport with my students that others on
campus spoke of me as 'a sure winner, a powerhouse.'

It was a custom at the college to offer a February lecture series for residents of the Lancaster-Reading-Allentown axis. There was no fee and three of the best older professors lectured on their specialties, hoping to bring the public up to date on recent developments in these areas, but it was also an opportunity to introduce two younger members of the faculty, always one woman, one man. During my first half year on campus, I was chosen for this honor and the hall was nicely filled when I spoke, for people were aware that I was a local lad who had done well at Columbia.

After considerable thought I decided to start my professional career with a bang, for the new confidence that had come to me after my experiences in Venice and Athens had converted me from a shy fellow into a self-assured scholar with something to say. I told myself: 'This is a propitious time to unveil my eight choices for the American novel, four commendable, four expendable.' But how propitious it was going to be I was not aware. Two reporters of local newspapers had slipped in to hear what the newest addition to the faculty had to say, and they heard what they termed 'an earful.'

I began on an austere note: 'Ladies and gentlemen, I do not wish to waste your time or mine, so I will launch directly into the heart of what I have wanted to say for a long time. In the steps of my distinguished professor at Columbia, the visiting professor from Cambridge and Oxford in England, F.X.M. Devlan, who in turn borrowed this concept from his own mentor F. R. Leavis, considered the preeminent English literary critic of this century, I invite you to wander with me through the rich meadow of the American novel, picking those blooms that will last forever and others that will fade before sunset. It seems to me, and to many like me who have studied the matter, that there are four American writers who understood what narration was and wrote books of lasting merit from which we can all learn. I'm sure you're acquainted with them. In chronological order, they are Herman Melville, Stephen Crane, Edith Wharton and William Faulkner.'

After the whispers subsided, I defended my choices, allocating most of my time to Crane and Wharton, as if they required defense while Melville and Faulkner did not. In the course of my remarks I revealed my criteria: honesty of purpose, simplicity of statement, artistry in portrayal and a mysterious, indefinable 'sense of what the novel should ideally be.' I managed to convince some of my audience, but less than half, and many of those I did win over deserted me during the second part of my lecture.

'Now, opposed to these four artists, and I think we can accept that they are artists, we have four other writers who have achieved some popularity but whose work is almost laughable from an aesthetic point of view. Again in chronological order: Sinclair Lewis, Pearl Buck, Ernest Hemingway and John Steinbeck. From an artistic point of view, they are hardly worth reading.' With that I stared down the baleful looks being leveled at me, and then proceeded to analyze and downgrade the works of the four. I considered their work facile, meretricious and deceptive in that they promised more than they delivered. My final opinion caused audible protest throughout the hall: 'Their most deplorable weakness was that they did not approach the novel seriously. They shied away from great challenges. They were too easily satisfied, and that was caused by the popularity and prizes that came to them too easily. They are novelists whom the serious student or reader need not take seriously, for they teach him nothing.'

When the time came for questions, it seemed that everyone wished to debate, and with what skill I could muster I had my eyes darting about the hall as I designated men and women to speak, and I had good luck in selecting one lively person after another who had something important to say and who said it well. The first set the tone: 'Professor Streibert, how can you nominate Stephen Crane for the top category? He wrote only one significant book, and many consider it very slight.'

I nodded, but then pointed out: 'We do not judge ultimate talent by poundage. If we did, Sir Walter Scott would have to be judged infinitely superior to Gustave Flaubert, which few would concede.

'Also, Crane must be considered in the same category as E. M. Forster in England, who wrote very little but dominated his period, especially when compared with a flatulent type like Hugh Walpole. Crane burned with an incandescent flame, Sinclair Lewis with a smoky smudge that never really caught fire.'

I was lucky with my next questioner, for the woman, in an agitated voice, pointed out: 'In the four you reject with scorn stand four of our people who've won the Nobel Prize and we're very proud of them. What do you think that tells us about your opinions?'

Very gently I replied: 'I think it tells a great deal more about the Nobel committee than it does about me.' Fortunately the audience broke into laughter, thawing the ice and allowing me to thrust and parry with my questioners while keeping the debate on a friendly level. At several points I said easily: 'You're right. My judgments may be either ill-considered or wrong, and I would certainly never badger you into surrendering yours.' But drawing upon experience acquired in my long debates with Devlan, I defended my selections, and in such a way that for most of the time the audience was laughing with me. I was forceful but not pompous and at one point won considerable favor by admitting: 'I realize that I'm throwing a lot of weight around tonight with my opinions and predictions, but I want you to remember that I'm the man who also said, "Pizza will never catch on in the United States. Too doughy." '

The evening ended with applause, the audience having decided that since I had not bullied them into surrendering their love for the four Nobel Prize winners in favor of four others whose books were so unpalatable that few in the audience had ever finished one of them, I could be accepted as a bright young fellow with a mind of his own. They also concluded that I would probably be an excellent teacher.

But my real rewards of the evening came from two unexpected quarters. One of the newsmen in the audience wrote an informed and witty report of the lecture and the subsequent discussion, and a wire service picked it up, along with a table entitled HE SAYS GOOD AND BAD, and included photos not only of the eight novelists but also of me. The amusing article was widely reprinted and occasioned a deep debate that put both Mecklenberg College and me in the headlines.

Then things quieted down, but in 1982 a Philadelphia television company engineered a talk show in which three critics defending traditional values hammered at me, but with witticisms and mannerisms acquired at Columbia I fended them off. The program became a lively affair and was rebroadcast by public television stations.

A second broadcast in the winter of 1983 was quite different, involving no facile wit or clever comment. A station in Allentown awoke to the fact that if I taught at Mecklenberg, I must operate close to where the popular novelist Lukas Yoder worked, and reporters arranged a half-hour show presenting me as a brash young man and Yoder as the sedate older writer, with both of us responding to questions from a woman professor of English from Bryn Mawr.

A host of viewers called the station to say: 'That was a stunning show,' and the reason was simple. I had never before met Mr. Yoder and was awed by his sales record if not by the quality of his writing, so I did not allow myself to posture as an ill-mannered Young Turk attacking a revered figure. Halfway through the show I thought to myself: I like this old duck, he knows how to handle himself. But the clever professor wanted to ignite fires. When the professor commented: 'Obviously, Dr. Streibert, if you apply the standards you have in dismissing our four Nobel Prize winners, you'd surely have to dismiss your neighbor Lukas Yoder, who falls in the same category,' I smiled and said: 'Anytime I have as my neighbor a man with his distinguished track record, I'm not going to be petty about it. Mr. Yoder is a damned fine writer.'

'But not your type?'

'I must confess, I favor the younger approaches, the newer challenges. But I take my hat off to anyone who can write five good novels. That's rare.'

'Make that six,' the woman said. 'Mr. Yoder told me before we gathered that he's working on his next book in the series.'

'A sextet!' I cried, for the first time using that word in connection with his books. 'I'm sure they'll be around these parts for a long time.'

'And in the other parts?' the shrewd professor asked, hoping to goad me into making an offensive statement or Yoder into giving a defensive one. She failed, because before I could respond, Yoder said: 'I believe a book finds its own level and its own longevity. I'd hate to prophesy what's going to happen to mine, and I'm sure Professor Streibert wouldn't want to be put to the test, either.' Then, with a wink, he added: 'I find that professors are little better than writers in making predictions about topics that are current. But give them fifty years, they usually make the right judgments.' And before either of us could speak he nailed down his thoughts: 'But of course, at the end of fifty years, other critics will be coming along to revise all estimates. I would expect a *tremendous* revival of Dickens before I die. They'll see he was truly one of the greats, Streibert.'

'Well, they may,' I conceded, and the program ended with a display of genuine amity among the three participants, especially when the Bryn Mawr professor said in closing: 'My friends who have been listening to this discussion, you have heard a rare treat, a gentlemanly conversation between a radical young man who knows where he's going and a distinguished older writer who knows where he's been.' I broke in: 'And a shrewd professor who knows how to keep us talking without tearing at each other's throat. It's been a privilege for me to be here today.' Yoder said nothing, simply allowing his puckish Dutch smile to convey his approval.

So my maiden speech achieved two desirable ends: nationally it earned me attention, locally an acquaintanceship with Lukas Yoder, but my most surprising reward came in an unexpected letter from New York. It was from a woman whose name I had never heard, Yvonne Marmelle of Kinetic Press, and it read:

> Dear Professor Streibert,
> Like others, I have followed with keen interest the results of your lecture at Mecklenberg College and find myself supportive of your views about the nature of the novel. If you are soon to be in New York, I hope you can have lunch with me because I would enjoy exploring your ideas in some depth, and I suspect you might also profit from such an exchange. Please call me.

I did not then know that Ms. Marmelle was Yoder's editor, but I did know that Kinetic Press published a wide spectrum of books, from the sensational novel of the day to reliable standbys like the works of Lukas Yoder and the experimental novel of the beginning writer. But I was not aware that Kinetic also published some of the best criticism both of literature and of sociopolitical conditions. Nor could I guess what interest Ms. Marmelle might have in me or what concerns we might have in common. But I called promptly, heard a pleasant voice and agreed to come to New York on the first weekday I could break away from teaching, for she had warned: 'On Saturday or Sunday I would not even see Thomas Mann or Marcel Proust.'

When I reported to her office on Madison Avenue one Friday in February and saw the early stages of the remarkable wooden panel PORTRAIT OF AN EDITOR I gasped at the pitiful record of Lukas Yoder's first four books in his Grenzler series: 'Total sales, 4,961. You mean to tell me Kinetic held on to him with that record?'

'Yes,' she said, 'and look what happened with Number Five.' '

I had no idea! That quiet gray-haired man we see on the campus
now and then. A record as dramatic as that.'

'That fifth book is what publishers dream of finding. Maybe one
in each decade.' Flinging wide her right arm, she said gaily: 'Yoder
paid for all this. He also paid for this,' and she tapped herself on the
chest. 'Men like him keep us operating, and don't you powerhouse
critics forget it.'

As I looked at her in that moment of free movement and free
thought, I saw a woman in her late thirties, some years older than
myself, artfully dressed in expensive clothes that proclaimed 'editor'
and not 'woman executive.' She wore her black hair in a neatly
trimmed bob, halfway down on her brow in front, barely touching
her dress collar in back, and everything about her bespoke a crisp,
eager approach to her job, at which she was apparently quite good.

'Give me two more of him,' she said affectionately as she indicated
her board, 'and I'd be considered a genius. As it is, I'm just a woman
who has a keen sense of what's happening, what ought to happen,
what will happen. My interest in you, Professor Streibert, resides in
the second category.'

Accepting a chair that faced her cluttered desk and not the broad
picture window, which confirmed her success within the company,
I asked: 'What is the second category, and how do I fit in?'

'You weren't listening,' she chided with a warm smile. 'What
ought to happen. You seem like the man who ought to write a book
we sorely need. Starting with your notorious lecture on who's hot,
who's not, you ought to codify and substantiate your thinking on
where the American novel is going, and where you think it ought to
go.'

'Who would read it?'

'Not many. But among editors and professors and writers there's
an intense interest—a constant speculation about such matters.

Reading is becoming more popular than ever, since television is
sliding ever deeper into ruts that are beneath contempt. Writers like
Saul Bellow, John Cheever, John Updike, Joyce Carol Oates have no
trouble finding readers, and an honest workman like Lukas Yoder—
look at the readers he's collected.'

'Let's suppose such an evaluation is necessary. Am I the one to
write it?'

'I'm the authority as to whether it's needed or not, and I say yes.
Also, I'm the one who takes a chance every time I recommend a
writer for a specific book, and from what I've read of you and your
ideas, I'm willing to take that risk, to make that commitment right
now—or almost right now. I want you to think it over and let me
know how secure you feel with the challenge.'

'Do you propose books like this all the time? To all your writers?'
The idea appalled me, and my near disgust must have been so palpa-
ble that Ms. Marmelle smiled: 'With novelists, never. That would be
risky and probably self-defeating, that is, of course, unless your
writer was someone who wrote whatever schlock was put into his
head. I don't have such authors, but if I did I'd not hesitate to tell
them what to write. But real novelists, never. I wouldn't even dare
ask such writers a rhetorical question like "Have you ever thought
of doing a novel on the radical changes in modern courtship?" And
do you know why I avoid it? Because the novel that resulted would
be crap.'

I winced at her strong language: 'Professor Devlan said almost the
same: "A novel about something is sure to be a bad novel." '

'But in nonfiction, Dr. Streibert, thoughtful editors who keep their
fingers on the public pulse propose somewhat more than half the
successful books, and sometimes three fourths of the big best-sellers.
I won't bore you with my track record, but it isn't trivial. And I have
the gut feeling that a book of the kind I have in mind, and which I
hope you'll get in your mind, could be a substantial success.'

'But you just agreed with me that it might not find many readers.'

'Normally it wouldn't. Satisfying numbers but not large. Your job and mine is to make it so compelling that it will command ten times the readership you would imagine—five times what I would hope for.' Before I could reply, she said brightly: 'I'm starved. Let's have lunch,' and in this abrupt manner I had my first literary lunch at the Four Seasons. Senior officers from other publishing houses stopped by our table to pay their respects, and in hopes of meeting whatever new prospect Yvonne had uncovered, but she volunteered no introduction and no one deciphered who I was. Our talk focused on the specifications of the kind of book she wanted: 'I visualize it as no more than about three hundred pages, no longer. It must be tightly written, punch, punch, punch. A minimum of clever anecdotes, but a wealth of significant frinstances.'

'What?'

'You state a major point, then cite at least two powerful short examples. We call them *for instances*, elided to become one word.' Before I could respond to any of her suggestions, she put down her fork and asked bluntly: 'Dr. Streibert, have you the capacity, do you think, of becoming a superior literary critic? A man who truly has something to say?'

'My professors have thought so.'

'But in analyzing whether you're really intelligent, they wouldn't have a clue. What do you think?'

Feeling challenged, I realized that this was a far more penetrating interrogation than I had experienced in my orals for the Ph.D. and to my own surprise I wanted to fight back, to prove to this bright woman that in any respect she chose I was her equal: 'In Athens this summer I argued with Professor Devlan for eleven unbroken days, at the very highest level he could reach, and he's one of the best. I stayed with him every inch of the way. I believe I could carry on where Auerbach stopped in his *Mimesis*.'

THE CRITIC

· ·

238

At my mention of this name, she smiled: 'If you say so, I'm inclined to accept your judgment,' and she began to lay out the eight or nine significant themes my essay would have to deal with if it was to have any merit, watching approvingly as my eyes lit up when each was mentioned in logical order. 'You can see the outline of each chapter right now, can't you?' she asked and I replied: 'So, obviously, can you. Why don't you write the book?' and she replied: 'I'm fantastic on erecting the superstructure. I fail when it comes to citing the frinstances.'

As we were about to leave the dining area, she warned: 'Nothing has been agreed on today. I'm not omnipotent, you know. I have to subject my ideas to an editorial committee. But I feel I can persuade them to allow me to approach you with a serious proposal. That would empower me to come back at you to satisfy myself that you can really do what you think you can. If I'm reassured, you could have a contract by the end of October. I'll want to talk with you again.'

'On what?'

'For your book to have relevance, and for it to gain the initial attention it will need, you must have not only the old-time American novelists that you like and dislike, but also the contemporary ones. Along about Chapter Seven you must say something like: 'The reader will have perceived that I am talking about . . .'"—I think this had all better be in the first person, but not aggressively so—"that I am talking about matters of great moment, using criteria that apply to novels in all languages and writers of all decades, especially the current decade in America and our writers." Then you say that you are going to follow the criteria postulated in Chapter One, and you cite four contemporary writers you approve of because they conform to those criteria and oppose them with four you reject because they don't even tackle the criteria. And in each category you must use names that are immediately recognizable, and the more frenzy you create, the more your readers will like it, because that's what attracts attention, and attention is what sells books.'

She did not allow me to walk her back to her office: 'Waste of your time and mine. I have meetings, you have work to do.'

I demurred: 'I thought we might go over my two lists for Chapter Seven.'

'Oh no!' she cried as she broke away. 'You do that work in silence, with the best brainpower you have,' but when she saw my disappointment she delayed her departure: 'Dr. Streibert, I'm much heartened by your description of yourself. I think you have the capacity to be a first-rate critic, and I'll help you.' Then with surprising speed she was gone.

On Monday I received a confirming note: 'I will be presenting my suggestion to the board on Wednesday and shall communicate soonest. Yvonne Marmelle.'

Wednesday afternoon about five-thirty, I received a phone call in which Ms. Marmelle could scarcely hide her delight: 'They've given me the green light. But only if—and underscore that heavily, *if*—you and I can satisfy each other that it's a workable idea, and *if* you can assure me that you'll be able to go right to work, and most important of all, *if* you have something substantial to say about our contemporaries. So sharpen your pencils and put your thinking cap on.'

'I have. When may I come to see you?'

'Better yet—I'm coming to see you. Saturday. Lunch at the inn in Dresden.'

'My goodness! I thought you never saw anyone on Saturday or Sunday.'

'At my office never. At the Dresden China, a lovely country inn, yes.'

'See you at noon, pencil sharpened.'

'And mine.'

Much later I would learn that Ms. Marmelle followed the rigid convention that kept senior editors out of trouble: 'Never, on pain of death, allow one of your older writers to know, when you visit him, that you're also visiting a younger one of great promise.'

So she was coming to Dresden not primarily to see me but to perform a much more important editorial task: to work with Lukas Yoder on the redrafting of troublesome passages in the manuscript that would be of such crucial importance to each of them. *Creamery* he was calling it, a tale of how the Pennsylvania Dutch lusted over land and agricultural property, and they both knew that his future, and perhaps hers, too, hung on the proper presentation of this novel. They had shared four heart-stabbing disappointments with his first Grenzler novels, and despite his startling success with *Hex*, they could recall numerous instances in which a struggling novelist had finally broken through with a work that was a resounding success, only to fall back into obscurity with its successors. They did not want that to happen.

It was obvious to me that Kinetic had more at risk in Yoder's *Creamery* than he did, for she realized that if he could follow through with another smashing success, and there was always that chance if factors remained favorable, the first four books in the Grenzler series would enjoy a rebirth, and since all costs on them had already been amortized, any unexpected sales would be clear profit, less minor charges for warehousing and binding sheets already in print or slipping the existing plates back on the press for another run. Kinetic had a huge financial interest in ensuring that Yoder's next book was a success.

Furthermore, with any series that might prove as popular as Yoder's Grenzler books, there would be a good chance that collectors would want to have a complete set, first editions especially, and she could see his first books skyrocketing in value, if first editions could be found. So it was no ordinary visit she was making to the Dresden China; two vital interests were at stake: a possible repeat by

a best-selling author and a possible nominee to write a first-rate
critical book that would have a chance of catching on for a respectable sale in universities. Rarely did she set forth on a weekend
mission so fraught with possibilities.

So, unbeknownst to me, she had slipped into town Friday afternoon and had worked diligently with Yoder at his farm. Now, on
Saturday afternoon, she was ready to deal with me, and when she
entered the Dresden China, where she had stayed when nursing *Hex*
to its glory, she gave me the impression that she had just driven in
from New York. But to protect herself from some inadvertent revelation by a hotel clerk or some townsman who knew her, she immediately revealed: 'Checked in last night. And how are you, Professor?'

'Fine,' I said, and we went right to work, spreading our papers
over a table tucked into a corner surrounded by glass cases containing Meissen ware. She began with a warm assurance: 'It's done, Dr.
Streibert. If we decide in the next two hours that you have an
appropriate editor and I a capable author, we shall have a contract
by the middle of next week.' When she saw my eyes brighten, she
corrected: 'What we'll have, of course, is a letter of intent from me.
That Kinetic intends to issue a contract along the financial terms
proposed. It usually takes some time to work out the details, but as
for you and me that letter is a contract. Do you have an agent?'

'No.'

'No reason why you should. At this stage. Hopefully you'll need
one soon. But I assure you, we'll give you the standard.'

'Which is?'

'I don't really know in your case. I suppose ten percent of list. If
the book sells for twelve dollars, you get a dollar twenty per copy.'

'Will it sell for that?'

'A book not yet written, length not assured, who can say? But
don't start dreaming about wealth untold. I suppose you know what
the average author like you earns from his first three or four books?

About sixteen hundred dollars a book, if he's lucky. The important duty for us right now— This is my lunch, by the way.'

'Not on my turf, it isn't.'

'Oh, all right. Well, what have you come up with?'

'I find myself totally at ease with the chapters we more or less decided on.'

'Nothing's decided, Dr. Streibert, until we nail it down, with notes—today.'

'I'm ready to do some nailing.' I liked her forthright approach to matters relating to books. You asked her a question, she shot back an answer.

'Good. I should think it would be advantageous to say at the start that you got your idea of the four acceptable, four nonacceptable from a distinguished critic. F. R. Leavis.'

'Yes, but you understand, he gave only the four acceptables. It was my Professor Devlan who improved the lecture by adding the unacceptables.'

'Is Devlan dead also?'

'No, he's alive.'

'All right. I think it most effective when a scholar admits right up front: "As the leading literary English literary critic F. R. Leavis said in his notorious Oxford lecture in nineteen something . . ." A statement like that informs the reader that you're not some smartass trying to take all the credit for yourself. It gives your ideas a genealogy, a respectability.'

We marched thus through the first six chapters, laying the groundwork for the hard analysis that would come later, after the principles had been established. She wanted ample reference to all the good men and women who were writing about American fiction, and she did not seem to care whether I agreed with the experts or not but was concerned only that I be familiar with their criticisms. But she did counsel: 'It never hurts a really bright young man to tackle the biggest panjandrums. Look how far Bill Buckley got by lambasting the stuffed shirts at Yale.'

When we reached Chapter Seven, I laid out my four goodies, as she called them, Melville, Crane, Wharton, Faulkner, as opposed to the baddies, Lewis, Buck, Hemingway, Steinbeck. She immediately jabbed her finger at Stephen Crane: 'I don't think he belongs.'

I tensed, and my face must have reddened. During my public lecture many had questioned the inclusion of a talent so apparently slight as Crane, and in subsequent weeks, when the list was commented upon widely, the harshest criticism fell on my suggestion that he was a major figure, until retaining him became the litmus test of my integrity. Quietly I said: 'I'd feel I'd abandoned my principles if I eliminated Crane. He represents all that Devlan and I stand for.'

'Devlan's not involved in this.'

'Oh, but he is!' I cried, with a quickness that brought new blood to my face, and at which she must have said to herself: So that's how the wind blows! Aloud, she said: 'Let's restrict this to American judgments,' and I nodded, but I did not retreat: 'I would feel deprived if I had to lose Crane.'

'There is a better one.'

'Who?'

'Nathaniel Hawthorne. Infinitely richer. Has infinitely more to say to us moderns.'

'I'm afraid I find Hawthorne rather dull,' I said curtly, as if addressing a presumptuous student. The words fell with an angry thud, as if I had dismissed as unworthy the reasoned judgment of a practiced older woman, and I could see that she resented this, but I bumbled ahead. She contained her anger, saying brightly as if opening an entirely new subject after a pleasant break: 'Well, any changes in the right-hand column? Or are we still disposing of our four Nobel winners?'

'No changes.'

'This could be a very powerful part of the book.'

'I'd like to make it so.'

'But I wonder if you really want to ridicule Hemingway? He's a rather impressive figure.'

'You've hit exactly the right word. A figure, not a writer.'

'Now, just back off a bit, young man.' She could sense that I resented this condescension, but I believe she used the phrase intentionally, to goad me, to test my mettle. So, to complete the testing, she added: 'I'm much impressed by the testimony of a well-known critic who had completed a world tour in which he met a lot of young writers: "Wherever I went I talked with writers of other nations who assured me: 'I don't want to write like Hemingway,' but they all did. Never did they not want to write like Camus or Faulkner, because these two didn't matter. They wanted to avoid a test of arms with Hemingway, because he did matter." I think that states my view.'

'No, Hemingway was the great poseur, not the great writer. Feigning to be so modest and not wanting to be recognized in public, but wearing the unmistakable beard. Posing as the invulnerable macho but, when the going got rough, ending it in suicide. He deserves to stay where he is and young writers ought to hear what I have to say about him.'

I could see that she was of two minds. As one who loved literature, she wanted to protect Hemingway's reputation, but as an editor who wanted her books to sell, she realized that if I blasted the icon, controversy must result, and our book would be helped. But something else, undefined, irritated her, and when I asked: 'What is it, Ms. Marmelle?' she smiled forgivingly as if I were her grandson: 'Has it occurred to you, Professor Streibert, that not once have you asked my opinion on this matter?'

Chastened, I asked: 'What *is* your opinion?' and she said in measured phrases: 'On the drive down I thought: In the negative part, drop Hemingway and substitute James Fenimore Cooper, who's a real bore.'

'Why didn't you speak up?'

'Because I suspected I might have to husband my resources to do some real battling on your contemporary lists.'

In this mood, each of us tense, we reached Chapter Eight, and from a carefully prepared slip of paper that contained many deletions and late corrections, I read the names of the four fellow writers I intended praising for their perceptiveness, their attention to major topics and their skill in execution. 'J. D. Salinger, Ralph Ellison, Saul Bellow, Bernard Malamud.'

The names hung in the air for a long moment, then Yvonne said reflectively: 'Three Jews and a black. No woman. You really do intend to kick the establishment right in the groin, don't you?'

'The mix hadn't occurred to me.'

'To me it's the first thing that did.'

'What change would you suggest?'

'Answering without time to consider all angles, and maybe that's the best way to answer, because it's less inhibited, I'd say drop Malamud and replace him with Joyce Carol Oates.'

'I'll also respond on the spur of the moment. He's one of the great professionals. She's untested.'

'I thought we were looking for that rare quality that reaches beyond mere professionalism. If that's all you want, take Louis Auchincloss. He writes wonderful books.'

'The rich man's Edith Wharton,' I said, to break the tension.

'You're satisfied with your four?'

'I am.'

Trying to mask her obvious displeasure, she said almost sweetly: 'Now let's hear the shockers,' and she leaned forward as I read out the names of those I proposed to condemn: 'Herman Wouk, Gore Vidal, Leon Uris, Lukas Yoder.'

I had barely uttered the last name when she said firmly but quietly: 'You can't use Yoder.'

'But he's the most windy nothing of all. He's an okay guy but as a writer he's the one who really sets my teeth on edge. I know the Pennsylvania Dutch country, I'm part of it. And his books—'

'But *Hex* is this decade's sensation.'

'And sensationally bad. I'd not want to bother with writing our book if I couldn't take off on his empty pomposity.'

'If there is one man in this world who is not pompous, it's Lukas Yoder. Find another adjective,' she said quite crisply, as if she did not propose to discuss it further.

'I'll withdraw "pompous." What I mean is that his style, his entire management of narrative, is inflated, early nineteenth century.'

'Some good books came out of that period.'

'Not for today's needs.'

Growing increasingly irritated with what she construed as my arrogance, she obviously felt that the moment had come to introduce me to the realities of publishing and my potential place in it: 'Lukas Yoder is not just somebody. He's not Leon Uris or Gore Vidal, or some able young man who writes good books. He's my writer. I'm his editor. Kinetic is his publisher. He's the author of a sensationally successful book after four misses. And next year the financial stability of our firm will depend on him. For me to allow you to denigrate him in a book I sponsored would be suicide. I'd get fired, and rightly so.'

'Ms. Marmelle, I have no animosity toward Yoder. I like him. We did a television show together and it was a pleasant experience. But in this book we're after the truth, and the truth is—'

'Truth, bullshit!' she cried. 'Do I have to spell it out, word for word? There is not a chance in hell that I would be able to publish your book if it were not that Lukas Yoder has brought in so much money with what you call his worthless *Hex* that we can afford to mess around with rank amateurs like you. Because I championed Yoder during the bad years and nursed him along to the great success of which I knew he was capable, the firm gives me, as a reward, freedom to publish you and other smartass young men and women who among you will never publish a single book as good as his, nor as good as his future books are going to be.'

I was so staggered by her assault and the language in which it was delivered that I could not respond, so she rose and said with controlled fury: 'The dinner is ended and so is the interview.' And then she called loudly: 'Waiter! Waiter! The check, please,' and against my wishes she paid the bill. But she was a professional editor who did not want to throw away a good book if she could salvage it, so when I trailed her to her car, she did give me a last chance: 'If you come to your senses, drop me a note saying so,' and she spun her wheels in the gravel, angry at herself for having lost her temper but even angrier at her inability to maintain control of her conversation with me. She had allowed me to make the early decisions without insisting that I attend seriously to her reasoned judgments. In the end, losing all patience with me, she had blown up. It had been a most disappointing session, one that had to be disillusioning to each of us, and I was not pleased with my performance.

Back in my rooms at the college, I castigated myself for having behaved so inadequately. That was the only word I could use; I was angry not at arguing so forcefully—because I was right in what I defended—but at showing such ineptitude. I could not sleep, and as was my custom at such times, I went out into the night and walked along the Wannsee, trying to decide what to do. I feared that I had killed any chance of publishing with Kinetic, and that was appalling, for I remembered Devlan's constant hammering: 'The overarching job of any writer is to get his manuscript finished and printed. That's how reputations are made.' I agreed, but I also had an unselfish reason for wanting to maintain contact with Kinetic. That house had a commendable reputation for publishing young writers, and if I established a connection with it I would be free to recommend those of my students I deemed eligible for professional attention. And secretly I had a more personal reason. Since I had this hankering to publish one of my own novels someday, I must not alienate Ms. Marmelle or cut my ties to Kinetic.

So, swallowing the brave words I had uttered about the integrity of the critic, I went to my typewriter toward dawn and wrote a brief note to Ms. Marmelle:

> Sorry. In classics to be praised, Crane is out, Hawthorne in. In moderns praised, Malamud out, Oates in. In classics lambasted, Hemingway must stay in. In modern luminaries rejected, your Mr. Yoder safely out, Cheever in. Hope we can work together on what can be a fine book.

In other words, I surrendered almost every point to her sagacity except Hemingway, and by return mail I received a brief note that encouraged me enormously:

> Your four decisions are not only acceptable but right. Contract along lines suggested will be forthcoming, but this letter is binding. Advance on signing contract, $1,500. Make it the most perceptive book ever.

Like any fledgling writer, I spent that day gloating over the fact that I was to have a hardcover book of mine published by Kinetic, one of the great houses, for I knew that most university teachers of writing would commit mayhem to achieve such a goal. But toward evening, as the glow subsided, I had to face the fact that in order to become an author I had surrendered my principles. Yoder was a dreadful writer, a man who ought to be named as such in any serious book of criticism, but my voice had been strangled and for the basest of reasons. To Kinetic, Yoder meant money, and as such he had to be protected. I had sold out to defend my personal interests and no would-be critic could be proud of that action.

But I had another accomplishment in which I could take satisfaction, my college teaching, and during the time I was battling with Ms. Marmelle—and mostly surrendering to her—I was also teaching a heavy schedule and doing all I could to help my students acquire the skills they'd need if they wanted to become writers. So during the Christmas break I said to myself: If I'm getting this $1,500 windfall, let me spend some on my students, and I did something I had long wanted to do.

At my own expense I employed a Dresden sign painter to transfer onto a wall of my classroom the intricate chart I had sketched three years earlier in Athens and verified by careful research in Mecklenberg. When the painter saw the two sheets on which I had worked out the relationships he had two reactions: 'I could make the chart look quite handsome, with different colors to show different things, but all those words at the bottom. I could never letter all that stuff.'

'No, no! Only the chart goes on the wall. We give each student a Xeroxed copy of the legend.'

Only when the job was completed did I inform the administration of what I had done, and the buildings supervisor, after voicing furious objections before he saw the wall, relaxed when he saw how handsome it was and what a superior teaching tool it could be. And when my students filed in on the first day after winter break, they caught the significance of the wall, and my popularity as a professor increased.

When my book, *American Fiction*, appeared in the winter of 1984, I was propelled for the second time into the midst of a vigorous debate, and to the astonishment of both Ms. Marmelle and myself, much of the criticism focused not on my castigation of Hemingway but on some harsh words I had written, almost as an aside, about James Fenimore Cooper. Many readers felt that although Cooper

was no Thomas Mann, he was our first serious novelist and a fine
storyteller: 'How could we have developed without the encouragement he gave?' And several acerbic writers suggested that I was
rather young to be casting aspersions on one of our greatest, although
there were those who agreed that Cooper was something of a bore.

But after the first blasts had been delivered and resolved, a serious
discussion ensued regarding the contemporary writers, with some
arguing that Ellison and Salinger had both produced so little that
they could not merit top approval, while to downgrade proven storytellers who had something valid to say, such as Vidal and Wouk, was
so arbitrary as to be ridiculous. Cheever also had strong supporters.
But when the fires died down, I proved to be the winner, for one of
the newspaper syndicates, seeing how interested readers were in my
unequivocal judgments, invited me, for a welcome fee, to provide a
long article in which I listed the fifty books from all nations that I
felt would reward readers.

My list included certain books of such vintage that no one could
deny their viability—*Les Misérables, Anna Karenina, Great Expectations, Huckleberry Finn*—and others less familiar but perhaps of
superior merit, such as *Oblomov, The Plague, The Mayor of Caster-
bridge, The Trial* and *McTeague*. To the editor's relief, I added a
personal epilogue: 'I cannot quit this exercise of juggling the great
and near great without sharing with you the names of four books
which, in my idle moments, I have read with sheer delight and which
without trying to categorize their standing in the world of literature,
I recommend to you as joyous reads: *Green Mansions, The Member
of the Wedding, The Constant Nymph* and *The Count of Monte
Cristo*.'

The wide dissemination of this chatty but instructive essay led not
only to numerous invitations to lecture at other colleges and universities but also to requests by magazines and newspapers for reviews of
new books. In these traditional ways I found myself a member of the
hierarchy of those who deal with books in their various manifesta-

tions. Associates realized that I might be on my way to becoming a major voice in my field, a fact that was acknowledged by the college: I was promoted to assistant professor, then to associate, and there was every likelihood of a full professorship before I reached thirty-five.

But my obvious success in teaching and criticism never dimmed my aspiration to produce one or two novels that exemplified my theories of what good writing should be. More and more I found that I was spending my spare time not in preparing for my seminar or in honing my essays on other people's novels but in planning my own, and I convinced myself it would be a major contribution.

In the winter of 1984 I brought to the campus some attractive professional writers for a series of lectures, and they delighted both my students and the townspeople from the German cities who joined the audience. It was at one of the most exciting of these evenings that I met the young man who was to have such a great impact on Mecklenberg and on my life. This seminar had been conducted by a pair of poets flown down from Boston, a man from Harvard, a woman from M.I.T.—university rumor was that they were lovers— and after the seminar we all convened at the Dresden China. The Harvard man said: 'It's a cultural anomaly. A century ago we had a group of very bad poets, each with three names, that everyone worshiped. Henry Wadsworth Longfellow and the rest had enormous audiences and great income but nothing to say. Today we have a group of very good poets whom no one appreciates, who have no audience, no income, but a great deal to say.'

The M.I.T. woman broke in: 'And what we have to say deserves to be heard, needs to be heard. We're entitled to vast audiences and we get none.'

'We're the vestal virgins of American literature,' the Harvard man said. 'Maintained off to one side in untouched sanctity, to bestow validation when required.'

A professor from Lafayette, in neighboring Easton, said: 'But you've made your poetry so precious the ordinary reader has no chance of comprehending it. The difference between you and the nineteenth-century poets you seem to scorn is tremendous—an unbridgeable gap.'

This spurred the M.I.T. woman to go to the heart of the matter: 'If one were capable of estimating the cultural, moral and political influence of poets, one would probably find, the world over, that poets living today enjoy a greater influence than at any time since the days of those great poets of ancient Greece and Rome.'

There was such a murmur of objection to this that she raised her right hand, palm out, in a pacifying gesture: 'Now, wait. Look at the role of the poet in Russia, in the Latin countries, in Europe generally, except England. Look at who wins the Nobel Prize in literature— half are poets because judges who really understand the world know that singers are inherently more valuable to society than people who mumble in prose.'

Such vigorous debate followed this declaration of war that the woman withdrew temporarily, but when the storm had subsided somewhat, she came back forcefully: 'I do believe there is a hierarchy of values. Novelist A of only modest competence may sell a hundred thousand copies of his latest piece of nonsense, all air and no substance, but the intellectual and social values of each of his readers may have an index toward the bottom of the list—say, two. Poet B, one of the ablest in the world, may acquire only a thousand readers, but the index figure of his typical reader may be two hundred fifty. So while the novelist has a total influence on his society of two hundred thousand because of his enormous popularity, the quiet poet will have an influence of two hundred fifty thousand because of the relevant things he says to the relevant people.'

'What do you mean by *the relevant people*?'

'Those legislators who write the laws, the political leaders who set the agendas, the clergymen who define and defend the moral codes, the professors, the editors, the village philosophers, the heads of our great corporations, our military leaders and all those who, on their own account, strive to make a positive difference in the world. Those are the relevant ones, the ones whom we poets address.'

'Only one in a hundred of that gang reads modern poetry,' a gruff-voiced man claimed, and the woman snapped back: 'But he's the one who makes the difference. For the human mind cannot improve unless it sings.'

The Harvard man said: 'In the next century novelists will find themselves where we are now. Can't you see it coming? Television will replace the novel, that's for sure, and it will be so bad that no one will waste his mind upon it, supposing there's any mind left. Novelists in 2084 will be traveling from one university or perhaps from one monastery to the next, because at the rate universities are drifting downward they'll be no better than glorified shopping centers—'

He was not allowed to finish his analogy because a distinguished-looking woman in the audience, a Mrs. Garland, who sat on the board of our college, interrupted rather forcefully: 'Do you mean that if I were still alive I wouldn't be reading good novels as they appeared? Unthinkable!'

Very calmly the Harvard man said: 'Let's not go forward a century, let's go back. You're in Concord, Mass., and Ralph Waldo Emerson is lecturing and he says: "I can foresee the day a century from now when no one will be reading poetry. They'll be reading only turgid novels like those of my friend Hawthorne." And you would have risen to your feet and cried: "Unthinkable!" Well, it's happened, and poor poets like Miss Albertson and me tour the provinces like the scops of old.'

'What's a scop?'

'Thanks for asking. It means troubadour. I do love words that allow me to show off. That's what a poet is—a word show-off.'

Neither he nor the woman would back down from their basic prediction as summarized by the man: 'Within the century the job of the novelist will be not to entertain the masses but to communicate with his or her peers on ever higher intellectual levels—to keep the national culture vigorously alive.'

It had been an electric evening, and when it ended, Yoder, in attendance as usual, maneuvered rather aggressively, I thought, so that he could grasp me by the arm: 'A remarkable evening! Six new ideas a minute.'

'I heard it years ago from Devlan.'

Yoder smiled: 'So down I go and up they go,' pointing to the visitors from Boston.

'But remember, they said the novel doesn't disappear until 2084. You've got a hundred good years, and the way you're going, Mr. Yoder—'

'Please call me Lukas, because we are landsmen.' He pronounced this in Yiddish style, *lahntz-m'n*, suggesting much to my displeasure that we were two rural bumpkins from the same farming district in Poland. Failing to see my irritation, he burbled on: 'Last year on television we proved that critics and novelists can work together.' Then he added: 'And I heard from one of your students that you may soon be published as a novelist. Then we really will be landsmen.'

Aware that I must say something to terminate this unwelcome conversation, I said, somewhat coldly I must confess: 'I hope I can do half as well with the short novel I'm trying to write as you do with your long ones,' and I left him, for I wanted to explore further with the two poets their concept of writing for the elite.

But I refrained from approaching them because they were in a corner talking animatedly with a sixteen-year-old high school student, one of the most remarkable youths I had ever seen. Not only was he conversing with the poets on their own level, comprehending all they had to say and asking questions that challenged their remarks, but he was almost unjustly handsome, with a beautifully modeled face that had yet to be shaved, black wavy hair, an infectious smile and a graceful bearing that showed to advantage in an expensive suit. 'How unfair!' I whispered to myself. 'All that and the ability to express himself, too.' I stood transfixed, comparing him at sixteen with the ungainly, tongue-tied lad I had been, and I wondered why he was so lucky.

Hoping to learn more about him, I elbowed my way into the group but was ignored. The poets had obviously classified him as one of their elite and they did not wish to waste their time on others. But I would not accept the dismissal, I even edged myself closer to the boy and heard him say in a voice that had only recently changed: 'I like Yeats and Eliot better than I do Frost,' and one of the poets said: 'Young intellectuals always do, but as they grow older they discover sweet merit in Frost.' And the group dispersed, with me knowing nothing about the boy but feeling that his aura would remain with me for a long time.

The final speaker I sponsored in that memorable winter was the woman to whom I was so deeply indebted and for whom I had growing respect. Editors and agents in New York, always on the search for talent, had formed the profitable habit of visiting schools of writing, paying their own way and accepting no fees, in order to meet the professors of writing like me and our abler students. They gave fascinating talks on the writing trade and their roles in it, and many students told me that such sessions were among the most rewarding I set up.

My visitor was Ms. Yvonne Marmelle, and her reputation had been so enhanced by her editorship of Yoder's novels that the auditorium was crammed with students and would-be writers. She spoke with an uncanny sense of what my young people would want to know, but during the long question-and-answer period the older townspeople ran away with the evening. A professor from nearby Lehigh University asked: 'Is there anything to the rumor that Kinetic may be bought by the big German publisher Kastle of Hamburg?'

Ms. Marmelle, indicating by a shrug of her shoulders that it would be improper for a member of Kinetic to answer that question, passed it along to another professor, who said: 'One would be foolhardy to discuss what those energetic German houses like Kastle and the English one with the weird name, Spider, might be up to. With the American dollar so low and the German mark so high, anything seems possible, and I've been warned that two or even three major American companies, one of them a paperback house, might find themselves with German owners.'

The knowledgeable questioner was persistent: 'Would Ms. Marmelle, as an executive at Kinetic, care to elaborate?'

'I only know what I read in the papers,' she said and the audience laughed. She added: 'And the papers have been saying for years that we were on the block. Regardless of who owns us, we still operate editorially as if we were independent and, if I do say so myself, we're one of the best.' Applause was dampened by another professor: 'You can laugh, but the threat is real. As you know, when Kinetic was a privately owned company, it was sold to Rockland Oil, the huge conglomerate. They soon tired of it and put it on the auction block. I understand that numerous potential buyers have nibbled at the bait, among them one of the Australian billionaires and a Japanese multinational. Is it not likely that Kastle might jump in with a quick sure-money bid and walk off with the company?'

Discussion then turned to what such radical changes might entail, and Ms. Marmelle said: 'Life in the home offices, the editorial ones, at least, would probably continue untrammeled.' But a speaker warned: 'We'd better be prepared to see substantial changes in our nation's intellectual life, because some of our great publishing houses are almost certain to be purchased by either a German, an Australian or a Japanese conglomerate.'

The questions then became more concerned with the editorial than with the managerial, and several people wanted to know whether there were any editors left who took the same care with their authors that Maxwell Perkins took with his. Somewhat to my distaste, for he was hogging the show, Lukas Yoder rose to say: 'I can testify that Ms. Marmelle is such a reincarnation. I owe most of my good luck to her.' This brought such loud applause that I felt I must, to divert attention from Yoder, make a similar speech: 'Ms. Marmelle sought me out and gave me such excellent counsel on my first book of criticism that it became a modest best-seller. I shall expect the same favors from her on my novel.' At this public revelation that I was working on a novel, the audience applauded just as loudly as it had when Yoder finished.

At the conclusion of her talk so many listeners clustered about to pepper Yvonne with questions that she held up her hands: 'Please. If you are so concerned about publishing, I suggest you join me in the lounge at the Dresden China, where we can chat comfortably,' When half a dozen professors from surrounding colleges indicated that they wished to talk further, she said with a relaxed smile: 'I invite all of you. Beer and pretzels, Pennsylvania Dutch style, in honor of my two Dutch authors, Yoder and Streibert.'

As we gathered in her corner by the Meissen ware, the questioning became pointed, with a professor from Franklin and Marshall setting the tone: 'Most of us in this group dream of publishing one of these days. And with a strong house like Kinetic. What would it mean to our chances if Kinetic were sold to a German house?'

She was frank: 'Since we are now out of public hearing, I can say that Kinetic's being kicked around like a football. I'm sure you know that Rockland Oil is finding that running a publishing company is far less glamorous than they thought. The meager seven percent per annum we return on their investment is far below the thirty-five percent they can hope for in what they call the go-go companies they own like oil and fast foods. Frankly, they're trying desperately to get rid of us. They'd sell us to anyone with cash.'

'Would the German buyer, if it turns out that way, keep Kinetic pretty much as it is now?'

She laughed: 'Some years ago a financial writer for *The New York Times* produced an informative book, *Welcome to the Conglomerate, You're Fired*. The new owner always promises "absolutely no changes," and three months later you're out on your keister.'

'But what does that mean to us?'

'You'll have exactly the same chance of landing a contract with Kinetic as you do now—for those same three months. Then they'll start cutting back on scholarly books like the kind you would probably want to write. With the new owners, your chances diminish, because all they'll be looking at is the bottom line.'

'Will they edit books toward a pro-German slant?'

'Heavens, no! They wouldn't be so stupid. You must remember, they'll also own firms in England and France. They couldn't afford to imperil their own business.'

Mrs. Yoder, who had accompanied her husband, astonished us by the depth of her business knowledge: 'Most of my husband's royalties are in escrow. Will they be safe under foreign ownership?'

'Your money is safe, but I must confess my job isn't.'

'Why not?' Emma asked, and Ms. Marmelle replied with a low chuckle: 'If the new owner has a lady friend who's always wanted to be an editor, I become expendable.'

'I would not be happy writing for a foreign company,' Yoder said, and the rest of us agreed.

———

I had now spent five full academic years at the college, and had published a second book of literary criticism. I continued to labor on a short novel. And during each of the previous summer vacations I had sped to Greece, two days after turning in my last grades. There, at the same congenial hotel in Athens, I would find F.X.M. Devlan waiting to resume our interminable discussions as we motored through the mountains of that endlessly fascinating country. One summer we had concentrated on the Peloponnesus, that forbidding land containing Corinth, Sparta and Patras; it had many sites associated with pre-Roman days and I delighted in old inns and mountain villages that rarely saw foreigners. We always felt vibrant in Greece, for it had been during our first visit here that we had realized that our mutual affection was more than a passing fancy nurtured by the magic of Venice, that we spoke and lived the same language, and that one was as concerned about the nature of writing as the other. To return to Greece was to return to first principles.

In the summer of 1983 Devlan surprised me on the afternoon we met in Athens by suggesting that we first go not to our familiar hotel but to an olive grove beyond the edge of the city. There he took out a paperback collection of Henry James's short novels and turned to the page on which the narrator, a stuffy young scholar, is trying with every ugly device to gain possession of the love letters of the dead American poet Jeffrey Aspern. Since they are being guarded by an old woman in Venice, he realizes that he can gain access to them only if he marries her pitiful, ungainly niece. The impasse is hammered home when the awkward niece proposes to him. Devlan, in the same low voice he had used in Venice when we first shared the ending together, said:

> 'Miss Tina, not knowing how one proposes marriage to a
> man, blurts out that if he were to become part of the family,
> he could gain access to the letters: "You could see the

things—you could use them." Then comes the terrible confusion, which she worsens by bursting into a flood of tears and pressing her proposal: "I'd give you everything, and she'd understand, where she is—she'd forgive me." '

Devlan's voice broke and he indicated that I should complete the story, so I took the book and read how the man rejected her:

' "I didn't know what to do, as I say, but at a venture I made a wild vague movement in consequence of which I found myself at the door. I remember standing there and saying, 'It wouldn't do, it wouldn't do!'—saying it pensively, awkwardly, grotesquely. . . . The next thing I remember is that I was downstairs and out of the house." '

Devlan, once more in control of himself, took back the book, and holding it in his lap to consult now and then, said: 'I have so wanted to make a point, Karl, to you and to everyone. This is what we struggle for when we write.' And he told of the young American's return next day with the tentative thought that he might indeed wed the spinster in order to obtain the precious letters. Skipping through the tense, beautifully written pages, he read aloud, in a voice trembling with emotion, the telling passage:

' "She stood in the middle of the room with a face of mildness, and her look of forgiveness, of absolution, made her angelic. It beautified her; she was younger; she was not a ridiculous old woman . . . this magic of her spirit transfigured her, and while I still noted it I heard a whisper somewhere in the depths of my conscience: 'Why not, after all—why not?' It seemed to me I *could* pay the price." '

Looking away from the book, he said with a powerful sense of self-identification: 'So he decides that he can marry her. The letters are worth it. And now, Karl, I want you to see with what exquisite skill James ends his story.' And he resumed reading:

' "Are you going today?" she asked. "But it doesn't matter, for wherever you go I shall not see you again. I don't want to." . . .

' "What shall you do—where shall you go?" I asked.

' "Oh, I don't know. I've done the great thing. I've destroyed the papers."

' "Destroyed them?" I wailed.

' "Yes; what was I to keep them for? I burnt them last night, one by one, in the kitchen."

' "One by one?" I coldly echoed it.

' "It took a long time—there were so many." The room seemed to go round me as she said this and a real darkness for a moment descended on my eyes. When it passed, Miss Tina . . . said: "I can't stay with you longer, I can't," and . . . she turned her back upon me, as I had turned mine upon her twenty-four hours before. . . .

'I wrote her that I had sold the picture, but I admitted to Mrs Prest . . . that it hangs above my writing table. When I look at it I can scarcely bear my loss—I mean of the precious papers.'

Devlan closed the book gently, but with such finality, as if a decision of great moment had been reached, one that tore at his heart, the way

Miss Tina's heart must have been wounded when the young man fled in horror from her proposal of marriage, that I had to ask: 'Devlan, what is it?'

'The end of the story.'

'But why did you read it? What does it signify?'

'I wanted to remind you, Karl, that the ending of *Aspern* is what we seek when we write. To fill a throbbing moment with revelation, with meaning, human passion.'

'Why are you telling me this?'

'Because your second book of criticism was shockingly mechanical. It had none of the flashes of insight that the first book had. You praised only works of competent organization and the marshaling of ideas, never those that are sharply perceptive or lay bare the seeds of passion.' Before I could interrupt, he walked away, then looked back like a playful leprechaun: 'You can accuse us Irish of many faults, but never a lack of passion. A wind off the sea, it can drive a homebound man crazy, or the memory of a beautiful child lost on the edge of a moor.'

'Devlan!' I said harshly, 'you didn't bring me to this olive grove to lecture me on Irish sensibilities. What is it, dear friend?'

Taken aback by the directness of my question, Devlan tried to form a reply, failed, and reached out curiously with his right hand as if to grab a pillar for support. While he continued to mouth unspoken words, he looked at me so pathetically that I cried: 'Michael! Are you having an attack?'

Shaking his head, he whispered as he sought a wayside stone on which to sit: 'I am indeed having an attack, my dearest friend, an attack of the worst sorrow a man can know.'

'What is it?' The fearful question betrayed the intense love I felt for one who had unlocked both my mind and my heart.

Suddenly Devlan, fifty-one years old that summer, looked up as if stricken, and said: 'The great pain assailed me before I ever left

Oxford, for I realized that I was coming to Greece to say farewell to the most precious thing in my life . . . to the one who gave me new vitality . . . and inspiration.'

'Michael!' Never before had I used Devlan's third name, and now I had spoken it twice within the minute.

Neither of us spoke for some moments, then Devlan reached out and drew me down onto the rock beside him. Pushing the hair back from my forehead, he said: 'Dearest friend, we must no longer see each other in Greece during the summer, when olives are ripe and ouzo flows. A terrible thing has happened that brings an end to Aeschylus under the stars.'

'What?' My voice was dry.

'A young man, as brilliant at Oxford as you were at Columbia, went at my urging for a year at Harvard. While there he excelled, of course, for I have always been able to spot true talent, you remember. But he also fell carelessly into contact with an assistant professor on leave from California—his teacher . . . you know how those things can happen.'

'And?'

'The Californian had the new disease, he had AIDS.'

'And?'

'He gave it to my prize scholar. We'd never heard of a case at Oxford, but here it was. The doctors were positive, experts came distances to study his condition.'

'Did he die?'

'Yes.'

'And you were so attached to him that you were desolate . . . still are?'

'I was, but no longer. While he knew damned well that he was afflicted, he continued to live with me on long weekends, and it was not until four days before he died that he told me.'

'And you . . .' I could not frame the words.

'Yes. The same great experts tried to track down everyone Peter might have contaminated. Karl, there were nearly a dozen, proof positive that he had been with them. When they found me, through reports of his landlady and two of the young men to whom he had mentioned my name . . .' He winced: 'I believe he told shameful jokes about me.' He shrugged: 'Well, these great experts who had proved to their satisfaction what had killed Peter looked at me with scorn and loathing. My age, my reputation, but most of all my position teaching the young. I think they were pleased to find me infected. And to inform me—a group of three staring at me with repugnance—that I would probably soon be dead, and for God's sake infect no one further in this daisy chain, as they termed it. . . .'

We two scholars, there in the countryside of Greece, sat silent among the olive trees watching peasants tilling a distant field. Then Devlan asked: 'Didn't you think it strange, Karl, that I was reserved when we met?'

'Yes.'

'When I saw you, my heart shattered. Finest student I ever had, England or America, my dearest companion, and I must never lie with him, for if I did, I would bring him certain death.'

'And you? What timetable?'

'Who knows? You must have noticed that I've lost weight. They tell me it'll go down, down, until the day when I'll look my very best, what I ought to weigh. However, that's the critical point, because I'll keep going down until I grow so weak that even a bad cold could be so perilous that it could sweep me away. And if it doesn't, something else . . .'

'Oh, my God!' I whispered.

'And that's why this has to be our farewell summer. I won't be able to travel next year, and when I think of the cruel thing Peter did to me, I could not conceivably do it to someone else—above all, not to you.'

'I want to go back to our hotel, Michael. To where we knew such happiness. I want to take you to some play that will be as profound an experience as *Agamemnon* was, to see those silver temples once more in the moonlight. But most of all, I want to talk with you. I've always valued your advice so, and now I need you to help me find out what's wrong with the novel I'm trying to write. You're a precious man, Michael, and I cannot let you go before you've shared more of your secrets.'

When we reached our hotel, Devlan slept for two days, for although travel had been relatively easy, he was exhausted, debilitated by his nagging illness. He was afraid to consult a doctor lest he be deported from Greece as a health hazard, a decision he said he would approve were he a Greek official; but with rest he did recover almost normal strength and was eager for the regimen I proposed. We took short trips out into the countryside and enjoyed picnics on historic sites six days out of seven. A Greek company was performing *Antigone*, which gave me an opportunity to compare Aeschylus and Sophocles. Having seen the monumental greatness of the former, I was at first disappointed in Sophocles, but as the torment of Antigone intensified under her uncle Creon's persecution the multiple glories of the Greek stage became manifest: the variety, the sweep, the power, and always the magnificence of the language. It was enormously moving—and a humbling experience for anyone presuming to create a world of the imagination, as I was.

My novel had not been going well, a disappointment I discussed with Devlan when the commanding preoccupation with death had receded: 'I didn't want to tell you sooner—didn't think it proper to bother you, but that novel I spoke about last summer, it's not doing what I'd hoped. I have such a clear vision of the end, but only a muddy concept of how to get there.' Before Devlan could respond, I added: 'Oh, I've got the characters—rather good ones, I must say—but how to present them and allow them to disclose their purposes seems quite beyond my powers. What to do?'

'When we last spoke you were undecided on the main thrust. Is that settled?'

'I've had in mind an American equivalent of *Marius the Epicurean*. I've wanted to do for contemporary America what Pater did for the age of Marcus Aurelius.'

'Isn't Pater a bit ethereal for raw American tastes?'

'In the original, yes, and in the Roman setting, but I'm placing mine in a big private university in New York City, something like N.Y.U., not Columbia. It gives me a fine setting, Edith Wharton's Washington Square, and some very real professors of strong character.'

'Got a title?'

'Working title, *The Empty Cistern*, basically your idea that popular art inevitably sinks to the lowest common denominator, leaving an empty cistern from which society tries in vain to draw its life-sustaining water. And a very strong support for your idea that the novel must become a dialogue between peers. My heroine could be Virginia Woolf, one of my principal movers Thomas Pynchon. But all very American, very contemporary.'

After contemplating what I had said, Devlan mused out loud: 'The basic image, not bad at all. Ideas that need to be ventilated. Yes, yes. But how do you objectify abstractions? Very dangerous terrain. One in a thousand is able to do it, and failures invariably read like Charles Morgan's *The Fountain*, impressive at first for their tenuous gentility, but in the end quite boring. The Irish had the right idea, even Bernard Shaw. Not lords and ladies but men and women who had to work for a living. I'd be more at ease, Karl, if it weren't N.Y.U. professors but farmers and small tradesmen in your own Dutch background, that splendid country you showed me on our two trips inland from New York.'

'Lukas Yoder has preempted my Dutch heritage. Writes his silly, empty books glorifying the Mennonites, offering hardly one word of truth about them. I'm very tired of that fellow but I'm afraid to show it at home lest I be accused of envy—that he's done it and I haven't.'

'*Are* you envious?'

'Of his success, yes. Of how he earned it, no—no. He's an empty windbag, and besides, you and I are talking about the elite, those capable of sustaining the life-giving dialogue.'

'I'd correct that, Karl. We're *thinking* about the elite, but we're *writing* about ordinary people whose native intelligence makes them the elite. There's a vast difference, which the best of the Irish playwrights always understood.'

We spent days dissecting my proposed novel—I did not confess that it was three-fourths finished and not at all what I had hoped for—and Devlan returned constantly to his warning to all would-be novelists: 'Get the characters lined up first, and make them real. Then have them move through the intricacies of plot and idea. Allow people to uncover the great truths upon which fiction rests, and from what you've been telling me, Karl, you're not doing that. You're putting your ideas, your message, first.'

After I had done my best to reassure him, as if I were again his student, he said: 'I'm not entirely secure about you, as a very fine critic, trying to write a novel. Requirements for the two tasks are quite different, you know, maybe incompatible.'

I argued back, as if defending my thesis before a doctoral panel: 'What about the two men you so frequently cite? Forster and James? Excellent novelists and quite acceptable critics, don't you agree?'

'Ah, but what a significant difference! Each of them proved first that he was a damned good novelist, then reflected later in life on what had made him good. Highly personal criticism, not at all the kind that I desire to specialize in. Quite unformed and undisciplined, really. Little more than ruminations beside a tankard of ale toward midnight.'

Devlan suggested many devices whereby my Pater-like novel

could be made acceptable, if indeed it had gotten off the track, which he suspected mine had. But everything he said had greater relevance to my literary criticism than to my novel. In other words, Devlan the critic could speak directly to me the critic, but he was powerless to communicate with me the novelist or perhaps I was unable to listen. And after our last prolonged talk I heard him muttering to himself: 'I'm afraid he won't make it. Didn't take in a word I said.'

One night after Devlan's revelations about AIDS, he had said as we ascended to our hotel room: 'I could take another room, you know, if you have fears.'

'Oh, Michael! I think God must have sent me here to care for you. I had thought, there for a while, that I should miss Greece this year. Stay home and polish off my novel. But something dragged me, some arcane force that I didn't fully understand. Now I do.' When we reached our room I cried impulsively: 'Michael, always remember that you found me a green boy in New York and by force of your personality and wisdom alone you converted me into a man in Athens. *American Fiction* is your book, as transcribed by a dutiful amanuensis.' After we had unpacked our traveling gear, never to be used again in companionship, I said: 'If you were to quit this room tonight, my heart would cry out with anguish,' and the subject was not mentioned again.

But there were moments of cruel pain, as when Devlan came naked from the bath to reveal unintentionally how much weight he had lost, and before he could cover himself with a towel it was made brutally clear that he had not only dropped to the ideal weight for a man of his height, but had continued to fall dangerously below it. If he maintained this precipitous descent, we both realized that the day would be at hand when even the slightest fever or infection would signal his death. We showed increasing tenderness toward each other, with any potentially disruptive subject like my novel avoided. We returned again and again to his basic theme, that novelists were obligated to maintain the exalted discourse that had always been maintained among the few since mankind first recorded its thoughts. 'We're the high priests of an increasingly pagan world, and we must keep the flame of intelligence alive. How many men in Florence comprehended what Dante was about? How many in Poland understood Copernicus? And look what the canaille did to Darwin!'

In the last week we walked slowly about the streets and monuments of Athens, savoring each familiar scene, both aware that this must be the last time we would ever see the radiant city together, or even apart, for I could not imagine returning here without him. Occasionally visitors to the city would pause to look at us as we passed—tall red-headed American and frail Irishman with the Julius Caesar haircut touching his eyebrows—and they would speculate as to who we were, but none came even close to guessing the powerful bond that held us together.

On what we knew would be the last night in our companionship we sat in a park where, with the aid of a rather dim streetlight, we read passages from *Agamemnon*. I interrupted the reading: 'Have I ever told you what I've done on the wall of my classroom?' And as I described the mural that outlined the deplorable behavior of the Atreus gang, as I called them, we irreverently laughed at the enormity of the actions that had led to such overwhelming tragedy. In the midst of our lighthearted talk, Devlan suddenly pressed his hands to his face and whispered: 'Oh, Karl! You must believe that Peter meant nothing to me—he was just a promising boy, that's all. We had a meaningless affair—you were away so long—and now this terrible penalty.'

In an attempt to console him and convince him of my deep love I added: 'You will be with me always, Michael. When I recall your puckish face, I will always be reminded of Shakespeare and Yeats, and we will forever be together.'

In the morning Devlan rose, shaved carefully to avoid cutting himself lest he infect me accidentally, and headed for the airport. In our previous departures it had always been I who flew out first, as if Athens belonged to him, but now, with all sense of proprietorship gone, he wanted to hurry home and prepare himself for death—in the way that great elephants are known to retreat to their cave when they feel the end approaching.

Upon my return to Mecklenberg for the fall semester of 1985 I participated in an unfortunate affair that sharply terminated my courteous relationship with Lukas Yoder. I had invited to the college's autumn poetry fest a fine young man from the University of Chicago who had published some strong poems in various little journals and whose reputation had grown so that he seemed assured of one of the next Pulitzer prizes, especially if he could somehow get a hardcover publisher to bring out a collection of his work. This would encourage the important journals to review him as a serious poet, which they refused to do so long as he had only occasional publication in fugitive magazines. 'We cannot be sure he'll build a permanent reputation among the poets,' the editors said, 'until he gets it together.' The last phrase meant: 'Until he manages a hardcover publication.'

His name was Heintz Bogulov, and he not only wrote good poetry but also displayed a raffish sense of humor, and when in the question period a woman asked what young men like him thought of the established poets like Longfellow, he used her as a springboard for savage burlesques of Longfellow's better-known lines: 'Tell me not in mournful slumbers' and 'Lives of bankers all remind us they have made their dough in crime' and 'When the G-men come to find us, in the clinker doing time,' and the risqué one: 'Let us then be up and screwing with a heart for any mate.'

When the first waves of laughter subsided, Bogulov moved as far forward on the stage as possible, adopted an orator's pose and recited with growing speed and mussiness of pronunciation his improvised version of the hilarious parody 'Hiawatha's Mittens,' set to the tongue-twisting rhymes and rhythms of Longfellow's poem. He broke up the audience with lines like this: 'Made them with the outside inside, made them with the skinside outside, never with the skinside inside, never with the furside outside, always with the furside her side.' At the conclusion of the hilarious jumble, and with his mouth awry as he tried to manage the various inside-skinsides he stopped abruptly and told the woman: 'That's what a modern poet thinks of your boy Longfellow.'

From the back of the room a small gentlemen in his sixties rose and began speaking in a clear voice that masked the emotion he felt. Since it was Lukas Yoder, whose latest best-seller, *The Creamery*, had leaped to the top of the lists, people wanted to hear how he would react to the buffoonery: 'We've had a delightful few minutes just now lampooning a poet who enjoyed a favorable reputation in the last century, and I agree with you that he is outmoded by today's standards, for he wrote poems that could be enjoyed, recited and shared, which our modern poets apparently can no longer do.' This insult to modern poets and their poetry caused a rumble of protest, but Yoder plunged ahead: 'I would remind you that Longfellow also wrote one of the finest single phrases in all of poetry: "Ships that pass in the night and speak each other in passing." Now, since most of us won't know *that* Longfellow, I'll admit that the next three lines fall apart, burdened as they are with his usual sentimentality:

' "Only a signal shown and a distant voice in the darkness;
So on the ocean of life we pass and speak one another,
Only a look and a voice; then darkness again and silence."

'As they say, "He should of quit when he was ahead," but he didn't. He never knew when to stop, always had to tack on his sentimental moral. But with his opening line he penned one that will live forever, and I doubt if there is any one of us in this room tonight who will do the same, so it does not behoove us to ridicule the silly old man. He was not always silly.'

With that he left his place, crawled noisily over the intervening seats, took his wife by the hand, and stalked from the hall. When many of the older people in the hall applauded his gesture, I felt that as chairman I must protect our visiting poet and, red in the face, I leaped to my feet and would probably have made an ass of myself had not Bogulov moved forward on the stage, saluted Yoder's back as the latter stormed away and said blandly: *'Chacun à son goût.'* Those in the audience who understood French chuckled, and soon the audience was applauding the adroit manner in which the poet had defused the tense situation. I was not among those who clapped, for I was staring at the spot from which Yoder and his little wife, Emma, had vanished. This disruption of my carefully planned poetry session was the act that broke the camel's back; from here on Yoder and I were enemies, for I saw in him every meretricious trick against which Devlan had inveighed.

Because I sought always to be forthright about my literary judgments, I prepared for the next issue of our college's paper, *The Martin Luther*, a short summary of what had transpired at the poetry session:

Last Friday at Alumni Hall I was honored to serve as chairman of the latest in our series of poetry readings and I had the pleasure of introducing one of our nation's finest young poets, Heintz Bogulov of the University of Chicago. Like most modern poets, he has a poor opinion of America's revered but inconsequential poets of the last century. Quite properly, in my judgment, he dealt humorously with many of Longfellow's pomposities and catchpenny moralizings.

A local novelist of some reputation, and a graduate of our college, felt constrained to rebuke Bogulov and to cite as Longfellow's claim to immortality one line from the poet's complete oeuvre:

Ships that pass in the night and speak each other in passing . . .

then making the extraordinary plea that this line, which does have merit, justifies considering Longfellow a real poet.

The evening ended too abruptly for me to rebuke the novelist's fatuous argument, but since many students may have taken his reasoning seriously, let me affirm now that not many thinking persons in this country take Henry Wadsworth Longfellow seriously. He was a poetaster, not a poet.

Karl Streibert
Professor of English

My declaration of war had been issued publicly, and I intended to abide by it.

My animosity toward Yoder had no time to fester, however, because an unexpected phone call diverted my attention to one of the most rewarding aspects of teaching, the enrollment of a gifted student worthy of special attention because of demonstrated skills. The summons came from President Rossiter, who said: 'Meet me in the Regents Room. We have a shot at an extremely bright young man.'

When I reached the well-appointed room reserved for the elder statesmen who ran the college and ensured its funding, I found Rossiter, an avuncular, handsomely dressed executive type in his early fifties, bubbling with excitement: 'Jane Garland, powerhouse on our board, said she wanted to see you personally.'

This surprised me, for although I was aware that Mrs. Garland, the wealthy widow of a former chief executive of a steel company, retained an interest in the college and a mansion some miles to the west, I had no reason to suspect that she had ever heard of me. 'She's tremendously important to us, Streibert. You must accommodate her if it's humanly possible. She controls a considerable fortune, and while she's been generous with her aid in the past, the bulk of her wealth is still unassigned. What's best, she's a delightful person to be with—extremely sharp.'

Before I could respond, the door pushed open with a purposeful snap and a stately woman in her late sixties entered briskly, her blue-silver hair neatly coiffed, her trim semibusiness suit impeccable. Her smile was warm and generous, not a polite smirk, and, with a nod to the president, she moved directly to me, extended her hand and said: 'I'm Jane Garland, and welcome to the room I call my second home. Could you promote something for us to drink, Norman? Let's not have this a formal affair.'

I had been so attentive to this imposing woman that I was not aware that something was brushing my leg, but when I looked down I saw a tan-colored Labrador, whose big eyes were staring into mine. 'That's Xerxes,' Mrs. Garland was saying. 'Gentle as a butterfly, and this is the reason for our visit, my grandson Timothy. It's his dog and I warned against bringing him.'

As soon as I looked at the boy I remembered him as the mesmerizing lad who had commanded the attention of the poets from Boston and the same electricity now emanated from him. I thought: How wonderful to see him again, and this time to be able to speak with him: 'I remember you. You're the fellow who preferred Eliot to Frost.' He obviously had no recollection of me, but he did nod politely. A strand of black hair had dropped across his forehead and his piercing blue eyes glinted as he looked about the room, trying to judge it and its occupants. He was neither excessively shy nor ill at ease and my first reaction was: 'This one is keen,' an assessment that would be verified as the meeting progressed. When cola drinks were served, Mrs. Garland said: 'Let's find comfortable seats,' and as young Tull slid into his, with Xerxes at his side, she added: 'President Rossiter, you may leave us alone. The professor and I want to test each other,' and her bright smile made it easy for Rossiter to withdraw.

As soon as he was gone, she began to speak in crisp, almost hurried sentences, for she had many ideas she wished to explore before deciding whether to place her grandson's future in my hands, but in fairness she wanted me to understand who the Garlands were: 'My husband, Larrimore, was chief executive officer of the largest steel company in the area. He was also chairman of this board of regents and a major supporter of the college football team. That portrait better than anything I can say illustrates the kind of man he was.'

The painting she referred to stood out boldly from other formal likenesses of self-satisfied businessmen in their sixties who so resembled one another that they could have been brothers, which in a sense they had been. Larrimore Garland had elected to have himself portrayed in a steel hat, not posing alone, but in the company of three fellow workmen. It was, said Mrs. Garland, 'the picture of a hands-on guy, which he was.' As she smiled at the portrait she added: 'When he died I was invited to take his place as a regent, but I declined. Membership, yes. Chairmanship, no.' She did not reveal that to honor her husband she had given Mecklenberg four million dollars, which had not been missed from the fortune Larrimore had built up through prudent management of his inheritance and salary.

At one point she asked her grandson to leave us for a while, whereupon he nodded politely, bowed to me, called: 'Here, Xerxes!' and withdrew. 'What a polite young man,' I said, and she laughed: 'You should have seen him two years ago. Candidate for reform school.'

In a burst of the amazing frankness for which she was noted, Mrs.

THE CRITIC

· ·
276

Garland explained: 'My only child, Clara, was a fearful disappointment, bless her rebellious soul. Failed to graduate from my old
school, Vassar, ran away to marry a really worthless fellow from the
mill, Thomas Tull, who was scorned even by his own mother. My
husband and I knew from the start that this sad marriage was
doomed, but even so we were stricken when it ended in a blinding
crash on the Rhenish Road just south of where I live. Both drivers
drunk, all six occupants killed.'

'And you assumed charge of Timothy?'

'Not satisfactorily, but I did. Very bright boy, but headstrong like
his mother. Had two difficult years in the public high school at
Reading, then by the grace of God he transferred to The Hill, a
school in Pottstown, just down the road. You must know its reputation, one of the best. Tough discipline, fine teaching, a good mix for
a lad like Timothy.' At this point she put her fingers to her lips and
gave a loud whistle, whereupon both the boy and Xerxes returned.

'I was telling Professor Streibert of your good years at The Hill,
that's how they like it to be called.' I noticed that Timothy did not
betray the unease that boys his age showed when elders talked about
them. Benignly, Mrs. Garland said: 'In his new school Timothy
snapped to attention and we all learned—Timothy, his masters and
I—that he had unusual ability, especially in the use of words. He was
quickly moved into a class reserved for those who had already passed
their College Boards and were headed for better colleges like the Big
Three, the Little Three or smaller places with respectable reputations
like Haverford and Trinity of Hartford.'

'Did he do well?'

'Timothy, show Professor Streibert the term papers you brought,'
and when I saw them my eyes popped: 'Narrative Devices in Günter
Grass's *The Tin Drum*' and 'Chushingura, Prototype of the Modern
Japanese Corporation.'

'How did you think up such topics?'

'I read a lot, I listen. An article in *Fortune* gave me a hint about the Japanese thing, and that started me digging.'

'But the German novel?'

'Magazines said it was first-rate, *Time* and *Newsweek* both.'

Tapping the two papers, neatly typed, I told Mrs. Garland: 'If these are any good, they'd be exceptional for a college senior.'

'They're very good. I've read them.' Timothy said nothing. She then revealed her reason for having invited me to meet with her: 'Come autumn, Timothy will be nearly seventeen. His exam grades qualify him for college—'

'His emotional, social maturity?'

'Well, there were those potentially ugly incidents at Reading High, weren't there, Timothy?'

He shrugged: 'No significance.'

'But that's what a strong school like The Hill is noted for. Knock some sense into fractious boys—'

'I was never fractious, just inquisitive,' he said, and I thought: Never have I had an interview like this. Either they're both nuts or geniuses. Mrs. Garland, on her part, kept barging ahead with revelations that would have appalled the average teenager, boy or girl: 'The head of the English department, a man with a sharp brain, told me: "I'd not be happy having him plunge into a huge place like the University of Chicago, living by himself in some off-campus rooming house, but since you're on the board at Mecklenberg, and it's only a few miles distant, I'd risk it. Your grandson is ready for college."

' "I'm too involved with Mecklenberg," I told him, and asked if he considered it a good college.

' "It's no Harvard, nor even an Amherst," he said, "but it's quite respectable. And they do have a strong teacher of creative writing. Some of our faculty heard his lectures—good man."

' "Your specific recommendation, please?" I said and he replied: "I'd say go for it." '

Mrs. Garland said: 'So my question to you, Professor Streibert, is: "Will you accept him as a student in your advanced class?" '

I had to clench my fists to keep from shouting 'Will I!' More sedately I said: 'I'd be honored to have a freshman who wrote papers like these.'

When young Tull arrived on campus in the fall of 1985, I decided it would be better for him if I did not take him directly into my advanced writing class but allowed him to fit normally into the college routine. I did keep a watchful eye and was surprised to see that he became almost indistinguishable from the norm: slightly taller than average, clothes a bit more expensive, hair much longer in back than had been allowed at The Hill but not so long as some, and a quiet demeanor that seemed to proclaim: I may not have been a football captain in high school, but I was sixth man on a good tennis team.

With other students he was not shy, but he did not seek companionship during his first semester; what he did was study furiously to see if he could keep pace with others who were somewhat older, and when he quickly satisfied himself that he could not only keep up but excel, he was ready to make his move.

I was astounded by the forms it took. He went out for the tennis team and made the indoor squad. He played a noisy game of touch football, and he attended all the school dances, where I often was one of the chaperones, and performed steps I'd not even seen before. He gave the appearance of a typical Joe College freshman, but this masked his drive for a powerful accomplishment far beyond his years. In the period between semesters in the winter of 1986 he approached me like any student with high marks in English who sought permission to enroll in my advanced writing class, and I conducted the interview as if I had never seen him before. But in a

twenty-minute discussion he displayed such a command of English
and interest in writing that I finally said: 'Of course I remember those
two term papers you shared with me when I met with your grandmother, but we have a requirement that applicants like you must
submit work you've done last semester. So type something up and
let me see it.'

'I don't type, sir. I use a word processor.'

'Do you do much correcting? By pen and ink I mean, on the
printouts?'

'I would never submit a first draft. Sometimes they're pretty
awful.'

'Could I see some of them? Maybe they'll fill the requirement.'

'Yes. I save everything,' and he disappeared for a few minutes to
retrieve a small file of material on which he had recently worked. I
saw that he corrected heavily by hand, then processed it twice. 'He's
already a professional,' I said to myself. 'He could be publishing
within a year, if he has anything to say.'

I told him: 'My class for the winter semester starts Tuesday at ten,
my room, and you're welcome. You understand that you'll be much
the youngest there, and the topics about which the others will be
writing may be out of your reach, but if you want to—'

'I work, Professor Streibert. If I get really interested in things, I
work.'

'And you're interested in becoming a writer?'

'Yes.'

Suddenly I felt a keen desire to know more about this boy and his
unusual skills. 'How did it happen? Your father, your mother, were
they heavy readers?'

'Both basically illiterate. Both killed when I was six. Grandmother
took over and she read to me every night. Not children's books, and
she encouraged me to write my own stories.'

'What kind did you write?'

'Every kind. Whatever kind I heard her read—if I liked it.'

'Do you still have any of those stories?'

'I never throw anything away.'

Accepting that what the boy said was probably true, I asked: 'When you go home next time, could you bring me—'

'I have a box of them in the dorm.'

'From all periods?'

'Yes.'

'Could you let me have three—early, middle, late?'

'I would be honored to have you take the time, sir.'

'Where did you learn to say *sir*?'

'The Hill. Grandmother was afraid I might be getting into trouble in public high school. I wasn't, just experimenting with different things, like motorcycles and word processors. Not studying much. So she sent me to The Hill, and they're pretty strict.'

'Were you on the school paper?'

'I wrote most of it. I'll bring you some copies,' and a few minutes later, when he placed before me three long stories and three copies of the newspaper, I accepted them formally and said: 'I shall read these with considerable care, because if you're as good with words and ideas as you appear'—I looked directly at Tull—'you're going to have a revolutionary time in my class.' I rose, shook hands and said at the door to my office: 'Get your affairs in order, Tim—'

'I don't like that name. Timothy, if you'd be so considerate.'

'Get your papers in order, Timothy, because we shall make a vital test—to see if you really are a writer.'

It was ironic. In the 1986 fall term, after I had declared war on Lukas Yoder, I was thrown into a dramatic confrontation that made me feel more charitable toward him as a person while remaining strongly opposed to his inane style of writing. One morning President Rossiter telephoned me while I was still in my room unshaved: 'I'm going to need you in the Regents Room almost immediately. They asked specifically that you be present at this meeting, but I must say, I don't know why.'

'Who?'

'Lukas Yoder and his wife. They do rise early, I must say!'

I shaved with such nervousness that I nearly cut myself, for I could not imagine why the Yoders would want to see me after that attack I'd made on him in *The Martin Luther*. Had they come to complain to President Rossiter, and was I, judging from the peremptory manner in which he had summoned me to the meeting, in serious trouble? 'Damn the Yoders,' I grumbled, for I had an abiding distaste for meeting my adversaries in public; I much preferred fencing with them through the published word. And this confrontation could become ugly because I'd been told that whereas Lukas himself was mild-mannered, his little wife was a tiger in defense of his reputation, which I had certainly attacked. I did not go optimistically to my early morning meeting.

Fifteen minutes later as President Rossiter and I looked out the window from the Regents Room we saw a sight familiar in the Dresden district. Up the brick footpath strode Mrs. Yoder, small and lively with a strong show of aggressiveness looking back now and then to be sure her husband was tagging along. And there he was, a colorless fellow with a half-smile plodding along, hesitating now and then to look at some bird or flower. Like Rossiter, I could not imagine why they were coming.

When they entered the paneled room I expected at least a coldness, more likely an immediate attack, but to my relief, they greeted me almost warmly: 'Good morning, Professor Streibert. Sorry to roust you out so early.' I breathed more easily.

Mrs. Yoder led the discussion: 'Lukas has had a striking success with his novels since *Hex*, and the officials at Kinetic, especially Ms. Marmelle, his personal editor—'

'Mine and fifty others',' Lukas broke in.

'They believe that he can do two or three more books, if he keeps them in the Grenzler series. The first four are having a rebirth—sensational, they tell us.'

'That must be the most gratifying part,' President Rossiter said, but Emma, who had studied economics at Bryn Mawr, corrected him: 'The most gratifying is a sale of almost a million copies of *The Creamery*, and Ms. Marmelle feels certain his next one will break that record.'

'There will be a next one?'

She reached over to knock her knuckles against wood. 'If he stays healthy,' and Yoder added: 'If we both stay healthy.'

Rossiter said: 'Yes, that would be necessary, wouldn't it? But you Pennsylvania Dutch farmers live forever, thank God.' He could think of nothing to add.

But Emma could, and she did so, boldly: 'We've been thinking. Lukas feels he owes everything to this college, and I agree. So we've decided to share our good fortune with you. We want to tithe, as it were, a share of the rewards he's earned from his past books, a promise of more if his next ones do well.' Before Rossiter could respond she added firmly: 'Of course, you'll understand that a share, not half by any means, will have to go to Bryn Mawr. I did help earn the money.'

'I heard about the years you spent in the Souderton schools,' Rossiter said, smiling at her, and Lukas said: 'Remember I do work at home, and that's demanding of a wife. She's earned half.'

'I don't want half,' she said, 'but women's colleges need funds, too, and I'll see that mine gets some.'

'Admirable idea,' Rossiter said, eager to know what figures they had in mind, but too polite to ask.

At this point I still had no clue as to why I had been invited to this session, and since neither Rossiter nor I knew what size of gift the Yoders were proposing, each of us waited in awkward silence.

Then Emma spoke: 'We've brought you a check, President Rossiter, with the promise of another next year, when we see how things turn out.' She produced it, but kept it in her hand.

When she finally handed it over and he saw the figure, one million dollars, he gasped and cried in honest confusion: 'Goodness me! Lukas, I knew you had affection for the college, but this is staggering.' Then he broke into a nervous laugh: 'No one told me that books sold like that,' and Emma said: 'Most don't. We've been lucky and we know it.'

The Yoders spent half an hour detailing the operating rules governing this gift and those that might follow. Emma did most of the speaking: 'No public notice. Only the regents to know. We don't want our names on anything. And most important of all, it must not be used for buildings, no kind of building. Others can be approached for that, promise them their names across the front.' At last she got to me: 'Our money is for books and all that relates to them—the students who will write them later on, the libraries in which the books are kept. Considering all these aims, we believe that Professor Streibert ought to have a major say in how the income is allocated.'

'Of course!' President Rossiter said. 'He's our resident expert.' Then he added quickly: 'Just as Lukas is our alumni expert.' But then his smile faded, driven off by a question he must, as president of the college, ask: 'There's no bad blood between you, is there? We couldn't sponsor a situation that might explode, to the college's detriment.'

'Oh no!' Yoder said brightly.

'I mean, that public difference of opinion about Longfellow?'

'Academic fencing,' Yoder said. 'Lifeblood of a good college.'

'And the rather forceful letter Professor Streibert wrote to our college paper?'

'I didn't see it,' Yoder said, his Dutch face wreathed in innocence. Mrs. Yoder explained: 'I saw it and I didn't like it, but Lukas tries never to read things written about him, so I didn't show it to him.'

I was staggered. I had thought I was dueling with a significant adversary over a significant point, the nature of poetry, and he wasn't even aware that I had fired. What was even more incredible, as my intellectual foe he was offering me custodianship of one million dollars, as if nothing had ever happened between us. I felt dizzy, and then I realized that this quiet little man really did live off by himself, ignorant of everything that he did not accept as touching him in a significant way. He was a primitive artist, totally self-directed and impervious to criticism. I was awed.

Now he spoke: 'We've drafted a memorandum covering the stipulations my wife has just spelled out. We mean every one of them—we mean them rigidly. Call in a notary and let's notarize this now,' and when the assistant registrar arrived with her ink pad and seal, Yoder placed a white sheet over the body of his letter so that the exciting information could not be read, and the formalities were concluded.

In moral confusion I watched. I had rejected Yoder because he represented the literary standards I despised—popular culture, novels empty of significant content, and a writing style I found boring— yet here he was giving me a million dollars to speed the work in my department. I was too perplexed and ashamed to thank him, but President Rossiter took care of that.

When he and I walked the Yoders to their aged Buick, which few students would care to own, he told them: 'All colleges receive gifts, thank heavens, but rarely so generous in amount and never more generous in spirit.'

'There'll be more,' Emma said, 'if I can keep him at his typewriter,' and as they drove off, the President said to me: 'Streibert, we're giving you a lot of fresh responsibility. Don't foul the nest any more than you already have.'

In 1987 in those nebulous weeks between Thanksgiving and Christmas when nothing substantial seems to get done, Ms. Marmelle took up residence in the Dresden China without any professional reason for doing so; she was on vacation, and for the first time I caught a hint of what was driving this extraordinary woman. Her life in New York had become routinized. Her parents were dead and she had few personal friends, only business associates. What was of considerable importance was that the city had become dangerous for a woman living alone, with the result that by comparison our quiet little town must have seemed a refuge, especially during the holiday season when people seek companionship. In addition, she had two of her writers near the town and, through my recommendation, was about to acquire two more. It was obvious that she'd decided to make Dresden her emotional home.

Her ostensible reason for coming was that Yoder had informed her that he had finished the first draft of his seventh Grenzler novel, a dreary thing called *The Fields*, and suggested that she take a look at it with a view to publication in 1988. Calling me to say that she'd be at the inn with time to see me briefly, she rushed down, hurried out to Yoder's farm, picked up the manuscript and scanned it avidly back in her Meissen-ware corner.

When I found her there reading, she said: 'It's standard Yoder,' adding quickly: 'And very good.'

Then, as if to assure me that I too played a significant role in her plans, she said: 'Your letter about the young man of promise in your class excited me. It's a situation New York editors dream about. A trusted teacher of writing at a good university sends an enthusiastic message: "I believe I've uncovered a really fine writer. Please take a look." ' This time it was I who had sent her the message: 'This lad's only nineteen but he could be the new Truman Capote. Same kind of saucy mind. Please call me the next time you drift this way.'

My wording had been exactly right, a lure to any editor who had

dreamed of spotting the new Gore Vidal or a clone of Françoise
Sagan. As Yvonne had once phrased it: 'To get a real talent
launched, and a fresh one, would be a relief after processing the
predictable schlock ground out by tired hacks in their fifties who
never had anything original to say, before or now.'

I told her: 'His name is Timothy Tull. His grandmother is the
grande dame of these parts, quite wealthy. Her daughter—that is, the
boy's mother—made a horrendously inappropriate marriage to a
nothing named Tull, who sired a son, then killed himself and his wife
in a drunken auto accident. The boy—he and his grandmother will
be here in a moment—was precocious, almost busted out of one
school, excelled in a better, and fell into my hands two years ago. I've
done little to mold him, actually. Totally self-propelled, and to my
astonishment has come up with a completed manuscript, which is
going to startle you. I think it's publishable, right now, but after you
pick yourself up off the floor when you finish reading it and go into
a dead faint, you may say "Not quite yet." ' I halted my first frenzy
of words and said with more restraint: 'But sooner or later, this
boy—'

'You told me how old he was, but I don't remember what else you
said in your letter.'

'Almost twenty.'

'He's eligible. But I always remember the case of the Putnam boy.
Great start in his teens. Fizzled. Same with the young daughter of
the South Seas writer, Frisbie. I'm cautious.'

Before I could add to this portrait of my prize pupil, Timothy Tull
and his grandmother entered the lobby and walked directly to where
Ms. Marmelle and I waited. Timothy introduced himself and his
grandmother and said with no hesitancy or embarrassment: 'It's
rather silly of me, isn't it, to bring my grandmother along? But she
runs things, including me.' I could see that Ms. Marmelle liked him
immediately.

But she was not remotely prepared for Tull's manuscript. It had been elegantly typed on 256 pages of expensive white paper that almost crackled, it was so heavy and costly. The pages were not numbered in any visible way, and appeared with the text in four positions: upside down, sideways, sideways upside down, and in the ordinary right-side-up position. They had been typed in six different typefaces, six different spacings between the lines, with now and then a whole page in italic, another in boldface. They formed a magnificent jumble, each page a complete item in itself, beginning in the middle of an undefined sentence and ending the same way. Most important, they were not arranged in any kind of order. Any one page could fit in anywhere. They were an astonishment and justified the title the young man had given them.

'I call it *Kaleidoscope*,' he said, as if naming a new baby of which he was proud. 'That toy in which fragments of glass and metal at the far end of the tube seem scattered and variable, but as you turn the tube and look at them through the magnifying glass at the near end, they form patterns that can be beautiful.'

'Have you written that description down?' Yvonne asked, and he replied with an airy brush of his hand: 'It's in there somewhere.'

'You hope to be a writer?' she asked, and I interrupted: 'He already is one.'

'I asked Mr. Tull,' Yvonne said, and Timothy replied: 'I'm determined to be one.' And I added: 'And Ms. Marmelle's the one to help you.'

After some polite conversation, the boy and his grandmother took their leave, Timothy smiling at us as they left the room.

I lingered and was sorry I did, for she gave me a shattering report on my recently completed novel: 'Karl, our people have labored over your manuscript and, to put the best face on it, they have doubts about it.' When I just stared at her she hurried on: 'No one likes the title, *The Empty Cistern*, and for a sound reason as Jean pointed out in our editorial session: "It's a temptation for some smartass reviewer to chirp: 'The cistern isn't the only thing that's empty.' " And that kind of snide crack we must avoid.' She had the decency to refrain from telling me what I learned later: it wasn't some fellow editor called Jean she was quoting; she herself had said it.

'What should I do?' I asked in a tremulous voice, for my stomach had constricted into such a knot that I could scarcely breathe. To learn from a knowledgeable editor that my novel, on which I had pinned such exalted hopes, had been deservedly shot down was too painful to accept. She must have seen my distress and did not wish to see my face grow even paler, for she made no reply to my appeal for help. Instead, she twirled her sherry glass: 'What lovely patterns the Bristol Cream makes.'

'What must I do?' I asked, more insistently than before, and again she refused to answer. Instead she said brightly: 'Karl, you and I seem destined to work together on many projects. I think it's time you called me Yvonne. I'd like that.'

I don't know what prompted me to respond as I did, but I blurted out: 'So you've more bad news to deliver?' and she replied with hardly a change of tone: 'You're at a perilous point in your career as a critic when a fall backward would start tongues wagging: "See, he never had it to begin with. Flash in the pan." ' She kept her eyes on me to watch how I accepted the kind of criticism I had the habit of heaping on others.

'You don't believe that, surely?' I asked, almost pleadingly.

'The judgment, no. But that the judgment will be viciously circulated, yes. I advise you to withdraw your novel. Let's make believe Kinetic never saw it.'

In my desperation, I grasped for any support: 'Professor Devlan had great faith in this novel.' This was a lie; Devlan had had serious reservations based on what I had told him. 'And I'd like, in honor of him—'

'You miss him a lot, don't you, Karl?'

'I do. The novel's dedicated to him, as you probably noticed.' I did not tell her that Devlan was dying and that I thought of *Empty Cistern*, which he had inspired, as my final gift to him.

'I did, and had the feeling that you'd be doing him no honor to attach his name to such an incomplete work.'

Her device of using Devlan to support her own judgment was so improper that I tried to calm myself by focusing on a Dresden doll representing a Court of Versailles milkmaid. Then apparently realizing how cataclysmic her report had been to me, she asked softly: 'Karl, what do you propose?'

With a firm voice I said: 'We'll publish it as is,' but as soon as I uttered the words I realized that this was not my decision to make. 'That is, if Kinetic will permit me.'

'With your record, Karl, you have the right to demand publication, and we've agreed to accept your decision.'

'You went so far in your office? To discuss rejecting it?' I was aghast.

'The vote was three to two against. I was one of the two, but since my vote counts triple, it was three against, four in favor. And there it will remain until you decide.'

'I just decided. I could do no less for Devlan. He fathered this book.'

Yvonne was a tough editor, one of the hardest grained in New York, and she had not acquired that reputation by being afraid of her writers, no matter how famous they became. Her motto was: 'If I don't tell them, who will?' In pursuit of that custom she asked a most damaging question: 'I must ask again: Do you really believe that a noted critic like Devlan will want you to attach his name to an amorphous book like yours?'

I must have blushed, for she did a most unexpected thing. Reaching out, she pressed my hand as if I were a child needing reassurance: 'Let's change the subject. I'd like to see what your phenom Tull has accomplished. If he's half as good as you say—'

'Let's not change the subject. I've definitely decided in these last few minutes that I will publish,' and she said quickly: 'Then I'll help, and I wish you a world of . . .' She drew back from finishing with the word *luck*, which would have been demeaning, as if that were the only way of salvaging my manuscript. She had the decency to express her wish as *good fortune*, which sounded more civilized.

But she did want to dig into the Tull manuscript. Putting the box in front of her, she lifted the lid and confronted a collection of 256 pages that bore no numbers; some pages were printed upside down, others sideways on the page. As she shuffled them, taking out four arbitrarily, I said: 'It's a true hodgepodge, but not a chaotic one. It really is a kaleidoscope, which your mind begins to arrange in meaningful patterns.'

'Did you help him devise the plan?'

'Heavens, no! This young fellow does his own devising!'

It was early next morning when my phone at the college rang: 'Karl! Yvonne here. Your boy really has constructed a kaleidoscope, and I'm completely taken with it. The boy's clever. It's intriguing, the way proper names appear arbitrarily and without definition, and the way the rich array of themes comes and goes. It's a bravura performance, and if I can get it properly presented and supported, we could have a big winner.'

'You think Kinetic will want it?'

'It's my job to make them want it. We really must not plod along publishing one Grenzler after another.' She must have realized what an improper thing she had said, for she quickly apologized: 'It was dreadful of me to say that. Forget I did.'

'I shall remember only that you published my novel.'

'Yes. Kinetic's going to publish *Cistern* and *Kaleidoscope*, whether they want to or not.'

purchased by his great-grandfather in the early 1880's and kept thereafter as a work of honor in the family's library den. Scores of visitors during the intervening century had tested the remarkable chair and given enthusiastic testimony to its merits, some spending two or three hours in it, their fundaments at ease, their eyes gratified by the practicality of the attachment, which relieved the tedium of reading heavy books.

In this generation Albertina had made the chair her personal possession, 'her throne,' Dortmund had called it, 'from which she dispensed her obiter dicta.' She smiled at such comment and diverted it by handing anyone interested a one-page sheet on which she had Xeroxed an explanation of the chair, its essential paragraphs reading:

THE MARVELOUS UTILITY OF THIS FAMOUS CHAIR IS A TESTIMONY TO THE FACT THAT ANY HUMAN ACTIVITY TO WHICH RAW HUMAN INTELLIGENCE IS APPLIED HAS A FIGHTING CHANCE OF PRODUCING SOMETHING FINE AND LASTING, AND IF A SENSE OF ART IS ALSO FACTORED IN, THE POSSIBILITIES FOR GOOD RESULTS ARE DOUBLED.

WILLIAM MORRIS (1834-1896), AN ENGLISH POET, ARCHITECT, BUILDER, FURNITURE MAKER AND SOCIAL REFORMER, APPLIED ALL HIS TALENTS TO WHATEVER JOB HE ATTACKED. WHEN HE DESIRED A CHAIR HE LISTED THE CHARACTERISTICS THAT WOULD MAKE IT SUPERIOR. THESE SEEMED TO BE: COMFORTABLE TO THE BUTTOCKS, HENCE THE PADDED CUSHION, RESTFUL TO THE ENTIRE BODY, HENCE THE AMPLE ARMS, AND ADJUSTABLE TO THE MODE EITHER OF LEANING FORWARD INTO ONE'S WORK OR WELL BACKWARD TO REST, HENCE THE MOVABLE BACK WITH A HINGE AT THE BASE, AND ARMS EXTENDED BACKWARD WITH SLOTS SO THAT A CROSS STICK CAN BE MOVED FORWARD OR BACKWARD IN THE SLOTS TO MAKE THE BACK UPRIGHT OR SLANTED TO THE REAR. IT PROVED ONE OF THE BEST CHAIRS EVER MADE.

WHEN THE FIRST MORRIS CHAIR APPEARED, THE PUBLIC APPLAUDED, AND MY GRANDFATHER BOUGHT ONE OF THE EARLIEST, BUT HE QUICKLY SAW THAT AN IMPROVEMENT COULD BE ADDED, ONE THAT MADE IT POSITIVELY IDEAL. HE BUILT ONTO THE LEFT ARM A BROAD DESKLIKE AFFAIR MADE OF OAK, WHICH COULD BE SWUNG ACROSS THE KNEES, BRINGING WITH IT A LECTERN ON WHICH A BOOK COULD BE RESTED, WITH CLAMPS TO HOLD THE PAGES OPEN, WOULD THAT MEN WOULD APPLY SIMILAR INTELLIGENCE AND INVENTIVENESS TO ALL THINGS THEY MAKE.

Sometimes she spent entire days in her chair, books piled beside her as she alternately leaned forward to compose her poems or leaned far back to rest and stare out to sea for the refreshment it brought; occasionally toward the end of a creative day Laura would enter the study to find her mistress sleeping in the laid-back chair as soundly as if she had been tucked into bed.

Albertina said: 'When I die, give this chair to that museum in Doylestown,' but this proposal so enraged Dortmund that he

*the late afternoon heavy with gloom, made more ominous by the howling
of the wind and the whipping of a rope-end against the shingles. But this
was the kind of storm she relished, for as she had told him several times
when they walked together inland toward the glade they had discovered:
'Storms remind me of meaningful blood hammering through my veins,'
and it was during such a storm that they had taken refuge in the shack
under the oak trees and engaged in the tender lovemaking that had now
grown so perilous.*

*As this day's storm increased and she lay back in her chair, watching
the rain beat against the windows, she caught herself wishing that she
might be in that other storm and in the shack with him once more: 'Let
it thunder!' she cried aloud, testing her voice against the tempest.*

*'In playful mood?' came the voice from the hall, and before she could
reply, Dortmund entered, stood before her and asked brutally: 'Is this the
kind of storm you were thinking about when you wrote him this letter?'
and with thumb and forefinger he dangled the gray-colored paper before
her.*

*'Whom did you pay to steal it?' she asked quietly, deftly maneuvering
the backrest so she could sit upright and face him directly, but she had not
completed the shift when he dropped the letter and sprang upon her,
forcing the rest so far backward and with such sudden force that the
guiding staff, more than a century old and the veteran of much use,
shattered with a resounding crack.*

*'Damn you!' she cried, struggling to free herself from his enormous
weight and feeling her arms and legs pinned hopelessly into the chair as
he raised his right fist to smash her in the face as he had done the other
night.*

*'No, by God!' she cried from her helpless position and shifted her
pinioned shoulders at the last moment to avoid the blow to her face.*

*This so infuriated Dortmund that he thrust his left elbow across her
throat and prepared to hammer with great force, but at this moment her
right arm worked free and in its mad fumbling came upon the letter
opener that she kept at hand as she worked. Gripping it firmly, she raised
it as high as she could and with all the force in her imprisoned body
brought it down into the middle of her husband's back. There was a gasp,
a convulsion, and a roar: 'What have you done?' Before she could answer
or exult in her release from imprisonment she fainted, while he remained
unconscious across her body, slowly staining with coagulating blood
his clothes, and hers, and the cushions of the Morris chair in which the*

pulled remorselessly by the tide ever farther from the shore. Between gasps
he caught sight, over his left shoulder as it cleared the waves, of the headland on which Albertina's green cottage stood, and his first taste of panic came
when he was assailed by the wild thought: Will I ever see her again? Fighting

to repress such destructive reactions, he burrowed his head into the waves,
kept the saltwater from his eyes and nostrils, and drove his frantic arms so
powerfully that he could see the cottage growing larger as he progressed toward
the shelving sand on which he would ultimately gain a foothold. But as he began

mentally to exult in that surge of hope, physically he caught a fearful message from
his aching muscles: I'm not going to make it! and dissolution set in, as if all
his muscles and nerve centers had fallen into wild confusion. "Help!" he tried
to shout, but when he opened his mouth a torrent of waves knocked him and his arms

birds from the taller trees swooped down, adding their melodies to the chorus until the entire meadow was swept by song. As the sun rose ever higher above the horizon, bathing the area in a cascade of red-gold light that muted even the greenness of the grasses, he felt a tremendous identification with this secret haven that he and Albertina had discovered and cherished. 'They're doing this for me,' he shouted to the heavens. 'The birds, those noisy frogs, the bending trees, the stars as they say farewell when light attacks them, and even that rolling

sun elbowing all things aside as it strides through the sky. Look at it muscle its way along, telling the shadows where they must fall.' And as he reveled in his proud possession of the glade and watched the trees as they teased the birds back to their bosoms while sun-burst peace descended over the area, he reasoned: I am like that sun. I must rise, dispel the night, bring order to this meadow, and build a refuge here for Albertina. Lure her away from that lonely headland and the turbulent sea. The sun controls life, not the swirling ocean tempests

Kinetic's 1988 publishing season was a hectic affair whose gyrations I followed closely. As might have been expected, Lukas Yoder's seventh Grenzler novel, *The Fields*, with its amber cover showing the spacious farms of Lancaster County, was a sensation; its first printing was 750,000 and there was a quick reprinting of another quarter million. It won honors in four nations, was translated immediately into eleven languages and was a total bore.

The sensation of the season, of course, was the publication of Timothy Tull's *Kaleidoscope*, the random collection of loose leaves providing no story line, no physical setting, no identifiable characters, and no ideological thread. Handsomely presented in a fabric-covered box whose top showed an artist's conception of an old-time children's toy displaying a wild mix of colors and forms, it was an inviting item in a bookstore and a focus of comment when taken home and left on a coffee table.

People railed against it, scorned it, parodied it, took it back for refunds, but rarely stopped talking about it. Young people saw what their contemporary was trying to say and applauded both his efforts and his daring. On television George Will cited *Kaleidoscope* as proof that American society was speeding toward total degeneration, and Bill Buckley said the Ayatollah had fingered the wrong writer. Cartoonists had a field day, especially those on the papers in the heartland, the best one showing Leo Tolstoy in muzhik costume and fur cap leading a pair of readers to a huge disorderly pile of loose manuscript pages marked *War and Peace* with Tolstoy telling the women: 'Grab yourself a handful.'

Yvonne, no novice in the handling of books, knew how to keep controversy bubbling, and behind the scenes she orchestrated efforts of Kinetic's publicity department to line up quotes in support of the book. She also drafted a statement she hoped Lukas Yoder might adapt for his own comment: 'America needs bold young voices and I am pleased to see that one of my neighbors, Timothy Tull, has come out with his version of the contemporary world.' Yoder, who loved the hustle and bustle of publishing, surprised us all; he gave a ringing endorsement, concluding: 'If I were a young man in today's world, I would certainly not write the way I do now. I might not mimic my gifted neighbor Mr. Tull, but I would surely come up with something more contemporary than my own *Fields*.' When Yvonne received Yoder's letter, she phoned me: 'The Dresden Cabal—you, me, Yoder—is operating full force to give Tull's book a powerful send-off.' When she read me Yoder's endorsement she said: 'It illustrates why I love that dear old man. Ancient history but a man of character.'

Yoder's statement, reprinted throughout the nation and in Europe, did much to gain Tull a hearing, and when the season ended, with twenty-seven thousand boxes sold, our Dresden Cabal could take credit for having launched a new force in American letters, the brilliant, highly trained and disciplined young revolutionary who knew exactly what he wanted to achieve. As a result of the fanfare the Mecklenberg faculty approved a recommendation that he be invited to become my assistant in our growing department of creative writing, an assignment that pleased me, since it meant that I could keep helpful watch on his progress.

Kinetic's conspicuous failure on its 1988 list was my novel, *The Empty Cistern*. What reviews did stagger in were so blistering that not even Yvonne's strong supportive efforts could give it life. However, Yvonne was manipulative enough to ensure that it was noticed by some of the little magazines, and a few of their editors, inoculated by the Devlanian theory of dialogue among elites, recognized what I was shooting at and gave the book strong notices. The major reviewers, responsible to the general reading public, turned thumbs down, with two of them, *The New York Times* and *Time* magazine, stealing the imaginary Jean's apt line: 'It really is empty,' meaning, one supposed, that there were no murders, no colossal thefts, no steamy love affairs and not much else except interminable conversations on the nature and responsibility of the arts.

But Yvonne, who had a keen nose for the realities of publishing, was able to write me: 'I would be a fool to mask the fact that in the general field *Cistern* has been a disappointment. Many copies shipped back from the stores, as you must have expected. But I can assure you that in the arena you seek to conquer and which F.X.M. Devlan defined so neatly, you've not suffered. Those you wanted to reach, you have reached and quite effectively. I want you to capitalize on that forward movement, slight as it may seem to you right now. Start work immediately on the task you can do better than anyone else, that is, your championing of Timothy Tull. Do a short book of criticism, *Our Bold New Voices*, and I will guarantee your prompt publication. All is not lost, not by any means. You're a powerful voice, Karl, one worthy to be heard.'

Yvonne's wise counsel prevented me from making an error that might have finished me as a critic, for when *Cistern* failed, I had taken an oath, which revealed my bitterness: 'Since they've rejected my novel, I'm going to hold those they accept to damned high standards. Drones, beware!' And I sharpened my knives to do some scalping. Her letter brought me back to basics; personal revenge had no place in criticism.

Walking by the Wannsee, I pieced together a philosophy that I hoped would serve for the rest of my life: I had written what I considered a fine novel and was desolated by its failure. But it's useless to argue that the public failed to applaud because it's been spoiled by the easy fiction of the best-seller lists. The fault was mine, for I could hear Devlan's words rushing back at me: 'The job of fiction is to bring to life real human beings in a real setting,' and his sage advice: 'Any novel about an abstract idea is bound to be bad—write about people, not prototypes.' It was a lesson I had repeated to my students but not listened to myself.

I now saw that a novel has to be born in life, with characters whose passions and pains the author feels as keenly as if they were his or her own. I had filled my novel with illuminating ideas acted out by ill-defined characters who moved in obscurity, and much as I hated to agree, Yoder was right: 'It didn't sing.'

In this pain of shattered illusions about myself, I had an obligation to become honest about who I was and was not. I was not a novelist. I did not have the insights and poetry required by the creative writer. What I did have was a powerful understanding of what good writing was. I had a nose that unfailingly identified rubbish. And I could teach others to do what I couldn't. Yvonne was right, I was the man to write *Our Bold New Voices*, for I had heard them singing.

Rumors had been circulating that affairs at Kinetic were in confusion. Rockland Oil, more determined than ever to rid itself of what it viewed as an albatross—all headaches, no profits—had entered into urgent negotiations with the five companies that had shown serious interest in buying the house, and it had become clear that the most likely to see the project to a conclusion was the German conglomerate Kastle. This was not a German word, but since the firm had as its logo a handsome medieval castle, and since the owners had foreseen that they would be doing much of their future work in England and America, they had kept their distinctive symbol and added the imaginative spelling. As those in the trade said: 'It's a bit of a misnomer, but it's a damned sight better than the name their London competitor uses, Spider.'

At the height of Kinetic's celebrations over Yvonne's successes, one would have expected her to be basking in glory. Not at all. One night she phoned me in great agitation, asking if she could come down to Dresden over the next weekend and hold an important meeting with Yoder and me. I felt uneasy at being constantly thrown into contact with Yoder when I felt such animosity toward him, but I had to say: 'Come along!'

When we met she went directly to the heart of her problem: 'The other day John MacBain, our president, summoned me to his office and closed the door.'

As Yoder and I leaned forward anxiously to learn what had happened, she gave an appalling account in her dramatic New York way of how America's big businesses sometimes operated: 'I was barely seated when he said: "Ms. Marmelle, I'm sure you've heard the rumors circulating around this building. I needn't tell you that most of them were just that, rumors."

'I said: "I'd be lying if I claimed to have paid no attention, but I did not believe them."

'He frowned, shook his head sadly and said almost in a whisper: "Well, this one isn't a rumor. We're this close to being snapped up—by Kastle."

' "Have you agreed?"

'He stared at me as if I were an idiot child: "Agreed! Ms. Marmelle, you aren't as sophisticated as I thought." '

Here she hesitated, apparently recalling a scene so painful she would have preferred to forget it: ' "Don't you realize that when an American conglomerate owns you, they never ask if you agree. They give you orders and you obey. And when the day comes for them to get rid of you, they do it like that." He snapped his fingers: "They don't give a damn what you think—they do not give one damn, because they own you and you dance to their tune." And suddenly from the gray pallor that swept his face I realized that he was in great pain, not the kind that stings but the kind that eats at the soul. I saw him as that fine man who had been given control of Kinetic when it was lagging, and because of his managerial insights and his humane treatment of his editors and writers he had turned the company about until it was flying high again. In the vast field of conglomerate enterprises, our Kinetic may be trivial but in the world's publishing business it looms large and honorable.'

Knowing that she must side vigorously with her longtime supporter, she had asked a series of rapid-fire questions:

'So you mean that Rockland would sell us without our approval?' Yes.

'Sons of bitches. And to a German company?' Yes, they're the only ones with money in the bank.

'Would they keep you on?' They always say so at first. Then they fire you.

'Would they allow you to keep me on? Seeing I'm Jewish?' They know that if they fired all our Jews, there'd be little worth buying.

'But I'm in a fairly important position, you know, thanks to your support.' They said specifically they wanted to keep the kind of ferreting nose, that's the phrase they used, which you've displayed so tellingly.

'To tell you the truth, Mr. MacBain, I'd not want to work here if you were gone. And I'm sure most of the others—'

'Ms. Marmelle, on pain of death, keep this secret. Kastle was even reluctant to let me speak to you.'

'Kastle was reluctant! Who in the hell is Kastle to give you orders?'

'From now on they'll be giving all of us orders.'

Yvonne told us that to her amazement and MacBain's, tears had come to her eyes, even though she had never been the crying kind. 'This is shameful,' she had blubbered and MacBain had said with a force she had never witnessed before, not even in the bad days: 'It *is* shameful. A great American company that published so many

books that were of significance to this nation to be tossed about in
the marketplace like a sack of potatoes. It's terribly shameful, but
I'm powerless to stop the sale. Rockland insists on getting rid of us,
and I've already been introduced to the man who'll be my new boss.'

Since Yoder and I were intensely concerned about who the new
owner might be, for our fortunes rose and fell with Kinetic, I asked:
'It couldn't possibly be a German?' and slowly she nodded: 'MacBain
told me the new head, Ludwig Ludenberg, was from Hamburg but
had been educated at Oxford: "Speaks better English than either of
us. Assured me that I would be kept on, of course, plus my top aides,
because he knew he needed our expertise." '

At this point Yvonne halted and asked me to order some tea,
which she poured like an English hostess. Thus fortified, she tackled
the ugly part of her report: 'MacBain told me that Kastle wanted him
to ascertain—delicately, of course, everything must be delicately
handled—whether any of our important writers—you two and Tim
Tull were on their list—would try to cancel your contracts if the sale
to a German firm went through.'

'What did you tell them?' Yoder asked, and she said: 'I leaped
from my chair and stormed about MacBain's office, shouting: "I'm
not going to spy on my writers, God bless every last one of them,
to assist a foreign buyer. A writer is a sacred commodity. That's why
mine stay with me, because I convey to them the fact that I believe
this, heart and soul. John"—this was the first time I had ever addressed him by his first name—"ask me no more questions. I would
be ashamed of myself if I answered them." '

Then I asked Yvonne: 'What did MacBain say to that?' and she
said: 'He allowed me to give vent to my righteous indignation, then
told me: "Remember, the deal isn't finalized yet. But I'm sure it will
go through and if it does, I want the transition to be peaceful.
Everyone's afraid of a replay of those distasteful events of some years
back when one of the big houses discovered that lots of their best

writers would flee the company if certain unpalatable sales went through. The deal died. So it's very important for the Germans to know who'll stay and who'll go. If you won't tell me, I'll have to guess, and if I guess wrong, the onus will be on me." '

Yvonne stopped, blew her nose and confessed: 'Those were ugly moments. When, as a matter of principle, I refused to share my guesses as to who would quit, he produced a list of all my writers and ticked them off, one by one, asking if they would stay or go. Horrified by the traitor's role I was asked to play, I would not speak, but I did nod yes for those who would stay, shake my head for those who would probably quit.'

'When he came to our names?' Yoder asked, and she said frankly: 'I said that Timothy Tull as a young idealist would probably walk out. I said that you, Lukas, as a German and an older man, would probably stay. You, Streibert, I not only didn't know, but I wasn't sure how I'd advise you if you asked.'

'Why not?' I asked, and she said: 'Because your career is in mid-flight. What you do next is crucial.' She stopped, smiled at me and said: 'My career too. I don't know what I'll do.'

To my surprise Yoder volunteered: 'Ms. Marmelle, the day you leave Kinetic I go with you. If I lost you I'd be like a young lamb left in a storm,' and before she could respond I added: 'I'd walk out the door with him.'

Giving each of us a kiss, she said: 'I've learned to avoid exhibition-istic gestures. We have maybe a week to weigh our options. But if the worst happens, get the name of our new boss right. Kastle with a K.'

In the fall term of 1989 I stopped worrying about the takeover of Kinetic in New York because I had to attend to the interests of two of my writing students. Mecklenberg, like all serious colleges, distributed questionnaires at the close of each semester asking students to evaluate their professors, and, at the close of Timothy Tull's first year, the results were so favorable that the dean of faculty summoned me: 'Streibert, it looks as if you've picked a winner in this lad Tull,' and when he showed me the tabulations I saw that they were truly superior. My judgment in selecting him as my assistant had been ratified, but the dean called my attention to a fact I had been ignoring because I did not want Timothy to leave our college: 'You must warn Tull that if he hopes to stay on here he must get his Ph.D., and he should do it while he's still youthful and the counterpull of a professional writing career has not become overpowering. I needn't remind you that if you hadn't left here to get your doctorate, your life would have been quite different. Encourage Tull to get on with it.' But when I hurried to tell Timothy how proud I was of his acceptance by the students, a chap in his hall told me: 'He's off-campus, participating in a seminar at Princeton,' and I gave a bittersweet smile: I was very proud of Tull but last year it had been I who was invited to do that job. This year similar invitations from the important schools were not coming my way.

The second student problem that preoccupied me was the arrival in my writing course of a disruptive tornado named Jenny Sorkin.

I was seated in my office in mid-September when a brash young woman in her early twenties banged her way in, wearing a T-shirt emblazoned in bright red with the words: DON'T JUST STAND THERE. DO SOMETHING. She wore her tawny-colored hair in a ponytail and was dressed in ragged blue jeans, with her rather large feet in marine combat boots. Before I asked she told me her name, that she was a graduate at twenty of Brandeis, had done postgraduate work at Berkeley and a stint as a waitress in a hash house in Oklahoma, and had spent the previous year at the University of Iowa's writers' workshop.

Startled by her general appearance and her boldness, I asked:

'How in the world did you ever hear of this college?' and she flattered me by saying: 'You're highly regarded in certain circles. Your *Cistern* spoke loud and clear to some of us in California and Iowa, and I bring with me a finished novel that needs some sharpening. I figured you were the current guru,' and with this she plunked down on my desk a boxed manuscript whose pages were far neater than their author.

Unable to estimate either the seriousness of the young woman or her capabilities, I said: 'I'll read it tonight. Drop by tomorrow about this time and we'll talk.'

The night was well spent. Her novel, entitled *The Big Six*, contained that number of chapters, each dealing with the adventures of an Oklahoma hillbilly girl, probably the author, as she fends off the advances of a prototypical football hero in each of the Western universities in the conference that used to be the Big Six but had now grown into the notorious Big Eight: Oklahoma, Nebraska, Kansas, Colorado, Missouri, Oklahoma State, Kansas State and Iowa State.

I read three of the episodes—about an all-time thug from Oklahoma State, an all-American Boy Scout from Nebraska, and a hilarious character from Missouri who could not decide whether he wanted to be a football hero or a poet—and through each of the episodes moved that heroine, one of the most lovable, illiterate rascals in recent fiction, perpetually beat up by her men but more clever than any of them. Jenny Sorkin could write, and when I went to bed it was with regret that I hadn't the time to inspect how she handled her clowns from Oklahoma, Kansas and Colorado.

The next afternoon when she slumped her way into my office I caught the feeling that she was trying to live out, here in my proper Eastern college, the role she had created for her heroine as the latter careened through her Western universities, because her new T-shirt read: WHAT I SEEK IS A MEANINGFUL OVERNIGHT RELATIONSHIP. Taken aback, I said: 'Judging from your ambulant billboard, you're

a young lady seeking rape,' and she laughed: 'You're catching on.'
Then, becoming a professor, I pushed her boxed novel at her and
said: 'Miss Sorkin, you're for real,' and her gamine face broke into
a smile as big as a rising full moon: 'I was terrified you might think
it too territorial—too Oklahoma.'

'Nothing wrong with any marketable state. Steinbeck did pretty
well for himself with Oklahoma.'

'Yes. But he got his people out of there pretty quick and into the
real world, California.'

'You've also done rather well with the Western plains.'

'Then you'll take me on as a student?'

'I'd lock the doors if you tried to go elsewhere,' and I took back
the manuscript: 'I'll finish it tonight and lay out a program for you
tomorrow.'

'Does that mean I can register?'

'You came to see me without having been formally accepted by the
college?'

'I can't waste money. If you'd said "No" I'd have been on the
night bus back to Iowa.'

In the next two weeks I more or less lost sight of Miss Sorkin, but
humorous stories about her audacious behavior began to circulate.
She was fond of amusing our staid Mecklenberg students with outra-
geous stories in Jewish dialect and shocking our prim Lutherans with
her religious travesties: 'What did the Virgin Mary call Jesus?' 'My
son, the rabbi, he's such a nice boy.' And 'What did the Virgin Mary
tell Jesus?' 'Eat the chicken soup, you'll like it.'

During these opening weeks, although I saw little of her, I did
have a chance to read her three stories, which all new students had
to submit with their applications, and they confirmed my first impression of this volatile, irreverent young woman. She could write.
Some days later, when I had to call Ms. Marmelle about my own
work, I told her: 'Thanks, Yvonne, for getting me off trying another

novel. The book you suggested—critical essays on our bright young writers—is forging ahead. Could turn out to be a modest success.'

'Karl, I'm so glad for you.'

'Even better, I may have found you another really fine young writer. Young woman this time. Name's Jenny Sorkin. Brandeis with high marks. Scholarship to Iowa, where she did well, but recently transferred to Mecklenberg because she liked what she heard of our program.'

'You say she's good?'

'Very.'

'How can you tell? You said she arrived in your hands only recently.'

'That's right. But she brought with her a completed manuscript and, Yvonne, it's sensational.'

'What's it about?'

'She calls it *Big Six* after that football conference out in the boondocks.

'How old is the writer?'

'Twenty-three.'

'How can a child of that age write a book like the one you've described?'

'How, indeed: When you see her you'll wager that someone did it for her. Tall, thin as a reed, ponytail, sloppy manner, you'll doubt that any man would look at her, but she's done a short story for me that's so good I've already persuaded a small magazine to take it. The girl could be the new Timothy Tull—on her own rowdy terms.'

'I'd better see her,' and it was arranged that when she next came down to consult with Lukas Yoder about the preliminary outline of what would be publicized as the final book in his "Grenzler Octet," a grim story of how Pennsylvania Dutch had abused their land, she would ask Emma to invite Jenny over to the Yoder farm for tea on Saturday afternoon.

When I reminded her once of her governing principles: 'Never talk to two writers on the same visit,' she laughed: 'You have a good memory, Karl. But this is such a different situation, you being her teacher, that I think you ought to join us.'

'Sorry. I've been invited to a meeting at Temple University in Philadelphia that afternoon,' and as I hung up I thought: Jenny Sorkin with her T-shirts and little Emma Yoder with her school-teacher ways, that's got to be a volatile mix, and I was almost sorry I was going to miss it.

On Friday evening, when Yvonne checked into the Dresden China, she had a premonition that she ought to telephone both Emma Yoder and Jenny Sorkin and suggest that the tea be canceled, and then Jenny could either come to the inn for the interview or arrange someplace on campus for Yvonne to meet her. But that did not seem a workable idea, especially since she didn't know where Jenny lived. I was absent in Philadelphia, conducting a seminar on recent American fiction and fending off ardent supporters of Gore Vidal, Herman Wouk, Leon Uris and John Cheever, who had their knives sharpened for me.

When I returned to Mecklenberg I heard from four different fac-ulty wives, breathless and giggling, the details of what had happened when Jenny Sorkin exploded into the middle of a faculty tea, and I was glad I'd taken refuge at Temple. Yvonne arrived at the Yoder farm in midafternoon to find that Emma had located Miss Sorkin and extended the invitation to tea.

The other invitees, faculty wives, also arrived early and the talk centered on the atypical Jewish girl who had stormed their campus: 'She's a Western firebrand with a vast contempt for our Eastern effeteness.' The speaker was corrected: 'She's from Brooklyn, went to Brandeis, then on to Iowa, to enlarge her perspective.' Emma asked: 'But why did she come to this out-of-the-way place?' and a faculty wife explained: 'I asked her and she told me she'd spent a

term at Berkeley to check on the radicals, then came here to investigate the conservatives.'

Yvonne, feeling that she must defend all writers, asked: 'Has
anyone met her?' and a shiver went down her spine when Emma
replied: 'I did. Reminded me of certain girls I knew at Bryn Mawr.
The type that took few baths.'

At about four the faculty wives in the Yoder farmhouse caught
sight of a tall, rangy girl coming up the walkway as the car in which
she had arrived started to drive off. Yvonne had the best glimpse of
her: unkempt hair, floppy skirt with an uneven hem, and a bold red
T-shirt emblazoned with heavy black lettering. She saw no more,
because Lukas went to the door, spoke briefly with the young woman
and said sternly: 'No, you may not come in, wearing a thing like
that,' and he dismissed her, slamming the door. Fortunately, the
driver of the car, whoever he was, had stopped to assure himself that
this was the Yoder farm, so she was able to catch a ride back to the
college, but as she was about to climb in, Lukas, ashamed of his
rough treatment, reopened the door and shouted: 'You'll be welcome
when you're properly dressed.'

When the women asked: 'What was wrong with her dress?' he
blushed furiously and said: 'Written right across her chest were
words in bold outline: SCREW YOU . . . OR ME, except that an even
filthier word was used.'

'Lukas!' Yvonne said reprovingly, 'we're grown up, you know,'
and he said: 'I do apologize for ruining your day, Ms. Marmelle. I
suppose that's the last we'll see of Miss Sorkin, and maybe that's
good. She seems a disagreeable lot.'

He was wrong because in the time it took for the car to speed at
seventy miles an hour over to the northern tip of the Wannsee and
back, Miss Sorkin was at the front door, knocking politely and
calling to her driver: 'Better wait, to see if I get kicked out again.'

She was admitted, but only because Emma reached the door before
Lukas. When she invited the young woman to enter, she burst into

laughter, for across her chest this time stood the bold letters IN CASE OF RAPE, THIS SIDE UP. Yvonne told me: 'When I saw the message, I chuckled, then guffawed, but Lukas was outraged and refused to shake hands.'

His embarrassment increased when Emma shared with Jenny and the faculty women a revealing story of her courtship with Lukas: 'He'd come down to Bryn Mawr to see me—it's only a short distance—and found himself amid a collection of girls from Penn and Vassar and Mount Holyoke. Maybe some Smith girls, too. It was an assembly on the rights of women, as I recall, and as Lukas and I were walking through a grove on campus, we crept up, unintentionally, on a group of visitors, and they were singing what they said was the Vassar alma mater. I'll never forget the jingle:

> ' "The first of May, the first of May!
> Outdoor screwing starts today.
> Hooray, hooray, hooray, hooray!" '

When the others chortled, she told Jenny Sorkin: 'Of course, they were singing the more vulgar word, the one Lukas intimated was on your first T-shirt.'

'What happened?' Yvonne asked, and Emma said: 'Lukas, as you might expect, was mortified. He blushed a deep red, realized that the girls from the other colleges had seen him, and fled, leaving me standing there.' Reflectively she added: 'I've always thought, Lukas, that your novels might have carried a bit more contemporary zing if you'd not been so self-conscious about sex.' And he was still so self-conscious that again he fled the presence of chuckling women.

When time came for tea, Emma said: 'I'll see if we can lure Lukas back.' When he came, rather sheepishly, he took one look at Jenny Sorkin's chest and broke into laughter: 'That's the damnedest thing I've ever seen. What's the purpose, may I ask?'

'Kids call it "a barrier breaker." A girl's whole problem is to get boys to notice her, to start a conversation. Anything that achieves that is a tremendous aid.'

'But you're no longer a girl,' Lukas said, and Jenny replied: 'You're a girl, in habit and thought, until you snare a man.'

'You deem it that important?' Lukas asked, suddenly interested in this strange young woman who presumed to be a writer.

'Even more than I can explain. You don't have to grab the man, but you do have to make him want to grab you.'

'And your proposed book. Does it consist mainly of football players grabbing?'

'Mr. Yoder, some of the best parts deal with a man who is as different from you as a man can be, my father, a football junkie, a dear galoot, and a consummate horse's ass.'

Turning to Yvonne, Lukas asked: 'And you think you can tame this wild thing into being a writer?' and Yvonne replied: 'If there's potential growth to work with, I can tame anything. It's when things are totally static that I have no chance. This one'—she looked approvingly at Miss Sorkin—'I do believe I can help tame her, but only if she cares to cooperate.'

'Cooperate? I'd rewrite every page, if you said the word.' Jenny paused: 'But you haven't said the word, have you?' When Yvonne shook her head, Miss Sorkin asked in a subdued voice: 'Would you be willing to consider my manuscript?' and Yvonne nodded.

The explanation I gave for not attending the rowdy tea at Emma Yoder's was the truth—I did have a seminar at Temple—but not the whole truth. I had gone there primarily to meet with a committee of three deans, but neither they nor I wished that fact to be known.

What had happened was this. I had received a letter from Dean Mendel Iscovich of something called the School of Social Communication which contained astonishing news:

> Our professors who have attended your various lectures and
> followed the track records of your graduates and your own

scholarship attainments have impressed me with what a valuable addition you would be to the program we are developing here at Temple.

Thanks to an unexpected grant of some dimensions from Walter Annenberg, whose offices in *The Philadelphia Inquirer* are down Broad Street from us, and from two generous gifts from other city industrialists, we find ourselves in a position to offer three new faculty members of established reputations positions in an exciting educational adventure. Would you care to meet with our deans to explore possibilities that could prove to be of mutual interest?

I did not want to leave Mecklenberg, and I certainly could not imagine teaching at Temple, which was in the midst of a turbulent city, but I did owe Dean Iscovich the courtesy of a response, and although my letter clearly indicated that I was happy in my present position, it was sufficiently collegial so that a committee of three Temple deans drove north the forty-odd miles to meet with me in an Allentown hotel, where they surprised me with their graciousness and knowledge in my fields of expertise. In fact, they made the intellectual and social challenges of moving to Temple so inviting and the funding of the school to which I would be attached so reassuring that I simply could not bluntly reject their enthusiastic invitation to visit them in Philadelphia. The result of what I again intended as courtesy led to my visiting Temple one weekend under the guise of conducting a seminar, and although I saw that all they had promised me was in position, the big-city setting was so alien to what I thought a great university should be that all I could promise when I left was: 'I'll need time to consider this dazzling invitation.' Actually I knew that I would require only a few minutes to reach my negative decision. When we parted, Dean Iscovich, a youngish man with degrees from North Carolina, Wisconsin and Harvard told me: 'Professor Streibert, do not take this invitation lightly. You're at an age when you ought to grapple with some big task, one you can grow with for the rest of your academic career. You're nearly forty. You have a quarter of a century left before retirement. Make those years count.'

The remainder of 1989 was turbulent for all of us, sad, but also rewarding. Jenny Sorkin was hammered at from two quarters: at college I labored with her, trying to clarify and simplify her syntax, while on her trips to New York, Yvonne was relentless in demanding greater depth.

I was present at one of Jenny's sessions with Yvonne. The editor wanted the six men in Jenny's novel differentiated in every regard 'so that a blind man could identify each on a dark night,' but Yvonne had only limited time she could devote to any one of her writers. 'The days of Maxwell Perkins hand-holding is gone. I can tell you what I think is wrong, but you have to fix it.'

'Tell me straight out, Yvonne. What's wrong?'

Quietly and looking straight at Jenny, Yvonne said: 'Wouldn't it be better if you called me Ms. Marmelle—until your first two best-sellers?' And then she smiled.

'I'm sorry. That's the kind of thing I came back East to learn.'

'We need . . .' Yvonne's use of that pronoun betrayed the fact that she had already adopted Jenny's manuscript as her own and would fight till she dropped from exhaustion to see it properly launched. 'We need six marvelous portraits. Funny, human, aggravating, pompous, macho. The portrait of your father and his crazy ways, perfect. And do you know why? You knew him. I don't get the feeling that you know your five football players. The Missouri poet? Well, yes, maybe.'

At lunch one day, Yvonne asked: 'Did you perchance ever sleep with one of your Big Six?'

'I avoid football players.'

'There's the trouble, you write about them ambiguously. You try to make them heroes, but you can't put your heart into it. Lay off the hero stuff, pin them to the pages of your notebook as if they were insects in your biology class. Sharpen, sharpen!'

Whenever Jenny tired of the hammering and the lack of specific instruction from her two mentors, she remembered something I had said at an informal party with advanced students: 'The sad fact is that most of the kids in the big class will never make it.' She was determined not to be one of that tribe, and one morning after having struggled with the portrait of her man from Oklahoma State, finally getting him into shape at two in the morning, she phoned Yvonne, telling her jubilantly: 'It feels so good, seven sheets reworked the way you and I wanted. All crud gone. Just the muscle, the music and the meaning.'

'You're beginning to sound like a professional,' Yvonne said.

Regarding Timothy, who had started so brilliantly and whom I had promoted to be my assistant in teaching the writing course, I wondered if he would be qualified to head the department if I ever moved on. He seemed to lack the patience required for sustained administrative work, and this was a difficult judgment for me to reach, because it was I who had recommended him for his present appointment and fought for him when older faculty members complained that at twenty-one he was too young. But one day when I returned unexpectedly to fetch some papers and found him lecturing, I was startled. Though young, he was so at ease and so obviously attuned to his students that I left wondering how these attributes came so naturally to him. He seemed to have absorbed all I had taught him but had transformed this knowledge with his natural gifts.

One afternoon as I walked across the campus I saw him in a rowdy game of touch football. All of a sudden he leaped high in the air like a young Icarus to snag a pass, and it was then that I understood that if his novel had vitality while mine did not, it was probably because

his life had vitality and mine didn't. Now at twenty-two he was a full
man, while I at nearly twice his age remained only a partial one.
When he made number five on the tennis team he played with such
grace that I found myself thinking: He's an Apollo and I'm some
grape-stomping clod, and against my will I began to envy him. I had
started our relationship as his mentor; now I saw him poised for
flight, and realized I had to let him go. The thought of losing him
was almost painful.

A few days later I suffered a crushing loss. One of F.X.M. Devlan's
associates at Oxford had written in late 1988: 'He asked me to inform
you that he was too weak to write and that the end seemed to be
closing in. I felt it proper for me to alert you, because he weighs no
more than 120 pounds and the decline of powers cannot be halted.
His spirit is bright, his attacks against mediocrity continue unabated,
and he sends his love.'

Because I could visualize Devlan so clearly, still valiant in his
dying moments, still firing shafts of mordant wit at the follies of the
world, I sent him three long letters in three days, reminding him in
each of the joy we had known in Greece and of the supreme influence
he had been in my life. I wanted to fly to Oxford to comfort him,
but could devise no excuse for making such a trip. I didn't feel I
could simply abandon my classes, and if I did get permission and it
was circulated through the student body and the alumni that I had
left to console what they would have termed 'his gentleman friend,'
or, what was worse, 'his close male associate,' I might be fired. And
so I stayed at my job, feeling miserable about doing so. As I walked
through the peaceful groves of the college and along the shores of
the Wannsee I saw myself in Oxford, walking to the digs in the
eighteenth-century stone cottage in which my friend lay dying, and
the pain became more than I could bear.

Finally, I burst into President Rossiter's office unannounced and looking rather disheveled, and blurted out: 'Sir, I must fly to Oxford immediately.'

To my astonishment he said quietly: 'Of course. When I learned about your friend's illness, I suspected you'd have to go. Tull has said he'd be proud to take your classes, give him a chance to test his skills at a higher level.'

'But what about the college community?'

'Streibert, if it were your father who was dying, of course we'd encourage you to go. Or when Anderson's wife was dying of cancer? Where else should he be?'

Totally unprepared for this degree of understanding and acceptance, I reached for a chair. 'May I sit?' and when he nodded, I'm afraid I burst into tears, for these had been confusing days. After a while he led me to the door, put his arm around my shoulder and said: 'Streibert, long ago the older faculty and the regents satisfied themselves that you posed no embarrassment to the college, you and Professor Devlan, I mean. That was settled long ago.'

At the door I said: 'I came here prepared to resign,' and he said: 'I'm sure of that,' and he suggested that I use the college car and its driver to speed me to Kennedy Airport.

By the goodwill of God I reached Oxford when Devlan was still alive and found him a shriveled little fellow weighing a hundred and two pounds, but still surprisingly lively. I believe he drew upon his last shreds of energy to talk with me, and the things he said almost broke my heart: 'What would I like to do in the time remaining? See the Uffizi again. Hear *Lohengrin*. Meet with my seminar one last time to share with them . . .' His voice faded, and when I leaned close to hear, he added: 'To hear the *Agamemnon* in Greek, in the old temple . . .' There came a long pause during which he took my hand: 'And to walk among the olive groves. We did once, did we not?'

He was buried in an Oxford cemetery, his grave marked by his associates with a small stone that says DEVLAN CRITIC, which is what he had directed me to provide.

Upon my return to Mecklenberg I fell into a malaise more depleting than I had known at the death of my parents. My hurtful experience with *Cistern*, whose weaknesses Devlan had spotted from a distance, had made me suspicious of my own self-direction: 'I too need helpful guidance just as Timothy Tull and Jenny Sorkin do. For no writer ever knows enough about his language, his characters or his art. Oh, Michael, I needed you then, I need you now.'

I had thought, as Devlan lay dying, that perhaps Tull could become the inheritor of the Leavis-Devlan-Streibert chain of insights and become master of the dialogue between elites. Certainly he was bright enough to fill that role, and after six or seven years at Mecklenberg he might be ready for a major appointment, especially if in the meantime he took his Ph.D. at some prestigious school like Yale or Oxford.

Mention of the latter name prompted a lively thought: With his record the lad could win a Rhodes Scholarship! But when I investigated I learned that students were eligible for only a limited number of years after graduation from college, and Tull had passed that date.

Then I smacked my brow in irritation: What am I thinking about? With his grandmother's millions he doesn't need a Rhodes. He could easily pay his own way at Oxford. Indeed, an article had recently appeared in *The Philadelphia Inquirer* pointing out the injustice in having Tull's *Kaleidoscope* on the best-seller list and coining more money for a young man who was already heir to his grandmother's millions, while two equally gifted mature authors in the city could barely earn a living with their writing. When I finished the insulting article I asked aloud: 'Who says they're equally gifted? More likely one-tenth as gifted.'

But even as I uttered this vigorous defense of Tull, a warning whispered: Streibert, don't make Timothy more important than he is. He's no more than one of your students who've displayed certain aptitudes. He's not a god. Let him find his own level himself.

Despite this sensible warning there was one aspect of his life about which I had to be concerned: I did not want to see him make some dreadful mistake by marrying too young—in haste—and to the wrong woman. Such as Jenny Sorkin, to whom he seemed attracted. This apprehension was intensified by a fact I could no longer mask: I actively disliked Jenny Sorkin, who constantly baffled me. Whenever I thought she was becoming civilized she would parade her latest outrage, but when I judged her to be beyond hope she would reveal some new aptitude that amazed me.

Her brash ways offended, her preposterous T-shirts were an affront to my college, such as the one that displayed an imaginative reworking of the warning that appears on side-view mirrors: OBJECTS HIDDEN BY THIS SHIRT MAY BE LARGER THAN THEY APPEAR. And, I must admit, her reliance on Yvonne Marmelle and Timothy Tull instead of on me for intellectual and artistic guidance was irritating. So one night, seeking only to protect Timothy, I knocked on his door: 'Timothy, I know I'm butting in, but I'm doing it not as a friend but as the head of a small corner of my college.'

'Sit down.'

'You could be edging into dangerous waters if you persist in seeing Jenny Sorkin socially. This is a conservative school, and the slightest breath of scandal, bang! The grenade of propriety explodes.'

'I went here, Mr. Streibert, remember?'

'But not as a young professor—teaching women students.' In the pause he glared at me but I did not back down: 'American colleges recently, especially those with graduate schools, have been plagued by scandals in which male professors have been charged, sometimes in court, with molesting women students.'

Tull broke into laughter: 'I'm not the type, Mr. Streibert. You know that. I date Jenny now and then, discussing her work. I'm twenty-two. I know what I'm doing.'

'And she's twenty-four. When the woman is older than the man, bizarre things can happen. Such women often start lawsuits just for revenge, if they fear the man is moving off to someone younger.'

'I'll take that risk.'

'But we don't know who she is—her hang-ups. I have grave doubts that she's a proper person for you to be affiliated with. It can lead only to trouble, Timothy, and you know I'm concerned only with your own good.'

Suddenly his eyes blazed, he leaped to his feet, and for the first time in our relationship he raised his voice in anger: 'This is crazy,' he shouted. 'Damn it, Mr. Streibert, you're way out of line.' I did my best to calm him, but he rushed on: 'I'm a college instructor with a good track record and a strong book behind me. Lots of people would want me if you care to give me the boot because I'm dating a grown woman just about my own age.'

'Timothy,' I said almost pleadingly, 'you refuse to listen. I'm warning you that a dozen universities have been scandalized recently by—'

'You already said that,' he snapped. 'And in many cases the women were justified and the professors were fired.'

'Teacher and student,' I said soothingly. 'A dangerous mix. And in your case you'd be a prime target, what with your family wealth and all.'

'You sound like something out of Kafka. A trial with no accusation, no evidence, no jury. I'm going to assume that this conversation never took place.' And when I sought to continue my warning he became so furious that he responded in a way I believe he must later have regretted: 'If I understand correctly, Mr. Streibert,' he said, spitting out my name, 'you weren't so meticulous in your small-town morality when you were a student at Columbia and your professor was nearly two decades older than you—and a man.'

It was brutal of him to sneer at my hallowed relationship with Devlan and of course it cut off any further discourse. But before I could rush from the room, a mist covered my eyes and I felt faint. Bumping into the doorjamb as I went I whispered: 'Professor Devlan died last week. Of AIDS,' and I left the room. During the next two weeks we did not speak.

I could not allow our relationship to end in such an ugly way, but I could think of no face-saving way of reinstituting it. Then, one day as we passed in the hall I stopped in front of him and offered congratulations on his able use of my diagram of the House of Atreus. Then I asked: 'And how's the new novel going?' and he said: 'Painfully. It's a protracted dialogue, the kind I believe you'd approve.' I said: 'I'll be eager to see it,' and he said: 'You'll be the first.'

One evening about nine, after a meeting with some students, I dropped by Timothy's room to find the door closed and to hear emanating from behind it the voice of a remarkable woman singer backed up by an orchestra playing music of extreme lushness. The voice was incredible, for it hovered between a deep-throated mezzo and a lighter soprano, rising to lyric heights, then falling away like a golden leaf drifting down or a silvery cascade. I could not determine what language was being sung, but it was clear that Timothy had acquired a compact disk of some remarkable music. Wanting to know more, I pushed open his door and found myself staring at Jenny Sorkin, stretched out on his bed, face down with chin propped on her clasped hands. Timothy was seated in the opposite corner in a chair beside his reading lamp, the disk player at his elbow, the two loudspeakers ranged against the opposite wall. He and Jenny were

THE CRITIC

· ·

320

obviously listening to the song and were in no way embarrassed by my entrance.

'What's that music?' I asked, remaining in the doorway.

'*Songs of the Auvergne,*' Timothy said. 'A collection of folk songs from Southern France.'

Jenny looked up from the bed: 'A peasant maid, afraid of growing old without a man, stands on one side of a river and sings to a young shepherd on the other side.' As we listened to the incredibly beautiful rise and fall of the woman's full-throated voice shivers ran down my spine; then I heard Jenny saying: 'That was the voice Ulysses heard when he was lashed to the mast, determined to resist the temptations of the Sirens, who turned men into swine.'

'With that wonderful deep voice, more like the Rhine maidens luring men to their destruction on the rocks,' I suggested.

'Let's not make it too arcane,' Timothy said. 'It's a woman in love with an abstraction and longing for the real man she sees on the opposite shore of the sea.'

'I thought you said it was a river,' I pointed out and Jenny smiled at me in her provocative way: 'When you're separated from your man a rill becomes a river, the river an ocean.'

The music so captivated me that the next day I looked into the background of the Auvergne songs and learned that this one, with the curious title 'Bailero,' was judged best of the lot; singers loved it and had recorded it in many countries, and how I had missed it perplexed me. But now as I listened to it in my own room on a record made by a French contralto, I realized that it bespoke a passion alien to my experience: the longing of a young woman for a man. Some nights later I went back to Timothy's room intending to speak with him, but as I approached his door I heard the enchanting music, the same murmur of voices, and I accepted the painful fact that I could not enter that room again.

In this dark period I tormented myself unnecessarily by remaining in my room after my evening sessions with students, listening to *Songs of the Auvergne* on my record player and imagining Jenny Sorkin singing those enchanting notes that rose and fell like the beating of the human heart while Timothy tended his flock on the other side of the stream. And the tremendous longing of which the human heart is capable overwhelmed me. As midnight approached I experienced a loneliness I had never known before.

It was at this low moment in my life that I began to doubt my usefulness at Mecklenberg, and then Lukas Yoder delivered one more body blow. But to give him credit I'm sure he wasn't aware that he was doing so. I learned about it accidentally.

One morning as Jenny Sorkin left my class she stopped to say breathlessly: 'At last I'm beginning to feel like a professional writer.'

'And what's happened in our class that occasions that feeling?' and she said: 'It's not your class. Lukas Yoder is taking Timothy and me into New York to meet with his agent, a Miss Crane, best in the business, they say. Believe it or not, she may want to sign me on as a client. Timothy she's sure to take, but Mr. Yoder has recommended me, too.' And off she ran, to find Timothy.

I was watching when Yoder drove up in his old Buick, picked up my two students and headed for New York. As I saw them disappear I felt devalued. I had been concerned with two major things: teaching them what good writing is and seeing that they fell into the hands of a strong editor. I'd accomplished both, and now to see them scurrying off with Yoder to attend to a problem on which I might have helped was galling.

During spring break, when the students were gone and I had the college to myself except for secretaries who remained to mail out grades, I enjoyed a string of uninterrupted days in which to assess my bewildering situation. I had fallen upon bad times. Nothing seemed to be going right in either my personal or my professional life. Devlan was dead, leaving me without an anchor. *Cistern* was also dead, leaving me with no illusions that I could ever be a novelist and with a real fear that I could criticize only the work of others and not my own. Which led to a frightening question: Can I even assess my own life honestly?

I was walking in the evening dusk beside the Wannsee when I asked myself that question, and I reacted to it as if to a physical blow. In my confusion I sought one of the benches under the trees that lined the lake, and sat there with my head bowed and my hands motionless in my lap. I conducted a brutal self-analysis and came to the conclusion that I'd been afraid to formulate because of its frightening consequences: That's it, you're tired of teaching, and you're merely marking time here at Mecklenberg. I was terrified by what those words signified, for this college had been my home. Unlike other unmarried teachers, I had no house in Dresden or Bethlehem; I'd always lived in one of the dormitories—in a fine suite, to be sure—but I was a prisoner within the cocoon I'd spun for myself. Had I the courage to leave it?

Shaking my head as if to erase that option, I turned to the other damaging weakness I'd been unable to face and said to myself: You're a critic, Streibert, and you had the possibility of being a powerful one, but you've lost your hard focus. I think it started when you were so eager to gain a book contract with Kinetic that you allowed them to talk you into killing your criticism of Yoder. That started the corruption, and what was worse, you stifled your criticism because Yoder had donated so much to your writing program. You've preached that the obligation of the writer or the critic is to stand in opposition to society, to help keep everybody honest. But when you faced the pressures of society you crumpled.

I rose, put my hands to my head and cried aloud: 'The dominoes are falling and I can't stop them!'

Professor Harkness of the chemistry department came by at this point, and while he did not hear my exact words he could see that I was in distress: 'Are you all right, Streibert? Your face is gray.'

'Wrestling with abstractions,' I lied, and when he asked if he could see me to my quarters I lied again: 'No, thanks. Too much work. I'm steady.' And I proved that I was by walking with him a short distance. He was unwilling to abandon me, but I insisted, and when he was gone I flopped onto another bench, and there I painfully drove myself to probe the basic truths about myself.

'No one's to blame but me. Not Devlan for having contracted AIDS. Not Timothy for having outgrown me. Not Yoder for having stolen Grenzler before I could get to it. And not the college for having failed to provide me with more challenging students. I've failed, and because of a weakness that is unforgivable in would-be critics or leaders of others: I've lost forward motion. I'm fighting for nothing. I'm lost in a terrible, deep rut whose sides are caving in on me.'

I have never been especially courageous, but I do believe that I'm not afraid to confront the inevitable, so at this low point in my fortunes I sat staring at the lake and, while gritting my teeth, re-solved to pull myself out of the rut I was trapped in. Mercifully, words spoken in the past came to console and guide me. The speaker had been Iscovich at Temple: 'You have a quarter of a century left before retirement. Make those years count.' On this troubled evening the invitation he had given that I had so cavalierly scorned now seemed alive with promise: It's a miraculous opportunity to escape the complacency I've been lulled into and to stretch myself toward momentous achievements.

Jumping from the bench with newborn enthusiasm, I hurried toward my room to telephone Dean Iscovich to report my decision, but there was one more hurdle to pass before I could claim my freedom. As I ran past the library I suddenly stopped and entered the nearly empty main room from which students had fled for their term break. Nodding to Jenny Sorkin, who labored in a corner, I asked the librarian for the Temple catalog. Tucking it under my arm, I went to my quarters to study the maps showing how the buildings at Temple were distributed haphazardly through North Philadelphia. When I realized that within this confined ghetto there would be no Wannsee, no gardened paths, no rooming houses with spacious quarters, my courage failed: 'God, Streibert! You must be insane! Such an unfair exchange!' But then came a voice as clear as if the speaker were at my elbow: 'Take the first step of your upward climb or forever lag behind.' Before I could waver again I called Temple and told the dean: 'Sorry to bother you at home, but I want to join your program. It sounds better and better,' and he, appreciating how difficult that decision must have been, said quietly: 'You'll never regret it.' But when I hung up and looked out my window to that glorious Wannsee, I knew that in some part of my being I would regret my decision every day of my life. But the real world was calling, and I could hardly wait to direct some Philadelphia sign painter in placing my DOOMED HOUSE OF ATREUS on a Temple wall. The confusions were past. I would be an honest teacher again, an honest critic.

My first task as a free man was not easy, but it could not in decency be evaded. Walking briskly across the campus to President Rossiter's home, I banged on the door and said: 'Please excuse this rudeness, but I had to tell you before I lost courage. I've decided, sir, that it's time I moved on. I'll be leaving at the end of term.'

Having conducted many such interviews, often at his instigation when firing someone, he showed no surprise. Instead he asked me to step inside, then retreated to the hackneyed statements required in such situations: 'I knew we wouldn't be able to hold on to a luminary like you forever, Karl. We wish you a world of good luck in your promotion. Where is it?'

'Temple. New program. Solid funding.' He was decent enough not to gasp at hearing that he was losing one of his stars not to Princeton or Stanford but to Temple, but his eyebrows did shoot up. 'Well,' he said, recovering nicely, 'big, stable institution. Doing fine work with inner-city young people, we hear. You'll have a notable opportunity. Our best wishes go with you,' and four minutes later he ushered me out. But as I left the porch he called after me: 'Karl, we'll keep this out of the papers, won't we? Student outcries when we lose a popular professor can become embarrassing, can't they?' and I agreed, for I was happy to be leaving on any terms.

It was in these moments of rebirth that I swore: 'At Temple, I'll allow nothing to divert me from trying to steer American writing on an honest course. The two seminars Iscovich has me scheduled to conduct, especially *Deconstructionism, the Pathway to Meaning*, will be a dialogue with my peers,' and I returned to my quarters elated.

For some years I'd been in the habit of reading the media pages of the *Times*, finding bits of inside information that made me feel as if I were a participant in the big games being played in the publishing community. One morning I found more than I bargained for:

> Rumors from top sources hint that the proposed marriage of New York's Kinetic Press to Hamburg's Kastle has collapsed. Blame is equally allocated, Kinetic wanting more assurances on policy continuation than the Germans were prepared to give, Kastle asking for more business concessions than the Americans could grant. Experts believe that both parties have moved back to square one, with every probability that an American white knight will rescue Ki-

netic, a house which in the past has published famous native writers and today boasts a list which is so diverse it contains both the elderly best-seller Lukas Yoder and the young iconoclast Timothy Tull. One competitor said: 'It would be salutary if ownership were kept in this country.'

Before finishing the article, I put in a call for Yvonne, but had no opportunity to convey my anxiety, for she cried in a voice of real agitation: 'Karl, thank God you called. Can I come down and talk with you?'

'How soon can you get to the inn?' When she said she thought she could make it by eleven, I said: 'Good. Do you want me to assemble Yoder and Tull and maybe Sorkin?' And she said firmly: 'Only you. And come with all decks cleared. Military action.'

When she arrived she was more nervous than I had ever seen her and sought to calm herself by ordering an atypical drink: 'Jack Daniel's on the rocks.' When it came she took a gulp and surprised me by reaching out to grasp my hands and saying: 'I'm so glad you could see me.' Then she settled back and said: 'Karl, you could do me a great favor. You're familiar with this town. If you come upon a really good house that's for sale, let me know.'

'What's happened? You quit? Fired?'

Laughing nervously, she squeezed my hand: 'No. I'm fine. Just waking up, as a matter of fact. These are days that send one back to fundamentals, and I realize that with both my parents dead and no siblings I'm really alone in this world. I have no real home. And I do not relish the New York I'm seeing. So much of my life centers on this village these days, it's become my home. I want to live where there are fields, and village policemen, and a corner store whose clerks know who you are.' She slumped, averted her eyes, blew her nose vigorously. 'I'm so glad you called when you did. I need judicious counsel and could think of no one in New York to give it.' She was so distraught, I decided that this was no time to tell her about my decision to leave Mecklenberg.

She launched into a detailed unraveling of the intricate corporate moves that had led to the breakup of the proposed Kinetic-Kastle union. But she had barely begun when she said abruptly: 'There's a tape recorder in the trunk of my car. Please fetch it. Here are my keys. I want you to get every word of this—and accurately.'

When I had the machine propped close to us, tape running, she said: 'You can turn it off for the moment. This next is very confidential,' so I flipped the switch: 'I understand that your short book on the younger writers is almost finished?'

'Yes, and I believe it's good.'

'I'm sure it is.' She tossed off this judgment in her anxiety to get to the real topic: 'Karl, a fine American publishing house is going down the drain. It's nobody's fault, and everybody's fault. What I want you to do, starting right now—put aside your other work—is to start researching and writing a really strong account of the assassination. I'll tell you all I know. I'll arrange for colleagues we can trust to give you long interviews. Get them on tape, and this new material, plus what you already know, which is substantial because you're more interested in publishing than any of my other writers, can be the backbone of a powerful article. I want you to call it *Murder of a Publisher*. And I know an editor at *The New York Review of Books* who is sure to like it. Like many people involved with books, he wants the story out in the open. Now, start the tape.'

She told me that when the deal between Kastle and Rockland Oil fell through ('We book people at Kinetic had nothing to do with it—just the money men') the basic reason was not ventilated because it might be bad publicity for publishing: 'A group of our best writers, none curiously in my stable, announced that they would not write for Kastle, would tear up their contracts and go to court to defend their right to do so. This altered the terms of the sale so critically that Kastle, justifiably in my mind, backed out.'

'The *Times* article didn't say anything about writers revolting—it said something about "business concessions," ' I said, and she added brusquely: 'Smoke screen to hide the ugly problems.'

An intense drive had then been orchestrated to keep the ownership in the United States, but one potential suitor after another inspected the books and backed off. A surprisingly able group from Kansas City included three members whose literary wives thought it would be marvelous to own a publishing house so that they could entertain famous writers, especially Lukas Yoder, and the sale came within hours of completion. But at the last moment the husbands looked at the real profit-and-loss predictions and the oldest member growled: 'What are we doing fooling around with this penny-ante business?' The men came to their senses and withdrew the offer.

For Rockland Oil that was the final straw. That very afternoon the big brass called the Kastle people in Hamburg and asked if they'd raise their bid by forty-six million if Kinetic promised that not more than six of their big-name writers would depart. But Kastle did want one assurance: 'Will Yoder and his editor, Ms. Marmelle, stay with us?' She told me that ten minutes before, when rumors of the first Kastle bid flashed through the editorial rooms, 'I had pretty much decided to walk out, taking my four Dresden writers with me, if they'd come. But when I realized that this might put the entire sale in jeopardy, and at a time when Kinetic desperately needed a home, I made a snap decision: I'll stay, and the deal was made possible. It hasn't been consummated yet.'

In the hectic weeks that followed I interviewed a score of people and found myself the nation's leading authority on the impending demise of Kinetic Press. I do believe I understood the dodges and desperation moves better even than the gray-suited lawyers who control so much of our national life. In what I now report I draw upon those interviews.

Yvonne had been correct in her assessment of why the first Kastle deal had fallen through: a group of writers had delivered an ultimatum, 'No German owners,' so the economic base for the sale had collapsed. She was also right in her guess that more than a dozen potential American buyers had nosed up to the trough but refused to feed. But she did not know that quite a few of these potential buyers had been put off by the arrogance of the Rockland Oil people, who considered Kinetic no different from an outmoded filling station in Albuquerque that had to be liquidated.

When word began to circulate publicly that German ownership of Kinetic might soon be formalized, employees of the firm started looking to their president, John MacBain, for guidance. But as Yvonne pointed out: 'We soon discovered that he knew no more than we. Neither Rockland nor Kastle bothered to inform him of how negotiations were going. He was treated with contempt.'

Through extensive interviews at the various law offices I learned that at the very time MacBain and his senior staff were trying to discover what was about to happen to their company—and mine, I was beginning to think—the deal was consummated along sensible lines, with both Rockland and Kastle getting much of what they had anticipated. But for three days, while papers were being signed, no one bothered to tell the people at Kinetic what was transpiring.

The time had now come when Yvonne had to inform MacBain of the commission she had given me surreptitiously and he said: 'Good. There ought to be an impartial record of this catastrophe in American publishing. Streibert will do an honest job.' To my surprise he was so eager to have a factual account rendered that he invited me to a session in his office, and after a few pleasantries in which he praised my books of criticism he said: 'We hope to enjoy a long relationship with you, Professor. You seem to have a judicious eye.'

'And ear, I hope, because as Ms. Marmelle told you, I've been investigating Kinetic rather carefully.'

'And what have you discovered?'

THE CRITIC

· ·
330

'There's an ugly rumor that Rockland Oil has not kept you informed of negotiations that everyone else knows are under way. Could that be true?'

'Absolutely.' He said this with such vigor and distaste that I asked bluntly: 'Would it be possible for Rockland to close the deal without telling you?' and he replied bitterly: 'In the past they've told me nothing. Why would they start now?'

The humiliation to which he was being subjected angered him so much that he rang for his secretary: 'Please ask the senior editors to join us. I want them to give Professor Streibert their full cooperation in the task he's undertaking,' and when the older men and women who had helped keep Kinetic vital through the years joined us, I could see in their faces the secret fears that attacked them in these days when they had no security in a company they had helped build.

At that moment the phone rang, and all of us in the room expected that it might be the president of Rockland informing us of whatever deal had been made. Instead it was a flunky in his office who said in a voice loud enough for some of us to hear: 'MacBain, this is Ralph Considine in President Cornwall's office. He wanted me to advise you that Kinetic has this day been sold to Kastle in a deal that looks profitable to both sides. Kastle has agreed to keep you on as head of Kinetic for two more years, after which you'll be eligible for a comfortable pension. There will be no mass firings, but deadwood will be removed as painlessly as possible.' There was more, but I forget the details.

When Mr. MacBain put down the telephone, I saw his ashen face. He told us the deal had been concluded three days earlier but no one had told him. He then looked at each of his staff and said: 'I suppose that by the terms of the sale, you seniors will be kept on. Those lower in the hierarchy may not be.' In the ensuing silence his fingers drummed on his desk, then he lifted the phone: "Miss Harcourt, please get me Mr. Considine at Rockland." When he was located,

MacBain said: 'This is John MacBain again. Since Mr. Cornwall did not have the decency to inform me directly that Kinetic had been disposed of, I feel no obligation to inform him personally of the move I intend to make. Tell him when he finds time to see you that I am canceling all my affiliations with Kinetic as of this moment, eleven-thirty-eight, Tuesday, February fourteenth, 1989. And say that this message was my Valentine.'

In the anguished silence that followed I studied the faces of the editors and financial officers who would be affected by the demise of this great American company, at least in its historic guise. Several of the women and one of the men wept; others blew their noses furtively, and all looked distraught. Yvonne showed from the set of her jaw that her teeth were clenched, and she was the first to express the emotion that everyone felt: 'We all ought to resign, too. I'm willing. Last month I promised to stay, but if they treat us this way, to hell with them, and I'm sure I can take most of my writers with me.'

When others made the same vow, MacBain surprised them by masking his own fury and speaking like the publishing statesman he had always been: 'Friends, friends! Don't make hasty decisions just because I had to. I've heard editors threaten before: "All my writers will quit with me," but they rarely do. Nineteen times out of twenty, upon reflecting, they discover where their interest lies and stay put. Besides, Kastle will inherit a strongbox full of signed contracts, and believe me, your new owners are the kind of hard-nosed operators who will sue to enforce compliance. Ours has been a great, proud company. I'm sure it can find a decent life under the new conditions. Stay with it, I beg of you.'

When murmurs of defiance continued, he said with that touch of humor which had made him so successful in working with editors and authors: 'Stop fighting the inevitable. In the early years of this century my grandfather ran a livery stable. When the automobile came he didn't rail against Henry Ford. He sold his horses, bought a Ford, and converted his stables into a profitable Ford dealership.'

When one of the editors pointed out: 'But Ford was an American patriot,' Yvonne, brought up in a strong pro-labor family that deplored Ford's behavior as a union-buster, growled: 'There were many who doubted that.'

At this gloomy moment one of the younger women editors said brightly: 'At an Irish funeral there's always food, and since this is a real funeral and I'm Irish, I'm going to get some beer and sandwiches.' I saw Mr. MacBain slip her two ten-dollar bills.

During the wake one woman editor said: 'I've followed this from the start and what appalled me was the contempt for books, the inability to find an American buyer for a great American company, the willingness of the money boys to ignore Mr. MacBain and even laugh at him. I feel humiliated, as if I too were being degraded, and I say openly: "Mr. MacBain, if you want to move to another publisher, I'm sure your editorial staff will go along if they're invited." '

MacBain would have none of that. Almost laughing, he told his people: 'Some of you would accompany me, and I love you for it, but, like the authors, most of you would finally see that you had to stay, mainly because jobs are not that plentiful out there.'

One editor, a reticent fellow who specialized in Western history and cowboys, startled me: 'You'll sound silly if you berate foreign ownership. Remember that much of our development west of the Mississippi was financed by foreign investors—our railroads, our irrigation ditches, our first factories.'

When one of the financial managers said: 'I wasn't aware of that,' he gave a wan smile: 'Most Americans don't know. When they see John Wayne swaggering across the prairie on the way north to Dodge City with Montgomery Clift, they never reflect that these Americans are working on a ranch owned by some capitalist in Dundee, Scotland. Most of the great ranches of the West

were financed and managed by men with names like Angus Mac-
Tavish, not an honest American in the lot. If the Germans give us
good management, we'll survive.' On that solitary ray of hope, the
meeting broke up.

Yvonne described the episode that summarized the situation pre-
vailing when the storms subsided: 'All senior editors were summoned
to a meeting with our new boss, Oxford-trained Ludwig Ludenberg,
whom we called General Ludendorff behind his back, and as the
meeting ended, he asked me to remain: "They tell me you've been
thinking of leaving Kinetic," and I replied: "You could say that of
everyone in the meeting."

'With great earnestness he said: "With Mr. MacBain leaving,
you're more needed than ever. With us your promotions are unlimited."

'I replied that I planned to stay for the time being. "And your
authors?" The way he asked this, with a mix of eagerness and apprehension, revealed that he was more interested in them than in me,
so I said: "Most of them, yes. Two of my Jews, no."

' "Ms. Marmelle, in Kastle there is no Jew or Gentile, no black
or yellow or white. Do you have a black woman as one of your
assistant editors, personally, that is?"

' "No."

' "Get one. Pay the going rate. Black, and a woman." We shook
hands and the interview ground to a halt.'

The debacle at Kinetic strengthened my resolve to begin a new
intellectual life, and I made a resounding start with my three-part
article in *The New York Review of Books*. It was so unequivocal that
perceptive readers had to see that I had returned to my earlier style
of deep commitment expressed in telling phrases. I felt that I was
back on track, and this newfound honesty occasioned three changes

in my life. I broke the seal of silence about my move to Temple, informing Yvonne of my switch at the end of term. When she heard the news she congratulated me on its boldness: 'Leaving the comfortable cocoon at Mecklenberg and diving into the maelstrom of a central-city university—that takes courage. I'm proud of you, Karl,' but then she grew pensive: 'Of course, I've noticed with writers that when you make a major change in one aspect of your writing life you can be expected to make comparable changes in all else. You'll probably be leaving Kinetic one of these days, which means that you'll be leaving me, too. And that's sad.'

I assured her that I had no intention of doing either: 'You and Kinetic launched me. Temple would never have heard of me otherwise. I'm yours for keeps.'

But I did make a complete break with my two students, Timothy Tull and Jenny Sorkin. At last I accepted the fact that I'd done all I could for them and that they must now go their own ways without further interference from me. I used the word *ways* in the plural because I still vaguely hoped that Timothy would not ruin the beginning of his adult life by contracting a hideously improper marriage with her, but even that I left to chance. I was no longer involved.

The third consequence of my articles on Kinetic was the most important. As if the gods wanted to test my new commitment to courage, the editors of *The New York Times Book Review* telephoned to say that with the forthcoming publication of Lukas Yoder's final novel in his octet they wished to show respect to both the book and his general track record, and since I was well acquainted with the Pennsylvania Dutch country, they were prepared to give me not only the front page for a review, but also a full page in the back for a separate wrap-up of the man and his works.

Since this was the kind of presentation that would confirm my rebirth as a serious critic I told the caller: 'I'd be honored. Send it down. I'll work to your schedule.'

But when I took one of my last walks along the Wannsee to plot the course of my review and the attendant essay, I gradually awakened to the many reasons why I should have refused: I'm too closely bound to Yoder to do either his book or him justice. I've grown to dislike him and his work. But I really can't ignore the fact that his generosity to Mecklenberg provided the funds on which my writing course prospered. However, I still despise his sententious display that night at the Longfellow talk when he prattled on about that sorry poet's one good line, 'Like ships that pass in the night.' Also, he hurt me deeply when my novel *Cistern* was so hammered by the critics. He added to the damage by saying: 'Karl's novel doesn't sing,' which was hateful. Of course, I learned later that what he really said was: 'It's a fine work in every respect but one. It doesn't sing.' Deep down I still resented his intrusion into the professional lives of my students Tull and Sorkin. And I confess that there was residual bitterness from that period when I honestly believed that I could write a better novel than he'd done. And finally it irritated me beyond words that he had preempted my Pennsylvania Dutch country in writing his successful books.

Had I been sensitive to the proprieties, I would have recognized that I had a score of reasons to recuse myself from writing a review of Yoder's novel, but at that point in my life I did not yet know the meaning of that profoundly moral word. A judge who knows that his personal relationship to the claimant standing before him is so intimate that he might be swayed either to favor the man unduly or treat him too harshly, is morally bound to inform the court: 'For personal reasons I recuse myself from this case.' In the same way, responsible critics recuse themselves when asked to review a book by a friend. In the Yoder case I should certainly have recused, but I didn't.

My reasoning, which at the time I deemed commendable, was that I wanted to use Yoder's bland, run-of-the-mill fiction as an example

THE CRITIC

. . . .
336

of the kind of writing I could no longer tolerate and which, from my
restored eminence as a serious critic, I had to oppose. After the most
severe self-analysis, I persuaded myself, as I took my place at the
typewriter to summarize Yoder and his work, that I had cleansed
myself of any animosity toward the man. If I was about to make
harsh judgments it wasn't that I disliked him but only his flaccid
novels. I never worked with purer intentions or produced more
sulfurous results.

I can only surmise what must have happened when my review and
essay reached the *Times*, but I'm told that someone at the paper
surreptitiously called Yvonne Marmelle and said: 'Sunday, two written by your Karl Streibert.'

I think that Yvonne, by one of the devices of which she was a
master, must have got hold of a copy of my review, or rather a
complete summary, for two days after I mailed it my phone began
jangling. A variety of friends in writing and publishing called to
inform me that she had spoken to them in honeyed phrases, striving
to establish Yoder and his book as ornaments in American intellectual life while crucifying me as a fool and an ingrate. It became clear
that she was engaging in what politicians in the last presidential
election had called 'spin control,' influencing public opinion either
before the event took place or soon thereafter.

She was selective in whom she called and overpowering in her
determination to nullify my adverse review. She also, as far as I could
judge from what my friends told me, hoped to persuade the *Times*
to kill my longer analysis of the defunct Yoder career, and I gained
an image of her as one of those fire fighters in Western states who
appear on television, tired and sooty, to explain how they are building backfires to deprive the big blaze of oxygen.

I doubt that she called the *Times* itself, because she once told me:

'Early in my professional life I learned a basic rule: "Never try to force a journal to alter a review, nor even to review a book when they've decided not to." I had one young man, fearfully proud of himself and his book, which wasn't worth a damn. I'd edited it only because Kinetic forced it upon me. I thought it so bad that I was relieved when the *Times* ignored it, but the young man mounted a savage campaign to force me to make the paper review his book. When I refused, advising him to let the matter drop, he wrote a vicious letter to the daily reviewer asking in insulting terms if the man had even bothered to read his book.'

Some days later the daily review began: 'Last week I received a plaintive letter from Harry Jackman asking if I had bothered to read his book *Desert Nights*, and when was I going to print my review? Yes, I did read it, and here's my review.' It was so scathing that Yvonne never heard from the young man again, but she made copies to send to young writers who insisted upon promoting their books by insulting newspapers.

There was a more important reason why she could not do anything to offend the *Times*; in the course of a normal year she would personally oversee the editing and publishing of at least eight books, so she dared not bellyache about bad treatment to Yoder, when doing so might imperil her other seven books. Her response to a bad review had to be: 'Better luck next time.'

But apparently the *Times* itself must have had serious doubts about my two papers, for one of the women at the *Book Review* called me at the college. She was told: 'Professor Streibert's in class and cannot be disturbed.'

'He must be disturbed. This is what you might call crucial,' and when I took the call she said: 'We have your two papers, the review and the accompanying essay. They're rather more negative than we expected. We've decided we must drop the essay, but, of course, you get a kill fee.'

'You asked for two articles of a certain length and I submitted them.'

'We'll run your review exactly as written, you're entitled to that, and we never censor except certain words we like to avoid.'

'It sounds like censorship to me.'

Gently she said: 'Professor Streibert, you must consider one aspect. Rumor is you're taking an important new position at Temple in Philadelphia. Don't start with what could become a scandal in the profession.'

This was advice so pertinent that I had to take it seriously. Personal spite had played no part in my essay on Yoder. I had been motivated only by a desire to elevate American fiction to a level far higher than his rather pitiful novels had attained or even aspired to, but if the reader interpreted my words as petty vengeance, I would be doing myself harm, and at the very moment when my career was on an upward course again. In a humbled voice I said: 'Consider it killed. But you did promise that the review would run as written.'

'That promise will be honored.'

I knew it was legitimate for Yvonne to try, discreetly, to ferret out what she could about the *Times* plan for my review, and I learned later that one of her friends at the paper told her they were appalled and would bury it on page 11 or 12. The informant said: 'So Streibert's demolition derby won't cover more than a quarter of a page,' but then warned that the essay wasn't dead, in that I might find a publisher among the little magazines.

I don't have to guess what Yvonne did next to protect her valuable property, because a bookseller in Bethlehem was chuckling when he called me: 'Karl, amigo, you must have dropped a bomb on Yoder. Yvonne just called, breathless. Said that the Sunday *Times* review was somewhat negative but to ignore it, because she was sending me post haste raves from half a dozen other important media. She said Kinetic was making *Stone Walls* their major fall effort and it was off to a magnificent start. I asked her: "What's this we hear about snide comments from the book clubs and orders slashed by the chains?" and she said: "No significance whatever. We're certain it will gallop to the top of the lists, thanks to the good work you men and women in the retail stores always do with a Yoder book." '

That covered, she seems to have telephoned individually each of Kinetic's top field representatives to inoculate them against bad news, and I heard from one of them I had interviewed when researching the Kastle story how she had massaged him: 'She was calm and sweet. Confessed up front that we'd been slaughtered in the *Times* but assured me that the other reviews fluctuated between very good and raves. She admitted frankly that millions of dollars were riding on this book, and assured me that Kinetic would be fighting all the way. More than half a million copies in print. She predicted it would remain near the top of the list for at least half a year, and she closed with a typical Marmelle zinger: "Paul, if you find in your sample case any copies of Streibert's own novel, burn them." '

A publicity person at Kinetic with whom I had become friendly when conducting my interviews on Kastle told me how close I had come to frontal assault by Yvonne: 'When her rage subsided she gave me three jobs. "Find me the lushest possible photographs of Grenzler terrain—Lancaster farms, barns, cattle grazing. Dig out the most favorable preliminary reviews and six raves on previous Grenzlers. And finally, I want a handsome photograph of Karl Streibert." '

'What was her plan?'

'She and I put together an eye-catching ad. Your picture real big, beneath the caption: "This famous critic who lives in Grenzler country did not care for Lukas Yoder's masterly novel *Stone Walls*. The rest of the nation did." '

'I never saw such an ad.'

'It never ran. When I had it laid out, with your photograph dominating, Yvonne came to my workbench, stood for some minutes tapping her heel, and finally placed her hand completely over your face. "Kill it," she said. "He's a man fighting to build a new life, and I can't roadblock him with a cheap shot." '

My review of *Stone Walls* evoked a storm, nowhere more virulent than at our college, where it was seen as one Mecklenberg graduate trashing another. When President Rossiter summoned me for a castigation, I saw a man very different from the official who fawned over potential donors. Like a bulldog protecting his turf, he growled: 'It's so damned juvenile, Karl. You're leaving us in a huff because you've made a mess of your private life. And, like a sixteen-year-old, you want to celebrate your going with an explosion. Well, you've done yourself more damage than you've done us. Any sensible faculty member of any college will see that it was reprehensible of you to abuse the man from whom you accepted a million dollars for your department.'

When I tried to defend myself he struck at me in an area where I belatedly acknowledged that I was vulnerable: 'Did you, as a professional critic, consider how inappropriate it was for you even to review Yoder's book, let alone condemn it? Had you praised it you would still be academically suspect—too closely related to the author, too personally involved. I hope for your sake that you behave more maturely at Temple than you've been doing here recently. You're wise in leaving, Streibert. You've worn out your welcome.'

Mrs. Garland also called to reprimand me: 'Infamous! You must have rocks in your head—or mush.'

It was from one of the students that I learned what Yoder himself thought, and his reaction surprised me: 'My aunt helps Mrs. Yoder clean on Thursdays and she told me that on Sunday he opened his copy of the *Times*, turned first to the *The Week in Review*, then casually flipped through the *Book Review* and saw at the top of page

12 the bold headline GRENZLER OCTET COLLAPSES NOT WITH A
BANG BUT WITH A WHIMPER. He stopped to notice that the review
had been written by Karl Streibert, but, as was his custom, he refused
to read it. And after a casual scan of the front page of the news
section he put the heavy Sunday edition down and walked out to his
carpenter shop.'

My student told me that Emma did turn to the review, which she
supposed would appear in this edition, and let out a roar when she
read the nine paragraphs in which I had skewered her husband and
his novel. Although she knew that Lukas tried to avoid such moments, she burst into his painting area: 'Darling, you've got to know
about the terrible thing that's happened—' With quavering voice she
read aloud my two closing paragraphs:

> ' "*Stone Walls*, coming as the capstone to the chain of tedi-
> ous novels, reveals in pitiful detail the wobbly base on which
> the whole was built. It is drawn out, sentimental, and care-
> lessly written. Its characters are wooden and their dialogue
> sawdusty. Action flags, plot creaks and the skill for descrip-
> tion for which Mr. Yoder is supposed to be famous is repeti-
> tious. Most reprehensible, he makes his fellow Pennsylvania
> Dutch amusing buffoons and misses entirely the grandeur of
> their stubborn resistance to a modern world they cannot
> trust.
>
> ' "That any supposedly serious writer would waste his time
> concocting such a confection is inexplicable. That any atten-
> tive reader would bother to read to the end of this wearisome
> guff is unimaginable. Just as the sixteen trifles in the *Jalna*
> series bear no discernible relationship to the Canadian expe-
> rience, so the eight *Grenzler* volumes relate not at all to
> America, past or present. And of the two sorry accumula-

tions this final volume of the so-called Dutch material is the worst. As the poet predicted, '*Stone Walls* do not a novel make.' " '

The cleaning woman said: 'When Emma slammed the review to the floor, she cried: "Well, Lukas, what're you gonna do about it?" and he said from the bench where he was cleanin' one of them hex signs he fools with: "Do? I'm gonna finish this paintin'." '

IV

THE READER

SUNDAY, **6** OCTOBER: I woke early this morning aware that today was special in the Dutch country. Books are so important to me, and I am so proud that my grandson has published one and seems to be completing another that I take special interest in any written by a neighbor. I was delighted when Professor Streibert at the college did his book on literary criticism and shared his disappointment when his novel turned out so poorly. But my joy for the past fifteen years has been the nationwide, indeed worldwide, reception given the novels of my friend Lukas Yoder.

Because I follow his career, I have been aware that the final novel in his Grenzler series, *Stone Walls*, is being published tomorrow, which means that the important *New York Times* review would probably be in today's Sunday edition. I'm ashamed to say I was inattentive when his first three novels appeared, and didn't even hear of them, though I live almost in the heart of the area in which they're set. But then, millions of other Americans didn't hear of them either, for the sales were either minimal or nonexistent.

There is in the Dresden Public Library a dear, thoughtful woman, who reminded me of my poor headstrong daughter in that she will- fully married a world-class zombie, but unlike my Clara, she had the sense to kick him out when she learned that he was foul-mouthed, a drunk and a womanizer. There are rumors that on her vacations she is apt to go where a married professor of English from Penn State is taking his, and this causes comment locally, but I feel that if she's worked out a satisfactory pattern of life, it's no business of mine.

She's just what a librarian should be, and fifteen years ago she did me a good turn when she said: 'Mrs. Garland, you really must read Lukas Yoder's new novel, *The Shunning*. It has a classic simplicity and a compelling sense of tragedy.' That's the kind of book I seek, something real and irresistible in its force, *Madame Bovary* for one, or *Anna Karenina*. *The Shunning* was such a book, with people in it that I might have met in the Lancaster markets at the turn of the century, and I'm delighted that it's in the process of becoming a motion picture.

But it didn't sell, at least not when published, although I'm told it's now being taken by all the European houses. I was impatient to learn how *Stone Walls* would be received, for I wanted Yoder to finish his career in a blaze of glory.

As I left my bedroom and started downstairs I stopped, as I so often do, at a landing from which I could survey the splendid room so symbolic of my wonderful husband, Larrimore, and the energy with which he faced life and the challenges of the steel industry. He had designed the room, supervised its construction, and to a large extent determined its decoration with a tasteful mix of Pennsylvania Dutch and American colonial. It was also he who had insisted upon a wall of windows looking south over the gently sloping lawn; these windows made it possible for anyone sitting in what was always called 'the big room' to have a panoramic view of whatever weather was sweeping the valley below.

When visitors entered this room, they had an immediate choice between two smaller rooms: to their left was a formal dining room seating twelve; to their right, a comfortable paneled library, whose walls were covered with books, not studiedly arranged in ostentatious order because these were books that had been read and reread. I thought of these three rooms as my special domain. Larrimore had named our place Windsong from the breezes that roamed the valley; locals still called it the Mansion. I thought of it as home.

On this morning I rang for Oscar with just a touch of urgency and when he appeared I asked: 'Have you gone for the *Times* yet?' and he said patiently: 'Madam, you know that on Sunday the last-minute sections arrive late. Have to be assembled with what came in during the week.'

'You told me, but I forgot. I am anxious.'

He laughed: 'You know that if I go now, I'll have to sit around and wait.'

'Of course. But please be a good fellow and get it as soon as you can.'

Sometime later, when he delivered the heavy Sunday edition, I shuffled the sections till I found the *Book Review*. I supposed that because of its importance, Yoder's novel would be featured on the front page and was disappointed when I did not find it there. Flipping the pages with growing concern, I came finally to page 12, where I found a savage review by Karl Streibert, my friend at the college.

Gasping at its annihilation of what I had been led to believe would be the finest of the Grenzler novels, I threw the *Review* onto the coffee table, upsetting an empty cup. Staring at the offending page, I muttered: 'Infamous! The men are neighbors! Almost colleagues.'

Retrieving the paper, I read each sentence with the care I had once expended on reading assignments at Vassar, and this made me even angrier. I had always loved books, and almost every room at Windsong had its own corner library; I couldn't take an insult like this to one of my authors silently.

Dialing with ill-controlled fury, I placed the first of the many calls I would make that day; it was to Streibert, but he was not in his rooms at the college. Shifting impatiently to my grandson's number, I did catch him before he was out of bed: 'Timothy! Have you seen Professor Streibert's review of Lukas Yoder's novel?'

'Yes. Thorough scrubbing, wasn't it?'

'It was infamous!'

'Grandmother—'

'But the men are friends—they almost work together—on good projects at the college.'

'Now, Grandmother! Streibert's review deals with standards that are of great significance to all writers—'

'But to go out of one's way to be insulting—to a friend!'

'He wasn't insulting. He was defining an intellectual problem, and disposing of it rather neatly, I must say.'

'Do you forget that Mr. Yoder supported you when you brought out *Kaleidoscope*? You're as bad as Professor Streibert—worse—you're ungrateful. And among gentlemen that's a dreadful charge.'

'Streibert and I—we're not monsters. You know I'm fond of Mr. Yoder and I am grateful to him. Simple fact is across America teachers of real literature know that Yoder's a dodo.' He paused, chuckled, and said: 'What a great title for my own essay, "Yodo the Dodo"!'

JANE GARLAND

· ·

347

'You write something like that, I'll disown you. Worse, I'll disinherit you.'

'Don't talk nonsense, you darling antediluvian.'

When I was left the sole guardian of my grandson I encouraged him to treat me not as some sacrosanct Grimms' fairy-tale grandmother but as almost an equal, and on this arrangement we thrived. Now he said: 'Go back and read *The Bobbsey Twins*, leave Yoder to us.'

'Why are you both so savage?'

'Because in the American system, a man like Yoder does a great deal of damage. He writes a book, or even a group of books, that may have been appropriate in its day. Never significant, never relevant to any major problem, space-fillers, but acceptable, I suppose, because they keep publishing houses viable.'

'What's dishonorable about that? He helped Kinetic to be there when you wanted it.'

'Honorable it is. Significant? No.'

'Then what's the trouble?'

'Men like Yoder preempt the space needed by real writers. They flood the market with junk, and Gresham's Law of Literature swings into action. Yoder's bad drives out Streibert's good.'

'Streibert's novel was unreadable, and you know it.'

'By the canaille. Those in the profession thought it significant. Spelled out the future.'

'God help America if *Empty Cistern* is the future. There goes any necessity for eyeglasses—nothing to read.'

'I love you, Grandmother. But we do have different ideas about what's worth reading.'

'And the money Yoder makes for Kinetic will enable you to get yours published.'

'Ta-ta, you darling. I'll send you an autographed copy of "Yodo the Dodo."'

My next call was to President Rossiter at the college: 'Have you seen your Professor Streibert's devastating review of Lukas Yoder's current novel?'

'Yes. I was shocked.' After we exchanged reactions to the various points the critic had made, Rossiter said: 'Jane, this is far more serious than you might think. . . . What I mean is, it's worse than you would be in a position to know . . . the details, I mean.'

Since he was far more agitated than I had expected, I said: 'Norman, you're mumbling. Please give me the details. I am a member of your board.'

'Privileged news, of course. But sometime back, as you know, Lukas and Emma gave me one million dollars, to do with as I thought best for the college. No announcement, of course.'

'From Yoder one would expect a rule like that.'

'What you don't know is that at the time they handed me the check they intimated that if things went well with their future books . . .'

'That they'd give us further gifts? They intimated that?'

'Much stronger than intimated.'

'But nothing in writing?'

'Of course not, but we have nothing in writing from you, either. Standard, I'd say. Advise me. Do you think Streibert's review, coming from the college, as it were . . . will it sour the Yoders on us?'

I reflected on this for some moments, then said: 'Emma will be furious. She may try to burn down Streibert's lecture hall. Lukas, I should think, will ignore the matter.'

'Ignore the review, perhaps. But will what's happened today strangle further gifts?'

More reflection: 'The Yoders aren't like that,' I said.

'What should I do?'

'What would I do? I'd convene a small cocktail party here at Windsong. I'll be hostess. You do the inviting. The Yoders, Yoder's

Dutch farmer friend, Zollicoffer, and act as if nothing had happened. The important thing, Norman, is to let Emma know that you treasure her husband, because she'll make the final decision.'

'What do you mean?'

'Consider a moment. The Yoders are exactly like me, only more so. We have no immediate children, I have only my grandson, Timothy, and the Yoders don't even have someone like him. So when we die, we have to do something with our funds. Emma knows this as clearly as I do, and she'll give to whoever treats her husband with respect.'

'In your recommendation just now, you meant that *you* would give the cocktail party?'

'Of course. I'll get the local librarian to come too, a fine woman named Benelli. That will make it a literary affair, celebrating his novel, and no one will see that you're sweating unmercifully.'

'Agreed, but I shall be sweating.'

My next calls were to the Zollicoffers, whom I knew only slightly but respected as the farmers who helped Yoder with his writing, and to Ms. Benelli, all of whom were pleased with the prospect of visiting Windsong on Wednesday.

That pleasant chore attended to, I prepared for a meeting I had long anticipated: an introduction to Miss Jenny Sorkin, about whom I'd heard a great deal from Timothy but had not met. Since it seemed apparent that Timothy was seeing her quite often, I felt I ought to know what kind of young woman she was. She was a new experience, tallish, slim, unkempt, a rowdy look, a twinkle in her eye, a ready smile and a T-shirt on which was printed: WHERE WERE YOU WHEN I NEEDED A DATE FOR THE PROM? When I saw it I had to chuckle. 'I had that problem at twenty. It was pretty awful to be at Vassar in those hectic years. The draft for World War II made men simply unavailable, especially if you weren't too good-looking, and I wasn't.'

When the two young people were seated facing the big windows through which the lights of cars driving the Cut Off were visible, I served sandwiches and a plate of Fenstermacher's new autumn scrapple fried so crisply it had become finger food. 'Now,' I said, 'explain if you can why you Young Turks feel you have to declare war on Lukas Yoder.'

'Wait!' Miss Sorkin cried. 'Don't include me. I'm quite fond of him and his books. Let's face it, we're pretty much alike. We write books that ordinary people can read and understand.'

I smiled at her and said: 'The minute I saw your T-shirt I knew I was going to like you.' Then, turning to Timothy, I said: 'So it's going to be two women who prefer books that can be read, against you and Streibert, who advocate books that nobody can read.'

'Talk about savage!' Timothy cried in mock horror. 'Grandmother, nothing I said about Yoder was half as brutal as what you just said about Streibert—that nobody read his novel.'

I said: 'I meant it in the abstract—that the general readership cannot absorb either his novel *Empty Cistern* or your exciting adventure story *Kaleidoscope*. Do you accept my kindlier interpretation?' My grandson snorted: 'You're digging yourself in deeper. Let Professor Streibert and me get on with our assassination.'

'No!' I cried. 'If he were here tonight instead of hiding down in Philadelphia, I'd spit in his eye. Here, have some more of Fenstermacher's scrapple. It's as close to the soul of Grenzler as Yoder's novels.'

'And just as lethal to the digestion,' Timothy said. 'In a time of growing cultural darkness, men like Streibert—in universities across the nation—are beginning to believe that the job of serious fiction is to maintain a dialogue of exalted meaning among the elite—the rare few who will be making the decisions that will keep society alive.'

'Does that eliminate people like me, who enjoy reading Jane Austen and Willa Cather?'

'No, no! You are the elite,' and he pointed to the two small bookcases that sat even in our big room. They contained, I must say,

an impressive mix of books: serious novels, essays on women, trea-
tises on, and analyses of, changing foreign policies. I have to admit
I was rather pleased at what I thought they reflected—the interests
of a concerned woman at the beginning of her seventies. As I was
immodestly preening, Timothy introduced a name that would
become of importance to me in the weeks ahead: 'I think our great
American poet Ezra Pound expressed it best when he was a prisoner
in St. Elizabeths insane asylum. He preached to those loyal American poets who braved public censure by visiting him in what
amounted to his jail: "Write only for your peers. Ignore the general
public. They always follow false gods." '

My husband and I had schooled ourselves to be suspicious of ideas
like the ones Timothy had been expounding, for we feared they led
to fascism. I had to protest: 'I don't believe I'd be comfortable with
the ideas of your Mr. Pound,' and Timothy explained: 'Professor
Streibert has taken Pound's concepts and elaborated them into what
he calls "the Imperative of the Now." '

'And what might that mean?'

'That an artist is obligated to wrestle with the problems of society
as they arise—in his day—in the understandings of his own particular time.'

I was about to say that to me this sounded like mere expediency
when Miss Sorkin said: 'Tell you what, Mrs. Garland, if you want
a taste of what Timothy's talking about, read the manuscript of his
new novel.' She explained: 'It borrows its title from the word that
Streibert and his fellow new critics like to throw around, *Dialogue*,
and it consists of a hundred and sixty pages of talk between a man
and a woman who are never named or identified in any way except
through their unbroken conversation. Their arguments, agreements
and reflections begin on page one in the middle of a sentence and run
unbroken to the end on page one-sixty. It's eight or ten pages before
you discover whether a man or a woman is talking.'

'But identities do emerge?'

'Yes! Quite definitely—and interesting they become, too—if you stick with it.'

'Sounds more difficult than your first one, Timothy.'

He shrugged his shoulders, obviously uncomfortable at hearing his unpublished work being discussed, but Jenny continued: 'The subtlety of the later pages—take my word for it—this one's going to establish the norm for the decade ahead. It's a brilliant book, Mrs. Garland, one you're going to be proud of.'

'Will I be able to comprehend it?'

'If you stay with it for fifty pages you'll catch on.'

'I'm like Snoopy. I want action in the first sentence. "It was a dark and stormy night," I joked. 'That's my idea of how to start a novel.'

Obviously eager to support Timothy's bold enterprise, Jenny said: 'It's a grand effort. To quote my grandmother: "Try it. You'll like it." '

'Are you going to let me see it?' I asked Timothy, for I was vitally concerned about his progress.

'Yes. I brought all but the last section,' he said, handing me a flat cardboard box. 'You know, Grandmother, I do appreciate your counsel—and act on it, especially when you don't drift back to the nineteenth century.'

'Have you ever read *Joseph Andrews*? Those rowdy goings-on in the eighteenth century might astonish you.'

We dropped that subject, and I asked: 'And what will you be writing, Miss Sorkin? After your football novel is published?'

'I'm trying to write a story specifically for you—one with a strong start and a striking conclusion.'

'I can hardly wait. The subject?'

'Well, now! If I've had good luck so far with football players and their hang-ups, why not do the same with the pompous faculty and board of regents of a well-respected college in—say—Ohio, where they have so many? Or perhaps eastern Pennsylvania?'

'Get that subversive woman out of here!' I cried, and she blew me a kiss.

As I led my talented young guests to the door I paused to take from one of the bookcases we passed a novel by Margaret Drabble, and as we stood together looking at the long sweep of lawn in the autumn moonlight, I held up my two hands: 'Left hand, Timothy's new novel to decipher; right hand, Miss Drabble's to enjoy,' and they booed me as they drove away.

WEDNESDAY, 9 OCTOBER: This afternoon I welcomed to Windsong four of our most congenial Grenzler citizens, the Zollicoffers and the Yoders. Two married couples in their sixties or slightly beyond, and in appearance prototypical Pennsylvania Dutch.

Lukas Yoder was a short man with a squarish face, sandy hair that looked as if he could produce a fine German beard had he wanted one, and the quiet bemused manner that Dutchmen often display when meeting strangers. His wife, Emma, a short little woman, looked as if she had been cooking for farmhands for years, so thin and active was she.

Their nearest neighbor, Herman Zollicoffer, was the darling of the group, a big, rotund Dutchman with a rumpled haircut, a round beaming face and the movements of an aging bull. He was noted for wearing both suspenders and belt, and for his reticence in talking before strangers until some topic arose on which he held strong views; then he would suddenly explode with an oration that might last instructive minutes, for he never spoke unless he had something cogent to say. Silent he was not; prudent he was.

His wife, Frieda, whom I had not met before, was the ideal Dutch wife: jovial, retiring in the presence of strangers, big round face, very round torso, huge round bottom all kept that way by a voracious appetite, as I was soon to learn. It would have been difficult not to like Frieda, especially when she spoke her Pennsylvania Dutch. The first words I heard her utter when she walked into our big room and stared down the valley leading to Rhenish Road were: 'Nice, aindt?' Then she jerked her thumb over her shoulder, pointing backward down the valley: 'Chust down there, Fenstermacher, aindt?' She pronounced *down* in a most engaging way: *dahnnn*. And when she looked at me for confirmation as to where our neighbors had their farm, I nodded.

I found that I was correct in my prediction as to how Yoder would react to Professor Streibert's bitter attack on *Stone Walls*, for when Ms. Benelli and the other guests assembled, one asked: 'How did you feel, Mr. Yoder, when you read that horrible review penned by your neighbor?' and Emma jumped in: 'A professional like my husband never bothers with reviews, especially when he's already sold more than half a million copies before publication.' I could see Lukas wince as if to say: I've tried to stop her saying things like that, but what can a husband do?

When someone pressed: 'But what did you do personally?' he said: 'I worked on my hex painting,' and this evoked numerous questions requiring him to explain how he searched for hex signs on old barns and converted them into what some critics had praised as collages of fresh concept and elegant execution. He himself dismissed such praise: 'All I do is try to rescue the fine traditions of our people—and touch them up a bit with my own fraktur.'

This word also occasioned questions, but at the end of his explanation he received gentle criticism from a quarter he would never have expected, for now Herman Zollicoffer was ready to speak: 'Lukas, I never really forgave you for the mean trick you pulled on them hexes. I warned you a dozen times but you wouldn't listen. Pennsylvania Dutch never believed that Gypsy business, hex signs wardin' off evil, or castin' spells on an enemy. But you went right ahead, even called it *Hex*.'

'What is a hex sign,' Ms. Benelli asked, 'if it isn't what the books say, something to ward off bad luck?'

'Simple designs. Brought over from Germany. Make a barn look proper. They're for nice, not ghosts.' Then, with the warmth he had always felt for Yoder, and proud of what his neighbor had accomplished in bringing Dutch ways to the attention of the world, Zollicoffer said: 'In your first four books you listened to what I said—you respected our traditions. That's why they were good. In *Hex* you tell all the fables, and it's no good.'

Both Yoders laughed, and Emma said: 'You have it wrong, Herman. When he followed your advice too closely, he couldn't give the books away, but when he used his own imagination, they sold like pork sandwiches at Kutztown Fair.'

This launched an extended discussion on how an artist ought to use raw material, and Ms. Benelli was helpful in her ability to cite specific examples of notable books that supported the most contradictory approaches to the problem. One speaker thought Herman Wouk had pulled a daring trick in adapting an entire world war to his purposes, but another said: 'If I could write, I'd try something like Tom Wolfe's *Bonfire of the Vanities*. Take one subject and really dig in—small canvas, penetrating focus.'

Emma said: 'Or one area of society, like Grenzler.' Everyone laughed at her eagerness to defend her husband, then Zollicoffer said: 'I'd like to apologize for what maybe sounded ugly a little while back. Stands to reason Lukas did all right when he listened to what I said about us Dutch, then gave it his own twist.'

'What do you say,' Ms. Benelli asked, 'to those who claim that the best book he's ever written was *The Shunning*?'

'Aha!' Mrs. Zollicoffer broke in with her heavy German accent: 'That's what the Mister said when he read the book the second time: "Chust wunst the young feller got it right." I think so too.'

'That's what I been tryin' to say,' Zollicoffer cried with intense excitement. 'A good mix, truth like I said, imagination like his brain saw it. What is the book? A story about a man's suspenders. None? Or one? Or two? I told him, but he told the world.'

The only hint Yoder ever gave that he had been irritated by Streibert's scathing review of *Stone Walls* came just as he was about to leave, for as he waited by the door for Emma to make her farewells, he took casually from a small bookcase tucked into a corner one of the Jalna novels that Streibert had compared to Yoder's Grenzler series, to the detriment of both. 'What were these books like?' he asked: 'I see you have six of them.'

'Polite nothings,' I said. 'But in her day Mazo de la Roche was a sensation.'

'Canadian, I believe?'

'Yes. The Canadians ridiculed her books—pure fairy tales. But women readers in England and the United States devoured them. I read *Whiteoaks of Jalna*, in high school, I think it must have been, and wept at what the heroine had to suffer. Or it could have been one of the other books, they did blend one into another.' Then I laughed and pointed my finger: 'And you claim you never read your reviews. How else would you have heard of Jalna—or been interested in the name?'

'Emma read the final paragraphs to me. I wish she hadn't,' and he would say no more, but I could see that my description of the famous Canadian books had displeased him.

Toward six, when the guests were ready to depart, I asked Ms. Benelli to remain and take a bit of supper with me: 'I've a question I've been wanting to ask, about literature,' and we sat in easy chairs facing the big window as dusk settled over the valley. Before I could ask my question, she asked: 'If Mr. Zollicoffer helps so much on Mr. Yoder's books, does he share in the royalties?'

'I happen to know the answer,' I said. 'A distant cousin of mine belongs to the Valley Mennonite Church "up against Souderton" as they say.' I pronounced it *Sawwwder-tunnn* in the Dutch way. 'That's the Zollicoffers' church, and when Mr. Yoder tried to pay Herman for his valuable help Zollicoffer said: "In the old days we all pitched in to help a neighbor build his barn. Today we help him build his book," and he would accept nothing.'

When Ms. Benelli marveled at such generosity, I chuckled: 'Never underestimate these Pennsylvania Dutch. Zollicoffer told Yoder: "For me, not a penny. But our church is tryin' to build an addition. You could help on that." '

'And did he? I mean Yoder?'

'Of course. He wanted to. But as soon as Zollicoffer had the promise he whispered to the church board: "Yoder will pay!" and the architect sat up all night enlarging his drawing of the extension that now serves as the meeting room. Next afternoon Yoder looked at the plans and said: "Nice. Go ahead." Now Zollicoffer's church wants to build what some would call a Sunday School, and believe me, they watch the best-seller list to see if Yoder will be able to afford it.'

When our laughter subsided I broached a more serious subject, one that had for some time perplexed me: 'Ms. Benelli, what do you know about an American poet who seems to exert an unhealthy influence on my grandson—Ezra Pound?'

She drew in her breath, and for some moments sat frowning in concentration: 'How to start? So many facets.'

'Let's try the beginning?'

Choosing her words carefully, she said: 'In the 1930s there was a little group of men at Cambridge University in England—and maybe the group wasn't so little—who in their intellectual arrogance betrayed England by committing treason in favor of the Soviet Union. Pound became so infected with the ugly spirit of the age that he betrayed the United States by committing treason in favor of Mussolini and Hitler. But he wasn't solely to blame. The times were so out of joint that writers fell into confusion: T. S. Eliot and his crowd were vicious anti-Semites, and it was popular to quote E. M. Forster's famous statement that he'd rather betray his nation than his male friend.'

'What an amazing statement.'

'Some experts claim that Forster never actually said *male* friend, but we know that's what he meant.'

'And Streibert adopted the ideas of these men?'

'To a limited degree. He's obviously not anti-Semitic. His editor is Jewish and so is the woman student he's pushing toward publication, Jenny Sorkin. And I'm sure he'd never consider treason. But he has evolved this dubious theory that a writer—'

I interrupted: 'What Timothy tried to explain? The Imperative of the Now?'

'Yes. Streibert claims that an artist must be judged by how he handles the great problems of his day. He doesn't have to write about them, you understand, just be conversant and allude to them in a consistent way. And it's obligatory that he break with the past in order to comprehend the now. He can study the past—should do so, in fact—to see its errors and the corrections that are needed.'

I said: 'That's a pretty heavy burden to place on the shoulders of a mere writer,' and she answered: 'Streibert preaches it's the only legitimate task. Polishing words and phrases was the job in the last century. Grappling with reality is the obligation in this.'

'Reality? Are you speaking of things like Pound's treason?'

'Yes. Men who extol Pound for his really fine poetry, and it's some of the best, and for the tremendous role he played in teaching other poets and even helping them revise their poems to make them more vivid . . . he seems to have influenced most of the good poets of his age. What was I saying?'

'That professors who extol him—'

'Intellectuals have been almost forced to make Pound their hero.

JANE GARLAND
. . . .

359

It's a litmus test: "Support Pound or you cannot stand with us on other matters." '

'If I were a fellow poet or an intellectual, I might feel the same way. Like airline pilots who go out on strike and later refuse even to speak with those sitting beside them in the cockpit who didn't. But tell me more about Pound's treason. I have only the vaguest recollection. Timothy said there was a hospital that figured.'

'Again the facts are indisputable. During the war Pound's broadcasts from Italy called for the defeat of England and the United States, perhaps not directly, but he certainly gave "aid and comfort to the enemy." He also supported the extermination of the Jews and, at the very least, harsh treatment of them. At the end of the war he was captured in Italy by Allied troops and was, I believe, held for a short period in a cage. When he was brought back to the States and indicted for treason, ardent supporters protested that he could not be tried for words he undoubtedly said but didn't really mean. To make their point these friends did something blatant. While Pound was in custody awaiting trial they awarded him the prestigious Bollingen Prize, confirming their claim that he was America's greatest poet. The Bollingen Foundation put up the money for the prize, but it was awarded under the auspices of the Library of Congress, and all hell broke loose.'

'But where does the hospital come in?'

'A sad affair. Unwilling to try Pound in a public trial as a traitor, in view of the strong support he had in the intellectual community, the government chickened out, declared him insane, and quietly incarcerated him not in a formal jail but in a wing of St. Elizabeths Hospital for the criminally insane in Washington, thus avoiding a public scandal.'

'That sounds like a mistake,' I said, and she agreed.

'They kept him there for twelve years. Other poets visited him and there's an entire literature about "the martyr of St. Elizabeths." An episode as shameful as anything Pound did in Italy. You know, he wrote some of his best poetry in what was an insane asylum.'

'Let's get down to cases. What influence do you think Streibert's ideas about Pound and the role of the artist might have on an impressionable young man like my grandson, who's had such a dazzling start? Might he become confused?'

Ms. Benelli did not hesitate, and from the force of her reply I judged that she, too, wanted to protect Timothy: 'It might lead to his membership in a coterie,' she said. 'Membership in a group of young people like himself who convince one another that they live in a special atmosphere in which they see things more clearly than others do—see them differently—are responsive to the superior demands of the immediate present.'

I had asked these questions because I was worried about my grandson's future, but now I broke into a quiet chuckle: 'I'm so pleased that Timothy's taken up with young Miss Sorkin, who said she was writing books I'd be able to understand. She seems a responsible sort—could prove to be his salvation. But this fascination with Pound and those rascals who betrayed England, I'm afraid I'll never comprehend them, and I'd deplore seeing Timothy follow in their footsteps.'

'Have you a VCR?' and when I looked blank: 'The gismo that plays movies through your television?'

'Had one, but could never figure out how to use it. Gave it away.'

'No problem. We have one at the library.'

'To show what?'

'The big video rental shop in Allentown has a wonderful film, a two-hour TV show, done at some university. Explains all you need to know about Ezra Pound.'

'It's important that I see that film.'

She said: 'Name the day,' and it was arranged that two days hence, if the film was available, she and I would meet in the library at five in the afternoon to see the film *The Prisoner of St. Elizabeths*.

FRIDAY, II OCTOBER: At five today in the Dresden Public Library, a rather small but tidy stone building in the center of town, I had a riveting introduction to treason and its genesis. I felt at home in the film projection room because, although Andrew Carnegie, the Scots philanthropist, had given the library to our town in the early 1900s, the modernizations had been paid for by my husband, upon goading by me, and after his death it had been one of my principal charities. I loved the staid old building and its sense of Scottish responsibility. Did a wealthy man ever make a better contribution to his society than Carnegie with his hundreds of libraries in towns like Dresden?

A prudent man, he would have been shocked by what unreeled in his library today, because Ms. Benelli easily fitted a cassette into her VCR, a machine that had defeated me, and we sat back to watch a harrowing summary of Ezra Pound's confusion, tragedy and ultimate triumph.

The film was composed of two parts, intricately interwoven: first, historic clips that had caught the arrogant poet in a surprising number of different situations and, second, a studio re-creation of the more important moments in his life. In these a British actor who had been made up to look like Pound did an amazing job of blending the real with the imaginary.

We saw Pound as a revolutionary young man from Nebraska, totally at odds with his generation, as a hesitant teacher, as an exile in Italy, as an apologist for Benito Mussolini and an advocate for the Italian and German victory in Europe and, by extension, the world. In these real scenes, photographed during the period when Mussolini appeared to be winning on all fronts, Pound revealed himself as contemptuous of all things American.

Extremely pitiful, regardless of what Pound had done, were the scenes that immediately followed the defeat of Mussolini and Hitler, for then the vengeful American victors, enraged by Pound's treasonous broadcasts during the war, arrested him and threw him into a small cage made of steel mesh and open on all sides, top and bottom, to the weather. Treated like a caged animal, he was visible to the public and scorned by all. Less brutal but more morally questionable were the episodes in which American government officials, afraid to try him publicly for treason because they knew they had only a fragile case against him—for he had merely harangued, not engaged in physical acts of treason—fell back on the device of getting some doctor to certify him insane. They then incarcerated him, without trial, in Washington's St. Elizabeths Hospital for the criminally insane for many long years.

I had to agree with the filmmakers that the steel cage and the spurious hospital imprisonment were blots on American justice, but even so I could not excuse Pound for his assumptions of superiority, his treason and his evil anti-Semitism. When Ms. Benelli asked me after the film ended: 'Any questions?' I shook my head 'No,' for there were too many to voice. But later, when I was alone in the big room, watching the lights of cars as they moved along Rhenish Road in the far distance, I burst into laughter: 'Those silly asses! Those contemptible traitors who thought they alone could assess modern history, who knew that Communist Russia must ultimately rule supreme, what would they say if they were alive now, when Communism has collapsed everywhere? Revealing itself to have been hollow all along?' And I thought of my prosaic husband, whom Pound would have scorned because he was a simple American trying to run a steel mill in an efficient, productive way. How right Larrimore had been in what he understood society to be, how terribly wrong Pound had been. I wanted none of his errors contaminating my grandson.

THURSDAY, 24 OCTOBER: Today I felt for the first time like an elder statesman. The elder part I experience constantly, for I am getting

on, and I feel it in my arthritic knuckles; it was the statesman part
that surprised me, for I was consulted professionally by two much
younger women.

First Ms. Marmelle, down on a working visit to her four authors
in our small but talent-rich area—one having led fortuitously to the
next—asked if I would allow her to pose a few questions and, supposing they related to my grandson, I agreed.

When she arrived at Windsong, she startled me with the frankness
of her approach: 'Mrs. Garland, I've been gratified with the protection you try to provide your grandson. Now I need some. You know
Dresden better than anyone. Would the town be ready to accept a
woman, alone, who wanted to buy a house here?'

'Of course—you'd be welcome here. You know many local people
already.'

'Where might I find a house?'

'Adam Troxel always has a dozen to sell, a trustworthy man. But
why would a city girl with a fine job want to lose herself in a little
country town?'

'Recent events have affected me badly in New York—the sale of
our company to the Germans, the death of my last surviving aunt—
they've sort of used up the city for me. I'm older, too, forty-seven,
so if I'm to make a shift it'd better be now.'

'You're not changing publishers?'

'Not for the present, but I do want to sink some roots outside the
concrete jungle. New York's not an especially hospitable place for
single women.'

I'd been told that Yvonne had been married in her earlier years
to a difficult man named Rattner—all talent, no character—and that
he'd been killed during some ugly affair in Greenwich Village. If so,
she handled her widowhood with distinction, and I liked what I had
seen of her. She was a sharp, courageous woman who had mastered
the art of survival in a man's world. Besides, she'd helped get my
grandson started right, and for that alone I was indebted.

'Leave your car here, and we'll have Oscar show us the area. Out in the country or in town?'

'In town. I want neighbors. In fact, I need them.'

As we drifted out past some attractive houses on the road to the college, she rejected each one that I proposed, but when we doubled back on College Road and approached Dresden from the northeast, I felt her attention quicken and was not surprised when she called to Oscar: 'Please, slow down here!' And there to our left, at the very edge of town, stood an old two-story house that exuded appeal; it seemed to cry: 'Stop and see what I have to offer!'

'Is this what you have in mind?'

'Could be. Oscar, can we turn left four times so that I can see it from all directions?' and as we finished the circuit she pointed to the sign: FOR SALE TROXEL & BINGEN. 'Are they reputable people?' she asked, and I told her: 'I've known Troxel for years. One of the best. Young Bingen I don't know.'

'Could we stop by their office?' and that was how a New York editor started proceedings that would lead to her emigrating to a small Dutch community.

My second consultation was even more startling, for having helped my grandson's editor find a home, I was now asked to help his young lady friend find a resolution to a writer's block that had immobilized her. It was Jenny Sorkin, whom I already liked, and when Timothy brought her to Windsong I saw that she was wearing a new T-shirt: IF YOU THINK YOU FEEL GOOD, YOU OUGHT TO FEEL ME.

I had no idea why she wanted to talk with me, but Timothy explained: 'Grandmother, Jenny's finished her football novel, but New York thinks polishing is needed and everyone's been giving her advice. Streibert did, he was her professor. I did, I'm her professor now. And Ms. Marmelle keeps heaping it on.'

'After that exalted barrage, what could I possibly contribute?'

JANE GARLAND
· ·

365

'A great deal, the capstone possibly. I mean, you're the only one of us, including Yvonne, who's a reader. You consume books, you don't write them. Jenny could profit from your touch, especially since Streibert's fled to Temple and left her stranded.'

'What's the book about? My knowledge of football is limited,' I warned, but with an ingratiating smile Jenny brushed that aside: 'The book's really about people, and about the kind of nineteen-year-old girl you might have been at that age.'

'I've never seen a novel when it was aborning. I'd be honored to take a try.'

'You saw mine,' Timothy said, and I replied: 'I meant a novel I could read—as if it were a book.' Turning to Jenny, I said: 'Come back in two days. I'm a fast reader.'

SATURDAY, 26 OCTOBER: I have rarely had more fun in reading anything than I did with Jenny's manuscript. It was a hilarious account of a naive-clever hillbilly type of girl and her misadventures with six football players from six Western universities, and the reason I enjoyed it so much was one that neither Jenny nor Timothy would have anticipated. My late husband happened to have been chairman of the regents' committee that supervised college sports at Mecklenberg, with heavy emphasis on football. He exulted with the team, of which he had once been captain, when it defeated Lafayette, groaned when it lost to nearby Lehigh, and was featured in *The New York Times* as the Mecklenberg alumnus who had placed his college in jeopardy by paying its athletes under the table. As a result of my husband's involvement I knew something about college sports and found Miss Sorkin's book refreshing even though I knew little about the Western universities she described.

But as a lifelong compulsive reader I could detect the strengths and weaknesses of her draft so that when she returned to Windsor this afternoon I was prepared with a page of notes and queries. As she arranged her chair to face me in the big room, I jumped right in: 'Utterly beguiling, Miss Sorkin.'

'You can call me Jenny, Jane.'

'You can call me Mrs. Garland, Jenny.'

'We could do a vaudeville skit with that, Mrs. Garland, and I appreciate what you just said about the manuscript.'

'I understand why Ms. Marmelle has accepted this. But . . .'

'But . . .' Jenny could not mask her disappointment: 'I can't think of a single thing more to do.'

'*I* can. It's been bothering me for the past two days, and at four this morning I finally figured out the weakness, and it's one that could limit this book. You've written it as a delicious comment on contemporary life among the best of our young people. But you didn't intend it to be only a comedy, did you? You were probing for something deeper, more significant, isn't that right?'

'I've vaguely wondered about that.'

'Good. No more apologies or evasions. Your novel cries out for some scene that adds a darker coloring, an almost tragic presentiment. The story must have it, or it remains only a superficial comedy.'

I saw that any inclination on Jenny's part to resist was vanishing and to my surprise she uttered a weak 'I agree.' I was disappointed that she had not fought to protect her position.

'Let's put our heads together and think of the one football player—or I suppose it could be the poet, although I'd respond less to him—to whom something vital could happen . . . the scene that would rivet the reader. Let's take the incident first.'

'No,' Jenny said with a forcefulness I did not expect. 'Let's take the player first, because I wouldn't want him to appear too early in the story. The overall mood of the novel wouldn't have been established.' I liked the way she was now defending her work; for some reason I could not have explained, I was rooting for her.

'We could switch the order of their appearance.'

'Impossible. That's been carefully orchestrated. An alteration of that kind—' She stopped. 'It would screw up all the values.'

'I'm glad to hear you say that. Means you've been thinking . . . even better, that, you have a gut feeling.'

'So I think we're stuck with Number Five,' Jenny said. 'You were right, the poet would give us nothing. And I've fallen in love with the gorilla at Nebraska State. "For away games we carry him in a cage." '

'I like that. So you've settled on Five?'

'Yes.'

Together we ran through a dismal roster of catastrophes that routinely overtake football players and I suggested: 'Maybe he gets caught taking drugs or steroids two weeks before the Heisman voting?' But she demurred: 'That's been overdone. Ben Johnson and the Olympics.'

'He gets tangled with gamblers and they escape but he's exposed?' Again she shook her head: 'No, the Pete Rose melodrama played too long on local television.' Then, to encourage me to make additional suggestions, she said: 'I never expected this, Mrs. Garland. You know your sports,' and I said: 'Why not? My husband was the czar of sports here at Mecklenberg. Castigated in the *Times* for financing near illiterates under the table. Could it be that your boy has parents who are in poor health, and because of poverty, have inadequate doctors? No, that was done on a television show last week.'

'Damn, you know books and sports on television. You're a triple threat.'

'Those are the sorts of things that keep you alive when you pass seventy.'

In mild but growing frustration we dismissed one plot device after another until I said: 'Let's go and walk on the lawn,' and as the brisk October air struck us, she said: 'Damn, this is real football weather.' Snapping her fingers, she said: 'Come on, between us we're bright enough to whip this thing.'

But my thoughts were elsewhere at that point. Very slowly I said: 'What really infuriates me about big-time college sports as I saw it with my husband and see it now on the newscasts is not the fact that a charismatic coach can earn a million dollars a year from all his extras like TV, camps and endorsements, while his players get nothing. What bugs me is the way male athletes all over the country think they have the God-given right to rape co-eds. Look at the cases in the last year, all parts of the nation. Three football players rape a freshman girl. Four hockey players, two basketball players, and any number of cases that don't get into the press. What's going on, that coaches seem to think their star players, to prove their manhood, can rape whomever they wish?'

Afraid that I had ranted, I drew back: 'I'll correct that. I doubt the coaches know. I'm sure they don't condone it.'

A long silence fell, and when I looked at Jenny walking slowly down the slope it was obvious that she was picking her way through a mental minefield. Finally she stopped, indicated a bench and invited me to sit beside her. Then she said quite slowly, choosing her words meticulously: 'So my Number Five, and he's the type, outstanding and upstanding—he rapes our heroine. She's so outraged she reports it immediately, but—and now I borrow from you—he's up for the Heisman. If he gets it, the university gets it, too. Great publicity, next year's recruiting that much easier.'

'Strong beginning.'

Jenny ignored this, for her mind was on the surprise ending to which she was leading me: 'The university lawyers, some of the faculty, the lesser coaches and especially the head coach, all pressure her to withdraw her charge—they muzzle her. They don't actually threaten her physically, but she's scared as hell. In the entire university establishment she has no friend except a black girl who has already fought all the battles a young woman can stand. She advises our heroine: "Forge ahead," and the following week the black girl's

JANE GARLAND
· ·

369

dropped from school. College authorities cite bad grades and infrac-
tions of rules.'

'You're writing a powerful revision.'

'But that's not the end. Our hero gets the Heisman. Our university
garners the accolades. And our heroine gets pregnant.'

Another long silence, then with extreme care: 'When this is verified, she goes to all the authorities who advised her before and asks
what she should do now, and it's the coach who solves her problem.
He provides funds and a doctor for an abortion, but our heroine says
she will not go through with it unless the black girl is reinstated. She
is, and they go together to the clinic.'

After some moments, I said: 'Eons ahead of anything I could have
devised. But of course you'll have to hang it on Nebraska State. Can't
use a real place.'

'No!' Jenny said with unexpected firmness. 'Nebraska State is so
richly rewarding as is, it must remain untouched. We'll invent another school.'

'What one?'

'How do I know?' and the force with which this exploded satisfied
me that Jenny had been more personally involved in this case than
she had revealed, but I knew that now was not the time to explore
that dark alley.

For a long time in the October sunlight we sat in silence, and as
I studied Jenny with sidelong glances I felt as if I were being granted
an interior glimpse of the writing process and I asked myself: 'I
wonder what happened to this young woman on those Western
campuses? Don't expect the truth from her. All writers are inventors,
even when describing a landscape. They have to be. They write their
interpretations and we're eager to accept them.'

Finally Jenny spoke: 'I'm sure I can guess what you're thinking.
No, I was not the girl who became pregnant and was so shamefully
treated. I've fudged the facts. That girl was black. The black girl in

my story, the one who did the befriending, she was white. And I'll
let you guess who she was.'

TUESDAY, 29 OCTOBER: I had decided when my husband died that
I would not become what the women in my childhood called 'a
wasting widow,' meaning a woman of some gentility and acceptable
appearance who considered her life ended, and who remained imprisoned in the house her husband left her, preoccupied with hoard-
ing whatever funds she had so that she could pass them on to her
children and grandchildren. None of that for me.

Sooner after the funeral than some of my friends might have liked,
I resumed the varied community activities that had in the past given
me a sense of accomplishment. And because I had been left a great
deal of money—it was as much as thirty million—I was able to do
the things I wanted.

Like my husband, I supported the town library and paid Ms.
Benelli a yearly bonus about which her board remained ignorant. I
gave to the college. I quietly put up the funds for Little League
baseball in Neumunster, and of course I helped rather generously our
small local hospital. The churches that Larrimore had supported I
continued to help, and so on.

But what kept me interested in local life, and protective of my own
welfare, was my friendly association with the farmers and tradesmen
of our community, so that when our new resident Yvonne Marmelle
needed a working introduction to her new community, I proved to
be the best cicerone she could have had. Starting at nine this morning, I took her for a sweep of our district, providing her with maps,
both printed and hand-drawn by me.

'This is where our road, Cut Off, meets Rhenish Road, and that
farm where the old barn has just been bulldozed is the Fenstermacher place, a mournful affair, really. Once had hundreds of acres,

but through the decades the family wasted them away. I've tried to help Otto, and I adore his wife, but I find their son hard to take. Larrimore and I gave him a kind of scholarship when he was at Neumunster, but he accomplished nothing with it. You'll come here frequently, I suppose, because Fenstermacher makes the best scrapple in these parts.'

When she asked what that was, I said: 'You're not ready for Dresden. It's what God invented after he made crusted apple brown betty. An indescribable Dutch meat dish that I cut into small strips and fry till they're crisp. You'll come here often if you like pork products. . . . Forgive me, do you eat pork? If not, there goes scrapple and maybe Grenzler, too.'

'Uncle Judah would rise from his grave if he caught me eating your scrapple, but so would he if he knew I was working for a German firm.'

'How is Kinetic?'

'Stabilized rather nicely, thank you. Uncle Judah saved my life, literally. I'll never forget the day in a Bronx public library when he led me away from the books of childhood with bright covers and showed me the more somber-looking books intended for teens. I was eleven or twelve, my right arm in a cast.'

'What had happened?'

'Broke it in a stickball game.' Then, as if she were hungry to confide in some friend in her new homeland, she made some extraordinary revelations: 'It was a baseball game, but that's not what was significant. The first male I ever loved, a red-headed Irish lad, pushed me away in disgust. I fell against the wall and broke my arm. Years later the second man I loved also pushed me away in disgust and again I broke that arm.' She held it out and started to pull up her sleeve, then stopped: 'Take my word for it, the two breaks still show.'

Though somewhat shaken by this disturbing account, I continued my tour: 'In that little house is Mrs. Dietrich, best seamstress in

Dresden. She'll fix your hem half an hour before a party. Needs the money and I try to give her as much business as I can. You should do the same.'

I especially wanted her to know the artisans who could be trusted: 'The two Moyer brothers over there run the most reliable garage in town, and this other Moyer down the road—you'll learn that half the honest people in Dresden are named Moyer—he's the carpenter Larrimore set up in business when Windsong was finished. Most of the interior features people admire were suggested by Moyer.'

'You seem to know everyone in town.'

'That was a decision Larrimore and I made when we started building our permanent home here,' and when I introduced Yvonne to our high school principal he told her: 'We consider Mrs. Garland an honorary member of our staff, she does so much to help us.' To my embarrassment Yvonne asked in her inquisitive way: 'Like what?' and he said: 'Like music scholarships, like a new chemistry lab, like prizes for our oratorical contests.' He overlooked the participation of which Larrimore was proudest, the three college scholarships for seniors in need of financial aid, some of whom have turned out to be our most productive citizens.

Our last stop was the library, where we met Ms. Benelli. She showed us the facilities Yvonne would be free to use when she became a resident: 'And what you see here is a mere fragment of what we have, because we're able to borrow by mail any book in the Pennsylvania state system, and, through that system, almost any book that circulates anywhere in the nation. Treasures, of course, don't circulate.' As we moved about, admiring the way she had organized her little domain, she came to us with a copy of that day's *Times*: 'Ms. Marmelle, have you seen the story about you in today's paper?' and we reached for it eagerly.

The item, which I read aloud, said that Karl Streibert, professor of creative writing at Temple University in Philadelphia, had decided to leave his current publisher, Kinetic Press, and his longtime editor, Yvonne Marmelle, and move to a smaller house whose well-known liberal tendencies were more in keeping with the values he stood for in his writing.

Up to this point Yvonne had merely listened intently, shaking her head sadly and saying: 'I suppose it had to happen,' but what I read next astonished her for some reason I could not fathom: ' "Professor Streibert revealed that he had signed a significant contract with Arthur Jameson of Pol Parrot Press. . . ." ' As I read these names Yvonne gasped, brought her hand over her face, then broke into a nervous laugh.

'It would be Pol Parrot!' she mumbled, but when I tried to discover why this had affected her so strangely she said nothing, so I continued reading: ' "With this departure of their avant-garde critic, Kinetic seems in danger of losing contact with younger writers, but Ms. Marmelle's standby Lukas Yoder is still a potent property and her new discovery Timothy Tull shows promise." '

When I stopped reading, she said quietly: 'Damn him, he could have departed like a gentleman—without those hellish quotes, He's a nervous little boy, striking out at his mother who won't let him have a sled.' Aware that she was even madder than she showed, I tried to divert her with one more local tip: 'Simon, over there, runs the best beauty parlor in town,' and she laughed.

When I deposited her at the inn she clasped my hand: 'I've already forgiven him. Thank you for having distracted me by showing me the riches of my new home,' but I entered a correction: 'You haven't seen the real riches yet. I'm giving a dinner party in your honor at our best-known restaurant, a place called Seven and Seven. It's some distance out of town, but we go there because it provides the famous seven sweets and seven sours that are supposed to be the basis for a decent Pennsylvania Dutch supper. And there will be other surprises.'

———

WEDNESDAY, 30 OCTOBER: Today Yvonne had work to do with the Yoders, and since I knew this involved business details, I volunteered to stay home, but she would have none of that: 'Time you saw how an editor earns her living,' and with Oscar driving we were off on a frenzied review of Grenzler at work.

Our first stop was the Yoders', where we heard Emma completing a call from Lukas's agent in New York. When she put down the phone she was eager to share the good news: '*Stone Walls* is going into three new languages. Swedish, Portuguese, Hebrew. That makes eleven so far, with more to come.'

Seeing that Lukas was embarrassed by our celebration, I tried to put him at ease: 'Is it true that you've written your last novel?' and Emma actually moved in front of him to answer on his behalf: 'It looks so. He's doing no writing, just working on his paintings.'

Yvonne, visibly distressed by this frank statement, broke in: 'Emma, you must not say publicly that *Stone Walls* is his last book,' and when the little Dutchwoman asked rather snappishly, 'Why not?' Yvonne gave what I considered a first-class explanation: 'If I should decide, later on, to leave Kinetic . . . it would be a lot easier for me to land a good job if Lukas came with me.'

When Emma looked mystified, Yvonne added: 'If I were to go alone, there'd be not much interest. If I took Tull and Sorkin to the new place, there'd be great interest. But if I keep your husband with me, I can write my own ticket.'

When Emma asked: 'You're thinking of leaving Kinetic?' Yvonne replied: 'Not now. But if things turn sour I need to protect myself. And believe me, your husband is my life jacket. Please take care of him.' This frank statement of her reliance upon Yoder was received with such warmth that on the spur of the moment Emma cried: 'You two must join us at the movie shooting tomorrow, down Lancaster way,' and I reciprocated by inviting the Yoders to my dinner tomorrow night.

Lukas was loath to accept: 'I've work to do,' but when I added: 'It's being held at Seven and Seven near Kutztown,' Emma cried: 'What a wonderful feast! We'll be there.'

When Yvonne revealed that she was contemplating the purchase of a house, the Yoders told her: 'Before you sign any papers, you've got to have Herman Zollicoffer check the place. He's a genius.' A phone call assured us that the big Dutchman was home, so the Yoders joined us on a quick drive to the handsome Zollicoffer farm, one of the finest in our region.

The Zollicoffers were excited when they learned that the house Yvonne was interested in was the old Hertzler place: 'Wonderful well built. Solid. Them floors won't creak.' We drove there, and Herman and Lukas inspected everything—roofs, gutters, cellar, water supply, electric wiring—with Emma standing by to write down each repair that would have to be made to make the house acceptable. As I watched these cautious Dutchmen probe into hidden areas that I had not known existed, I understood why their cautious ancestors had made Dresden such a habitable, sturdy place.

Satisfied that any minor weaknesses in the house could easily be corrected, we moved as a committee of six to the real estate offices of Troxel and Bingen, where the senior partner told Yvonne: 'You can buy it for two hundred forty thousand,' and Zollicoffer asked right away: 'Does that include the lot across the street?' When Troxel nodded, Herman whispered: 'That's a steal. Offer two hundred thousand, but only if the Hertzlers agree to make all repairs.' Mr. Troxel said he'd entertain such an offer and see if the Hertzlers would accept, but Herman warned: 'Be wary. The Hertzlers are mean, tough people,' and when Mr. Troxel asked: 'How do you know?' Herman said: 'Because my uncle married one of them.'

When some of us chuckled he said sternly: 'Don't laugh. How do you suppose Hertzler got the money to build that house you like? Huge insurance settlement, that's how,' and he proceeded with a rural yarn that sounded fictitious except that he had good reason to vouch for it: the wife involved was his aunt who had married Hertzler. 'Listen to the explanation he gave us later: "The missus and me was in our buggy travelin' a country road when we was hit from behind by a big black car that threw us out. When I saw my wife lyin' there unconscious and realized that the rich people in the car with their big insurance policies wasn't lookin', I had the presence of mind to kick her in the face." '

THURSDAY, 31 OCTOBER: Early this morning Oscar dropped me at the Dresden China, where I met Yvonne and the Yoders, and in their old car—I wanted Oscar to drive us in mine, but they said: 'On Amish roads a big Cadillac competing with buggies would look crazy'—we headed south. With Emma driving, Yvonne in the other front seat, and Lukas and me talking in back, we drove to where the cameras were set up on a dirt road east of Lancaster.

A crew of more than eighty was working at a stately pace shooting a simple scene, each of whose many parts had to contribute properly to the image of a peaceful Amish farm on an October day in the 1880s. All camera work had to focus on the north side of the country road, where no telephone wires intruded.

The basic take, as they called it, was not complicated, at least insofar as we visitors understood it. None of us could place the incident in the book, but an assistant to the producers explained: 'We needed a scene to depict the solemn, rural aspects of Amish life and our writers came up with this one. It's not only visually impressive, it also moves the story line forward. A traditional black buggy, drawn by a fine-looking horse properly groomed, will come along the road from right to left, driven by the young Amish man who is wearing suspenders. His wife is with him. From a distance to the left the camera will pick up a smaller black buggy, which contains only one man. He is surly and wears no suspenders; his buggy will pass closest to the camera, so that we can keep him in strong focus and see his grim expression.

'Obviously, the timing of the scene, especially of the progress of the two carriages, will be crucial, demanding quite a few dry runs so as to place the surly man coming from the left before the camera at the moment when we can watch his reaction when he sees his enemy in the other carriage. That timing's difficult enough, but to give the extended scene additional emotional content, we want two schoolchildren, a boy and a girl in their own distinctive garb, to be walking along the road, oblivious to the two buggies, which they see every day.

'Finally, cameras and carts and children must be so placed and timed that the rear of the picture will be framed by that handsome red barn whose sides were painted by our company artists with red and green hex signs. The Lancaster scholar advising us on the film warned: "Most Amish farmers refrained from painting hex signs on their barns not because they ignored superstitions but because sign painters charged too much." As one Amish man told us: "It would be chust like wanity." But the men producing the film pointed out: "A million people have read Mr. Yoder's other book *Hex*. We did, and we'll want to see hex signs, and there they are." '

It was several minutes before Mr. Saito and his partner from Israel learned that the author of their book was attending the shooting; when told, they hurried to greet him as an old friend: 'You bring us good luck,' Mr. Saito said, and he halted his preparations to introduce Lukas to the crew. But the Israeli cut the greetings short: 'We've got to get this shot within the next hour. Sun'll be getting too bright by then,' and Yvonne whispered to me: 'Now I see why it costs Kinetic only a few thousand dollars to produce a book, a film company a few million to make the movie.'

When the actors driving the two buggies had their roles letter-perfect for the scene, the horses acted up, and even soiled the road with their droppings. This called for a long discussion as to whether the balls of manure should be removed or not, and if they were to be removed, who was to do it. The adviser said: 'I wanted the manure there from the beginning, but this man said it would cost too much to set it up,' and the Israeli barked: 'Keep it.'

When men and horses were performing ideally, one of the children looked at the camera, and just as everything fitted gloriously like an intricate puzzle, a jet flew over on its way from Pittsburgh to Philadelphia and the take was ruined.

At the end of another forty-five minutes of useless shooting—the director had not yet called the magic words 'Print that one' because no shots were even remotely adequate—the Israeli grabbed a bullhorn and roared: 'We have fifteen more minutes of usable light. For God's sake, let's get this one right.' The director went to him in some anger and said: 'If we don't get it today, we get it tomorrow,' and the Israeli, uncowed, snapped: 'Why not? It's only money.'

After a flawless take in the thirteenth minute, the director cried: 'Print that one and let's try for three more.' So back went the horses at a mild trot, back came the two children to have their black uniforms—flat hat for the boy, lace cap for the girl—adjusted, and a second effort resulted in another 'Print that one.'

They missed badly on the third emergency backup; horses whinnied, children jumped, drivers lost control, but on the fourth try, as the October sun was about to throw too much light on the scene, all elements blended into an almost perfect depiction of life among the Amish, their fields, their children and their old-fashioned mode of transportation. The director applauded and the Israeli cried to the farmers who had provided buggies and the teams: 'Can I kiss those horses?' The Amish men looked at him as if he were crazy.

On the drive to Dresden, Lukas reported: 'All morning, eighty workers and six horses, they got one minute and twenty seconds' worth of finished film,' and Yvonne said: 'But if they got the right eighty seconds, it was worth it.'

When I asked the Yoders what they thought of the shooting, Lukas said: 'I was impressed. They were working so hard to get their pictures right. And I thought I had worked beyond the call of duty to get my words right. And Yvonne worked so hard to make everything mesh. I respect professionals'. And during the rest of our trip he had no more to say. But Emma did: 'Remarkable accomplishment. When those two were here last year they mumbled broken English. Today their English is fluent, idiomatic. I always admired students who mastered their assignments.'

The Pennsylvania Dutch restaurant south of Kutztown known widely as the 7&7 featured typical German country cooking—lying on a big table were dishes of ham, beef, chicken, scrapple in season, sausage, but no fish or lamb or veal—and fourteen small crocks, seven labeled SWEET in bright red, and the other seven SOUR in bright green, in honor of the Dutch tradition. At this restaurant, the only one in the region that featured the actual crocks, sweets would be spiced apples, apple sauce, sweet pickles, three kinds of jelly or other sweet concoctions; the sours would be pickles, relishes, a kind of sour mustard and other condiments.

We were eight in my party that night: The Yoders, the Zollicoffers, Yvonne, my grandson, Timothy, and his date, Jenny Sorkin, and me. The restaurant, pleased to have such distinguished visitors, had given us a semidetached room containing a huge central table crowded with the fourteen colored crocks, but when my guests entered to take their places they found that nine chairs had been provided, and Yvonne, who had done much of the inviting, started to ask: 'What's the extra chair for?' I refrained from explaining because I had arranged what I hoped would be a pleasant surprise for her, and here it came! Into the room strode Karl Streibert on his first return since his hasty departure to Temple, and I must say that I was both surprised and delighted by the dramatic change in his appearance. No longer a hesitant young man with slightly stooped shoulders, he now seemed more mature, with an erect posture and wearing a new pin-striped suit of the kind favored by executives and the department heads of prestigious universities. Ignoring the rest of us, he went directly to Yvonne, grasped her hands and said quietly: 'I owe you an apology. That newspaper story about leaving you and Kinetic was brutal. Worse, it was in poor taste. I owe you so much.'

When Yvonne did not choose to respond I jumped in: 'Then why did you make such hurtful statements?' and he said: 'It was a telephone interview. I couldn't see the questioner, who was just a disembodied voice. . . . I was disoriented and said too much. I'm truly sorry,' and he was so contrite that Yvonne said: 'When I read it I told Mrs. Garland that you were being a nervous little boy striking out at your elders. I was being ungracious, too, so it's only right that I accept your apologies,' and peace was restored.

As Karl took his seat beside her I happened to see Yoder's reaction to this extraordinary display of feeling; he raised his eyebrows as if to say: I don't believe I'd have said that in public, and I thought: What I'd really like to hear is Karl's explanation for that savage review of *Stone Walls*.

Before the food came, Yvonne made a gracious speech: 'How strange it is that I have found in the Dresden area four of my major writers,' and she named them, including Streibert, whom she mentioned last and said slyly: 'I guess we'll have to make that three, because recently I seem to have lost one.' Before anyone could comment, she continued: 'You may think it premature to include Jenny Sorkin in the category of major writers, for the public hasn't had a chance to read her book yet, but four of us in this room have, and we know it's a winner. Let's drink our first toast to the novelist yet to be born, Jenny Sorkin.'

When Emma asked: 'How can you say "yet to be born" if she's already completed her novel?' and Yvonne said: 'In our league it's not completed till it's published,' Emma commented: 'Not a bad definition. Lukas and I know a professor at Mecklenberg who can write about the Pennsylvania Dutch a world better than Lukas. But he can never sit down and really do a book—all the way through—and so it's never done,' and I noticed that Yvonne looked away, strangely.

Now three waiters brought in heaping plates of meat and the meal began, with Mrs. Zollicoffer eating prodigiously and her husband not far behind. The feasting was interrupted by a waitress who informed Yvonne that a telephone call had come for her, and as she left us she winked at the Zollicoffers and flashed them the good-luck sign of clasped hands.

The call took so long that I almost forgot she was part of our company, and I was further diverted by Jenny Sorkin, who leaned over to whisper: 'Have you seen that marvelous square face of Zollicoffer? Looks so much like a Mennonite barn you'd expect to see hex symbols painted across his forehead,' and as I looked not at his face but hers I was gratified that my grandson had come upon this girl who was both witty and wise.

When Yvonne returned, beaming, she remained standing: 'That was Mr. Troxel. He said the Hertzlers have accepted my bid for their family house— don't cheer yet—but they insist that I assume responsibility for all repairs— don't moan yet—because they'll give me back fifteen hundred dollars to cover those costs.'

To steady her nerves, she reached for her glass and pressed its cool sides against her forehead, then said, raising it high: 'To my longtime friends and my new-time friends, I am now one of you and could not imagine a more appropriate celebration.'

There were cheers, and both Streibert and Timothy came forward to embrace her. Yoder nodded. Emma grasped her hand. I tapped a glass and said: 'I propose a toast to our new taxpayer. *Salut!*' and both Zollicoffer and Yoder corrected me: *'Prosit!'* and the toasts were drunk.

Now the table was cleared. In the waiting period between courses, Streibert rose, cleared his throat modestly, and said: 'I was allowed this privilege of returning only through the thoughtfulness of my longtime friend, Mrs. Garland, whom I thank profusely. For the past year I'd been scheduled to moderate a symposium at Mecklenberg tomorrow night on a subject close to my heart, "The Place of the Artist in Society." Alas, I shall not be present, but you're all invited to attend as my proxies. It should be a rousing evening.'

When he sat, we applauded lightly and then I asked: 'How many of you noticed that the waiters, when they cleared the table, left one crock remaining? Marked SWEET, it symbolizes the most glorious sweet of all.' A cowbell sounded, the door to the kitchen opened, and the three waiters entered, each holding like a votive offering before him, in two hands, a deep luscious pie—apple, pumpkin or mince. One by one they were placed before our women, who were then given serving knives.

Cheers greeted the pies, and Emma, serving as mistress of ceremonies, cried as she brandished her knife: 'Take your pick!' Pumpkin seemed to be the favorite, but the knowing took mince, for it is the greatest of the German pies. Some asked for tiny slivers of two different pies, and Mrs. Zollicoffer wanted all three, with no mention of slivers.

As pies began to be devoured, with a surprising number of guests asking for seconds, Emma rapped on her glass and posed a riddle: 'Who can tell me what goes into the making of the mince pie? Dutchmen not allowed to answer.' The guesses were remarkably accurate: 'Apples, raisins, some kind of nut, candied citron, currants, spices, brown sugar.' Emma said: 'Very good, but you've left out the most important.' Guests tasted the savory filling again but could not solve the riddle.

'The name is mincemeat pie. Meat! Yes, shreds of beef and pork, that's what makes it so rich and good,' which caused Yvonne to say: 'Bits of ham and bacon in my lemon meringue pie. That'll take some getting used to.'

FRIDAY, 1 NOVEMBER: Since Yvonne had not intended staying in Dresden past Thursday night, her sudden decision to remain and buy the house gave me the opportunity for an important discussion I'd wanted to have for some time.

She could not have been prepared for our tea, because what faced her at Windsong was not an eighteenth-century affair, two gentle-women idly indulging in gossip, but a brass-knuckle interrogation on vital matters: 'I need guidance regarding my problems with my grandson, Timothy.'

'I should think any grandmother would be delighted to have what-ever problems that amazing young man produces.'

I leaned forward: 'Tell me. Is he really gifted?'

Struck by my intensity, she said with considerable care: 'Timothy is one in ten thousand. If he gets the cultivation he merits—from you—Streibert—from Kinetic as an institution, he can go to the stars.'

'I should like to speak with the greatest frankness, Ms. Marmelle. Timothy is twenty-three. He's already practically finished his second novel and it's revolutionary, like the first. As you may have heard, my husband, his grandfather, inherited a sizable fortune and multi-plied it many times with Bethlehem Steel stock when it was on its way to the top.

'Larrimore and I had one daughter, a brilliant child, headstrong as a hurricane, ran off with a wastrel who married her for her money. Both were killed when Timothy was only a child. I reared him, made mistakes, made some wondrously right decisions. The point of all this is, I have no other descendants, and when I die, Timothy is going to be very wealthy—destructively so, I sometimes fear. Can he handle a fortune and a writing career too?'

Yvonne pondered how to answer that question, and rejected several sharp ideas with a shake of her head: 'I grew up in Jewish genteel poverty, not many dresses but loads of books. I knew several other girls and boys my age who had everything. I didn't think then that they had it much better than I did. And looking at them now, I see that they were damaged by their affluence, but there was another girl I did envy. Her parents were rich by our standards—lavished everything on her, but they also gave her a lot of love, security. She went to Barnard, swept the honors and now she's the wife of a liberal university president in the Midwest and has three kids. I still envy her.'

'You think Timothy is made of strong stuff?'

'He's willing to fight with me. And I've heard him give Professor Streibert what for.'

I asked abruptly: 'And your opinion of young Miss Jenny Sorkin?'

'Very gifted. A most solid young woman. I'd be proud to have her as my daughter.'

'I'm delighted to hear you say that. Timothy has, as they used to say, "taken up with her," and I see her as a possible salvation for him, an anchor to reality.'

'In my book she's Miss Reality, and Timothy's lucky to have found her.'

Reassured, I shared a quick meal with her. Then she drove us the relatively short distance east to the college, where we found an excited crowd assembled for the symposium. The chairman, a professor of art from Ohio State, explained: 'The format, and indeed the list of speakers, were organized a year ago by Professor Streibert, who, alas, is not able to be here tonight, but whose brilliant concept "the Imperative of the Now" motivates and drives our discussion.'

Hard facts were introduced by the professor from England's Nottingham University, who gave a brilliant synopsis of how the intellectual life of Europe in the 1930s had converted excitable men like Pound and Eliot into virulent anti-Semites and seduced the weaker young men at Cambridge University into committing actual treason against the Allies, especially the United States, and in favor of Communist Russia. Having laid this groundwork, he then plunged into the middle of the controversy that still raged about Pound:

'We are indebted to Professor Streibert for the phrase that scholars are now increasingly applying to this phenomenon, "the Imperative of the Now," which gently pushes any young artist or intellectual toward the edge of that perilous chasm called treason, and not necessarily treason to one's nation, but to one's religion, one's mode of earning his livelihood or, especially in Britain, one's class.

'Consider the great anomalies. In Mexico there are no statues to their greatest hero, Cortés, because both the Spaniards and the Indians considered him a traitor to their interests. In South Africa there are no great memorials to their noblest son, Jan Christiaan Smuts, because the Boers are convinced that in World War II he might have been one of the saviors of Britain but was certainly a traitor to Boer interests. And here in the United States, who is indubitably your greatest man of the century? Franklin D. Roosevelt, but you are not allowed to erect any memorials to him because the conservative people who dominate decisions in your nation will not allow it. They know that Roosevelt in striving to aid the common man was a traitor to his class.

'Artists are like the great political leaders. They tend to reject their own class, they attend to the imperative of the now, the problem at hand, and the establishment abhors them, designating their behavior treason.'

It was a bravura performance, delivered in an energetic style, and the audience cheered.

Then my grandson approached the podium, and I was proud of his manly bearing, his mature self-confidence and the able manner in which he marshaled his ideas. He at once put forth in simple terms the gist of his argument:

> 'I doubt if anyone here tonight would argue with the fact that Ezra Pound, who certainly attended to "the imperative of the now," was three distinct persons: one of America's greatest poets, the world's foremost teacher of other poets, and a notorious wartime traitor to his own country. But I want to speak of him in his fourth category, the one of which this nation cannot be proud, the tortured prisoner of St. Elizabeths.'

He then proceeded to give a harrowing account of the twelve long years Pound spent in the asylum for madmen because the government simply declared him insane, without a trial.

> 'Thus our government itself converted this great poet into a symbol of all artists who rebel against authority, who ask impertinent questions, who by one trick or another infuriate the establishment. Pound reminds us of the dangerous tightrope on which the artist balances between regard for the past and vision of the future. The young man or woman who aspires to become an artist but who is not willing to take that risk will have no chance whatever of being remembered. Art is a confrontation in which one gambles his or her life.'

Timothy's peroration drew such vigorous cheering that I had to approve of his performance, even though I rejected his conclusions. When the applause continued, as if he had uttered divine truth, I felt that someone with a more considered grasp of values must remind the audience of the greater truth. Rising from my seat, I signaled for the floating microphone, and when an usher brought it to me, the chairman said from the dais: 'We're so fortunate in having with us tonight a woman who supports the arts in a magnificent way. She gives us funds to run them. Mrs. Jane Garland, of our board of regents.'

Grasping the microphone with a firm hand, I said: 'Tonight we've been hearing a great deal about the obligation of the artist and his freedom to behave as he likes. We have in our audience a man who has probably done more actual writing than any of us, who on a daily basis has wrestled with these abstract problems in the arena of actual performance. I refer to Lukas Yoder, well known not only in these parts but in America generally, and I wish he would come forward and share his views with us.'

I could see that Lukas was not inclined to join the discussion, for he remembered the debacle that had ensued in this hall when he defended Longfellow, and he wished no repetition of that anguish. But Emma prodded him: 'What have you to lose?' and he proceeded to show her.

With his first words, Yoder detonated a bomb: 'We've heard a great deal tonight about the heroism and intellectual grandeur of Ezra Pound, but every speaker has evaded one terrible fact regarding this man, the fact that in my mind supersedes all others. How many in this audience are Jewish? Raise your hands high, please, because you are testifiers to the point I hope to make.' When a considerable number of hands lifted, including that of Jenny Sorkin but not of Ms. Marmelle, Yoder said gravely: 'Thank you. If Ezra Pound had had his way, you would not be here tonight. Indeed, you would never have existed, because your parents would have gone the way of the Jews of Germany and Poland and Greece and Czechoslovakia. They would have been exterminated.'

His words created a furor, with the English professor crying: 'Oh, that's infamous,' and another professor from Penn shouting: 'Let me respond!' Some students, led by my grandson, booed Yoder while others, including Jenny Sorkin, applauded and tried to drown out the boos. President Rossiter, who had become increasingly uneasy with the tenor of the talks, stared ahead impassively until his wife goaded him into action. Then without much conviction he moved toward the microphone and was able to restore a semblance of order, muttering: 'This is a college audience and we must observe the rules of comity. Our good neighbor Lukas Yoder was summoned to the microphone. He didn't grab it on his own. Please, I beg of you, let him speak.'

Lukas, who had said nothing during the near riot nor made any move to protect himself, stood at that moment at the conclusion of a working life; he had a universe of ideas he wanted to share; but when quiet was restored he shot off in a direction that astounded us all, even Emma:

'I have written my last book [There were many cries of 'No! No! but he ignored them] and I've written in a style that is clearly old-fashioned, even outmoded.' [More protests.] But if I were starting over tonight as a beginning writer I wouldn't dream of doing it the way I did. I would be adventurous. I'd use new styles, new forms, new discoveries in psychology, new approaches to the reader, new everything. I am addicted to constant change in all things.

'To tell you the truth, I sometimes find my Amish friends' adherence to outmoded customs preposterous. But the way they adhere to the fundamentals pleases me very much, and in my own work I've tried to copy their stoutness of character.

'So in the discussion tonight I find myself heartily in favor of young artists being bold enough to break bonds, but I also believe that the artist has an obligation to his or her society—to help the disparate elements cling together in mutual interests—to support good government—to care for the unfortunate, and give assistance to young people who yearn to become artists. I find myself in harmony with them.

'But I am not in harmony with anyone who argues that a drive for freedom of expression entitles him to engage in treason against his nation or advocate the extermination of people he doesn't like.'

He retired from the front of the hall to modest applause from his supporters and silence from the thoughtful, but all seemed moved by his revelations about himself as a writer and by his willingness to remind his colleagues of the permanent moral values of the human race. When he reached his seat Emma said simply: 'It had to be done. Let some fresh air into this room.'

For me at least the symposium had thrown such blinding light on Pound's treason that I was hungry for further exploration of a crucial point I had not been sufficiently forthright to raise in my long afternoon discussion with Yvonne. So when she drove me home in her rented car, we sat for some moments in the driveway as I asked the question that tormented me: 'Ever since Streibert quit his job or was fired—no one will tell me which—Timothy's been driving down to Temple to meet with him. Says he needs Streibert's help on *Dialogue*, but I'm worried that it could become something, shall we say, more complicated?'

'You mean is he, shall we say, a negative influence on him?'

'You really are helpful.'

'Mrs. Garland, this afternoon I told you as strongly as I could, your grandson is totally self-directed. No one has undue influence on him.' Then she laughed and made a point I had never considered: 'Mrs. Garland, your grandson also works with me. Comes sometimes to New York to do so. Do you ever torment yourself with the question: "Might she lead him into error?"'

'You're saying he's so strong he's in no danger?'

She evaded my question: 'Besides, who invited Streibert to your party last night?'

'I did. I like him. Always have. I find him a wonderful man. Besides, who ran up to kiss him last night?'

'I've always respected him. Still do, despite what he said in the papers. I just hope he gets his act together.'

I said: 'But an elderly woman can enjoy Streibert for herself yet fear him for her grandson.'

'You asked if I thought Timothy was strong. He's a bulldog. I'd hate to get in his way.' Then she added: 'I consider him the finest young fellow of his age in America. He really has everything going for him, so rest easy,' and her statement was so clear and unequivocal that I went to bed saying to myself: To have a son of proved talent who is properly launched, that's what parents long for. And my sleep was undisturbed.

EARLY MONDAY MORNING, 4 NOVEMBER: On this date, for reasons that will become clear, I left the page blank but some days later Ms. Marmelle was required to give the police a statement detailing how she had spent November 4. The police stenographer took it down verbatim and I have deemed it best to incorporate her narrative instead of trying to reconstruct my own.

Office of the Chief of Police
Dresden, Pennsylvania
Wednesday, 6 November 1991
Statement of Ms. Yvonne Marmelle
Kinetic Press, New York City

Early Monday morning, 4 November 1991, to beat the heavy traffic returning to New York, I drove my car in darkness past the fields of my new home state, Pennsylvania, and into suburban New Jersey, where dawn was creeping in. As I approached the New Jersey entrance to the Lincoln Tunnel, my car radio brought an announcement that gripped my attention. On the heels of news from a meeting of heads of state in Brussels, the newsman said: 'Last night one of America's highly regarded authors died in a mysterious . . .'

I had now penetrated so deep into the tunnel that the broadcast vanished, so in the depths of the tunnel, far below the bottom of the river, I rode in silence, speculating on who the deceased man might be, but as I began to run through the men who would fit the brief description 'one of America's highly regarded writers' I concluded that if it had been Yoder the announcer would surely have said 'one of America's best-selling writers,' for that was the accepted characterization. 'It could have been Streibert,' I told myself, 'but he probably wouldn't have been given such air time.' After that I ran through other writers, and as I neared the Manhattan exit of the tunnel I cried: 'Doesn't have to be a man. The announcer said nothing about a man,' and before the radio came back I rapidly ran through women writers in my mind but, of course, to no avail.

Then suddenly out in the open the radio blared quite loudly, for in trying to keep it alive in the tunnel I had turned up the volume: 'The President has said firmly that if the bill is presented to him with those stipulations he will veto it.' Irritated, I spun the dial as I drove up Tenth Avenue so slowly that cars began honking. I heard the tail end of several early-morning newscasts and then: 'Other writers and critics who commented on the death said that Timothy Tull was one of our most promising . . .' A police siren blared, lights flashed, and I was edged over to the side of the avenue.

When a policeman bent down to my car window and started yelling at me, I looked at him with what must have been visible terror: 'Sir, I'm an editor at a publishing house, and I just heard that one of my authors . . .'

'Yeah, that young fellow in Pennsylvania Dutch country, beaten to death, quite horrible . . . Lady! Lady! Hey, Max! She's fainted!'

When the police revived me I said weakly: 'I'm sorry. Can you verify the young man's name?'

'No. But they're sure it was murder, and in Pennsylvania. That's why we're checking the tunnels from Jersey.'

'Can you help me? I feel very weak. I must make a phone call. . . .'

'Lady, you can't stop here. Monday-morning traffic.'

'The dead man might be my author.'

'Hey, Max! Protect the car. Just a minute.' He took me to a phone, helped me as I rummaged through my purse to find my address book, and lent me two quarters as I called a reporter on an early beat at the *Times*: 'Izzy, Yvonne Marmelle. Do you have an overnight on the murder of a writer in the Dutch country in Pennsylvania?'

'Came in after midnight. Nothing in the morning paper but two writers are working on it.'

'The man's name?'

'Timothy Tull. Did that wild upside-down book, everyone said he was a genius, the new Truman Capote.'

'Brutally murdered?'

'I believe the first announcement, from the local sheriff, said "horribly beaten." '

Fearing that I might faint again, I appealed to my policeman for help, then gained control and walked with him back to my car. 'It was as I feared. A young man of unbelievable talent.'

'How far you driving this car?'

'Garage on East Sixty-ninth.'

'You sure you can make it?'

'Yes,' I mumbled, but when I looked at the officer's fresh young face I saw Timothy at the dawn of his glorious new life, and my legs began to buckle. I did not break into tears, but I did fall limply into the officer's arms: 'Please help me home. It would not be safe for others on the road for me to drive.'

When I reached my apartment and recovered with the aid of a soothing shower, I called one of the literary editors at the *Times*, announced myself and told the secretary who answered: 'It's vitally important. Please have Angelica call me.'

In a surprisingly short time my friend called back, prepared for my questions: 'We have a full report on the brutal facts. Absolutely nothing on the cause or the killer.' Sitting down, I said: 'Go ahead,' and Angelica spoke rapidly: 'Timothy Tull, twenty-three years old, son of blah-blah-blah, both dead, grandson of the distinguished steel magnate, Larrimore Garland, now dead, and his wife, Jane, still living and benefactress of the arts. Then there's a bit about *Kaleidoscope* and its upside-down pages, and you're mentioned as the editor who launched him.'

'The murder?'

'We'll get to it. Body found at four A.M. Monday morning, that's today. By the chauffeur, name of Oscar. On the grounds of Windsong, family estate, ninety yards from the house. Badly mutilated by some instrument that could not be identified—that is, not even its type could be determined. Dead dog lying nearby, name of Xerxes. No motive can be guessed. No identity of the murderer. Nothing on or near the corpse to indicate anything about the crime, except that Tull and his dog apparently tried to defend themselves. His right forearm was broken as if he had attempted to ward off a blow. No gunfire evident, no weapon found.'

My friend's next question was: 'Would you have any comments on his death?' and I said: 'Only about three hours' worth.' Angelica said: 'I'll have Paula call you. She's working on the story, I believe,' and when Paula called, eager for news that would intensify the public's reaction to the tragedy by bringing his death more intimately into focus, my grief became undammed, and I told of how I had met him, of his wit, his gentleness with his grandmother, and of how, at an early age, he not only wrote his amazing *Kaleidoscope* but also won an appointment helping to teach creative writing at Mecklenberg. I made it a glowing summary of a young life.

Then, to round out her story, Paula asked: 'Did he leave any unpublished work?' and I remembered that perfectly typed three quarters of Timothy's second novel, and I had a powerful premonition that I ought to establish right now, in the first moments after his death, that a nearly completed novel was in being. So without calculating the conflicts I might be setting in motion, I said with great care: 'On Friday, it must have been the first, I saw at the home of his grandmother an almost completed novel—probably seventy-five percent finished. I was allowed to read a substantial portion and I predict it will be a sensation.'

'Did you say that about his first book, when you saw it in manuscript?'

'It's on record that I did.'

'The title of the new one?' Without hesitation I said: '*Dialogue*, and it's going to be bigger than *Kaleidoscope*.'

It's important that the surprising things I did next be noted, and if anyone thinks that I was callous about this, or unmindful of the great tragedy in which I was involved, he or she is mistaken. I became an editor battling to protect both the survival and the validity of an important work of art. In these moments, I could think of only two things: the slain novelist and his unfinished work.

Within a minute after talking to Paula I was on the phone to Windsong, where Martha Benelli was handling calls on behalf of Mrs. Garland. I was insistent: 'It isn't that I must speak to her, she must speak to me. Tell her the fate of her grandson's reputation is in her hands. Tell her that, forcefully. . . .'

Apparently these were the only words that could budge the bereaved woman, for Ms. Benelli said: 'She's coming,' but it was many moments before she reached the phone, and when she spoke her voice was a shadowy whisper, 'Yvonne,' then silence broken at last by a sob: 'It's beyond understanding, but thank you for calling. I wish you were here.' Afraid that she was about to hang up, I said hurriedly and with force: 'Mrs. Garland, Jane, I need your help.'

'My help? I can hardly breathe.'

'Jane! Listen! You and I have much work to do—now—to save Timothy's place in literary history—in your world of books.'

There was a long pause, during which Mrs. Garland must
have been drawing on her deepest reserves of strength, for
when she spoke again, her voice was clear, her resolve firm:
'Tell me what I must do.'

'I believe Timothy left his manuscript with you that day
I saw it.'

'He did.'

'And you still have the pages?'

'I do.'

'Good. Mrs. Garland, you and I will fight to establish the
tremendous validity of Timothy's contribution. Now listen
carefully to what I say, for every instruction is crucial. Get
the manuscript, give it to Ms. Benelli. Have her take it immediately to a copy store in Dresden and have three copies
made of every page. At the bottom of each page show a
cardboard with today's date, 4 November 1991, and her
name.

'Then she must take the whole bundle to a notary public,
who will wrap one set of sheets into a tight package, seal it
with sealing wax and notarize it with the date and the librarian as witness. When that's done, she's to take the sealed
package to the bank, rent a safe deposit box in her name,
place the manuscript inside, lock the box and keep the key.
She can then return the original and two copies to you. You
keep the original and send me the two Xeroxes.'

Mrs. Garland asked: 'Do you wish to repeat those instructions to Ms. Benelli?' and I said: 'Yes, tell her to get a pencil
and paper.' Only when I was sure the manuscript would be
protected did I say to Mrs. Garland: 'I was terrified when I
heard the news. I fainted and a policeman had to drive me
home.'

'I can hardly bear it. I loved him so much, and he had such

promise,' and I said: 'It's to protect that promise that we must notarize everything we do. Years from now people will begin to claim that he didn't write his second book. That we fabricated it after his death.'

'You and I will not let that happen,' Mrs. Garland said. I then launched a blizzard of calls. To my office I reported that I must return immediately to Pennsylvania, and because of my fainting spell that morning, I hoped that Chuck from our office could come up, get my Olds from the garage and drive me to Dresden. That done, I knew I could not escape involving Karl Streibert at Temple, for he had known Timothy on the intellectual level more intimately than any of us. But this posed an ugly problem, since he had publicly rejected both Kinetic and me, and although we had repaired the damage that night at the 7&7, there was still friction between us because of his savage review of *Stone Walls*. What I would now require was almost daily contact with him as we discussed emotional materials and I did not know if either of us was equal to that strain. I knew I must call him, but a premonitory impulse warned me to call Jenny Sorkin first: 'Jenny? Yvonne Marmelle. Let's have no tears, neither you nor me. . . . Did Timothy leave any portion of his new novel with you? Oh, thank God! The better part of a chapter? Three individual scenes but not linked together? I'm going to give you mystifying but absolutely essential instructions, and I want you to follow them in every detail.' I repeated what I had told the librarian, and added: 'If you need money for this, borrow it. I'll be at the inn this afternoon. Tell no one of this. No one. We're taking these steps to protect the reputation of a remarkable young man, whom you and I knew, each in our special way. Help me.'

Only then did I have the courage to call Streibert, for I did not know how he would react to hearing from me, and it took some time to track him down at Temple, but when at last he came to the phone he cried: 'Yvonne! Thank God you've called!' and he broke down in tears. When he regained control he explained: 'I came to my class knowing nothing, but a student, aware that I had known Tull at Mecklenberg, blurted out: "Professor, did you hear that Timothy Tull was murdered last night?" I had to leave the lecture hall and come to the faculty retiring room, where I am now.'

At the end of this tearful outburst, I said: 'Karl, if we forget all that's happened recently . . .'

'Yvonne, I want to explain why I felt I had to leave you and Kinetic—'

'Karl, I said we'd forget it. I need your help most urgently.'

'What can I do?'

'Help me protect Timothy's reputation. His place in the world of books.' This challenge had the same effect on him that it had had on Mrs. Garland: 'What must I do?'

In the next minutes he revealed that Timothy had left with him two substantial segments of *Dialogue*, but again they were isolated segments with no linkage to other sections. Like Jenny, he had every reason to believe that Timothy had intended them as part of the closing section of his novel. As soon as I started to recite my instructions he stopped me: 'I understand your apprehension and share it. We must ensure authentication of this material. I'll have it dated and Xeroxed immediately.'

'And notarized,' and he said: 'Of course.'

'Could you drive up to Dresden? Meet me at the inn at three? I'm driving down.'

'I'll see you then.'

At last I telephoned the German president of Kinetic and told him: 'In the depths of this tragedy there is one glimmer of light. Timothy Tull left behind at his tragic death a splendid manuscript—I've read eighty percent of it—I've been assured that ninety percent is completed. I seek your verbal promise, which I will not publicize until you and I work out the details in writing, that if I can get this new work published in good form and with the wide success I anticipate, you will, on behalf of Kinetic and our continued concern over the finest in American fiction, donate either a lump sum or a portion of our profits to the Department of Creative Writing at Mecklenberg College, where Tull learned his trade and where he taught others. A deal? Good. No, I can't come in, because I've got to return to Dresden to help the boy's grandmother arrange the funeral. I have your approval of the gift and Kinetic will reap untold rewards.' That settled and with Chuck driving, I headed for Dresden, but I was asleep even before we entered the Lincoln Tunnel.

End of statement of Ms. Yvonne Marmelle.

Witnesses: Walter Stumpf
Leonard Dreyfus
Dresden, Penna.

Typist: Fanny Trumbauer

WEDNESDAY, 6 NOVEMBER: I will let Yvonne Marmelle's report to the police explain why I was unable during the first days of the tragedy to write of it. Timothy's death, that extinguishing of a life I had nurtured, the murder of a boy with such limitless promise and in such a horrible way, threw me into a state of shock that was intensified by the cold realization that with his death any hope of preserving the honorable name of Garland was also erased. I fell into such a trembling confusion that only Martha Benelli's assistance at Windsong and Yvonne Marmelle's calm voice in New York enabled me to get through that first day. By midafternoon, when Yvonne and her driver reached Dresden, I was functioning. When she called she asked me: 'Would you be up to seeing Karl Streibert at three this afternoon? I've asked him to drive up to discuss the manuscript.'

Since this was the day's first problem involving living human beings I said: 'High time you two started working together again,' but before either he or Yvonne arrived, Jenny Sorkin knocked at the door, and I embraced her as the girl who might have married my grandson.

As we sat in big chairs facing the wall of windows and staring down at the scene of the murder, I said, trying to fight back tears: 'I do wish, Jenny, that this were the incident I once read about in an eighteenth-century romance. My grandson has been killed fighting with the Duke in Flanders and you're the sweetheart he courted before leaving. You've come to tell me you're pregnant and that you and I shall raise his bastard son. Dear God, I wish that were your story, Jenny,' and I dissolved in tears. Before she could speak I added: 'That's what comes of taking you writers seriously.'

In her blunt way, which I so appreciated, she said: 'I'm afraid I don't bear his seed, Mrs. Garland, but I do have the germ of the closing to his novel, and Ms. Marmelle gave instructions on how we can preserve it.'

When Professor Streibert joined our solemn group we greeted him as if he were the prodigal son. Ms. Benelli said: 'It doesn't seem like the same library without you dropping by now and then,' and after Jenny embraced him warmly she said: 'Timothy and I missed you. You kept our noses pointed in the right direction,' and he had to dry his eyes.

Within a few minutes Ms. Marmelle appeared, and her first task, after consoling me, was to establish amicable relations with Professor Streibert, whom she was meeting for the first time since our dinner at the 7&7. And even though I was distraught I could see that he was more nervous about the meeting than she. 'Hello, Karl. I'm grateful you could come back to help us,' she said and kissed him on the cheek.

Then she became the Napoleon I had admired: 'Can we, among us, piece together Timothy's movements during his last days?' and as we began to explain what had become known since her early morning call to her friend at the *Times* she started her tape recorder lest she miss important details.

Jenny spoke first. 'On Saturday night he had a date with me at the Hex, that's the college hangout, where we met with two other couples. One couple walked Timothy to his rooms, the other took me to mine. No heavy date or anything. That was one in the morning.'

On Sunday Timothy in company with four other men and two women, all from the college, hiked down the entire length of the off-road border of the Wannsee, a distance of twelve leisurely miles, while Jenny had Timothy's car waiting at the end of the hike. In rather brisk November weather containing a hint of frost, they had a cookout on the campus, at the end of which, at about seven at night, Timothy said: 'I'm sleeping at Windsong tonight. Grandmother lives alone and enjoys companionship now and then.'

Authority for his movements now shifted to me, and painful though it was, I managed, with frequent pauses to dry my eyes, to share as much as I knew: 'What Jenny says sounds reasonable, because he arrived here alone about seven-thirty. He said he'd already eaten but would join me in a bowl of rum raisin ice cream, which he knew I kept in the refrigerator on a regular basis. As we ate it, we talked of his manuscript, which I had found both professional and ingenious. I told him that although it was daring I believed he had pulled it off, except for one passage at about page ninety. He asked to see that section and cried: "No wonder! The typist left out a whole section," and he borrowed my pen to make a mark so that he could insert the missing paragraphs.

'We watched the end of the J. B. Fletcher show as she solved her weekly murder, and then we trundled off to bed. No one saw him alive after that, except the murderer.'

Now Ms. Marmelle took over, beginning with an apology: 'I may sound ruthless raising these matters at this time of mourning, but we four are responsible for the literary reputation of a gifted young man, and the steps we take in the next few days will determine how the public, now and later, will remember him.

'First of all, Mrs. Garland, have you any document that gives you title to the manuscript? Is it yours?'

Calmly I said: 'With foresight our lawyer insisted upon two wills. Mine gave everything, after gifts, to Timothy; his gave everything to me.'

'Good. We're free to go ahead.' Then she asked Ms. Benelli: 'You had the manuscript Xeroxed, notarized and stowed in a locked box? Good. This can be a tremendously important book—if it's presented right. Karl, I see a five-signature book—a hundred and sixty pages— if we can reconstruct the closing pages, so I want you to write a one-signature essay up front, thirty-two pages on how this work was conceived and perceived by Timothy, the conditions under which it was written, and most important, his habit of showing you and Jenny, his colleagues, segments as they came along. You must establish that he shared with you two, as his co-equals in the writing program, his hopes and plans for the completed book.'

At this point she snapped her fingers: 'Did he ever read portions of his text to members of his class? Great! Jenny, I want you to get notarized statements from half a dozen students testifying to what he told them about his work in progress. Karl, try to remember the one who writes best and I'll invite him or her to do a two-page piece on Timothy reading, and let's make sure our writer specifies what it was he read.'

Continuing with Karl, she warned: 'You're to be a most meticulous chronicler, because if you are, you justify our combined efforts to complete his manuscript. Thus you write your own credentials.'

'Sound strategy,' Streibert said, and I agreed.

She interrupted her instructions: 'Please clarify one point. I've been using three different percentages, seventy-five, eighty, ninety. Can we agree on how much of the manuscript he completed—in the typed form I saw?'

Streibert and Jenny each said eighty, and then Yvonne said: 'Now the crucial part. You, Karl, have two segments he gave you to read, and you, Jenny, have three.' Streibert looked at his former student. 'But do either of you have pages on which he was still working—not typed out properly?'

Both did, and from their briefcases each produced pages showing how Tull had worked and reworked passages. 'Marvelous,' Yvonne said. 'Four of these must be reproduced photographically in your essay, Karl, to establish authenticity.' Returning the pages, she asked: 'Have we any clues that can be substantiated as to how he planned to finish the book? Any notes? Fragments?'

When Streibert remained silent, Jenny said: 'He talked to me about it. I have a fair idea of what was in his mind.'

'Hearsay. Any notes from him?'

'No, but if you'll look at the Xeroxes of my pages you'll find three places on which I wrote notes telling him how I think the pages he'd let me see would fit or not fit into his overall plan.'

'Where? Where?' and when Jenny produced the pages she referred to, we plotters saw that they were exactly as she had described them. There were her notes, tying the tentative pages into the complete plan, and his curious notation: 'Okeh,' a variant of O.K. 'These are precious,' Yvonne cried. 'The manuscript can be completed, and thousands of people are going to read it, hundreds of thousands.'

She then gave a series of crisp directives, allowing no deviations: 'Karl, can you get to work immediately on your essay? Document everything. Let's call it something like "Tull at Mecklenberg." But first, Karl and Jenny, have dinner with me at the inn, and we'll try to fit your five segments into some kind of sensible sequence. In the published book, we'll give the reader three clear indications: the part finished and edited by Timothy, the five segments written by him but not polished or edited, and those short linkages proposed by us but with no original verification by him. Every word completely honest and aboveboard.' Rising from her chair, she came to me: 'It's going to be a sensationally good book, one that'll be studied for decades to come,' and I said: 'That's what I want. More important, that's what he would have wanted. When he handed me the unfinished manuscript he said: "This one'll be much better than the first." ' Yvonne turned and said: 'Did you get that on the tape, Karl?' And as they left, I heard her say: 'Now tell me about this fabulous new department at Temple.'

THURSDAY, 7 NOVEMBER: For the past four days I've been having constant reports from a man for whom I have developed considerable respect. Captain Walter Stumpf of our Dresden police looks like a junior Herman Zollicoffer, for he's a rotund Dutchman with a bullet head, thick neck, powerful shoulders and short pumping legs that seem tireless. Red-faced and inclined to sweat, even in November, he works energetically. He speaks in a modified Dutch accent; that is, he uses proper English learned at Franklin and Marshall but with a rural pronunciation that seems at times illiterate but is always amusing. From what I can see of him or learn about him, he's a bulldog of a man; each time we part he says: 'Mrs. Garland, we'll find out who did it.'

I first saw him around four o'clock in the morning on the day of the murder. Oscar, my chauffeur, had heard a dog barking at two and deduced that it must be Xerxes, though why he was out at that hour he did not know. He went back to sleep. At about four he awakened, left his quarters to investigate where Xerxes was and found the body. Bellowing, he ran toward the house, awakened me, and in my night-dress I ran down the lawn to see the horrible sight. It was so awful, blood everywhere, and the dead dog so protectively close to Timo-thy's face, that I began shaking uncontrollably, but Oscar, quite properly I think, said: 'Stay here. I'll go call the police.' He left me his flashlight but I turned it off, for I could not bear to look at the carnage, and there in the cold darkness I assessed the destruction of my world. I was numb, but not from the cold.

I guarded the body till Captain Stumpf roared up in his police car, siren shrieking and lights flashing. When he flashed his light on the broken bodies of Tim and Xerxes he muttered: 'A madman,' and that started his three-day effort to line up the facts.

Using his radio to summon assistants, he posted them so that no one could molest the body or trample such clues as the lawn grass might hold. Then, standing back to view the crumpled body, he swore to his men: 'We'll find out who did this.'

Before the sun rose at six-thirty he had begun assembling known data on my grandson, his associates and his movements in recent days. Members of his staff had alerted the Philadelphia and New York newspapers, while he hurried off before breakfast to the college to interrogate Timothy's associates, among them Jenny Sorkin. Uni-versal shock greeted the grisly news he bore, and President Rossiter rushed out wearing a mix of nightclothes and the formal wear lying beside his bed following a college dinner party the night before. Everyone testified to Timothy's fine character, his intellectual bril-liance and his lack of enemies. From Mecklenberg Stumpf picked up not one clue.

Doubling back, he spent two hours in the village of Neumunster questioning anyone who might have specialized knowledge of Tim's associates or movements, and wherever he probed, Stumpf heard the same report: 'Fine young man. Never attended our little school after the sixth grade, but not stuck up, either.' Had he dated any of the local girls? 'He wouldn't have been allowed to do that. After his parents were killed in that crash on the Cut Off, his grandmother took over, and she ruled with an iron hand. Sent him to the expensive private school in Pottstown.'

'I thought he went from here to Reading?'

'You're right. He did. And I believe he ran with the fast crowd there. At any rate, his grandmother yanked him out and sent him to the private school. Discipline was better.'

Visits to both Reading and Pottstown produced only standard information: 'It's wrong to say that Timothy ran into trouble here in Reading. Bad study habits but never bad personal behavior. He associated with only our best boys. Girls? None that we know of.'

At The Hill word of his murder had come in over the morning radio, so that officials had already begun assembling a verifiable profile, and it was exemplary: 'Superb student. Passed his College Boards with highest marks his junior year. Played moderately good tennis. Excelled in writing and won the Edmund Wilson Prize, named in honor of the great literary critic who got his start at this school. Trouble? Timothy never came close. Bad companions? We have none at The Hill. A few in the local community but he never associated with them. Girls? Not as far as we know.'

Since Windsong lay only ten miles from the heart of Allentown, Stumpf also hurried there after leaving Pottstown, but the dead man's name was not even known by the police in the city, and there had never been a single incident involving an Allentown hoodlum and Windsong: 'The feeling among our hoods was that the place was too well guarded, and patrolled by you fellows in Dresden. Our police agreed, so Windsong just didn't surface in Allentown calculations.'

Frustrated in that quarter, he sped along the crowded highway to Bethlehem, so close at hand that he, like most of us, was never aware of when he had left Allentown and entered the industrial center. In the offices of the steel company he asked probing questions about whether Larrimore Garland could have generated any conspicuous hatreds or actual enemies during his tenure as a major representative of management at the great mill: 'Anytime you have a strike, tempers are apt to flare, but Larrimore was such an understanding man that he kept the differences restricted to money matters only. Never allowed arguments to degenerate into personal hatreds.'

'With labor, yes. But how about jealousies in management over things like promotion?'

'None of that. I honestly believe we all grieved when that good man died.'

'Managers of competing mills?'

'We don't play that way.'

'But someone had a vicious hatred of his grandson. That I saw at four this morning.'

'Captain Stumpf, in this industry the sins of the grandfather, if there are any, which I doubt, are not visited upon the grandson.'

'Someone visited Timothy Tull real heavy. I'd appreciate any leads that might come to mind later in the day.'

So at five-thirty Monday afternoon, just as our meeting at Windsong of the people interested in Tim's manuscript was breaking up, Stumpf stopped by to report, and when he saw my three guests, he remembered that Yvonne had consulted him about the purchase of her house: 'Did you have a good deal with Troxel?'

'We were both satisfied.'

'Now since you're all here, and interested in your own way, let me give you a brief report. The coroner believes he must have died about two in the morning. Police photographs show he could have died from any of six or seven different blows, so some could have been delivered after he was already dead. I'm sorry, ma'am.'

'Go ahead,' I said.

'I've checked the local school, the one in Reading, The Hill in Pottstown, the college. Not a clue. No bad companions, no boys hated him, no girls wanted to get even. No family enemies at the steel company, no records of any kind in Allentown, and we don't even have a reckless driving charge against him in our files at Dresden.'

'What do you have?' I asked, and he said: 'Nothing, except a powerful determination to solve what looks right now to be a mystery, but can't remain one, considering the brutality, the amount of blood spilled, and the exposed place of the killing. Somebody had to have seen something.'

It was something of a study in contrasts that Captain Stumpf blusteringly dispatched his men on investigations that accomplished nothing, while Ms. Marmelle quietly and efficiently directed Streibert, Jenny, Ms. Benelli and me in our task of assembling materials for 'Tull at Mecklenberg,' and then saw to it that we did our jobs. Streibert immediately attacked his assignment, the thirty-two-page essay. Jenny began transcribing her memories of Timothy. Ms. Benelli helped with reference books and literary data, and Ms. Marmelle herself sat in the Dresden China checking the accuracy of her very full memorandum, from which I quoted. I spent my time verifying data.

This evening Yvonne assured me: 'We're producing a book that will be read by everyone who loves literature. A cult book, if you will, but of the highest authenticity.' With that benediction she boarded the bus back to New York.

At the end of his three exhausting days Captain Stumpf could merely repeat his stolid promise: 'We'll find out who did it.'

WEDNESDAY, 13 NOVEMBER: While watching the energetic but fruitless efforts of Captain Stumpf, his force and the several state police who cooperated with him, I became aware that two private citizens were also preoccupied with this case. Knowledge of their activity reached me when the college held a planning session regarding the fund Lukas Yoder had given, and he pushed his way forward with uncharacteristic vigor to express his condolences: 'Everyone who knew Timothy shares your sorrow. He was a rare lad and we shall find the criminal who did it. Mrs. Garland, we shall find him.' He seemed so personally distraught that I quietly sought Emma: 'Is anything wrong with Lukas? He seems so unnerved,' and she gave a doleful answer: 'Everything seems to be going poorly for him. The murder has affected him far more profoundly than I would have expected. He's told me several times: "A thing like that oughtn't to happen in Grenzler," and he's developed a bitter hatred for the murderer, as if the savage had attacked him personally. And to top it all, his painting, *Hex XXIV*, isn't going well and he was psychologically bruised by the fracas he got himself involved in over Ezra Pound.'

'Watch over him, Emma. Good men are precious in this world.'

'In times of depression like this, he's always found consolation in his evening visits with Herman Zollicoffer. He says: "Herman is of the earth, and his sensible attitudes bring me back to earth." But now even that friendship fails to solve the problem, because when Lukas visits him, all Zollicoffer wants to talk about is the murder. They're a pair of fanatics.'

When I heard that my two Dutchmen, Yoder and Zollicoffer, were struggling to identify my grandson's murderer, I became hungry to know what they had learned, so I asked Emma: 'Could I come by tomorrow to speak with you?' and when I reached their farm she and Lukas, as well as Zollicoffer, were waiting for me. Lukas spoke first: 'I was very fond of Timothy and I respected what he was writing. We had our differences of opinion, as when he spoke rather harshly against me in the Pound affair, but at his age he should have.'

When I nodded my approval of his reaction, he told me: 'The two sources I visit for my news about the murder produce two radically different types of information. At the post office I get sporadic gossip, one item rarely relating to the next, guesswork at best. At Zollicoffer's I get the patient, shrewd deduction of a longtime Dresden man who has seen crimes that seemed completely insolvable at first yield to either analysis or inspired intellectual police work. As a result of watching numerous such performances in surrounding communities, from Bethlehem on the north to Lancaster on the south, Zollicoffer has deduced certain immutables: "Lukas, the two rules still hold. If it ain't sex, it's got to be money." You'd be surprised how often that rule has helped the old fellow to deduce the specific motives that ultimately identified the criminal.'

I did not know Zollicoffer well, had spoken with him at length only twice—when the Yoders brought him and his wife to my cocktail party and when we had dinner at the 7&7—but what I now heard him say made me appreciate his robust common sense. 'Any girls involved that we know of?' he asked.

'None,' Yoder said, 'except a responsible young writer named Jenny Sorkin . . . if the police are telling us what they know.'

'They're not obligated to, but I haven't heard of any others, have you?'

'Not a whisper,' Lukas said, 'and college kids do like to whisper.'

'It's got to be money.'

I was impressed with Zollicoffer's common sense and asked: 'Have you anything else? Even something that seems unimportant?' and Zollicoffer said: 'There was that story in the Philadelphia newspaper, remember, about your boy. Maybe—'

I stopped him: 'Lukas, may I use your phone?'

When Stumpf came on the wire, I asked: 'Are you aware that some years ago *The Philadelphia Inquirer* carried a story about Timothy's upside-down book and it informed the public that my grandson was

a millionaire, or words to that effect? Couldn't that story have triggered some sick mind?'

I could tell from his reaction that Stumpf was irritated by my
intrusion: 'Mrs. Garland, we had a copy of that paper by three
o'clock on the day of the murder.'

'Good police work,' I said, and he added: 'The story did carry your
boy's picture and it did suggest that he was very rich. So your hunch
was a good one. We're going to find the killer.'

When I reported Stumpf's words, Zollicoffer nodded: 'He's right,
you know. We will find him,' and I was gratified that this stubborn
neighbor was on the trail.

SATURDAY, 16 NOVEMBER: The fact that Yoder and I have had to
meet with the college authorities on various issues has been rewarding in two respects. It's kept me from brooding on my terrible loss,
and it's given me a rich opportunity to know a man whom so many
Americans love. But recently there has been a third boon: a chance
to watch intimately how the concept of a novel arises in the mind
of the writer. To an inveterate reader this has been a privilege.

It came about by accident. At the end of one of our meetings at
the college I realized that I had not instructed Oscar about when he
should return for me. I was left without a car, and Lukas suggested
that he drive me home. We left the college and instead of heading
directly west toward Windsong, we wandered the lovely back roads,
which showed our area in its finest dress, and as we went he mused:
'If I were forty again I could perform an important public service,'
and when I asked him what that might be, he said as if talking with
a stranger who had no emotional involvement with my grandson's
murder: 'I'd start to build a novel on this tragedy. The Grenzler
setting. My familiar characters. The peaceful countryside and then
smash! The intrusion of this horrible murder.' He paused to consider

how he might handle it: 'I'd not have the courage to depict what you saw when you went down the slope. Too awful. But the setting, the values involved, and the ultimate meaning, I could use them to great purpose.' And he seemed to dismiss the concept.

But then he started running through a list of other potential writers of such a novel, for I could see that when he visualized a work of fiction it became a precious object, worthy of reverence: 'Streibert couldn't do it. Jenny Sorkin might, but she's too personally involved, and a stranger to our local ways and history. There's that promising young fellow in Reading, he could do it if he were old enough, and I have great respect for that teacher of writing at Lafayette College in Easton, but he's following his own low-keyed agenda.' Then he was struck by a startling idea: 'The man who could have done it perfectly was Timothy Tull himself! Some radical new approach. I don't know what, but there'd be flashes of insight, broken narrative, characters flitting in and out. He'd have come up with something dramatically appropriate to the action of the novel. The result could have been overpowering.' Yoder was now so involved with the idea of the murder, and with the irreplaceable loss society had suffered on the death of my radiant grandson, that he avoided Dresden and the superhighways, electing instead College Road, which enabled us to make a distant circuit of Mecklenberg, as if he expected to meet Timothy hiking the dusty back lanes, and he had to stifle a sob.

We had become more or less lost, and when we discovered where we were it was clear that a sharp turn to the right would land us close to the Zollicoffers': 'We'll drop in and see if he has any news,' and when we entered the kitchen we found Frieda and Herman preparing for supper. The cooking odors were seductive, and Frieda cried in her loud voice: 'We'll chust call Emma and make a feast already.'

Herman took Yoder and me aside: 'I been thinking; about what I said relatin' to the newspaper article concernin' Tull and his millions. Who in this area would see a paper like that from out of town?

Not the ordinary scoundrels in Neumunster or Dresden, the ones the police already know. More likely college students, they have the papers in their library. My guess, you're goin' to find the murderer among his college friends.'

Lukas was interested in an entirely different approach: 'I thought as I drove home by the back route, daydreaming maybe, of the great job Timothy Tull might have done with this story, a writer who understood the area and its Dutchmen. My question for him, if he were still alive, would be this: "Knowing us Dutch as you do, what kind of man or woman among us, no outsiders, would be likely to do such a thing?" Now imagine yourself as young Timothy. Same question: "What kind of Dutchman, Herman?" '

Zollicoffer leaned back in his kitchen chair, his suspenders and belt showing, and reflected upon his neighbors: 'Good question, Lukas. Let's suppose it was one of us.' Slowly he began to draw a portrait, composed of elements from people he had known. 'Not our age. We're too old to risk a deal like that, too weak to act in a rage of such power. Aindt easy to break heavy bones.'

'They were broken?'

'Didn't you study the coroner's report? Right arm, left shinbone. Powerful blows.' I shuddered, but Zollicoffer plunged ahead: 'Lukas, it's got to be a man. Even strong women don't have the power. Under forty-five, I'd think. Hotheaded, because he must have continued hittin' the boy even after the worst had been done.'

'You're leading toward a monster.'

'Oh, no! A lawyer, a minister, they can do dreadful things if they're taken by surprise, can't they, Mrs. Garland? Or if they're—scared. There was a dog at the scene, right?'

'Yes,' I said. 'A handsome Labrador named Xerxes.'

'But kept inside?'

'Yes. When Timothy stayed with me, Xerxes slept on his bed.'

'So what we're left with, hidin' among us Germans, is a man

between the ages of, say, eighteen, strong enough to do the damage, and forty-five, still crazy enough to do it. Probably a farmer, with those muscles. Heard about Tull bein' a millionaire. Brooded three full years before he had the guts to do it.' He stopped: 'Let's say he read the paper or heard about it when he was nineteen or twenty. Hadn't the courage then. Now he's twenty-two, twenty-three. Think along those lines.' But as soon as he said the words, he modified them: 'No, I still think that kind would never have seen the newspaper article. It's got to be a college boy—maybe a football player. With that steroid thing they can become pretty powerful. Remember, Lukas, the killer has to be nearly a gorilla. Hang on to that.'

Hoping to bring realism to the discussion, I pointed out: 'Whoever the killer was, he stood to make no money from Timothy's death. Was it to be a kidnapping?'

Zollicoffer, amazed at what he considered a ridiculous question, said patiently: 'Mrs. Garland, never in a hundred years did he intend to kill your grandson. And a kidnapping was physically impossible, Tim was a big, strong boy. The killer was taken by surprise. Tim and the dog coming at him, he just lashed out. Automatic, you could say.'

'What did he intend?'

'Robbery. It was supposed to be a simple robbery. He carried some tool to break into your house. All he wanted to steal was some money if he found it lying around, maybe a TV or a VCR. A robbery that turned sour.'

Before I could say how horrible it was to think that Timothy might have been killed protecting his belongings, we heard Emma bringing her small car off the main road and into the Zollicoffers' driveway. When she entered the kitchen she rebuked her husband: 'I had supper waiting. Where've you been?' and he pointed at me: 'At the college.' She embraced me and said: 'You're wise to keep busy,' and I watched with awe as the four energetically dug into Frieda Zollicoffer's good food.

'You eat like a bird!' Frieda clucked at me, but I thought I'd been eating like a proper pig.

FRIDAY, 29 NOVEMBER: I noticed that in my bereavement two factors seemed to dominate. As in every previous crisis I found positive relief in reading, and I chose to revisit old favorites that had charmed me at various times in my life: *Green Mansions* when a girl, *Precious Bane* when older, *The Constant Nymph* when a young married woman, and *Anna Karenina* from the dark days following the death of my daughter. But, if I may say so, they were all more or less in the same mold, storytelling in the great tradition and language used in traditional ways, and each was by a European writer. With them I mixed the latest well-reviewed novels by young American writers, and some of them were so fresh and delightful, and even daring, that I lived a spiritually satisfying life. I did not require how-to books on living with pain or surviving the loss of a loved one. My therapy came from great thoughts and adventures related in great languages.

The second factor that helped me to retain my sanity was a surprise. I had been reared in a proper family, had married a proper man who worked in a proper corporation in a proper American city. You might say that I was socially deprived, for my circle of friends comprised no blacks, no Jews and very few Catholics. My family had no prejudice against such people, nor the Slavs and Czechs and Poles that made up the work force in a steel mill; my parents simply taught me to ignore them. I did not even appreciate the rather amusing Pennsylvania Dutch who lived at the edges of our society.

But now, left alone with my books, I found myself with two wonderful Jewish women as my close friends and two quintessentially Dutch families as the ones who gave me the greatest solace. In these tortured weeks of November I realized that I loved Yvonne Marmelle and Jenny Sorkin for their vibrant attack on life, and I treasured the Yoders and Zollicoffers for their solid attachment to the land and the ancient rules of thumb by which good men and women have lived through the millennia. These six were harbors along a tempestuous shore, lighthouses marking the dangerous head-lands.

In these days I was thrown increasingly within the orbit of Ms. Marmelle, and she helped keep my mind away from the tragedy in an unexpected way. Although I had always loved books, to me they had been mysterious entities, finished products I found on library shelves, as if they had sprung from some magic source without human assistance. But now, in overhearing her telephone calls to her office, I caught stray information about how books are made. One day I heard her say on a telephone call to New York: 'I asked that all widows be killed,' and since I was one—and I believed her to be, too—I thought this order strange if not inhuman. When I protested she explained: 'In making a book we look at how the lines of text connect from the bottom of one page to the top of the next. We try to avoid having the bottom of a page end with a single line from a new paragraph. We abhor having the top line of any new page contain only a few words as a continuation from the preceding page. We call such lonely words widows.'

In return for her kindness in explaining the workaday aspects of her profession, I was helping her in establishing her new home. I was working with her on the presentation of my grandson's unfinished novel, and I was taking vicarious pleasure in her successes as an editor. She was adjusting comfortably to her German superiors, which was not surprising, for Yoder's novel led the lists, one of her other books had been taken by the Literary Guild, another had been picked up by a Hollywood independent for a TV miniseries, and Jenny Sorkin's rewrite incorporating the abortion affair at the imaginary university turned out to be not just satisfactory but positively brilliant and the manuscript was already being prepared by the copy editor for setting into galleys. Publishing friends said of Yvonne: 'She's on a roll.'

But I saw that her greatest satisfaction came from her acceptance by Dresden. An able carpenter had required only two weeks to dispose of Emma's list of defects in the new house. With considerable help from Streibert, she had her house in condition for occupancy, three-quarters ready, by the fourth week in November and, to her amazement, had celebrated Thanksgiving there with the Yoders and Zollicoffers, who had provided such a plethora of typical Pennsylvania Dutch dishes for her holiday feast that her new refrigerator now contained enough deep-frozen food to last till Christmas. Thanksgiving Day dinner in itself was somewhat spoiled by the two Dutchmen arguing about who might have murdered Timothy, a topic that continued to obsess them.

Another source of satisfaction, she told me, was the mature manner in which Professor Streibert had responded to her call for help: 'It couldn't have been easy for him to come back to Mecklenberg after such a tempestuous departure. Or to work with me again after having dismissed me.'

'I still can't justify the unfeeling things he said about you. He owes you everything and he shouldn't sully that debt.'

'When an ambitious man struggles to rise in his profession, or to stand up for what he believes in, he often must step on a few toes.' Then, deeming this an unworthy characterization of Karl, she offered excuses for his behavior: 'He may have felt forced to leave Kinetic—he didn't find the German management congenial, and our steady drift away from the kind of literature he espouses may have seemed to prevent him from uttering the critical judgments he feels compelled to make.'

'But to leave you?'

'There's a chance he may have outgrown me, too.'

'Are you defending him? After the way he insulted you in public?'

'An editor has certain deeply ingrained attitudes. We're gratified when someone we've worked with does a really fine book, regardless of who publishes it. Such success ratifies our earlier judgment. And in Karl's case I have to accept him because we need his help on your grandson's novel. His imprimatur will make it legitimate. Besides, I've always been fond of him.'

I had to admit that he was doing a splendid job in his essay by positioning Timothy in the category of those who had died young, such as the poet Sylvia Plath and the novelist Nathanael West. Karl's foreword was going to be definitive. Even more satisfying was the reconstructive work we all contributed during sessions at Windsong when I led the gifted trio—Marmelle, Streibert, Sorkin—in putting in the proper sequence the five fragments indubitably written by my grandson and then linking them to the poetic material that he had completed and polished. It was as if he were being called back to a second life, and I was grateful to the magicians who were ensuring his survival, especially Streibert, my rediscovered friend.

But the time had come when he had to return to his teaching at Temple, and on his last afternoon with us, Yvonne and I sat with him before the big windows and spoke of his future. I told him: 'Karl, it's preposterous for you to cut your ties with this community. You were born here, you had your education and your principal accomplish-ments here—and your friends . . . Timothy, Yvonne, me, you'll find no better.'

This did not trigger a sentimental reaction: 'You can't imagine how rewarding my new work is. And Philadelphia can be quite attractive, with new friends at Penn.'

'But don't you often regret not seeing the Wannsee, and your friends here?' After a long pause he said: 'Yes,' and while Yvonne sat silent, listening, I continued: 'Karl, Philadelphia isn't far. What? Forty miles. Many men commute that far daily.'

'I couldn't.'

'I wasn't suggesting that. What you could easily do is establish a home here. Come here for your weekends. Keep in touch with your homeland—your college.'

With his chin resting on his knuckles, he thought for at least a minute, which can be a long time when two interested people await your answer. Then he said something neither Yvonne nor I could have anticipated: 'I've rather felt that Lukas Yoder stole my homeland from me. I have no taste—'

'Oh, Karl!' Yvonne cried. 'You're on your way to a notable career, I'm sure of that. It could be even more powerful if you keep in touch with your roots. I know, Karl, because I'm fighting that same fight. I need a foothold in reality.'

Now it was my turn: 'Has it ever occurred to you that with the death of my husband and grandson I have a house here that is too big for me alone? It would be no trouble to make part of it an apartment—which you could have . . . or rent, as you wish.'

And then Yvonne added: 'I now have a roomy house. A separate outer door could be cut that would open into your own rooms.'

At this Streibert rose to his feet and cried, almost in pain: 'Why are you doing this to me?' and I said: 'Because we love you. Because you're part of our lives—an important part.'

The idea that two people unconnected in any way to his major concerns could be so actively interested in him that the word *love* was not inappropriate was so revolutionary to him that he could not digest it, and the three of us sat in silence. As we looked out toward the gathering dusk we saw a lone figure tramping over the ground where the body had been found. It was Captain Stumpf, bullet head bent forward as he tried unsuccessfully to reconstruct what had happened.

TUESDAY, 3 DECEMBER: A day of intense emotion for everyone and it was only by accident that I found myself in the middle of it all. It started innocently with Emma Yoder telephoning: 'Can you come

over here and help me knock some sense into my dumb Dutchman?'
Eager these days to leave the house on any pretext, I asked Oscar
to drive me by the back Valley Mennonite Road to the Yoder farm,
and there I found Emma waiting in her kitchen. Her husband remained out in his workshop, from which I could hear not typing but
sawing.

'What's he doing?' I asked, and Emma said: 'He and Zollicoffer
are working on a hex painting. Take a look.' And when I walked
back to the workshop I found the two men busily engaged, Zollicoffer sawing boards for frames, Lukas adding fraktur drawings to
enhance the weathered hex he had rescued from some doomed barn.

'He's creatin' a real work of art,' Zollicoffer explained and I could
see the pride these sturdy Dutchmen took in their work. 'What he
does,' Zollicoffer continued, 'is find the hex on the side of some dyin'
barn, rebuild the wood by injectin' some of this epoxy glue, find the
right hunk of wood for the panel, add the little paintin' of Dutch life,
and it's done.'

As I bent down to examine what was becoming a significant work
of art, I saw that despite the careful work of the two men an imper-
fection marred the finished appearance, but I felt unqualified to point
this out. However, Yoder, always sensitive to people's reactions,
noticed my slight frown and asked bluntly: 'What is it you don't
like?' and his forthright question forced me to be equally honest:
'You left this scar in the wood unattended. And it stands right in the
middle of your picture.'

'Not a mistake,' Lukas said, almost snappishly. 'I left it there on
purpose. To represent the withering of age, to remind the viewer that
this hex had served on a real barn—that it's a fragment of Dutch
history.'

This adroit explanation satisfied me but not Zollicoffer, who bent
close to the hex and said: 'But this scar aindt old. Done recent, like
a sharp ax scrapin' acrost it.'

I happened to be looking at Yoder when this was said and I saw him freeze. A heavy silence filled the workshop as if an evil hex had drifted in. Zollicoffer, looking up from the picture, saw that Yoder had been startled by something, or had perhaps been struck by a sudden illness: 'What is it, Lukas?'

With an ashen face Yoder said slowly: 'What did you just say?'

'I didn't say nothin'.'

Lukas pointed to the blemish: 'About that line across the hex?'

'Oh, that? I thought you ought to fix it.'

'The other part?'

'You said it was old, I said it was new. Look for yourself. Like an ax drawn across it.'

Lukas moved quietly to the door, satisfied himself that it was firmly shut, then said in a whisper: 'You're right, Herman. Did I tell you that last October, when I took the finished manuscript to you, I bought these three hexes from Otto Fenstermacher?'

'You didn't tell me.'

'I think I must have. Anyway, when Otto and I started to cut the hexes from his old barn, the job became pretty rough, so he called for his son, that big fellow they call Applebutter. The boy groused. Said he had things to do. When his father insisted, saying I needed help, the kid cursed at me, under his breath, but I heard him. Then, in a fury, he tore at the barn to hack out the last hex, using a huge ax. Striking out with no control, he dragged the ax across the face, just as you pointed out. When I cried "Hey, watch it!" he looked at me as if he wanted to use the ax on me. I can still see his distorted face.'

As I leaned forward Zollicoffer said, almost in a whisper: 'Tell me again,' but all Yoder saw fit to say was: 'A big ugly-tempered fellow with a huge ax.'

Zollicoffer said: 'He'd be bigger now, more powerful.'

Yoder added: 'I remember having the feeling that if we'd been alone, just the two of us, he might have come at me with his ax,' but Zollicoffer, always alert in his reasoning, pointed out: 'There was no ax at the murder, we know that,' and Yoder said: 'But he might have been there with whatever weapon he'd picked up.'

Zollicoffer did not respond to this; instead he bent over the damaged hex, studying the scar: 'You say he did this with a swipe of his ax? Sort of out of control?'

When Lukas nodded, Zollicoffer sprang into action: 'We've got to see Stumpf!' and, bursting open the workshop door, dashed right through the kitchen, heading for his pickup, with Yoder and me trailing behind. When Emma cried: 'Where're you going?' Lukas called over his shoulder: 'We'll be back soon.'

When it was apparent that the three of us would have to crowd into the front seat of the dusty pickup, I suggested: 'Let's use my car. Oscar can speed us there.'

As we drove along, Zollicoffer said: 'Only time I ever been in a car like this was at my aunt's funeral.' Speeding into Dresden, we drove directly to police headquarters, where Zollicoffer announced in a respectful voice that he wished to see Captain Stumpf. 'All of you?' the young officer asked, and Zollicoffer said: 'We're all involved.'

When Stumpf passed through the waiting room, he recognized me and took us directly into his office, where Herman said: 'What we got isn't a proper clue but it is something that stopped Lukas and me cold.' In his shrewd way he told of how they had eliminated one logical possibility after another, but these were paths Stumpf had gone down a dozen times.

'Get on with it, please.'

Zollicoffer could not be budged from a rational explanation: 'We said it had to be a young feller, very powerful, who knew the area, maybe even the house.'

'We decided that a month ago.'

'But it's what happened today.' There followed a description of

Yoder's hex painting and his method of adding frakturs around the edges. Mystified, Stumpf looked at me in bewilderment. Then, triumphant, Zollicoffer turned the reporting over to Yoder, who told in short, quick sentences of buying the Fenstermacher hexes, cutting them out of the rotting boards, and of the ugly role played by the boy they called Applebutter. Lukas spoke so fast, with such obvious distaste for the boy, that Stumpf asked him to repeat his story slowly. At the conclusion he said: 'There was no ax at the murder.'

'We know,' Yoder said, 'but we're convinced—*I* am, at least—that Applebutter was.'

'Jesus,' Stumpf growled. 'No self-respecting police department could tell the press that it was hot on the trail of a guy called Applebutter. What's his real name?'

'Otto.'

'Almost as bad. Now, gentlemen, not a word of this—not even to your wives. Otto has not been on our list of suspects, Mrs. Garland, but now he is.'

'What're you goin' to do about it?' Zollicoffer asked and Stumpf said: 'That's not for you to know. But we do thank you for your help.'

Before my two amateur detectives left, Yoder tried to say: 'When Tull's book was published there was this story in the *Inquirer*—'

'Mr. Zollicoffer pointed that out—weeks ago,' and as we left he added: 'I shall enter into the record that on this date Mrs. Garland, Herman Zollicoffer and Lukas Yoder stopped by to discuss the murder.'

TUESDAY, 17 DECEMBER: In the days that followed our visit to the police, Captain Stumpf's men worked overtime trying to understand Applebutter's behavior patterns. Stumpf himself dropped by Windsong periodically to keep me vaguely informed about what was happening, and I learned that the young man was noted for his quick

temper, insolent ways and misbehavior with cars, both his parents'
and those he borrowed, with or without permission. His football
coach said he was one of the best; his principal, one of the worst. The
police had nothing substantial except that he had ugly manners and
was grossly overweight. But they did start quietly to track his movements, and on December fourteenth, when he ran a red light in
Dresden and betrayed just a touch of alcohol, they had enough to
arrest him, hold him in jail and, while he was there, to obtain a search
warrant for cause, which allowed them to go carefully through his
home—despite wild protests from his mother and threats from his
father. In the middle drawer of a dresser in the boy's room they
found among a mass of junk, including books missing from the high
school library and empty Coke bottles, a copy of the article with
Timothy Tull's photograph and the story that he was probably a
millionaire.

Then the grilling of Applebutter began, and since it was two days
before his parents, who had been properly advised of their son's
Miranda rights, had the sense to call a lawyer and have him apply
for a writ of habeas corpus, persistent interrogation began to reveal
one suspicious fact after another. Stumpf, who assured me he followed the questioning attentively but without personally participating, kept warning his men: 'Nobody touch that kid. Remind him of
his rights at every session. Water to drink whenever he wants it. Time
for sleep. And I want you, Hickham, to keep an hour-by-hour log
of what's happening.'

On the second day, when Applebutter—the officers called him
only that—was punchy, one asked him: 'Why didn't you use a gun?'
and he made his first mistake: 'Everybody knows. You get into
trouble if you use a gun.'

'Why didn't you use that ax you were so good with? Fellows say
you're a wizard with the ax,' and he made his second slip: 'Wouldn't
I look crazy, goin' around with an ax in my pickup?'

'What did you take with you, Applebutter?' and suddenly the dam broke: 'There was that dog comin' at me and I had to hold him off.'

'With what?'

'The steel bar.'

'Why would you have a steel bar?'

'To pry open a window, if they was all locked.'

'You were going to look for money in the Mansion?'

'Yes. Then a light went on and a man came runnin' toward me, and the dog leaped at my throat. I had to defend myself, didn't I?'

'Did you hit the dog?'

'Yes. I knocked him back.'

'Did you hit the man?'

'No. But the dog didn't stop, so I had to kill it. The man tried to protect the dog and I didn't mean to hit him, but he got in the way.'

'He was hit many times, Applebutter.'

'He kept barkin' at me and I swung.'

'The man was hit many times—maybe a dozen times.'

'I didn't mean it, I just kept swingin' at the dog.'

'Did you get any money?'

'Another light came on in the house and I ran to my pickup.'

'What did you do with the steel bar?'

'Threw it in the Wannsee.'

'That's a far piece.'

'I was afraid to go home on the Cut Off. I eased around.'

'Did you know you'd killed the man?'

'No. But I did hurt him some.'

When Applebutter's lawyer finally appeared on Wednesday he was appalled to learn that his client had talked so freely and shouted: 'You denied him his *Miranda* rights,' and Stumpf showed him the record: 'At the beginning of every interrogation from the moment we arrested him for drunk driving a different officer read him his rights. Nine different times.'

'You haven't a single clue,' the lawyer said, and Stumpf replied: 'But three divers in Arctic protection gear are searching the shore waters of the Wannsee right now, with powerful metal detectors.'

FRIDAY, 20 DECEMBER: At eleven this morning Captain Stumpf called in the press but ordered Zollicoffer, Yoder and me to stay at home and see no one for the next two days. Waiting till police reporters from the three German cities arrived, he announced, in carefully chosen words, which my two Dutchmen and I heard on the television in the big room at Windsong, that intensive police work, 'plus helpful hints from concerned citizens,' had solved the murder of the famous writer Timothy Tull. A young man, after being carefully told of his *Miranda* rights, had confessed and the murder weapon had been retrieved from ten feet of icy water in the Wannsee. When reporters demanded the accused's name, Stumpf said very carefully: 'Otto Fenstermacher, nineteen years old, who lives on his parents' farm at the junction of Rhenish Road and Cut Off.'

Minutes after the briefing ended, photographers and reporters swarmed over the Fenstermacher place, but one especially bright young woman from the *Allentown Call-Chronicle* ignored the farm and dashed through Dresden interviewing people at random. She learned that the killer's nickname was Applebutter. The national frenzy was on.

When other reporters studied their tape-recorded notes and remembered that Captain Stumpf had used the phrase 'plus helpful hints from concerned citizens,' they pestered him to learn who those citizens were and what hints they had contributed. Having anticipated such inquiries, he said that in view of the coming trial he could not reveal facts that had been brought to his attention, and flatly refused to identify his informants; he knew that once he mentioned Yoder's name, the press would be climbing all over his farm, and if he mentioned Zollicoffer, the talkative Dutchman would promptly involve Lukas, who, after all, had flashed the signal that had set the wheels of justice into motion.

MONDAY, 23 DECEMBER: Both Emma and I quickly perceived that the arrest of Applebutter and the attendant publicity had a curious effect upon Lukas. She told me over the phone: 'He's begun leaving home early in the morning and driving his car slowly along back roads to Neumunster to study the town where Applebutter went to school, then through the underpass to remind himself of how Windsong looks in various lights. He slows almost to a walk driving down Cut Off to the Fenstermacher farm, where he sometimes sits silent in his car, trying to absorb details about the old barn, now razed, the new shed, the way the farmland rises and falls. With his eye he outlines the homestead as it must have been at the turn of the century, before the present generation sold off many of its best fields. Then he drives east along Rhenish Road, as if imagining the Fenstermachers in their relationship to Dresden.

She told me that as noon approached, he would reverse his route and study the same landscape from opposite angles and in the harsh light of a cold December day. He would wind up at the Zollicoffers', phone from their kitchen and tell her he was taking lunch with Herman. Then he and the Zollicoffers would review the sordid facts of the murder. Lukas seemed to have an insatiable hunger for information about the way Herman had reacted to the various aspects of the crime.

She said he would return home about two, take a short nap, rise, get into his car and reverse his original morning route, eager to see the locations at dusk, then wait till almost seven at night for a rapid spin around the entire circuit, detouring to see where along the Wannsee Applebutter had thrown the steel bar. He would return late for dinner, and when Emma asked what he had been doing he would give the same answer: 'Scouting the land.'

———

TUESDAY, 24 DECEMBER: This afternoon, as has been my custom through the years, I piled our car with carefully wrapped gifts and had Oscar drive me through the countryside so that I could deliver them in person. At Yvonne Marmelle's new home I was greeted with the news that our manuscript was in promising shape, and at the motel where Professor Streibert was staying I received an actual draft of his essay, which was a greater gift to me than I could have given him. Thrilling reading, it made Timothy spring alive.

At Zollicoffer's I had to stop for spiced cider and Christmas cookies. The couple told me that Yoder dropped by almost every afternoon to ask endless questions about the murder and their reactions to it, and Herman added: 'He's a bulldog till he gets everything straightened out in his head.'

I therefore approached the Yoder farm with some apprehension, and as soon as I entered that warm and lovely kitchen redolent of Christmas delicacies I realized that the debate over the murder was as active as ever, for Emma greeted me with: 'How fortunate you came! Lukas is on the verge of starting a new novel, and I'm trying to warn him against it.'

Lukas, sitting in his favorite chair, looked up sheepishly and said: 'No, no! I'm not. Not at my age.'

'But I know how you work, Lukas,' she said as she tended her cooking. 'You memorize the land—keep talking with people like Zollicoffer you may want to use as models for your characters.'

'It's just that I'm preoccupied with Timothy's death—and the clever way Zollicoffer guessed what must have happened.' He addressed this to me, but Emma answered: 'I'm warning you, Lukas. Neither of us is capable of facing another siege.'

'Why does she keep calling it a siege?' he asked me. 'It would only be the kind of work I've always done.'

'But it *is* a siege, Lukas. For both of us. And I'm too tired to attempt it another time.'

I broke the impasse by saying: 'Aside from making my deliveries, I also came to invite you to the midnight Christmas Eve service at Valley Mennonite,' and they both cried: 'Yes! Yes!'

Toward eleven that night Oscar drove me back, and we picked up the Yoders and Zollicoffers and drove the short distance to the church that overlooked the rolling farmland toward Dresden.

Many of the women who attended wore the white-lace Mennonite bonnets while their husbands displayed their best black suits. The children, of whom there were many, were dressed in such bright colors that they brought a mournful pang: on the Christmas after Timothy was orphaned by that hideous crash I thought he might be cheered by a new set of clothes for Christmas, and I chose an outfit in colors suitable for infants, forgetting that he was six. When he saw it laid out on his bed he looked at it, and then kissed me and said: 'You told me I must be a big boy now.' We passed his new babyish clothes along to the roly-poly Fenstermacher boy who would later be nicknamed Applebutter.

Dismissing the pain, I surrendered to the spirit of gaiety and Christmas cheer that enlivened this plain but handsomely designed church. Branches of spruce decorated the windows; a tree rose in austere beauty; along one wall stretched a putz, the local name for a German nativity scene in which some two dozen very old figurines, many brought over from the Rhineland in the 1700s, depicted the sacred scenes of Saint Luke. There were black princes come to worship the infant Jesus, emirs in flowing robes, Roman soldiers staring menacingly at the Mother and Child, and, as befitted what was essentially a Pennsylvania Dutch farm scene, a host of farm animals, not carved to scale, so that a pig might be as big as a cow or a calf no bigger than a plump chicken.

When I, a woman whose Christmases had been pure Charles

Dickens, visited Valley Mennonite, I was reminded that Christmas in America was essentially a German tradition and that only the Pennsylvania Dutch knew how to celebrate it properly.

At the far end of the putz stood two tables laden with the rich food of the valley, cakes and pies and cookies and canned goods galore; they were for the impoverished and the homebound. When the unfamiliar German hymns reverberated, I caught the feeling of what Christmas must have been like in colonial days, but finally the choir came to a sequence of the timeless English carols, with which I was familiar, ending with 'Silent Night' in German, and on this first Christmas Eve following the death of the last member of my family, my heart filled with love.

WEDNESDAY, 25 DECEMBER: On Christmas Day I joined Yvonne's new neighbors at her new home as we brought her gifts. We had an enjoyable visit, and toward two in the afternoon Professor Streibert stopped by, accompanied by Jenny Sorkin, who had invited herself to Yvonne's party and was most welcome.

While Streibert and we women discussed the manuscript, which was almost ready for typesetting, Yoder and Zollicoffer sat off by themselves reviewing aspects of the murder, and once when I chanced to look in their direction, I saw that Lukas was ashen and his lower lip trembling. 'Mr. Yoder!' I called. 'Are you ill?' He replied in a quavering voice: 'I was thinking it must be a cruel Christmas at the Fenstermachers',' and although he fought against it, tears came to his eyes and he was unable to speak. It occurred to me as I looked away from his stricken face that he *was* Fenstermacher. He was not with us. He was in that farmhouse with the murderer's parents, and their emotions were his. That was the secret of his writing: he became the people he wrote about, lived in their skins, suffered in their hearts, shared their mental confusion. We others could ignore the Fenstermachers on this Christmas Day, but not he, and I suppose that was why he was a novelist and we were not.

Mrs. Zollicoffer broke the spell: 'Partly their fault. They did allow their son to sass them fearful—even curse at them. First time a son tried that on me, the Mister would of broke his jaw.'

'And accomplished nothing,' Emma said, always the determined little schoolteacher. Frieda replied: 'It would of stopped his cursin', wouldn't it?'

A few days later Emma told me something that illustrated her husband's ability to project himself into the lives of others: 'When Lukas was writing *Shunning*, I found him using suspenders to hold up his trousers, something he'd never done before. But he was using only one of the straps, over his left shoulder, and when I asked: "What are you doing?" he said: "Trying to imagine how your grandfather felt." A week later he was wearing neither belt nor suspender and I teased him: "So now you're the brother," and he said: "I am." '

SATURDAY, 28 DECEMBER: For the account of what happened to the Yoders in the next three days I'm indebted to my friend Emma, who told me the facts, sometimes with the mist of affection clouding her eyes.

'On the day after Christmas,' she began, 'Lukas disappeared altogether, not even stopping at Zollicoffer's for lunch, and when he came back at dusk I really lit in. Said I could not stand by and watch him kill himself with overwork. He didn't want to listen, promised me he wasn't working on a new book. But he added: "If I *were* to try another, and I'm not saying I am, it would be entirely different. Not the way I used to write. Some of Streibert's ideas make sense. New approaches are needed. New ways of looking at things—expressing them."

'I asked if he was out of his mind, and he replied: "No. Jenny Sorkin—she's teaching at the college now—took Tull's place. She asked me to read a chapter she's recently finished. Strong stuff. A white football player rapes a coed, then forces her to have an abortion. She's black and the entire university establishment jumps on her—"

'When I asked why, he explained: "To save its reputation and to protect the boy's chances for getting national publicity and a lucrative professional contract."

'I asked him what kind of book it was and he said: "A very powerful one, the way she writes it."

'I told him to let the young people do their thing, as they say. He wasn't obligated to write violent love scenes, for instance. It wasn't his style, and besides, he'd be too nervous if he tried. He replied: "That's not the point, Emma. She's writing about football as it is. I've been thinking about describing Dresden as it is now." '

At this point Emma stopped to press her fingers against her eyes: 'I was terrified by what he was saying. I could see him plunging headlong down a mountainside, as it were. But since writing is a vital part of his life, it has to be of mine, too. So I asked him what he had in mind at his age, this breaking of new paths? And he said: "I'd like to show how the stolid, unyielding ways of the Dutch could produce a murderer. No long descriptions, no formal introductions as if it were a play. Certainly no chapters of explanation. Scenes would flash by and dialogues would be half as long as I used to make them." '

'How did you respond?' I asked, and she said: 'Although I could foresee only disaster in such a drastic reversal of style at his age, I knew I had to stand by him. So I went to his chair, hugged him and told him that he wasn't obligated to write like the young people. He listened, nodded, then said: "But the problem goes deeper. When I read their material I find it scintillating, but not one of them knows how to tell a straightforward story, keeping it fresh and moving ahead. I'd like to marry their new skills to my old ones. That could be explosive." I looked away.'

TUESDAY, 31 DECEMBER 1991: When I accompanied the Yoders on a holiday walk through the town, viewing the Christmas decorations and greeting friends, Lukas told us: 'Wait a minute,' and darted into a stationery store. He reappeared shortly with two small wire-bound notebooks four and a half by three inches.

As soon as Emma saw them she cried: 'Lukas! You bought them to take notes for a novel.' Then turning to me she said: 'He insists on starting a new novel in a new style.' Eager to avoid a domestic spat, I left them as they entered our little market with the amusing name of Superette, and as I watched them grab two carts for their year-end grocery shopping I said to myself: Look at that pair! I calculate from what Yvonne tells me they'll earn well over three million dollars this year. But it wouldn't occur to them that they could afford a maid. A cleaning woman once a week, yes. But a cook to intrude on Emma's kitchen? Never.

Back at Windsong, I helped Oscar and the maids complete arrangements to receive the neighbors, who soon came streaming in to offer condolences for the death of my grandson. I shook hands warmly with each couple, glad to have their friendship, and when several wanted to tell me how appalled they were at what the Fenstermacher boy had done, I let them know that I had no further interest in that Neanderthal: 'I worked diligently to help identify and apprehend him, but I was never driven by a desire for revenge. Rather by a compulsion to learn who had done it and why. Today I have no yearning to see him electrocuted, even if Pennsylvania law permitted it.'

By four the guests had left. I took a leisurely bath and found enormous comfort in the fact that at eight o'clock that night the

people I called the Timothy Tull Cadre would be coming to Windsong for a quiet dinner, at the end of which we would greet the New
Year. Yvonne Marmelle, Jenny Sorkin and Professor Streibert were
precious to me, and when they entered my house I embraced them—
in Jenny's case, as if she were my child or grandchild.

At ten that night, in the intimacy of the book-lined library, I
served a light French dinner with apologies: 'This is a poor thing
compared with what we had at Seven and Seven, but we all have to
work next year and a dinner like theirs could incapacitate a person
well into March.' But toward the close of the meal, to get my friends
laughing, I rang a cowbell and the two waitresses, assisted by Oscar,
brought in for dessert three enormous pies he had purchased the day
before from 7&7—apple, pumpkin, mince—and we had a true Dutch
ending to a relatively austere dinner.

When we returned to the big room, talk once more became literary: 'I've been thinking,' I said, 'or, more appropriately, brooding
about the great ones who died young. Chatterton, Keats and my
beloved Kit Marlowe. What a wonderfully gifted man he was, rois-
tering at the Mermaid, writing little in his brief twenty-nine years,
but all of it touched with the fire of genius. In many lines he even
excelled Shakespeare.'

'I find that hard to believe,' Streibert said, whereupon I sent a
maid for a notebook in which I had written Marlowe's soaring line:
'Was this the face that launched a thousand ships, and burnt the
topless towers of Illium?' and below it Shakespeare's maladroit re-
creation: 'Was this fair face the cause why the Grecians sacked
Troy?'

'I stand corrected,' Streibert conceded.

'But one passage in Marlowe has always haunted me, from the
time I memorized it in college. We gave a performance of *Doctor
Faustus*, all young women, and I was the elder who lamented the
death of the necromancer:

' "Cut is the branch that might have grown full straight,
  And burned is Apollo's laurel bough,
  That sometime grew within this learned youth . . ."

'The last line really ends with learned man, but in these days I've modified it to my purpose.'

I visualized the mighty Marlowe being slain in a barroom brawl and asked: 'What might he have become, had the branch not been cut?'

'Who?' Jenny asked, 'Marlowe or Timothy?'

'I'm not sure . . . whom I intended.'

'You can be sure, Mrs. Garland, that Tim was destined for greatness—in his own sphere. . . .'

'Do you honestly believe that, Jenny?'

'I do. Working on the concluding pages of *Dialogue* convinced me. I'm sure he was moving toward some stunning departure from conventional writing.'

Having said this, the young novelist excused herself: 'I promised my students who remained on campus that I'd help them kick in the New Year with a beer bust.'

Soon we heard her car wheels whipping through the gravel. When the sound faded, Yvonne said: 'You can't believe, Karl, the giant strides that young woman has made in her third draft. But what gives me confidence in her future is the ease and naturalness with which she uses simile and metaphor.' She showed us several pages of manuscript on which she had marked lightly in pencil phrases and sentences she had liked: 'As frenzied as a mother trying to squeeze three kids through a revolving door.' Her description of a line coach at Nebraska: 'He would have been invaluable when Hannibal was trying to get those elephants over the Alps,' or the way she skewered a show-off quarterback who could never deliver: 'With him it was always The Night Before Charisma.'

'I suppose I was prejudiced in my judgment of her and her work,' Streibert said. 'I saw her only as a bad influence on Timothy.'

But I had seen her as his salvation. This evening I was not unhappy to have her go because I wanted an opportunity to speak with Streibert and Yvonne alone, and now I broached a subject that concerned us all: 'We've so much in common. We're the ones who lost our beloved. For me, three times, my husband, my daughter, my grandson. You twice, Karl, the Irish professor you visited in Greece, and now Timothy. You, Yvonne, that gifted fellow who could talk but not write.'

'How do you know so much?' Yvonne asked, and Karl echoed good-naturedly: 'Yes. You are a snoop.'

'I had to be careful whom my grandson chose as his mentors. He chose well—I like veterans of the human wars who are scarred.' I added: 'I started out afraid of you, Karl. You could have proved a very bad influence on my grandson, but fortunately Jenny came along to point him in a safer direction. And I was also afraid of you, Yvonne. I feared you were too brittle, too much of what I heard a student call "a smartass Jewish intellectual, no heart." The way you nurtured your writer friend is the best love story I've heard in recent times.

'So in the knowledge of pain you are my brother and sister. And now I propose that we pick up the conversation where we dropped it some weeks ago. Karl, are you going to resume your private life here in Dresden? And if so, on what terms?'

He sat silent, so at ten to midnight, I turned on the television and as the final minutes of 1991 ticked away, I said: 'Good riddance! Who could tolerate another year like this?' But I eased my judgment: 'There were good moments, but I suppose there always are if you live enough days.'

When the silver ball dropped in New York and cheers from that vast crowd filled the big room, I rose, kissed Streibert and embraced

Yvonne, managing it so that they were left standing side by side and could not escape greeting the New Year with a kiss.

As they were preparing to leave I took from the small bookcase in the big room an anthology my husband had given me years ago during a tour of Great Britain: 'On wintry nights like this I do enjoy *The Eve of St. Agnes* and imagining myself immured in that medieval castle on the night of January twentieth.' When they departed I sat down in a deep chair, with a light over my shoulder and the book in my lap. The maid extinguished the other lights and I was left in near darkness, reading.

Then a frightening thing happened. As I looked at the familiar lines of *St. Agnes* I had the overpowering sensation that they had lost both their vitality and their relevance to me. They were from another century, clichés almost, wordy and signifying little. They were rhythmic and predictable, with nothing fresh or meaningful about them. As I skipped here and there through the long poem I saw the phrases as different only in skill from the platitudinous rhymes of Longfellow that my grandson had ridiculed, and at last I understood what Karl Streibert, Ezra Pound and F.X.M. Devlan had been sponsoring: a dialogue between people of intelligence, heightened in significance and intensified in emotion.

As the book lay in my lap opened but unread I was chastened to think that I was now accepting the very reasoning for which I had rebuked Yvonne when she said: 'Lukas Yoder with his sentimental novels depicting the Dutch milieu and Jenny Sorkin with her amusing description of the football arena are writing interesting books that anyone with a grammar school education can read and enjoy. Streibert, Pound and Timothy were reaching for a communication far more powerful.'

It was toward two that morning when I saw the frightening consequences: Streibert was right. If the popular novel of today stands where popular poetry stood in 1850, then our novel will surely follow the destiny of our poetry: better and better novels read by fewer and fewer people. Such a prospect for a devoted reader like me was so depressing that I could not sleep, so I remained in my chair, the book of poems unattended.

New Year's Eve did not end on that mournful note, for as I was about to go upstairs to bed, my phone jangled and a voice cried: 'Mrs. Garland?' and it took me a confused moment before I realized that Yvonne Marmelle was speaking. 'Where are you, dear?' I asked, and she said: 'At my house. May I drive over?'

'At this hour of the night? It wouldn't be safe. But we do have much to discuss.'

'When Karl drove me home, I hoped he would come in, and he did. We spoke first about the good work he'd done on Timothy's manuscript. And although he's always been suspicious of Jenny Sorkin, he seemed honestly pleased when I told him that Book-of-the-Month quietly slipped me word that if we can delay publication of her *Big Six* till the start of football season they'd probably take it. What a start for a beginning writer!'

'You didn't call to tell me that.'

'No. I was as agitated as a schoolgirl who's about to be kissed for the first time. Didn't know how to start, but finally blurted it out: "What Mrs. Garland said made sense—you could quite properly move in there—there's a big enough difference in ages so that there wouldn't be gossip." '

'What did he say?' I asked and she said: 'Nothing. Just stood there. I don't think he heard me. I believe he was thinking of his great god Devlan, for he took out his handkerchief and dabbed his eyes.

' "For God's sake," I cried, "blow your nose like a man." It was a horrible thing to say, but out it came.'

'He must have reacted to that!'

'No. He asked a question in a very weak voice: "Are you lonely, too?" and I replied as gently as I could: "Terribly. Why else would I have moved to Dresden? To find someone real like Zollicoffer. Or Mrs. Garland. Or you." '

'And then what did he do?'

'He stepped back and studied me, and as I looked at him I saw an entirely different man. No more the tentative intellectual crippled by the death of Devlan. No more the young professor traumatized by the murder of his star pupil. He seemed taller, straighter and his voice was certainly stronger.'

'What did he say?'

'You won't believe it. Oxford University has invited him to come there for a full academic year to teach American literature!'

'How wonderful! I'm so glad for him.'

'And Temple has received additional funding for his department. He's to have three Ph.D. students to assist him.'

'And his return to Mecklenberg? Did he react in any way to our invitations?'

'He rejected them both.'

When she heard me express my disappointment, she broke into robust laughter.

'You couldn't possibly guess what he said.'

'It must have been something sensational or you wouldn't have called at this hour.'

'He said, and I quote exactly: "As Mrs. Garland said, you and I need roots, so three days ago I purchased an apartment in that new condominium at the edge of Dresden." '

It was now four in the morning, and as I looked through the big window to the valley beyond I was driven to impose my gnawing sorrow on another: 'It was at this hour on that other night when we found Timothy down there on the lawn, and grief chokes me when I think of what you and I have lost in his death.' Then, forcing myself

THE READER

· ·

440

to turn from such thoughts, I asked: 'What do you think Karl will
do with his newfound vitality?' and she replied: 'After he gets to
Oxford and weeps at the gravestone he erected for Devlan he'll begin
to think: "Those are two bright women back in Dresden. They know
what they're talking about." And he'll begin weighing the two invitations you extended. The more important question: What do I do if
I've grown to love the gentleman? The new gentleman, that is, the
one who's painfully made himself into a man?'

She asked this with such obvious hunger for guidance that I concluded her long-ago lover must have been a self-pitying whimperer,
and I wanted to lend her the courage to take another shot at life:
'Yvonne, you wait. The good things in life are like the birth of a child.
Ninety percent waiting.'

WEDNESDAY, 15 JANUARY 1992: Yesterday I had a sobering experience. As my recent notes will show, I've been engaged in an intellectual struggle to judge honestly what I think about the writers who
have come to mean so much to me. Some years ago I thought Lukas
Yoder was the dean of storytellers, but then Professor Streibert with
his penetrating evaluations forced me by the sheer brilliance of his
logic to question that early opinion. My grandson opened my eyes
to what a newer, bolder type of writing might offer, and I felt in
Jenny Sorkin's brash irreverence a clean new wind blowing away old
cobwebs. And fundamental to all was the reasoned judgment of
Yvonne Marmelle, whose task it was to keep a great publishing house
on course. She served as my cicerone, offering her developed opinions
and fortifying my nascent ones.

I really believed I had fathomed the secrets of literature and
wrapped them in neat bundles. But yesterday when I stopped by to
chat with Emma Yoder about the gifts she and I are making to the
college, I asked as we sat in her kitchen: 'What's Lukas doing these

days?' and she said: 'You'd be interested. In this quiet period following the festivities he applies himself to what he calls "my burden." '

'What's that?'

'Answering his mail. An enormous amount piles up after publishing a new book.'

'*Stone Walls* came out months ago.'

'Yes. But his earlier books keep getting printed in various countries. To those readers they're new.' She took me to his crowded
study, where he sat at his typewriter, studiously engaged in sending
letters to all parts of the country. 'This is also part of the profession,'
he told me as he paused over the keyboard of his old-fashioned
manual Royal.

'Do you really answer all of these?' I asked, indicating a waiting
pile of at least eighty.

'I do. These are the people,' he said, tapping the letters beside him,
'who've kept me going.'

'May I read some of them?'

'Read them all,' he laughed. 'I do.'

And that began my introduction to a world I had not known, the
world of hundreds, thousands, of people much like myself to whom
the reading of books was a precious experience. I knew that I thought
so; I had not known there were so many like me.

In the warm sunlight of a winter's day in Dresden I began first to
skim the letters, and then read them, and saw that they fell into three
categories. There was obviously a lot of junk mail in the batch,
students asking him to tell them 'all about writing,' mature men
begging for autographed photos for their collection, and a surprising
number who had found in one of his books a character who bore the
same German name as they: 'Could your storekeeper have been
modeled after my uncle Isaac Schmandtz? It's not a common name.'
But the more serious letters were a revelation.

The first group, but not the largest, said simply that through the years the reader had come to trust Yoder as the teller of honest stories based on the experiences of men and women of significance whom the reader would have liked to meet and who lived in places worth visiting. Such writers were apt to say: 'You are my favorite author, probably the very best writing today, and I eagerly await your next book.' I had the suspicion that some of these correspondents had not read widely the works of other writers.

The second group moved me deeply, because each could have been written by my husband when he was alive:

> I work with such concentration in my business that I truthfully have no time for reading. My wife heckles me about this, says I'm allowing myself to degenerate into a typical redneck. Some years ago when your popular novel *Hex* came out, she talked so much about it, assuring me that I'd like it, that in self-defense I had to give it a try.
>
> Your book knocked me off dead-center. It was so good, so real, that I asked: 'What else has he written?' and she told me about *The Shunning*, said it was even better than *Hex*. She was right, and I'm proud to tell you, Mr. Yoder, that I have now read all your books, and those of other writers, too. You brought me back to the world of ideas bigger than those of my business, and for this I thank you. Ten times I thank you.

That was precisely Larrimore's experience. He had read little but steel-business reports until I practically forced him to read *Hex*. Then he too went back and read the others, and more besides.

But it was the third group of letters that stunned me—so many I could scarcely believe the readers had written in almost identical phrasing:

When I approach the closing pages of one of your novels, a feeling of profound regret comes over me, for I realize that I am about to sever a relationship with characters I have grown to love. And to abandon a corner of the world in which I have spent rewarding weeks and even months, for I read slowly and carefully. I feel, when the pages dwindle, as if something good were being stolen from me, something precious that would not be replaced.

You may laugh at what I say next, but when I realize how few pages are left I ration myself, only so many each day, and when the final one looms, and I close the book, I stare at the back map for many minutes, aware that something precious has touched my life.

Pushing the letters away, for they were in a sense painful to read, I looked at Lukas as he typed away. He did not look like the sort of person who could evoke such reactions.

'Have you always received such mail?'

'It started with *The Shunning*. Since then it's never stopped.' He pinched his upper lip as if embarrassed by this admission, then pushed another pile my way, smaller than the first, which he said he would be answering tomorrow. I was surprised to see by their colorful stamps that they came from all parts of the world, every continent, from nations large and small. And it was interesting to see that the writers, having come to his books in a nonchronological way, depending upon when some publisher in Germany or Brazil or Sweden had translated an individual book, wrote to him about novels he had published decades earlier as if he had written them yesterday.

It was as if all his books were alive this week, as if they had just now sprung off the press, for a book comes to life not on the date it was published in New York, but on the happy day when it falls

into the hands of a reader in Johannesburg or Buenos Aires or
Istanbul, three cities that happened to be represented in the letters
I held in my hand at that moment.

I was humbled. When I saw the passion, the identification my
quiet little Dutchman had been able to evoke in all sections of his
own country, and in various nations of the world, I had to look at
him in a different light.

'You wield a powerful pen, Lukas.'

'I've been lucky to come along when I did. And especially lucky
to have found a woman like Yvonne Marmelle to defend me.'

'Do letters like this'—I indicated those from foreign lands—'mean
a lot to you?'

He leaned back from his typewriter, reflected for several moments,
then smiled in his almost wizened Dutch manner: 'Well, when Professor Streibert's rather harsh review came out in the *Times*, the one
that agitated you and Emma so sorely, you asked me how I had
reacted. I told you I hadn't read it, nor had I reacted when Emma
did read parts of it to me.' His smile became the infectious grin of
a schoolboy who has caught on to a secret: 'Mrs. Garland—'

'For God's sake, call me Jane. We're practically partners at the
college.'

'Well, Jane, when a man receives a batch of letters like this almost
every mail day of his life, he can afford to ignore criticism. They fuel
an inner fire that keeps him warm.'

I left his littered study an enlightened woman, for I had been
allowed to see a new world of writing, and when I returned to
Emma's kitchen I said: 'Maybe a man or a woman who can paint
fine canvases or write good books is obligated to keep on doing
so—as long as the fires last.'

'You think Lukas should try one more?'

'I do.'

'Looks as if you'll get your wish.' She said this while tending a pot
bubbling on the stove, and when she turned to face me, I could see

that she was quite tired. As she joined me for a cup of lemon tea, she said: 'It was on New Year's Eve that I finally saw I could no longer oppose him. I didn't want him, at his advanced age, to tackle another major novel, especially since the Grenzler series had been so nicely put to bed. But after we and the Zollicoffers had greeted the New Year at their place, we drove home, and instead of going to our room, Lukas went to his study. Last thing I heard as I fell asleep was him typing.

'It must have been about two in the morning when something wakened me, and when I heard him still typing, I went in to his study and cried: "Lukas! What are you doing?" and he shoved at me a handsome map he'd drawn and colored of the area between the Fenstermacher farm and Windsong, extended to show Neumunster, Dresden and the shore of the Wannsee where the murder weapon was found.

'I shivered when I saw the map, for it meant that he had finally committed himself to writing an entire novel in some bold new way that critics like Streibert would approve of. It also meant that even though both of us are older now and failing in energy, the grand chase for facts and characters and significance has once more begun.

'So there I sat as three o'clock approached, looking at his notes for the novel. He'd already chosen the title, *The Crime*, and identified its central figure as someone like Herman Zollicoffer, an adherent of the old ways. The villain would be a repulsive slob like Applebutter but with a less ridiculous nickname. Lukas had two traditional Amish alternatives penciled in—Strong Jacob and one that had been widely used among the Dutch, Huddle Amos—but he said he didn't feel happy with either. In the center of the novel would be the tragic figure of a man like the elder Otto Fenstermacher, who had always intended good but who had lost his way, selling off bits of his farm while proving himself unable to keep his insolent son from getting involved with drugs.

'I could see it was going to be a powerful novel, but at three-thirty

I said: "Lukas, have you any idea what time it is?" When he looked up it was clear he had been lost along the back roads of Dresden and I said: "Time for sleep." On the way to our bedroom he put his arm around me and said: "Thank you. I have great hopes for this book. And do you know why?" He laughed at himself in the way that makes him so easy to live with: 'Remember how we used to dismiss Streibert and his pompous Imperative of the Now that no one understood? Well, he was right. I'm driven by the very impulse he described. I no longer want to write about my colorful Dutch as they used to be, but the way they are now. How a chain of wrong choices and obstinate behavior can lead to murder.'

'Despite my reluctance to have him start another major book, I was happy to hear him speak with such conviction. In the early stages of his other books he had spoken that way, so it was a good omen. I still felt as tired as I had in the argumentative days before Christmas, but I remembered his cry: 'Writing is what I do. I have to do it," and when he climbed into bed I leaned over and tucked the blankets about him.'